THINK ZEBRAS

THINK ZEBRAS

A Novel

Kathryn Scott

Think Zebras

Charles Clivie Publishing

Editing and design by Indigo Editing & Publications

ISBN: 978-0-692-66125-3

For Deane—and for public health nurses, who endeavor to keep individuals and communities healthy and thriving.

Acknowledgments

It is with much gratitude that I thank Vinnie Kinsella and Susan DeFreitas with Indigo Editing & Publications for their professionalism and talent in making *Think Zebras* a reality. They gave a first-time novelist the encouragement she needed to see the book through to its completion. I extend my sincere thanks to Michelle McBride for her thoughtful comments on a draft and ideas for future directions for the characters. And it is with deep love that I thank my husband and daughters—Deane, Emma and Clara—for giving me the time and space to write this book. Our family is my life's greatest blessing.

Contents

Friday, April 25, 2003

Mary Campbell, the nurse supervisor for the Revere County Health Department Communicable Disease (CD) Control Unit, entered Erin O'Donnell's cubicle and smiled at the intern. Mary leaned against a gray, four-drawer filing cabinet and began to sort through the letters and messages she had picked up from her mailbox. The first was from the State CD Program. It declared that her county's quarterly rash illness report was overdue.

Of course it's late, she thought with irritation. *You told us not to send them anymore.*

The second envelope contained a colorful, glossy flyer recommending an introductory emergency management training for local health department personnel. Mary scoffed. The word *recommended*, when used by the state, usually meant *required*, and that meant precious time for her nurses away from their busy workloads.

A pink message slip had been slipped into the stack of mail. Her counterpart in DePaul County, home to one of the largest cities in the state, had returned her call. The message said they had not seen any norovirus outbreaks that month.

"Weird," Mary muttered. Her unit had investigated three such outbreaks since the beginning of April, but none of the counties that bordered hers were seeing anything unusual.

Erin heard Mary's utterance and indicated that she would be off the phone shortly. "Yes, ma'am, I did read this morning's headline," she said to the caller. She tucked a strand of her straight honey-brown hair behind one ear and added, "If it makes you feel any better, I don't think Supervisor Cahill has the authority to stop those services. The federal government funds the program."

Mary watched Erin roll a pen between her fingers At twenty-nine years of age, Erin was smart and enthusiastic. She had left a business career to pursue nursing and was turning out to be a godsend. She worked the CD phone like she had been born for the job, and the unit felt sufficiently staffed for the first time in months. If Erin continued to perform this well, Mary would recruit her for a vacant nursing position. She was only waiting for Administration to give her permission to post the job.

"I understand it's upsetting," Erin continued, "but the health department has no plans to end the program." After a brief pause, she said, "Thank you for calling, and I'm glad to hear your partner is doing well. Don't hesitate to call back if you have any other questions." She hung up the phone and turned to Mary.

"Another call about the article?" Mary asked.

Erin nodded. "That's the fifth one this morning. They all want to know if we're shutting down our HIV/AIDS services. Could the Board of Supervisors really do that?"

"They could refuse the federal funds," Mary replied, "but we have the third-largest gay population in the state. It would be political suicide to anger that community."

"I don't think they care about that, boss," said a gravelly voice.

Mary turned to see Stella Cooper, one of the unit's two full-time public health nurses, at the opening of the cubicle. She held a copy of the local newspaper, the *County Courier*, in her hands. A tall woman in her sixties, Stella carried her thick, muscular torso on long, trim legs. Her pale-blue eyes were a striking contrast to her white, wavy hair and perennially sun-kissed cheeks, which came from working her family's dairy farm.

"What do you mean?" Erin asked.

"Cahill and this new crop of supervisors are bat-assed crazy," Stella answered.

2

"Shush," Mary scolded her. "They approve our budget."

"I know," Stella replied only a little more quietly, "but did you read what Cahill said? I swear, it may be time for me to retire."

"You're not allowed to retire," Mary teased, but only half-heartedly. She could not imagine running the unit without Stella, who was the unit's most knowledgeable and experienced nurse—their anchor.

Stella began reading from the front-page article. "Listen to this," she said. "'I want a review of all county programs using tax dollars to promote immoral human activities, in particular sexual relations between members of the same sex.'" Stella lowered the paper. "If Cahill is that comfortable talking to the press about her homophobia, then she's not afraid of political suicide. She's a zealot."

Cass McGovern, a nurse who split her time between the CD and Field Nursing Units, suddenly stepped into what little space remained in the cubicle. She wore a flowing mauve skirt that reached her ankles and a matching vest over a pink T-shirt. A soft maroon hat with a pink flower attached to its hatband rested on top of her curly, thick, waist-length brown hair. "Are you talking about the Cahill article?" she asked eagerly.

"Morning, Cass," Mary greeted her. She saw that the woman's eyes were rimmed red. "You look like springtime itself today," she said kindly. Three months earlier Cass had broken up with Jill, her partner of ten years, and she was still struggling emotionally.

"What are you doing here?" Stella asked. "I thought this was your field nursing day."

"My nine o'clock family canceled. I want to be busy, so I thought I'd work on my backlog of hep C cases or see if you need any help with the outbreaks."

"I do," Stella responded appreciatively. "Mary, I can take over the phone now that Cass is here."

"Good," Mary replied. "That means I can keep my appointment at the Administration Office."

"Lordy. What do you need to go over there for?" Cass asked.

"I don't want to," Mary said, "but I have an appointment with

Suzanne to talk about the DePaul County database." Suzanne Henderson, MD, MPH, was the county's health officer. "Since it was built with public funds," Mary added, "DePaul County will give it to us for an annual maintenance fee of only fifteen hundred dollars. Admin can't possibly object to that amount."

"Don't bet on it," Cass muttered.

Mary grabbed the stack of active case reports next to Erin's computer and held them up. "Just think," she said, "we'll be able to track our case and outbreak information electronically."

Stella smiled. "I love your youthful optimism," she said. "Can you also ask about our vacancy? Work is really piling up. A database isn't going to do us any good if we don't have people to use it."

"I always do," Mary answered. What she did not mention was her worry that Admin might defund the position. During a recent budget meeting, Suzanne had asked her, in front of the other managers, "So, what exactly do your nurses do all day long?" The question had stunned Mary. Her staff consulted regularly with Suzanne on its investigations. If she did not value their work, then it was unlikely that Carl Zielinski, the director of the health department, would either, and he controlled the budget.

Mary turned to Erin. "Would you like to come with me, since you haven't met Suzanne or Carl yet?"

"Sure!" Erin replied.

"Do you really need to spoil the kid's day?" Cass asked.

Mary laughed. "It's only an introduction."

Cass said nothing, which Mary knew probably required a fair amount of effort on her part.

Stella tactfully changed the topic. "So, how was the morning here?" she asked. "Anything new come in? And where's Lourdes?"

Lourdes Contreras was the unit's only other full-time nurse. "She's watching our TB patients take their meds," Mary replied as she thumbed through the stack of case reports. She stopped and gave the bundle to Erin. "Why don't you give the morning report?" she suggested.

The intern looked startled but stood to address Stella and Cass. "Um, we got a positive lab result for a calicivirus—likely norovirus," she began.

"Really?" Cass said excitedly. "Does it belong to the Rose Park outbreak?"

"Yep."

"Bingo! I love it when we get lab confirmation."

"What else?" Stella asked.

"Two campylobacters, three salmonella, and a giardia came in over the fax last night."

"Our usual poop problems," Stella noted.

"And two new hep Cs," Erin added.

Cass extended her hand. "I'll take those." She was the unit's lead for hepatitis reporting.

Erin handed her the faxes and said to the group, "I left messages with the docs for the new cases, except your hep Cs, Cass. And it turns out that the person with giardia is the same guy who was reported to the unit for malaria a few days ago."

"Remember him, Stella?" Mary asked. "The missionary from Ivory Coast? Doc Hansen ordered an ova and parasite test for his diarrhea."

"Really?" Stella commented. "That gal is so good."

"Is that unusual?" Erin asked, puzzled.

"Yes," Mary, Stella and Cass replied in unison.

Jeanitha Vong, who worked as the administrative assistant for both the CD and Field Nursing Units, appeared at the cubicle entrance and handed Mary a pink message slip. Mary read it and muttered, "Damn."

"What's wrong?" Erin asked.

"A Rose Park nursing home resident died," she sighed. "Complications from norovirus."

"Let me have that," Cass said, reaching out for the message. "I'll call them for more details."

"Anything else, Erin?" Stella asked.

"Jane Holcomb from Highland Hospital called about a probable pertussis in a five-month-old infant."

"Another pertussis?" Mary groaned. "What does that put us at, Stella? Twenty-nine cases?"

"Thirty," the nurse corrected her.

"Jane offered to do the initial interview with the family," Erin continued. "I faxed her a case report form."

"Good. That will help," Mary said.

"That's all I have to report," Erin said, "except for a few calls from the public. One was a client of yours, Cass."

Cass had returned to her cubicle, which adjoined Erin's. "That was probably my nine o'clock." She paused and then declared, "Could we possibly generate more paperwork? I have about an inch of free space on my desk."

Jeanitha reappeared and said, "You can have these hep B lab results that just came in."

"Gee, thanks," Cass grumbled.

Stella laughed. "Be thankful it wasn't hep A in a food handler," she said.

"Hush your mouth," Cass scolded her. "It's Friday, for God's sake."

Mary grinned at Erin. CD workers held a superstition that diseases like hepatitis A or bacterial meningitis, which required their immediate attention, were always reported on Friday afternoons after 4:30 p.m. They would blame these weekend-consuming events on the wrath of the epidemiology, or epi, gods.

"Thanks for your good work everyone," Mary said to the group. "I'm off to Admin. Erin, are you ready to go?"

"Hey, boss?" Stella interrupted her.

"Yes?"

"Just a heads up that Suzanne and Carl may have a surprise for you."

A worried expression appeared on Mary's face. "What kind of surprise?" she asked.

Stella shrugged. "It's about the new operations manager. Try not to look too shocked."

Mary studied the nurse's face. The Administration Office was renowned for its political intrigues, and over the four years Mary had held her job, she had learned to distance herself from them as much as possible. On several occasions, Stella, who was a union steward, had discreetly warned her about the antics of the agency's executives. But Mary knew she and Stella had to tread carefully about the information they shared with each other. Mary was management and Stella was staff. Everything known could not necessarily be shared openly or in its entirety.

Stella shooed Mary and Erin away with a wave of her hands. "Go on with you now. I've got an outbreak to deal with."

× × ×

Mary grabbed her satchel from her office, which was on the second floor of the former furniture store that now housed most of the public health programs. The building was located on Seventh Street in the downtown area, while the county's public health clinic and regional laboratory were situated on the opposite side of town. The Administration Office, where Mary and Erin were now headed, sat in the county courthouse on Tenth Street.

Mary joined Erin outside of her office, and the two women walked past the photocopying area, a cluster of cubicles, and the staff break room before reaching the top of the building's broad, central staircase. Mary considered this feature to be extraordinarily elegant for a county government building. By all other measures, the Seventh Street structure conformed in color and style to the typically bland approach to government decor. This staircase, however, reminded her of the scene from the musical *Funny Face* in which Audrey Hepburn floated gracefully down a flight of steps, gossamer fabric billowing behind her as she called out to Fred Astaire's character, "Take the picture! Take the picture!"

As they descended the stairs, Mary looked out over the expansive sea of tightly packed gray cubicles, nearly half of which were empty, and recalled the effort that had been required to move out of their former location. That site had suffered from black mold and peeling asbestos ceiling tiles. Additionally, eighteen CD and field nursing staff had shared one large room that should have held only eight employees. Only after an anonymous complaint was filed with the state's Environmental Health Division had the County Board of Supervisors been embarrassed into relocating the health department and complying with its own safety and workplace codes.

Mary saw Jackson Barnes, the department's first bioterrorism coordinator, approach the staircase landing. A tall, lean man in his late fifties, he favored cowboy attire and a sharply defined white crew cut. He had once been a military police officer and security specialist. To his new public health colleagues, encountering him in their day-to-day jobs was as remarkable as encountering an extraterrestrial being. To Mary, he represented yet another example of Admin's fondness for assigning unnecessary work to her unit.

Jackson greeted the two women in his usual upbeat manner. "Good morning!" he said.

Mary thought that if he had been wearing a cowboy hat, he would have tipped it to them.

"Good morning," Mary replied. She did not slow her pace.

"Mary?" he asked when they were next to each other. "Can I have some of your time to talk about the training I'm planning?"

Mary and Erin walked passed him. "Sure," she answered, barely glancing at him. "But maybe next week. I'm busy today."

Out of the corner of her eye, Mary saw Erin gaze at her and then back at Jackson. Mary knew she had brushed off Jackson's request, but she had real work to attend to.

× × ×

As they neared the county courthouse, Erin asked Mary, "So, is this Carl Zielinski fellow not well liked?"

"What?" Mary asked.

Erin explained herself. "It's just that people don't respond very well whenever you mention his name."

Mary considered Erin. The intern was savvy and had probably seen her fair share of maneuvering in the for-profit world. She could probably handle a taste of the political reality of the health department. "I don't think Carl is liked or disliked any more than any other administrator," Mary began. "He restructured the department over a year ago, which caused some resentment. The state had lost millions in the energy crisis and dot-com crash, and county budgets were slashed as a result. Around the same time, our operations manager retired, and Carl eliminated the position. He said it was a cost-saving measure. We understood that the department couldn't create new jobs, but we hated losing that one. It was the glue that held our programs together. Then, about six weeks ago, Carl surprised everyone by announcing that he was reopening the position. We finished the interviews a few days ago."

"Did you get someone good?" Erin asked.

"I think so," Mary answered, hoping her voice did not betray her worry.

The two women climbed an inside stairwell to the suite that housed the Administration Office. "Wow. Nice digs," Erin exclaimed as they stepped through the double glass doors to the reception area. The suite's decor was impressive by county standards. It was not as sleek as the private law offices Mary's brother had once worked in, but it was elegantly decorated and had an air of sophistication not found in the Seventh Street building.

Mary approached the receptionist, who sat behind a semicircular desk made of highly polished wood. The woman greeted her pleasantly. "Why, hello, Mary."

"Hi, Rosalyn. How are you?"

"Fine," she said.

"Rosalyn, this is Erin Williams, our new public health nursing intern. Erin, this is Rosalyn Moore."

Erin extended her hand. "Nice to meet you," she said.

"You too," Rosalyn replied.

As the women shook hands, Rosalyn performed her usual visual inspection of a new female employee. Rosalyn was an oddity among the earthy, practical public health sisterhood, who liked to look nice but did not spend much time in the effort. A full-figured woman in her forties, she favored pencil skirts, tight sweaters, and high heels. Mary wondered what was going through Rosalyn's mind as she sized up the lithe and beautiful Erin.

"So, what brings you here?" Rosalyn asked.

"I'm meeting with Suzanne," Mary replied.

"Do you have an appointment?"

"I do," Mary stated confidently. "I blocked out fifteen minutes on her calendar."

Rosalyn's face dropped its pleasant expression. "So, you didn't make the appointment through me?"

Oh no, Mary thought. *Now what?* Each encounter she had with Administration lately seemed to involve a new rule that was not shared with others until it was broken by the uninformed victim. "No," she replied. "Was I supposed to?"

"Yes!" Rosalyn declared. "I make all of the appointments now for Suzanne and Carl—and anyone else in Admin for that matter. You wouldn't believe how many meetings I've had to remove from their calendars because people didn't talk to me first."

Mary clenched her teeth at the self-important tone in the woman's voice, but she expressed no outward displeasure. She knew she had to stay on Rosalyn's good side if she wanted to get anything done with Admin in the future. "I must have missed that memo," she said apologetically.

The receptionist studied her for a moment and then broke into a smile. "That's okay. Since this is your first offense, I'll see what I can do. Have a seat."

"Thank you," Mary replied. She turned away, and Erin raised an amused eyebrow at her. The two women sat down in the soft leather chairs to the left of the double doors. Mary felt like a schoolgirl waiting to see the principal, but she soothed her annoyance by imagining her fully staffed unit using the DePaul County database to track their case and outbreak information.

Focus on getting Suzanne's support, she told herself.

An office door opened just as Rosalyn began to dial the number. Mary watched as Suzanne and Carl walked into the suite's central area with a young man Mary recognized as a candidate from the first round of interviews for the operations manager position. She had been a member of the interview panel.

He can't possibly be the one, she thought with horror. He had been so ill qualified for the position the panel decided Human Resources must have made a mistake in advancing him out of the applicant pool. They had interviewed him, but only out of courtesy.

Suzanne glanced in her direction. "Mary!" she exclaimed.

Mary and Erin stood and walked over to the trio, and Mary thanked Rosalyn on the way. The receptionist nodded appreciatively.

Suzanne was stylishly dressed in a pale-green suit that complimented her strawberry-blond, shoulder-length locks. The outfit was accented by a dark-green patterned scarf around her neck and open-toed green pumps. "How are you?" she asked.

"I'm fine," Mary replied. "Rosalyn was just going to buzz you to see if I could take a few minutes of your time to talk about the DePaul County database. I'd also like to introduce you—and Carl—to our new intern."

Carl, who stood to Suzanne's left, glanced briefly in Mary's direction but continued talking quietly to the young man.

"Actually, we have an introduction to make to you too," Suzanne said brightly.

Suddenly, Carl stepped over to Suzanne and took hold of her elbow. "Suzanne, this isn't the best time. Jonathan and I need to get to that Board of Supervisors meeting."

"It will only take a minute," Suzanne replied testily as she glanced at Carl's hand on her elbow.

"I'll be quick," Mary stated, seeing the tension between the two. "Erin, I'd like you to meet Dr. Suzanne Henderson, the Revere County public health officer. And this is Carl Zielinski, the director of the health department. Suzanne and Carl, this is Erin O'Donnell."

Suzanne, Carl, and Erin exchanged brief greetings, but neither Carl nor Suzanne introduced the young man. He smiled in a rather goofy manner, and Mary thought he must be nervous.

After an awkward pause, Suzanne said, "Erin, we need to speak with Mary in private."

The intern understood she was being dismissed and looked to Mary for direction. "I'll meet you back in the unit," Mary said. "See if you can help Stella and Cass with the outbreaks."

Now clearly irritated, Carl grumbled, "I need to get to that meeting."

In response, Suzanne ushered everyone into her office and addressed Mary first. "We're going to make the formal announcement tomorrow during the all-staff meeting, but since you're here—Mary, this is Jonathan Cox, our new operations manager."

Mary felt physically ill at having her fears confirmed. But she extended her hand and said, "Yes, I remember you from the interviews."

"Oh! You were there?" The young man chuckled.

Mary gave Jonathan a weak smile and glanced at Suzanne. The health officer wore the pleasant but unrevealing expression she used for television interviews. Mary looked back at Jonathan. He resembled Carl a great deal. Both men were big. In height, each was over six feet tall. In girth, the long-term effects of gravity had dragged down the once considerable musculature Carl had developed in his first career as a firefighter. Jonathan's soft bulk, however, suggested he had never held physical exertion in much esteem. In contrast to the young man's open expression, Carl wore the practiced poker face she had often seen on law enforcement and military personnel. Mary knew it was probably a demeanor necessary for their work, but she had observed that the emotions behind their eyes usually betrayed their stern bearing.

Carl pulled himself up to his full height and said in short, direct sentences, "Mary, Jonathan will be my assistant. He will assume Suzanne's supervisory responsibilities for the CD and Field Nursing Units. Suzanne will still be available to you for medical consultation."

Mary was shocked. "Your assistant?" she asked awkwardly, trying to contain her emotions. "Does that make him the deputy director?"

Jonathan guffawed.

"No," Carl answered with a steely voice. His eyes bore into hers. "But as I said, he will report to me."

Confused, Mary looked to Suzanne for clarification.

"Mary," Suzanne began soothingly, "Carl and I have our hands full with administrative responsibilities. We thought it best if someone took over the more burdensome aspects of our jobs so we can concentrate on high-level policy activities."

Mary drew in her breath at Suzanne's use of the word *burdensome* to describe what apparently included supervision of the public health nurses, but she swallowed the insult and addressed the man who was to be her new boss. "Jonathan, as I recall, you aren't coming to us from another health department."

"That's right," he chuckled. "My last position was down in the city."

"And remind me what you did there?"

"I was a purchasing specialist with the city's Contracts and Procurement Office."

"But you've worked in the health field at some point, no doubt."

"Nope." The man laughed. "I've always been in procurement—dealing with contracts, invoices, that sort of thing."

"So you've never worked with PHNs?"

"What's a PHN?" Jonathan asked nervously. He shifted his weight from one foot to the other, as if beginning to understand that Mary's questions were pointing to inadequacies on his part.

Mary blinked at him in disbelief. "*PHN* stands for public health nurse. They make up the bulk of the staff you will be supervising and—"

"Oh, that." Jonathan laughed.

Carl interrupted their exchange. "I assure you, Mary," he said imperiously, "Jonathan is highly qualified for the job. As you know, we held an extensive search for the position."

Jonathan moved closer to Carl upon hearing his words of support and mimicked the director's authoritative stance and stern expression. Mary held Carl's hard gaze. Her fears had turned to anger as she envisioned what lay ahead of her with Jonathan as a boss.

Is it too much to ask for a supervisor who understands our work? she thought.

Suzanne offered brightly, "No doubt Jonathan will face a bit of a learning curve, but we have every confidence he'll do a fantastic job. And I'm counting on you to help him learn the ropes!"

Mary said nothing. The cheerleader quality in Suzanne's voice only fueled her dismay, but she knew she could not express any more of her concerns in front of Jonathan.

"I'm finished here," Carl stated as he walked away. Jonathan followed him, but he glanced back uneasily at Mary as he closed the door.

Suzanne seemed eager to change the subject. "So, how's your work with Jackson going?"

Mary regarded her with alarm. "Suzanne! Why has a purchasing specialist with no public health experience been hired as our operations manager? This isn't going to work."

Suzanne walked to her desk and began to straighten up the papers on it. "Jonathan is going to do just fine," she replied. "I'm still here, and Carl will have the final say on decisions."

And that's a good thing? Mary wondered.

Carl had been hired by Revere County after resigning from a county manager position in Florida. When a rumor began to circulate that he'd left his previous position under questionable circumstances, Stella did some investigating and found a newspaper article describing how Carl had been accused of, but never charged with, taking kickbacks from a waste disposal company in exchange for a county contract. Carl had found redemption in Revere County, however. He'd started out as the health department's chief financial officer but quickly impressed the Board of Supervisors. A deputy health director position was created for him, and within a year, he became the director. The deputy position had never been refilled.

"Jonathan is just going to be Carl's point man," Suzanne continued. "You take your needs to Jonathan, and he, in turn, will discuss them with Carl and me. It's that simple."

"Suzanne, the last thing this place needs is another layer of bureaucracy. It's hard enough to get our work done. How can Jonathan speak for our programs when he doesn't even know who we are or what we do?"

"He'll learn!"

Mary wanted to trust Suzanne. She wanted to believe that she had the unit's best interests in mind. They had met ten years earlier as volunteers at a free clinic for the uninsured. Mary had just finished nursing school, and Suzanne was a medical resident. After Suzanne finished her residency, she began her public health career in Revere County as a program manager. A few years later, when Mary decided to move home to help her parents, she applied for a job with the county, in part because she was excited about working with Suzanne again.

Suzanne pick up her briefcase and said, "It's going to be okay." When she walked toward the door, Mary realized she was leaving.

"Wait," Mary exclaimed. "I want to talk to you about the DePaul County database."

"I need to get to the city for a meeting," Suzanne replied, reaching for the door knob.

"But I found out the database will only cost us fifteen hundred dollars a year."

Suzanne waved back to her from the middle of the suite. "Talk to Jonathan about it," she called out.

× × ×

Raymond watched Geoff Landers, the administrator for the Sumner Care Assisted Living Facility, from the doorway.

Geoff looked up from his desk, startled. "Done already?" he asked.

"I interviewed your director of nursing," Raymond said, "but Mrs. Clayton is asleep. I'll have to talk with her tomorrow."

"But that's Saturday," Geoff countered.

"We're allowed to do our assessments on off-hours," he stated with authority.

"But I won't be here," Geoff persisted.

Raymond grew angry at the man's resistance, but forced himself not to show it. "Well, I can interview you today after I've looked over the facility. You could let the front desk know I'm coming tomorrow for the quality of life evaluation."

Geoff sighed. "I suppose. I really wish you'd tell me more about the complaint against us."

"We keep that information confidential. All I can say at this time is that it deals with the care of a resident."

Geoff nodded. "Okay. Do you need someone to show you around now?"

"No, that's not necessary."

"You certainly have your own way of doing things," Geoff said.

"I'm sorry if it seems like that," Raymond replied. He really did not care what the man thought of him. "We usually send out more than one person to conduct these surveys, but we're short staffed. It's made me a little scattered."

"Okay, okay," the administrator snapped. "Just come find me when you're ready."

"Do you mind if I leave my briefcase in your office?" Raymond asked. "I only need to carry my checklist with me at this point."

Geoff pointed to a small round table. "You can put it over there. I'll keep an eye on it."

Raymond set the locked briefcase down and left the office. In the reception area, he encountered a group of elders who were making their way to the dining hall. One woman inched along on slippered feet with the support of a walker. Two others used weak, choppy arm movements to maneuver their wheelchairs forward, and a man leaned on the arm of a nurse's aide to maintain an upright position. None of them seemed to notice Raymond as he wound his way through the group and entered a stairwell. He climbed to the second floor and turned left into the empty hallway. At room 231, he slowly opened the door. As he had confirmed earlier, the residents were not present. He stepped into the small space and adjusted his silver-framed eyeglasses. Then he removed the surgical gloves that were secured to his clipboard and pulled these over his hands. He next let slip from his shirt sleeve a one-ounce spray bottle. It was filled with an opaque solution. Raymond stepped further into the room and sprayed several objects. When he was finished, he returned to the hallway and coated the handrails and doorknobs with the substance until the bottle was empty.

Tuesday, May 20

The disheveled teen walked to the top of the on-ramp at the rest stop just outside of Elkhart, Indiana. He was cold, so he set his backpack down, stepped into his sleeping bag, and pulled it up around his shoulders. Last night's spring sky had been brilliantly clear, and the morning air was surprisingly biting. He used his left hand to hold the sleeping bag in place and his right hand to signal his need for a ride. He had been on the road for a week but was not nearly as far along in his journey as he had hoped. He cursed his best friend, who had told him it only took three days for his family to drive across the country. He had wanted to take a train from DC to San Francisco but had learned that, as a fifteen-year-old, he could not travel alone without parental consent. He cursed again, but this time at himself. His troubles were his own; he could not blame anyone else.

The teen felt nervously for his wallet, which held all of his money. He had earned it doing chores for his neighbor, Mrs. Anderson. She would often tell him how much he reminded her of her son, and she fed him after every chore, and often beforehand. His stomach growled at the memory of her.

A car shot by along the interstate. The driver was moving an electric razor over his neck and face. Another car soon followed. The woman behind the wheel did not even glance at him.

Am I that invisible?

He thought of his parents, and his head began to throb. Nothing made sense to him. They had never given him a good reason for why they split up. They only said they had grown apart.

"Grown apart. Whatever that means," he grumbled as he rubbed his right temple to ease the pain.

"Mark, you're always welcome to visit me," his father had whispered to him before he left the house for good. He had come into his room one night and cried against the frame of the bunk bed. "I love you, son. No matter what."

It had been a year since he had seen his dad, and he hoped his father's offer still held.

An oversized, gleaming white pickup truck approached, and the boy took a step toward the road. But he forgot that he was standing in a sleeping bag and nearly fell over. In the time it took to steady himself, he almost missed flagging down the vehicle. He quickly stuck out his thumb, and the truck came to a stop about thirty feet from where he stood. Mark stumbled out of the puffy material, gathered up his belongings, and ran to the vehicle. The driver rolled down the passenger seat window. Mark heard a loud male voice on the radio stridently defending the U.S. invasion of Iraq.

Mark studied the driver. The man's appearance did not fit the teen's image of someone who would drive such a souped-up truck. He was middle-aged with a weak chin and an overbite. Aviator sunglasses were perched high on the bulge of his prominent nose. What looked like a light rash accented a deeply receding hairline and a broad, shiny forehead. A photograph of three children and a woman was tucked into the lowered sunshade on the driver's side. The man took off his sunglasses and turned down the sound on the radio. His eyes were red and watery.

"Where are you going?" he asked Mark.

"As far west as you can take me," Mark answered. He decided the driver looked harmless enough.

"I'm headed to Illinois," the man stated. "How does that sound?"

"Great!"

"Hop in, then." The driver leaned over and unlocked the passenger door but coughed with the effort. The teen slung off his backpack and stuffed his sleeping bag into it. Then he climbed onto the passenger's seat and placed his belongings on his lap.

"I'm Eugene," the man said.

"Mark," the teen replied. "Is that your family?" he asked, pointing to the photograph.

Eugene looked at the picture. "Yes," he answered.

Mark waited for more information. When none came, he examined the picture further as Eugene maneuvered the vehicle onto the interstate. A plump woman stood behind two girls and a boy. The son appeared to be about his age. His expression held a cold anger.

Eugene said little as he drove, and Mark's eyelids grew heavy as he watched the flat northern Indiana landscape roll by from the warmth of the truck's cab. He had slept little the night before. His last ride of the day had dropped him off at the rest stop close to midnight. He had found a secluded spot in which to sleep behind one of the buildings that housed the toilets but was awoken by what he thought was a fight. When he realized people were having sex inside the building, he moved to a picnic table, nestled near a distant stand of trees, and tried to fall asleep.

"You look tired," Eugene said in a fatherly manner. "Feel free to nod off."

"Thanks," the teen replied. "I think I will."

Eugene smiled. "I'll wake you if anything exciting happens."

Mark leaned against the door and at first slept fitfully. His head bobbed on his neck, and it occasionally banged against the window. Eventually, he drifted into a deeper sleep and dreamed.

Kurt stood behind his mother. The man towered over her and taunted him. Mark faced his mother, but only as a small boy no higher than her waist. He shouted to her. He warned her, but she did nothing. Kurt grew taller, and he reached around the woman for the boy. Mark screamed and pleaded with his mother. She vanished, and the man lunged at him. The little boy turned to flee but could not move quickly enough.

Mark's head hit the passenger window hard, and he opened his eyes. He forced his brain to right itself and take in his surroundings. The pickup truck was no longer on the highway; it was parked on the sloped shoulder of a country road. When he felt a hand squeeze his inner thigh, he thought of Kurt. His heart began to pound, but his body froze in place. *Am I still dreaming?* he wondered.

The teen shifted his gaze down to his lap without moving his head from its awkward resting place. Fear surged through him as he watched Eugene stroke his thigh. Now breathing shallowly and quickly, Mark found the nerve to shift his weight. Eugene continued his groping, and Mark edged further toward the door. He looked into the man's eyes.

Without a hint of embarrassment, Eugene cooed, "Finally awake, sleepy head?" He drove his strokes closer toward Mark's penis. "You must be hungry. I know I am."

Panic surged through the teen's body. His muscle and skin recoiled toward bone, and he looked out the window for an escape. A line of trees stood to either side of the road, as windbreaks for the barren fields. In the distance, a housing development abutted acreage of spent cornstalks that had not been plowed under after the last harvest.

"I thought you and me could have a picnic," Eugene said.

Mark stared at the man.

"I've got a cooler in the back with roast beef sandwiches, potato salad, chocolate cake, and beer. A nice lunch made by my adoring wife."

Mark heard the eager anticipation in Eugene's voice.

The man leaned back into his seat and began to unzip his pants. "Now, what would a good-looking boy like you do for beer and a roast beef sandwich?"

× × ×

Mark ran hard for the housing development through the rough field, stumbling over the broken cornstalks.

"I'm calling the cops, you punk," a furious voice shouted after him. The teen turned and saw Eugene spit blood from his mouth.

With a thick tongue, he hollered, "They'll hunt you down. You hear me? I'm a big man in these parts. I know people!"

After a few minutes, the pain in Mark's ribs forced him to slow to a limping jog, but he did not stop moving until he came to a strip mall. There, at a small convenience store, he found a concrete column to hide behind. He leaned against it and vomited what little food was in his stomach. He gasped for air as he tried to process what had happened to him. Eugene had grabbed him by the collar when he reached for the door handle and then begun to punch him in the head and ribs. Some part of Mark's brain had taken over despite the disorienting blows. He had drawn his knees up to his chest and delivered a double-footed kick to his attacker's torso. The force had caused Eugene to hit his head against the driver's door and to bite his tongue. Eugene's shock at the pain and blood had given Mark the time he needed to flee the vehicle. Now, as he crouched over and worked hard to slow his breathing, he peeked around the support column to see if Eugene had followed him. The area was quiet except for a customer who walked out of the store carrying a large bag of chips and a jumbo soda.

Mark pulled a dirty T-shirt from his backpack and pressed it gingerly against the gash above his now swollen eye. He looked again around the column for Eugene and spotted a stack of newspapers in a bin. He walked over to it, cautiously. The words *South Bend Tribune* were displayed across the banner. The name sounded familiar. Mark hurried back to the safety of the column and pulled a neatly folded but well-worn map from his backpack. He expanded it to look at Illinois and scanned the bold lettering for the name, *South Bend*. When he did not find it, he anxiously folded the map back to Indiana. Tears welled in his eyes. He was still in that state. Eugene had driven him no more than thirty miles.

× × ×

"God, Mark, I can't believe you're here!" his cousin yelled at him later that night. "By yourself…in West Lafayette! And what happened to your face?"

Gary had been ranting at him ever since he picked him up at the bus station. Mark had not minded at first because he was so relieved to see someone he knew, but as they approached his cousin's off-campus rental, he began to have second thoughts about his decision to contact him.

His cousin glared at him as they pulled up to the curb in front of the house, and he repeated the words he had already stated several times. "Are you crazy? Hitchhiking by yourself? You're only fourteen years old, for God's sake!"

Mark retrieved his backpack and sleeping bag from the huge trunk of the tan 1970s Oldsmobile. "Fifteen," he replied as he slammed the door to the compartment shut. "My birthday was two months ago." In an attempt to lighten the mood, he added, "And you know, Gary, you shouldn't use the Lord's name in vain like that."

Gary's family were Pentecostals. Mark hoped to calm him down by drawing attention to his language, but Gary only poked him hard on the sternum and growled, "Don't get smart with me, kid."

The rebuke vividly reminded Mark of his cousin's anxious, inflexible nature. He had not seen Gary in three years, and he knew that contacting him was risky, but after his encounter with Eugene, a switch seemed to have flipped on in his brain that kept him in a constant state of fear. He also realized his remaining cash would probably not see him to the West Coast, given how long it had taken him to get to Indiana. Gary was the only person he knew in the Midwest. Being family, he hoped his cousin would help him.

"I'm calling your mom," Gary declared. They were now sitting in the living room of the old house, and his cousin reached for a black phone over the arm of a couch, which was frayed and stained from years of college life.

"No!" Mark cried out. He lunged for Gary's hand. "Please, no."

"Why not? You haven't given me one good reason why I shouldn't call her."

At that moment, one of Gary's housemates strolled into the room and introduced himself as Ross. He was of average height and build and wore thin, pink, plaid flannel pajama bottoms that had probably once been red. A T-shirt with the Purdue Boilermakers' logo adorned his torso. Ross collapsed into a sagging brown chair, threw a leg over one of its arms, and proceeded to eat cereal and milk out of a large mixing bowl as he watched the two cousins.

"You can't," Mark pleaded. Desperate, he added, "It's not safe. You can't tell anyone I'm here."

"What do you mean, it's not safe?"

A second housemate, Nick, entered the room and playfully slugged Ross on the upper arm. Then he threw himself into a worn green chair, which had lost most of the padding from its seat cushion. As a result, the young man's knees were above the level of his waist when he sat down.

"Guys," Gary snapped at his housemates. "Do you mind? We'd like some privacy."

"Why?" Nick asked. "I can hear your yelling upstairs."

"Yeah," Ross agreed.

After producing a glare that left his housemates unfazed, Gary turned back to Mark and made a strained attempt to understand him. "What's going on?" he asked awkwardly.

"I can't be around her boyfriend anymore," Mark replied. "Don't ask me why. I just can't. I want to get to my dad." The words released a flood of emotions, and when he began to cry, he hung his head in shame at showing such weakness in front of the others. The room was silent except for the sound of a spoon softly hitting the inside of a bowl.

"Do you even know where your dad is?" Gary asked. "Aunt Helen told my mom that he dropped off the face of the earth after their divorce."

"That's not true! Mom just doesn't want me talking to him," Mark replied angrily. He recalled the many times his mother had hung up on his father when he had phoned. She had also torn up the birthday and holiday cards he had sent Mark after first taking out the money. "I've got an address," he declared defiantly. Then he lied. "And a phone number."

"But are they right ones?"

"Yeah."

"How do you know?" his cousin demanded.

"I just know, all right?"

"Have you tried calling him?"

"Yes," Mark answered looking down.

"And?" Gary demanded again.

The teen hesitated. "There's no answer, but he might be out of town."

"Or he doesn't live there!"

Mark hung his head. He had not allowed himself to think about that possibility because it was the only known location he had for his father. On the night he decided to leave, he had searched for a number in his mother's papers but had found nothing. The only relatives his father had who might know where he was were stepsiblings, and Mark had met them only twice in his life.

"We've got to call your mom," his cousin insisted. "She's probably worried sick about you."

"No, she's not."

"Sure she is," Gary persisted. "You're just mad. You're not thinking straight."

Mark heard a tone in his cousin's voice that he knew well. Gary was plotting a way to get himself out of the situation. His cousin was brilliant and would probably be the outstanding engineer he was studying to become, but he had never dealt well with disruption and uncertainty. He liked well-defined rules and routines that allowed no deviations. At their family reunions, Gary's father would force him to interact with his cousins, but he was an oddity among them. The ever-changing and free-flowing nature of their games had led the boy to impressive heights of frustration. Gary, the man, appeared to be no less troubled by the present situation.

Nick saw the impasse and leaned into the conversation. "Gary?" he asked cautiously.

"What?" Mark's cousin replied sharply.

"It may not be my place—"

"Damn straight it's not."

Nick ignored Gary's anger and suggested diplomatically, "Why don't we ask Mark what he needs from us?"

Gary considered his housemate for a moment and then threw up his hands and fell back against the couch. "Whatever," he said dramatically, but Mark could see the relief on his face that the pressure was off of him momentarily.

"Mark?" Nick asked gently. "How can we help?"

Mark turned to the young man. Nick was slender, dark-haired, and spoke with an East Coast accent. He looked at Mark with a calm, nonjudgmental gaze. Mark was quiet for a moment as he realized he did not know what he wanted of Gary.

"See!" Gary yelled upon seeing his cousin's hesitation. "He doesn't know what he's doing. We've got to call his mom."

Nick lifted a hand in Gary's direction. "Hold on," he said.

"I know I want to get to the West Coast," Mark replied, looking only at Nick.

"And how do you plan to do that?" Gary asked, exasperated. "Keep hitchhiking and you'll get yourself killed. I thought you were smarter than that."

"I am!" Mark replied angrily.

Ross put the now empty mixing bowl down on the dusty hardwood floor. "Gary, relax," he said. "There's no emergency here. We'll figure this out."

Mark watched as his cousin let out another heavy sigh, and for a second time, threw himself back against the stained couch. The teen glanced shyly at Nick and Ross. He was grateful for their presence.

× × ×

"Hey, kid, wake up."

The male voice penetrated Mark's sleep. Adrenaline surged through him at the nudge of a foreign hand on his shoulder, and he sat up suddenly.

"Easy," the voice whispered. "It's okay. It's just me, Nick."

Mark forced himself awake. His brain registered a faint light seeping through the living room curtains. He soon recognized the objects in his cousin's house, and his heartbeat began to slow.

As Mark untwisted himself from the blanket, Nick asked quietly, "Kid, are you sure you don't want to see your mom?"

"Yes!" he declared loudly.

Nick shushed him and said, "Gary called her after you fell asleep last night. She and a guy named Kurt are flying to Indianapolis this afternoon. Gary told them he'd keep you here."

"He did what?" Mark gasped. "I can't...I can't..."

The previous night, Nick had persuaded Gary to let Mark stay with them for a couple of days while they tracked down his father. Ross was confident that a friend who worked in the campus police department could help them. Gary had agreed on the condition that if Mark's father was not located in two days, he would tell his own parents that Mark was with him.

"It's okay," Nick said. "If you're sure you don't want to see them, I can help."

"How?"

"How much money do you have?" the young man asked.

"About two hundred and fifty dollars."

"That should cover the bus fare," Nick whispered, "and I can give you a little more for food." Meeting the teen's eyes again, he suggested, "Look, if you're up for it, I can get you on a Greyhound bus to Chicago. From there you can make a connection to the West Coast."

"Yeah?" Mark asked, his panic abating. "That would be great."

"I can drive you to the station, but we've got to leave now. I need to get back before Gary wakes up. His name is on the rental agreement for this dump, and if he finds out that I helped you, he'll kick me out."

Mark looked at Nick intently. "I don't want to get you in trouble. It's okay. I can find my own way to Chicago."

Nick grinned. "Don't worry about it. I want to help."

"Why?" Mark asked.

Nick's dark eyes grew serious. "Let's just say I know something about creeps. Mine was a baseball coach."

A thud sounded from above, and Mark jumped. The two looked up at the ceiling and waited. When the noise did not repeat itself, Nick said, "You pack up while I get dressed. I'll be right back."

But shortly after Nick walked out of the living room, a toilet flushed upstairs. Mark froze. When he heard two voices talking, he hurriedly gathered up his belongings and fled the house. He left only the blanket crumpled at the end of the tattered couch.

Wednesday, May 28

"Jonathan, the DePaul County database is a cost-effective solution for us," Mary explained yet again. "We need ways to work more efficiently, especially since we are short staffed."

Mary's topic was last on the agenda for the managers' budget meeting, and she could tell that Jonathan's capacity to focus was nearly depleted. The man stretched his arms over his head. "Excuse me!" he yawned. "Fifty-six pertussis cases doesn't sound like a lot, Mary."

"It is when each one has about eight contacts that need to be interviewed," she insisted. "We average about twenty-three cases a year, and it's only May."

"Mary?" said Kim Carter, the nurse supervisor for the Field Nursing Unit. "Maybe my team could help. They could add some side trips—"

"No, they can't," Jonathan interrupted testily. "The field nurses have their own work to do." He glared at Kim, but she held his gaze calmly until he lowered his head and took another sip of his soda. Then she mouthed to Mary, "Come see me."

Mary smiled. Despite her unassuming manner, Kim was an extremely smart and effective manager. Before she was first hired to lead the county's Field Nursing Unit, which supported medically at-risk children and their families, the state had put the program on notice for not meeting its contractual agreements. In her first twelve months on the job, Kim had brought the program into compliance, and after three years, it was considered a model program for other counties.

Jonathan turned his attention back to Mary. "We don't need to spend money on computers," he said. "You know what I think? We could save a big chunk of money if we only did the work required of us by law."

"That's ridiculous," growled Nettie Breach, the department's powerful Community Health Program manager. Jonathan's suggestion, if implemented, would effectively eliminate all of Nettie's outreach programs.

Jonathan flinched at the rebuke but said to Mary, "Your girls do a real good job with what they've got. You should be proud of them. Why aren't you proud of them?"

Mary drew in her breath. "They're not anyone's girls, Jonathan. I've asked you before not to call them that."

"Sorry," he replied flippantly.

Mary took a deep breath. *Four weeks*, she moaned. *He's only been here for four weeks.* She had always considered herself the type of person who could work with anyone, but Jonathan was proof she had her limits.

"And, again, we're not asking for new computers," Mary reiterated. "DePaul County has developed a surveillance database. It's software. Since it was built with public funds, they can give it to us in exchange for a fifteen hundred dollar contribution to the annual maintenance fee. All I'm asking is that you present their offer to Carl—unless you'd like me to."

"No," Jonathan bellowed immediately. "Talking to him is my job." He took another sip of soda, and Mary decided to launch her final tactic, one she hoped would appeal to Jonathan's image of himself as a rising executive.

"Jonathan, imagine that Suzanne is preparing for a press briefing," Mary began. "She gives you thirty minutes to put together a summary about our pertussis cases. She wants to know the average age, gender, and ethnicity breakdown for the cases, and how many contacts are on prophylactic antibiotics. If that happened today, we couldn't get her the information, because we would be thumbing through paper files. With the DePaul County database, we could print out a report in a few minutes."

Jonathan pouted. "There's that word again."

"What word?" Mary asked, confused.

"Pro-phy-la-xis," he enunciated. "I had Rosalyn take it out of a Board of Supervisors report. If I don't know what it means, I'm pretty sure they won't."

Mary heard someone snicker at the end of the table.

"Prophylactics prevent things," explained Kim. "For example, a condom is a prophylactic."

Jonathan choked on his soda. "Ha! That's a good one, Kim. I'm going to tell that to my wife. Speaking of condoms, did I tell you she's pregnant?"

The meeting participants became silent. Nettie looked over the top of her black-framed, half-moon reading glasses and said sarcastically, "So, another Jonathan is coming into the world. How nice."

"Yeah, isn't it?" Jonathan exclaimed.

Whoever Mary had heard snickering at the end of the table earlier was now coughing to cover his laughter. She brought the conversation back to her topic. "Jonathan, if you could get a summary to Suzanne that quickly, she would be very impressed with you." Mary hated the cloying sound of her voice, but the tactic seemed to work. Her supervisor's eyes widened, and he lowered his soda to the table.

"I know what I'll do," he declared. "I'll ask Carl what he thinks. Yep, that's what I'll do."

Mary sighed, but with relief, at finally getting Jonathan to agree to this small concession. He stood up, as if to leave, and Mary turned to Nettie. She steeled herself—getting a favor out of Nettie was never easy.

"Nettie," she said, "would you mind if Linus helped the CD Unit for a few days?" Linus Baldwin was the health department's epidemiologist. Although, by policy, communicable disease investigations took precedence over other department activities, Mary knew she did not dare engage Linus without first seeking permission from Nettie, his supervisor.

Nettie gave her a suspicious look. "Why?" she snarled. "He's busy writing a grant for me."

Jonathan immediately sat back down when Nettie spoke, and Mary took pleasure in watching him do so. Although he was at least twelve inches taller than the woman and likely outweighed her by a hundred pounds, Jonathan was terrified of Nettie. He had learned quickly that she went after anyone who threatened her interests.

"The norovirus outbreaks haven't stopped," Mary answered. "I would like Linus to review our reports and see if he can find any pattern or connection that explains why they're occurring. He might catch something that I've overlooked."

Nettie removed her reading glasses and waved them dismissively. "Please. Norovirus isn't even a reportable illness. It's harmless."

"Yeah," Jonathan interjected importantly.

"Individual cases aren't reportable, but outbreaks are," Mary explained. "And it's not harmless. We just got word of a third nursing home death."

Nettie sighed heavily. "All right, Linus can help." She pointed the reading glasses at Mary and added sternly, "But limit your use of him. I want that grant done on time."

"Thank you," Mary said.

Jonathan leapt out of his chair and declared gleefully, "Okay, then. See you around, everyone! I'm off to see Carl."

× × ×

Mary decided to stop by Linus' office to give him the news about working with her unit. She peered down a dimly lit passageway to the right of the grand staircase. At its end, a thin vertical line of yellow light streamed out of his office door. Mary walked to it. After knocking a second time, she peered inside and saw the reason why no one had answered. Erin was holding Linus' left hand in hers. The two were focused solely on each other.

"Is it sore when I do this?" Erin asked.

"Ow. Yes!" Linus winced. He was about Erin's age, but his shy countenance made him appear younger, and his manner of dress only added to the effect. He wore Birkinstock sandals and a bold Hawaiian-print shirt over blue jeans.

"How about this?"

"Yes!" He grimaced but then laughed. "You call yourself a nurse?"

Mary cleared her throat, and the pair turned toward the sound. Upon seeing Mary, Erin released Linus' hand and stepped away from him. A blush quickly spread across Linus' face.

Erin said to him in her most professional voice, "You should ice that and take regular breaks from the keyboard. You don't want to develop carpal tunnel syndrome."

Mary grinned and made a mental note to congratulate Lourdes, the department's matchmaker, on pairing up these two. Mary had put a quick stop to Lourdes' efforts to see her coupled with Linus. He was a valued friend and colleague, but he reminded her too much of her brother. The romantic spark between Linus and Erin, however, was clear; their attraction lit up the dim office.

"Well, I should let you two talk," Erin said as she headed to the door. She gave Mary a chagrined smile. "See you later."

"Glad to see you're finally getting some help for your hand," Mary said after Erin left the room. She was teasing Linus, but the cause of his discomfort was obvious all around the office. His bookcase was filled with data reports. Papers spilled off of his computer station and even more covered his desk. Although Linus had specialized in infectious diseases in graduate school, he was expected to be a generalist in his present position. As the sole data analyst for Public Health, he worked on topics ranging from teen pregnancies to pesticide exposures.

Linus lowered his gaze and smiled. "How's your day going?" he asked, quickly.

"I just got out of a budget meeting, if that's any indication."

"Did you get any movement from Jonathan on the database?" Linus asked with hope in his voice.

"He said he'd talk with Carl."

Linus laughed. "Well, Jonathan's pace is glacial, but that's progress, at least."

"What's so hard about understanding the value of that database?" Mary asked, throwing her hands up in the air. "If a bioterrorist attack ever did occur, the mayor and governor would be all over us for updates. What are we supposed to do? Show them a bunch of papers and say, 'We'll get back to you in a couple of weeks, after we've figured out what's going on?'"

"Actually, they'll probably get the information from CNN," Linus retorted.

"That's not funny."

Linus laughed again. "It's the truth. It's not like we've got people to send out into the field."

Mary acknowledged his logic with a nod. "The reason I stopped by," she said, "is that I've got some good news, although it means more work for you."

Linus looked at her suspiciously.

"Nettie has given you permission to help the CD Unit for a few days."

"Really? With what?"

Mary heard the excitement in his voice. "The norovirus outbreaks," she said. "I'd like you to review our reports to see if there's a connection or pattern I've missed."

Linus smiled. "Sounds like fun. Have you asked the state if they're seeing anything unusual?

"Not yet, but I'll do that when I get back to my office," Mary answered. "Can you meet with me later this afternoon? That'll give me time to pull the materials together for you."

"Tomorrow morning would be better," Linus replied. "Suzanne wants some graphs and charts from me by four for a presentation she's giving." He pulled a black Palm Pilot from his pocket and punched at the instrument with its stylus. "How about 9:30, after your morning report?"

"Perfect," Mary said

× × ×

"I think my husband got everyone sick," the caller confessed anxiously.

"Why's that?" Mary asked. She was covering the CD line while Stella, Lourdes, and Erin were at lunch. The caller had told her that eleven of the nineteen guests who were at her home for a soccer-team party two nights ago had come down with a gastrointestinal illness. Concerned, the caller had meticulously gathered information about the party's attendees. As a result, she was able to give Mary detailed responses to each of her intake questions. State law mandated that health care providers and laboratories report over sixty communicable diseases to local health departments. Members of the general public, like this team parent, also called in their suspicions. For this, Mary was grateful. These calls could save her staff significant time in identifying and initiating investigations.

"He had stomach pain and loose stools before the party but didn't tell me. It was only later, when I found him upstairs, hugging the toilet, that I knew he was sick."

"How's he doing now?"

"Oh, he's fine," the woman replied. "He was laid up for about a day. But the thing is, he prepared some of the food and used the guest bathroom—along with everyone else."

"Ah," Mary said knowingly. "Well, based on the symptoms you described, and what we're seeing in the community, it's likely your guests were infected with norovirus. Would your husband be willing to give us a stool specimen so we can have it tested?"

Laboratory tests made it easy, most of the time, to identify the bacteria and viruses that caused communicable diseases. Modern medicine could usually treat the resulting illnesses, especially if they were diagnosed early. But it was Public Health that tracked down and prevented further spread of the diseases.

"Yes," the woman replied. "I'll see to it."

Mary smiled. The caller was so determined to make amends for the outbreak that Mary doubted the husband would have much say about producing a stool specimen. "Was he around anyone else with similar symptoms before he got sick?" she asked.

"He was," the woman confirmed. "He visited his mother at the Carriage House the day before the party. Do you know that place? They have some sort of stomach flu going around there too."

Mary's eyebrows rose. The Carriage House was a high-end retirement community with graduated levels of care for its elderly residents, from independent living to skilled nursing. She had visited the facility in search of a place for her father but had quickly realized it was beyond her family's financial means.

"Really?" Mary responded, hiding her irritation. By law, nursing homes were required to report outbreaks to the health department within twenty-four hours of symptom onset. "I didn't know that. I'll give them a call."

A probable norovirus outbreak, Mary wrote in her notes about the soccer-team party at the end of the call. She leaned back and thought, *I'd better look at our baseline numbers before I call the state.* She swiveled in her chair, opened a drawer in her filing cabinet, and found a single-page report that Linus had compiled for her the previous summer. It displayed a bar chart and a table of numbers. The information confirmed what she knew about the seasonality of the disease; most of their norovirus outbreaks over the past five years occurred during winter. The bar chart showed that outbreaks generally began in September and peaked in February. In previous years, only one outbreak had been reported, on average, in April, and none in May. The table of numbers also showed that more norovirus outbreaks were reported to her unit in 2002 than for previous years. The United States had experienced a pandemic strain of the virus that year. People exposed to the virus would have had little or no immunity to the new strain.

Mary looked at the call schedule for the State CD Program, which was tacked to the wall over her telephone. She was pleased to see that Sonia Wong, a medical epidemiologist, was the duty officer for the day.

That works well, she thought. *Sonia wanted an update on our pertussis outbreak anyway.*

Mary reached for the phone's receiver and dialed the long-distance number she knew by heart. The first person to answer would be the receptionist, Irene. As Mary waited, she quickly jotted down some notes in preparation for the usual battery of questions that came with these calls.

"Communicable Disease," a pleasant-sounding woman announced. "Irene speaking. How may I help you?"

"Hi, Irene. This is Mary Campbell from Revere County. Is it possible to speak with Sonia?"

"Hi, Mary. Sonia isn't here today. Are you calling for the duty officer?"

"Yes, but—"

"Okay, let me connect you," she replied before Mary had time to stop her. "Just a moment, please."

Mary felt a minor panic over not knowing who would pick up the phone next. She always dreaded talking to one person in particular.

"Please don't let it be Phil," she whispered.

Phillip Margolis was the medical epidemiologist who managed the State CD Program. On a good day, he only spoke tersely to her when she called with a question. On his worst, he seemed to enjoy putting Mary in her place with, as she regrettably had to admit, his considerable intellectual skills.

Irene came back on the line. "I'm putting you through now, Mary. Have a wonderful afternoon."

Mary heard a click on the line, and a man announced himself with a sharp-edged voice. "Margolis here."

Damn, Mary cursed to herself. In her best attempt to sound pleasant, she said, "Hello, Phil. This is Mary Campbell from Revere County."

"Yes, I know. Irene told me."

Mary fought a strong impulse to hang up the phone but, instead, said, "I'm calling to update Sonia on our pertussis outbreak. Will she back tomorrow? I can call her then."

"No, she's in Atlanta at a CDC conference for the rest of the week," he said flatly.

"Damn," she whispered more audibly than she realized.

"Excuse me?"

Mary stumbled over her reply. "Sorry. I mean, if she was around, then I wouldn't have to bother you, would I?"

Phil said nothing.

"How about David Ketchum?" she asked, trying not to sound desperate. "Is he there?"

"No, he's at the same conference." As if reading her mind, Phil said, "You're stuck with me. What do you need?"

Mary's shoulders slumped, and she resigned herself to the inevitable conversation. "I'd like to know if you're seeing any unusual norovirus activity."

"What do you want to start with, pertussis or norovirus?"

"The pertussis can wait—" Mary stated, but Phil interrupted her.

"No, I want to hear about it."

"Okay, then let's start with that," Mary said. She quickly reviewed her notes. "Five new cases were reported to us this week."

"Lab confirmed?"

"Not yet. We're waiting for the results of the NP swabs."

Mary was intimately familiar with nasopharyngeal, or NP, swabs. The instrument, which resembled a very long Q-tip, was slipped up through the nose and into the sinus cavity. Once there, it was gently turned to collect mucus, and hopefully, the bacteria or virus that had sickened the person. She and another classmate had practiced the technique on each other in nursing school. Mary had vivid memories of tearing up when her fellow student thrust the swab upward too vigorously.

"Are they epi-linked to confirmed cases?" Phil asked.

By epi-linked, Phil was referring to whether the new cases had been exposed to a known case whose clinical diagnosis was confirmed by positive lab results for the bacteria that causes pertussis, *Bordetella pertussis*.

"Yes and no," she replied. "Two were exposed at a slumber party held by one of our first cases, and we're looking into a possible exposure for the third one. The fourth case is from our west county region. The parents of that child refuse to talk to us, since we're with the government, so I've asked their family doctor to interview them. The fifth case isn't linked to anyone that we know of yet."

"So you're still seeing west-county cases?"

"Yes," Mary said. "You're familiar with this investigation?"

"Sonia gives updates on it during our daily wrap-up."

Mary was startled to find herself reassured by these words. It was as if, despite the ongoing challenges she had with her state colleagues, they were watching out for her unit.

"So, how many cases do you have to date?" Phil asked.

"Fifty six, with no let up in sight," she replied.

"How do you know?"

"Excuse me?" she asked.

"How do you know there's 'no let up in sight'?"

Uh oh. Here it comes. Mary realized her mistake. She had used a turn of phrase that had no epidemiological meaning.

"What do you mean?"

"Hasn't Linus been tracking your incidence rate?"

"No, he hasn't," she replied irritably.

"Why not?"

"Because he's not allowed to work with my unit much. Listen, Phil, I don't have time to talk statistics. We've been getting two to four new cases each week, and that's a lot when you're understaffed and each case has multiple contacts that need to be interviewed. I'll believe a let up is in sight when no new cases come in for a while. I don't need an epidemiologist to tell me that."

Phil said nothing. The line was so quiet Mary wondered if he had hung up, but then he said, "You've probably noticed that many of your cases are from the same pediatric practice."

"That's right," Mary replied, surprised that he knew this level of detail about the investigation. "West Hills Pediatrics. They have about five providers out there."

"And they participate in the federal Vaccines for Children program."

"Yes, that's correct."

"We may need to do a medical-chart review to see why so many of your cases are coming from there."

"Whoa. Hold on, Phil. My team doesn't have time for that and—"

Phil cut her off. "You wanted to talk about norovirus?" he asked.

Mary hoped his rapid change of subject meant he was not going to pursue the chart-review idea. "Yes. I was wondering if you're seeing any unusual activity in our region?"

"Other than as a result of the pandemic strain?"

"Yes."

"No, we haven't. Why do you ask?"

"We've had seven confirmed norovirus outbreaks since early April, and a presumptive report just came in."

"I take it that's above your baseline count."

"Yes, it is."

"What settings are they in?"

"The confirmed outbreaks were at a home-and-garden expo, a conference center, an elementary school, and four nursing home facilities. The presumptive outbreak involved a soccer-team party at a private home."

"That mix of locations suggests community spread. Have you ruled out a common source for the nursing homes, like a food supplier?"

"Yes," Mary replied. "Our environmental health specialist helped us with that."

"Have you looked at other possible links, like float staff who work at different facilities?"

"We did, and nothing came of that."

"Well, we're not seeing anything unusual in your region or any other part of the state," Phil said. "I wouldn't worry about it. You're probably having an extended season due to the pandemic strain."

Mary was disappointed with Phil's assessment. His conclusion was likely correct, but it did nothing to help her unit address the situation. "All right," she said. "That's all I wanted to talk about. Thank you."

She was hanging up the phone when she heard Phil's voice again.

"Mary? Are you still there?"

Mary looked at the receiver and thought, *I could pretend I didn't hear that.* Instead, she put the phone back to her ear. "Yes, I'm here," she said.

"It sounds like you have a lot going on up there."

No fooling, Mary felt like saying, but she held her tongue. It was not Phil's fault that she was tired and wanted nothing more than to go home and curl up on her couch. "We do," she replied. Then Phil surprised her again.

"Do you need any help from us?" he asked.

Mary thought a moment. Her calls to the State CD Program usually led to more work for her staff, not offers of assistance. Her unit could definitely benefit from the addition of another person, but Phil would likely send a student with little experience, or worse, a high-maintenance physician epidemiologist who would not want to do any scut work. She did not want to burden her staff with either.

"I appreciate the offer," she answered sincerely, "but no, thank you. We'll be all right."

After she hung up the phone, Mary leaned back in her chair and folded her arms tightly over her chest. *At least, I hope we'll be all right.*

× × ×

When Stella returned from lunch, she ordered Mary to take a break. Mary complied and exited the Seventh Street building through its north-facing door. Once outside, she was immediately enveloped by the sweet fragrance of jasmine from a vine entwined around a nearby trellis. A former employee with a passion for medicinal herbs had created a small garden out of the narrow space between the building's foundation and the sidewalk. The garden had lost much of its luster through neglect over the years, but the most tenacious of the plants persisted in the poor soil. Mary tilted her face toward the warm sun and breathed the scent in deeply.

She decided to eat at her favorite taqueria, La Cantina de Rosa, which was a short, two-block walk from the health department. She turned to her right and headed to the Seventh and Pine Street crosswalk. At the curb, she glanced around for oncoming traffic and spotted

Carl and Jonathan standing at the front entrance to the health department. The two talked as Carl concluded his customary premeeting smoke. He dropped the butt of his cigarette onto the sidewalk and ground it out with the toe of his tasseled, black shoe. Neither man looked her way, and she hurried across the intersection.

The taqueria was located on Main Street at the west end of the downtown area's large, grassy plaza. The restaurant's interior decor was simple yet colorful. Mexican blankets and posters adorned the walls. Mary used her high school Spanish, modestly enhanced by her many years in public health, to greet the staff behind the counter and to order two soft-shelled chicken tacos. She and the staff laughed together as she mangled their language.

While she waited for her food, Mary turned her attention to the midday news, which was showing on a television placed high in a front corner of the eatery. The station's longtime anchor was congratulating a colleague, Trish Matthews, on her promotion from entertainment reporter to coanchor.

"I'm excited and humbled by this responsibility," Trish told the audience. Then she smiled broadly and said, "And now we turn to Beth for the weather." But Beth did not appear on the screen, which left Ms. Matthews staring awkwardly at her audience. She swiveled to face a different camera and smiled eagerly. Then the professional headshot of an elderly man appeared next to her on the screen. Confused, the anchor's smile stiffened as she began to shuffle anxiously through her notes. Mary might have found this miscue amusing if not for the painful memories of her own mock on-air interviews during a mandatory county news media training.

Ms. Matthews wore a grave expression on her heavily made-up face when she next raised her head. "Joseph Tremaine," she began, "founder of Tremaine Wineries, died this morning at the age of eighty-seven of complications stemming from a sudden illness."

Mary recognized the man's name as the deceased nursing home resident she had mentioned during the morning budget-planning meeting. She was impressed at how quickly his death had become public.

Linus is probably right, she thought. *CNN will be the first to know what's going on during a bioterrorist attack.*

With her tacos in hand, Mary proceeded to a small round cafe table out in front of the taqueria. Dappled sunlight, filtering through the leaves of two fruitless plum trees, flickered on the red-and-white checkered tablecloth. She sat down and tried to free her mind from thoughts of work by watching passersby, attempting to decipher their body language and wondering about the topics of their conversations. She watched people meander in and out of the boutiques across the street and envied them their leisure time. Several teens dressed in various articles of black clothing socialized near the plaza's large water fountain despite the blaring of Beethoven's Ninth Symphony from a speaker mounted on a nearby building. Shopkeepers had hoped the music would drive away loitering youth, but the teens looked very content lounging around the water feature with the famous composition thundering at them from on high.

Over the past eight years, high-tech companies had moved into Revere County, drawn by its natural beauty and international reputation for wine, cheese, and specialty foods. Mary had watched, with mixed feelings, the metamorphosis of her hometown from one that catered to the working class to one that celebrated a sophisticated rural lifestyle. Main Street, on which the taqueria was located, had once been lined with simple shops that posted handpainted signs in the storefront windows. Now enormous bouquets of geraniums hung from English-style black street lamps; park benches were colorfully painted to celebrate the region's scenery; old buildings had been lovingly renovated into restaurants, with attention given to historical detailing; and at night, delicate little white lights lit up the trees and warmed the plaza with a festive, romantic glow.

Articles in the local newspaper, however, highlighted the ominous side of the county's growth. They featured stories about teachers and police officers who could not afford housing. Vineyard owners and environmentalists argued about the dangers of grapes as a monoculture while restaurateurs championed the farm-to-table movement. The financially strapped county government found desperately needed tax revenue in the building of vast subdivisions, but parents complained about overcrowded classrooms. Many feared that the growth would continue unchecked and the region would realize the ugly fate of other congested metropolitan expanses in the state.

Mary had returned home four years earlier because her mother, Carol, was struggling to care for her father, who had been diagnosed with Alzheimer's disease. He had been able to dress and feed himself for a while, but that ability disappeared during his rapid decline. His nighttime wanderings in the house, and his daytime escapes to the outside world, had driven her mother to exhaustion. Still, Carol had reacted angrily when Mary first suggested they find a facility for her father. Not until he was escorted home by the police in the early morning hours, confused and soiled with his own feces, did her mother finally relent.

Then her brother and twin, David, was killed in a car accident. His death had been a devastating blow, but she grieved on her own because her mother was even more crushed in spirit than she. Carol had almost withdrawn from the world entirely. Her outings were limited to the grocery store and trips she made with Mary to visit her husband.

As Mary finished her taco, a young father sat down with his toddler son and school-age daughter at the table directly in front of her. She watched as the man cut the children's quesadillas into small pieces, and she smiled at their laughter when sauce squirted messily from their father's burrito. She listened to the father ask his daughter about her morning in kindergarten, and the child relayed a story about being teased by two second-grade girls. The man's loving response triggered a deep ache in Mary for the comfort of conversing with her own father as he had once been. Tears stung her eyes, and her throat tightened. She stood up from the table and carried her tray to the trash bin.

Knowing Stella would scold her if she came back too early, she decided to walk around the plaza before returning to work. She crossed the street and passed a deli at which she never ate because she knew it received poor inspection ratings. A broad-shouldered police officer rode by on a bicycle, and she watched as he acknowledged nearby teens with a nod. He stopped to check on a homeless man who was lying on a park bench. A brown paper bag lay on the ground, under the man's fingertips. Mary could just make out the classic crumpling of the bag around the neck of the bottle.

When Mary reached the grassy knoll of the plaza, she shared a greeting with two teens but politely brushed off a request for money from a third. She noticed that a small crowd had gathered in the center of the park. They were listening with some interest to a middle-aged man with wavy, light hair. He was dressed in a faded African tunic and blue jeans. A young woman with straight brown hair that flowed to the middle of her back stood next to him. She held a baby and a handful of papers.

Mary stopped at the park bench from which the police officer had roused the homeless man. Its surface depicted a faded image commissioned years ago for the county's sesquicentennial celebration. On the left side, the artist had drawn a farmhouse surrounded by a small apple orchard. A fence separated it from a second house and a large oak tree in the middle of the scene. The background was filled with rows of tidy grapevines that flowed over rolling hills. In the foreground, two elaborate glass goblets stood amidst a cluster of purple grapes. Red wine spilled from one goblet into a river that coursed along the right edge of the bench.

Mary looked up when she heard someone cough. She saw a thin, disheveled teen standing alone at the edge of the crowd. Unlike his peers, he wore conservative attire: khaki-colored pants and a light-blue polo shirt. He seemed to sense her presence and turned in her direction. They held each other's gaze for a brief moment. One of the boy's eyes was bruised, and a cut ran along the brow. Mary expected a glare or a glance of indifference from him, but instead, she saw anxiety and fear in his eyes. Then the boy turned away to listen to the man addressing the crowd.

"Every action," the speaker stated with conviction, "every intention should be performed with awareness and purpose. That's how we live our lives at Dovestone. Our goal is to awaken people to the destruction we're perpetrating against our planet—our mother—and to offer practical solutions for everyday living. You're welcome to learn more about this work at our upcoming fund-raiser. Please take a pamphlet and come visit us."

Mary looked back at the boy. An older teen had joined him after the speaker and his companion began to hand out flyers. The older boy was dressed all in white, and his red hair was tied back in a ponytail.

Well, at least he's not alone, Mary thought, and she made her way back to work.

× × ×

Mark glanced back at the woman who was now walking away from the park bench. Moments ago, he had caught her studying him. On the road, he had been invisible to most people unless they wanted something from him. This woman had looked at him with genuine concern, but he had found her attention unsettling.

Take it easy, he told himself as he dug his hands into his pockets and followed his new friend, Skye. *Everything's going to be okay. You got this far.*

Mark was not quite sure what to make of Skye, but at this point he was just grateful for the kindness he had shown him. Skye had come to his aid earlier that day at the mall, after his arrival in town by city bus. Mark had shown the driver his father's address, and she gave him the number for a connecting bus.

"Mill Creek is a small town on the way out to the coast. It's best if someone can drive you there. It's only thirty minutes by car," she had said, "but ninety minutes by bus."

The driver had also told Mark that the bus would not arrive for another hour, so he'd walked across the street to a large shopping mall to find some food. All he had eaten that day was the remainder of a bagel and some cold, cigarette-perfumed coffee he had found on a counter at the city's bus terminal.

At the mall two men in their early twenties cornered him at the public phone near the entrance to the long hallway that led to the bathrooms. He had been looking for his father's name in the phone book. One thug had shoved him against the wall while the other searched him for cash. Mark had been assaulted like this in Chicago and had lost all but nineteen dollars of his money, but he had learned from the experience. He now kept his paper bills in his socks, under his feet, but left a couple dollars worth of change as bait in the zippered front pocket of his backpack. Mark claimed to have only that small amount on him as he was searched. He told the two men they could take his backpack too, but they laughed about how much both he and it stank.

The assailants fled after security shouted at them from down the walkway. When two guards reached the scene, they looked Mark over intensely. Not liking what they saw, they began questioning him. Then Skye appeared. He told the guards he had witnessed the attack and could vouch for Mark's story. To his surprise, Skye even pretended to be an acquaintance of Mark's from high school.

"Yeah, he was in a couple of my classes," the young man said. "He's okay, even if he is a bit of a slob."

Mark played along with the story by keeping quiet. Eventually, the security guards let him leave with Skye.

"Hey, thanks," Mark said when the guards were a safe distance away.

"No problem," Skye answered. "I thought you could use some help. You look pretty bad."

Mark felt the insult, but then saw his reflection in a storefront window. His once-lean frame was now almost gaunt, and his body, along with everything on it, badly needed a wash. "Yeah," he conceded as he raised a hand to smooth his hair, "I guess you're right. But what's up with your outfit?"

"This?" the young man asked. Skye tugged at his billowing white tunic, and Mark noticed the word *Dovestone* embroidered in golden-brown thread near the collarless neckline. "It's something I wear to honor my community."

"Community?" Mark asked, a bit alarmed.

"Yeah, my father runs an eco-spiritual group called Dovestone."

Kurt would love this, Mark thought sarcastically. His mother's boyfriend had openly mocked anything that smelled of environmentalism. Mark had once made the mistake of asking his mom, in Kurt's presence, to sign a permission slip for a school field trip to a wildlife refuge. The man spent fifteen minutes lecturing him about why the refuge was a waste of high-value land.

"Hey, are you hungry?" Skye asked. "I could use a bowl of fried rice. Want some? My treat."

Mark gladly agreed. In the mall's concession area, he chose a white plastic spoon over the cheap chopsticks so that he could get the food quickly into his mouth. As they ate, he learned that Skye had been at the mall passing out flyers for a Dovestone fund-raiser. Skye was easy to talk to, and with Mark's hunger pains abating, he was able to relax and listen to his companion talk about his father's work. He learned that over the past decade, Skye's father had tried, with limited success, to grow the Dovestone community. His father was working to restore a farmhouse and the land, but progress was slow because they were always low on money. Skye's father had hoped his outreach to the community and the steady stream of volunteers it attracted would bring in more funds, but they only seemed to drain money further away. As a result, his father worked odd hours as an aide in nursing homes to pay the bills.

"Our philosophy is pretty simple," Skye stated. "We take the best of other religious practices—tolerance, meditation, community service—and blend it with a lifestyle that has a minimal impact on this planet. You find God when you are in harmony with the earth." Then Skye made him an offer. "Would you like to spend the night with us if you can't reach your dad?"

Mark was taken aback. The concern must have shown on his face, because Skye asked him what was wrong.

"Listen," Mark began cautiously, "don't take offense or anything, but I've had a lot of trouble and…I mean…your group…they're not into brainwashing or kidnapping…things like that?"

"What?" the older teen asked.

Mark could not tell if the odd expression on Skye's face was from anger or amusement. "Well," he added defensively, "you talk about an eco-community and—"

"Eco-spiritual," Skye corrected him. "Haven't you been listening?"

"And you wear those clothes."

"I wouldn't be criticizing anyone's clothes if I were you," Skye retorted.

Mark slumped back in his chair, and the two young men sat in silence for a few moments. Then Skye leaned onto his elbows and looked at Mark earnestly. "Listen," he began. "I'm just trying to help. You look like you could use a friend. Like I said, we have lots of people—volunteers and visitors—coming and going from Dovestone all the time. One more person isn't going to make a difference. And they're all adults. It'd be nice to have someone my own age around, even if it's just for a little while. We're not into anything perverted or criminal. I promise."

Mark said nothing because he was fighting back the tears that seemed to come so easily these days. Skye sensed his mood and said lightheartedly, "Besides, I'll be doing the public a favor." Mark looked up at him for an explanation, and the older teen smirked. "You smell like a dump."

Mark laughed. He was exhausted, out of options, and had little fight left in him. "Okay," he replied. "Thanks. I'd like to stay with you."

Skye smiled broadly. "I just need to make sure it's okay with my dad. He's speaking over at the plaza. Let's go see him."

Mark rose from the table and followed the young man out of the mall. They walked past the bus depot to a broad, grassy area surrounded by shops. Skye pointed out his father to him and said he was nearly finished addressing the small crowd of people. Mark remained behind when Skye walked over to his father. After a few minutes, Skye returned and said excitedly, "It's okay with my dad. You can stay with us. He wants us to meet him at the car."

The vehicle, an old white passenger van, was parked along the eastern edge of the plaza. Skye introduced his father as Paul Merrill.

To Mark, he appeared to be in his early to mid fifties. His brown hair was turning white, and his blue-gray eyes were offset by lightly tanned skin. Unlike Skye, who was skinny and about six feet tall, Mr. Merrill was of medium height, with a fit build.

"Thank you for putting me up for the night, Mr. Merrill," Mark said.

"My pleasure," Paul replied as he studied his new guest. "From the looks of you, I'd say Skye was right to think you needed a soft place to land. How long have you been on the road?"

"About two weeks," Mark admitted.

"Are you feeling well?" Paul asked. "You look pale."

Skye laughed and nudged Mark. "Don't mind him. Dad was a medic in Vietnam. He fusses over people a lot."

"Look who's talking," his father teased.

Mark smiled shyly. "I think I'm just tired, sir."

"Sir?" Paul repeated, impressed. He grinned at his son and declared, "Now, this boy knows his manners."

The young woman with the baby who had helped pass out fliers joined them, and Paul introduced her as Willow. He told Mark she was also visiting Dovestone. Then a police officer approached them and asked that they move their vehicle because the farmer's market was going to open soon. Willow strapped her sleeping child into a car seat in the center back of the van, and Paul said to Mark, "Why don't you sit up front with me? And do you mind if we run an errand on the way home?"

"Not at all, Mr. Merrill," Mark replied, surprised that this man would be concerned about what he thought. "And thanks again for letting me stay at your home."

"Well, you seem harmless enough. And call me Paul."

After about fifteen minutes of driving, the van turned into a small shopping center and stopped long enough to let Willow out. Mark watched her hurry into the organic food store that was sandwiched between a chocolate shop and a bar.

"So, where does your dad live?" Paul asked as he pulled into a parking spot and turned off the engine.

"In Mill Creek."

Paul looked at him thoughtfully. "Skye told me you haven't been able to contact him. Is that right?"

"Yes," Mark replied, looking away.

"Do you have his address and phone number?"

Mark glanced at the man tentatively. He did not want to lie, but he was embarrassed to admit that he did not have a phone number.

"Just an address," he confessed.

If the man was surprised by this response, he did not show it. Instead, he asked, "May I see it?"

Mark leaned forward and rummaged through his backpack. He pulled out the envelope with his dad's address and handed it to Paul. He read it over and then looked at Mark with concern.

"Son, this is the address of a resort," he stated. "Pine Ridge Resort."

"I know," Mark said. "I think my dad's living there." He glanced back at Skye, who was watching him with concern.

"But resorts are like hotels, and Mill Creek is a popular tourist town," Paul said gently. "The population triples in the summertime, but there aren't many permanent residents."

Mark suddenly felt ill, like all the energy had drained out of his body. "So, you don't think my dad's there?" he stammered.

"It's a possibility," Paul cautioned him.

The teen turned toward the passenger window. A thick silence filled the van.

After a moment, Paul asked, "I take it that contacting your mother or another relative isn't an option?"

Mark lowered his head and shook it vigorously. Then he felt the man's hand on his shoulder. He flinched only a little at his touch.

"Well, let's not worry about anything yet. He was probably a guest at the resort. I bet the owners can look him up in their records."

Encouraged, Mark looked over at Paul. "Do you think so?"

"I don't see why not. We'll find him, and you can stay with us until you do."

"I don't have money to pay you."

Paul laughed. "Don't worry about that. You can earn your keep with some sweat equity. There's plenty of work to do at Dovestone. Right, Skye?"

"Yeah, way too much," his son answered.

× × ×

Dovestone was not nearly as impressive or intimidating as Mark had imagined. The white farmhouse was badly in need of a new coat of paint, but otherwise the area around it was tidy. The building was separated from a barn by what must have been a hundred feet of vegetable and flower gardens, which were well-tended. Mark understood the reason for this when Skye told him that much of the produce was sold to support Dovestone. Next to the ancient-looking barn stood the foundation and unfinished frame of a small cabin. Skye said that structure would eventually house overnight guests.

Through the door that opened onto the farmhouse's sagging back porch, Mark found a worn but large and airy kitchen. After everyone had a snack there, Skye offered to give Mark a tour of the property. Despite his fatigue, Mark thought a walk might feel good after being cooped up on the bus. The afternoon sky was clear, the air was warm, and the rural surroundings were soothing.

"Let's go to the elementary school across the street," Skye suggested. "It's up on a hill. You can see a lot from there."

The teens walked for about five minutes up the gently sloped gravel driveway to the two-lane road that defined Dovestone's property line on one side. At the top of the grade, Mark could read the name *Daisy Merrill Elementary School* on the building across the street.

"Any relation to you?" Mark asked Skye, pointing to the school.

Skye grinned. "I never met her, but Daisy Merrill was my grandmother."

The older teen led the way to the playground. Mark collapsed heavily onto a swing, taking in the beauty of the broad vista before him. From his vantage point, he could see that Dovestone was surrounded by acres of hilly land. Craggy oak trees, which dotted acres of long grass already turned brown, flowed into the horizon, and the curve of a river was just visible near a distant stand of tall pine trees to the north.

"There's something different about the sky out here," Mark said aloud, not expecting a reply. *Maybe it's the light*, he thought. The sky's brilliance and clarity were intense, but not so harsh as to drown out the landscape's rich colors. Under its expanse, he felt like he could breathe freely again, and the revelation lifted his spirit. After a moment, Mark pointed to the field behind the barn. "How much of that land is yours?" he asked. "It goes on forever."

"A lot," Skye replied. "Dad is talking with a local winery about putting in a vineyard and making an organic table wine to bring in money."

Mark thought about the wine-and-cheese parties his mother had hosted and laughed aloud. "The people my mom hangs out with would never drink anything organic," he said. "They're snobs about things like that." But the thought of his mother made his stomach knot, so he changed the subject. "How long have you and your dad lived here?"

"Ever since I can remember," Skye replied. "I was born in Oregon, but we came back here when I was almost two. My grandmother left a chunk of land in her will for my dad. She left some more for this school. That's why they named it after her. It just opened this fall."

"Cool," Mark replied.

"My uncle, Raymond, got the rest. He lives over there in my grandmother's house." Skye pointed to an area far to the left of his home. "See that fence just beyond the apple orchard? Uncle Ray's property starts there. The house my dad inherited belonged to my great-grandparents."

Mark had no trouble spotting the ugly mental fence that ran through the wild field. It reflected the sunlight harshly. In contrast, the neat rows of small apple trees to its left looked cool and inviting. Several acres of land separated Skye's home from that of his uncle.

"What does your uncle do with his land?" Mark asked.

"Not much, as far as I can tell," Skye replied. "He calls himself a farmer, but he works full time—something about licensing nursing homes. All he does around here is take care of those apple trees."

"He has the same job as your dad?"

"Kind of. Uncle Ray is more on the business side, I think. My dad actually takes care of people in nursing homes."

Mark noticed that Skye seemed uncomfortable talking about his uncle, so he did not ask any more questions. The two teens were quiet for several moments, but then Skye said, "My dad wants Uncle Ray to go in on the vineyard deal with him, but they keep fighting about it."

Mark heard the worry in Skye's voice. "Why?" he asked.

Skye glanced sideways at Mark. "There's bad blood between them," he confessed. "Until recently, Uncle Ray barely even talked to my dad, which is kind of weird because he's only a couple of years older than him. You'd think they'd be friends."

Mark leaned toward Skye. He wanted to ask what the bad blood was about but realized he did not know Skye well enough to do so.

Skye saw his interest, though. "It's got something to do with my mom. Dad doesn't talk about it, but I think Uncle Ray was in love with her or something. Uncle Ray doesn't think my dad should have inherited any of my grandmother's land."

"Why?"

"He says my dad never cared about it, that he was never around and never helped with the upkeep."

"Is that true?" Mark asked.

"I guess it was when he was younger," Skye replied. "My dad told to me he wanted to get away from his family. He said they were pretty messed up. That's why he enlisted and fought in Vietnam. To get away."

Mark said nothing. He fully understood the desire to flee one's family.

Skye suddenly laughed. "Dad won't let me go anywhere near a military recruiter's office." He tugged on his white tunic top and added, "Not that they'd even want me."

Mark laughed too.

"But my grandmother did leave my dad some land," Skye said. "He's been working on the place ever since, trying to make something out of it. My dad's got this dream about making the world a better place. It's kind of crazy, but it's kind of cool, too. He's a good guy."

"Maybe your uncle will come around," Mark suggested, "now that he sees how hard your dad's working."

"Maybe," Skye replied, "but it's been fifteen years since we moved back. Isn't that long enough?"

"You don't trust your uncle, do you," Mark commented.

Skye shrugged. "He's just really odd. You'll see when you meet him."

"And your mom? Will I meet her too?" Mark asked.

Skye kicked the dirt with the toe of one sneaker as he twisted on the swing. "She died from a drug overdose about a year after my dad and I moved back here," he said. "I don't really remember her."

Mark looked at his new friend with genuine sympathy. "I'm really sorry about that," he said shyly.

"Yeah, well, you know—my dad says everyone carries some sort of burden."

Mark wasn't sure what that meant, exactly, but he nodded. "What was her name?"

"Maureen Durand. She was a great artist," Skye stated proudly. "My dad's planning an exhibition of her work for our fund-raiser."

Mark smiled at him, and the two twisted in their swings in silence. Then Skye suddenly asked, "Is your dad gay?"

"What?" Mark asked, stunned.

"Is your dad gay?" Skye repeated.

Mark's body tensed as images of Kurt's angry face exploded in his mind. "What makes you think that?" he blurted out.

"Hey, I'm sorry. I didn't mean anything by it. It's just that, you know, his address is in Mill Creek. It's a really popular hangout for gay men."

Mark calmed down a little when he realized Skye had not meant to insult him, but he felt a gripping pang in his chest at the thought of his father. He had not seen him in over a year and feared he was forgetting what he looked like. After a moment, he replied, "No. He had me, didn't he?"

"Yeah, so probably not." Skye smiled. Then he asked tentatively, "Do you have a problem with gays?"

Mark saw an expression on Skye's face that he did not understand. He thought of Kurt and began to stammer. "I don't know…I guess…it's just that I haven't known anyone—"

Skye interrupted him. "Hey, it's okay. I was just curious." He changed the subject. "You know, during the summer the gay community holds really huge parties in Mill Creek. The restaurants hire extra help to handle the crowds. Maybe we could get a couple of jobs, if you're still here."

"I don't know," Mark stammered. "Does your dad mind if you work out there?"

"Hell no. He's glad I can earn some spending money."

The pair hung from the swings in silence for a while longer, until Skye asked, "What time is it? I'm hungry."

Mark looked at his watch. "It's almost six o'clock."

"No wonder. Let's head back and get some food."

"Okay."

Dusk had begun to soften the landscape. The bees and other insects that were so abundant in the grass earlier now seemed to have dispersed for the day. Mark stood up from the swing and looked west to the horizon. Startled, he pointed to it and asked, "What's that?"

"What's what?" Skye asked.

"That white stuff."

Skye laughed. "Oh, that. You can't see it from here, but the ocean is out there. That's the fog rolling in. Pretty impressive, huh? It swallows up everything."

Impressive was not the word Mark would have chosen. The opaque, slowly rolling cloud bank made him uneasy, and he shivered. Skye was already walking in large strides down the incline toward his home, and Mark pushed himself to catch up.

× × ×

Mary scanned the television section in the newspaper and called out, "Mom, *Oklahoma* is on tonight. Would you like to watch it?" She and her mother had just returned from visiting her father in the nursing home. When her mother did not respond, Mary left the living room and found her standing in the middle of the small kitchen.

"Mom?" she asked with concern.

Carol was staring into space. She had not yet removed her coat and was still holding her purse.

"Here, let me help you," Mary offered. She took the black vinyl clutch from her mother's hands and set it on the kitchen table. Then she gently took the coat by its lapels, slipped it off of her mother's shoulders, and laid it across the back of a chair. "Would you like to watch some TV?" she asked again.

"I hate leaving him in that place," her mother said angrily. "It smells so bad."

Mary drew in her breath. "It has a good reputation," she replied, trying not to sound defensive. "And the staff are kind. They're very fond of dad." She placed her hands reassuringly on her mother's shoulders, but Carol twisted away. As with many of her mother's movements, the snub had a theatrical air, but the emotion underlying this gesture was genuine. Mary felt the rejection keenly.

Her parents had been professional dancers who met in their twenties and managed to stay together despite their competitive careers. In their midthirties, when their bodies were no longer able to meet the demands of professional dancing, they settled in Revere County and opened up the Campbell Dance Studio, where they taught ballet, jazz, tap dancing, and stage movement. A few years later, they started a family. Neither Mary nor her brother had shown any aptitude for their parents' profession, despite being raised in the studio and spending innumerable hours backstage during rehearsals and performances. Now the inseparable couple, who always carried themselves as if they were about to step onto a stage, was being torn apart by dementia.

"Can I get you something to eat?" Mary asked.

Carol did not look at her when she said, "No, I'm going to bed."

Mary persisted. "It's only nine o'clock. I thought we might do something together, like watch a movie. Or we could just sit and read."

Carol turned on her daughter. Her face was stern and fixed. "I should never have let you talk me into putting him away," she snapped. "I don't know why I listened to you."

"Mom," Mary replied softly. "We've talked about this. Taking care of Dad was killing you."

"So what? That's what husbands and wives do for each other. But you wouldn't know that, would you? First your father and then my sweet David. It's too much. I can't take this any more."

Carol began to sob, and Mary moved closer to her. She fought back her own tears. David had died in a freeway accident two years ago. His wife and daughter had traveled out of town for a weekend soccer tournament, while he stayed home to work. But on Sunday he drove north to spend the afternoon with Mary and their parents. On the way back to the city, a semitrailer jackknifed on a sharp, fast curve, and David's car was pushed into the truck's underbelly by the vehicles behind his own. Mary still had nightmares about him calling out to her from under the truck. She would wake from those dreams sweating and sobbing from a grief that tore at her soul.

"Mom—" she said as she reached for her mother again, but Carol backed away.

"Go home, Mary," her mother insisted, as she hurried from the room. "Leave me alone."

Thursday, May 29

Mary entered the storage room near her office and unlocked the tall filing cabinet. She was glad to have an excuse to be in the little room because it afforded her some privacy after the rough start to her day. Before work, she had called her mother, who had promptly hung up on her. Then, at the morning check in, Cass, Stella, and Lourdes got into a heated and uncharacteristically accusatory argument about how to best document follow-up tasks for an investigation. Mary regretted only a little the sharp words she used to stop the quarrel.

She stood on her toes and thumbed through the tightly packed files in the back of the top drawer. She was looking for closed norovirus investigation reports to add to the active outbreak files she had photocopied for Linus. She was grateful for the epidemiologist's assistance but worried about his reaction to the tedious task she was going to ask of him. After she found the necessary files, she secured the stack with a rubber band, locked the cabinet and storeroom door, and returned to her office. Jackson and Lourdes were waiting for her outside.

"Mary," Jackson asked, "may I have a word with you?"

"Can it wait?" she replied tersely. She slid past him to get to her desk. "I've got to get ready for a meeting with Linus."

Jackson hesitated but then said stiffly, "I guess it will have to."

Mary glanced up from her desk in time to see the expression of sympathy Lourdes gave Jackson before he left the office.

"Is there something you need?" she asked the nurse.

Lourdes raised an eyebrow at Mary's curt tone but only said, "I want to tell you about a new twist to our pertussis outbreak. I got a call from a lawyer representing the parents of two of our cases. The older child, a third-grader, brought the illness home from school. She caught it from an unvaccinated child in her classroom. Her sibling, an infant, got sick and was hospitalized. The family's lawyer wants me to give him all of our outbreak information. His clients plan to sue the parents of the daughter's classmate and the school district for not following the law requiring unvaccinated children to stay home during an outbreak."

"Really?" Mary said. "Well, I guess something like this was bound to happen."

"Shall I refer him to the county Legal Office?"

"Yes, but call Legal first and give them a heads up. And send Jonathan and Suzanne an email about the situation."

At that moment, Linus poked his head around the doorframe to her office. "Knock, knock," he chirped.

"Hi," Mary called out. "Come on in. I'm just about ready for you."

Linus looked at her nervously. "I've got someone here who wants to meet you."

Mary peered through the partially open blinds that covered the window next to her office door and saw a man standing outside. She eyed Linus quizzically. "Why are you hanging back like that?" she asked.

Linus looked nervous. "Well," he said, glancing behind himself.

"Bring him in," Mary insisted.

"Okay," he said with trepidation.

Linus stepped back and let the guest enter Mary's office. The man smiled at her, and she took a quick measure of him. He was young and attractive but not someone who would necessarily stand out in a crowd of handsome men. His gray eyes looked out at her from under a gray Scottish cap that, when he removed it, revealed closely cropped, light-brown hair. He was a couple of inches taller than Linus and had the build of an athlete—not the delicate physique of a runner or cyclist, but the thick body of someone who played a contact sport. His solid build suited the square lines of his face.

"Mary, Lourdes," Linus began, "this is Joe Becker." Linus took a step backward when he added, "He's an epidemiologist with the State Health Department."

"The state?" Mary asked, raising an eyebrow at Linus.

"Uh huh," Linus affirmed.

Joe extended his hand first to Lourdes and said, "Hello."

"Hello!" she replied with a flirtatious lilt to her voice.

Joe then stepped toward Mary. When she took his hand, she felt a warmth that gave her pause. She tried to pull back, but he held on. "It's nice to meet you," he said.

After Joe released her hand, Mary glanced at Lourdes and was annoyed to see an impish grin emerge on her face.

"So, what brings you up here, Joe?" Mary asked, cautiously.

"You didn't get my message?"

"No. I don't believe so," she replied.

Joe looked from Linus to Mary and said, "I was sent up here to help."

"To help? By whom?"

"Phil Margolis," Joe answered.

"Now, why would he do that?" Mary stated, turning an angry gaze on Linus.

Linus raised up both hands defensively. "Don't look at me."

If Joe was unnerved by the tone of Mary's voice, he did not show it. "Phil wants me to validate the immunization histories for your pertussis cases," he said.

"Oh, he does, does he?" Mary replied as she crossed her arms over her chest. "I told him yesterday that we—"

Linus interrupted her. "Suzanne didn't say anything to you?"

"No."

"Maybe we should back up a bit," Joe suggested with a wry smile.

"That's a good idea," Linus said. "Let me start. Mary, the state thinks that our pertussis outbreak may be related to an event that occurred at the West Hills Pediatric Clinic five years ago."

"Their vaccines were stored improperly for nearly a year," Joe added.

"I heard about that," Lourdes commented. "Stella said it was quite a mess."

"According to the State Immunization Program," Linus continued, "the temperature readings for their biological refrigerator were all over the place."

"The clinic held a revaccination campaign," Joe said, "but—"

"Let me guess," Mary said. "Since it's a west county clinic, not many people showed up."

"That's right," Joe affirmed.

"Apparently," Linus added, "since you told Phil we're really busy, he asked Suzanne if he could send someone here to gather the data instead of asking us to do it."

"And here I am," Joe declared with a broad grin and outstretched arms.

Lourdes laughed. Mary wanted to also, but she held on to her annoyance. "Why didn't Suzanne say anything to us?" she asked. "All it would have taken was an email or phone call."

"You know how these things go," Joe answered. "The bigwigs at the state have to talk with the bigwigs at the county—"

"And sometimes they forget to tell us little people," Linus said with a grin.

"Sometimes?" Lourdes stated sarcastically.

Joe placed his gray cap over his heart. "In my defense," he began, "I did call before I left this morning."

Mary picked up the stack of papers in her in-box and thumbed through them. A small pink message note slipped out from between the larger sheets and floated down to her desk. She read it and held it up to Joe. "Is this you?" she asked.

"Yes, ma'am." He grinned.

Mary was quiet a moment and then said, "Look, Joe, I understand that Phil has assigned you a task, but helping the state with one of its academic studies is just too much of a luxury for us at the moment. My staff, and certainly Linus, don't have the time to support you."

"But get this, Mary," Linus said eagerly, "we can use this guy as we please." He turned to Joe and said, "No offense."

The man laughed. "None taken."

"How's that?" Mary asked.

Linus stepped to her desk and leaned on it. "Phil told him to help us out with whatever we needed, in addition to doing the validation work."

Mary could not help but smile at her friend. He spoke with the energy of a salesman pitching a high-performance sports car. "Really?" she asked. "That doesn't sound like Phil."

"That's what he told me," Joe said. "Basically, I'm yours to do with as you please…as long as I get him the data."

Mary uncrossed her arms. "Okay, now that sounds like Phil. But we would still need to free up staff time to orient you, and I haven't had the best experience with state staff trying to learn local—"

Linus interrupted her again. "But Joe's worked at the local level."

"What do you mean?" Mary asked, intrigued.

"I've held epi positions at two local health departments over the past seven years," he explained.

"Then what are you doing at the state?"

The man shrugged. "I'm not quite sure. I just started the job. I was hired to support the counties." He smiled disarmingly and added, "I guess you're my test case."

Mary raised an eyebrow. "How much time can you spend with us?"

"I wasn't given a limit. Between you and me, I think Phil was just happy to have someplace to send me. But to answer your question, I thought I'd spend most of my time here to start."

Mary glanced at Linus, who wore a boyishly hopeful expression on his face. He could probably tell that her resistance was weakening.

"Oh, come on, Mary," Lourdes said. "Let him stay. I'm curious to see what the man is made of."

Mary was impressed that Joe did not flinch at the nurse's blatant flirtation. She sighed and said, "I'm not your supervisor, Linus, and I don't know what, if anything, Suzanne had in mind for Joe, but until we learn otherwise, I'd like you to be responsible for him."

Linus grinned broadly. "Great!" he exclaimed, clasping his hands together.

Mary could not help but smile at his excitement. "He can have the empty cubicle next to Jackson."

"Okay!" Linus said. "You don't have to worry about anything, Mary. I'll orient him and set him up with a computer. But what about our meeting this morning?"

Mary turned to Joe. "We might as well throw you right into the work." She looked at Linus. "Why don't you show him his cubicle so he can put his things away? You can fill him in on our investigations, and then we can meet."

"Sounds good."

As Linus steered his new charge toward the door, Joe glanced back over his shoulder and smiled at Mary, again. Mary felt Lourdes eyeing the exchange, but she did not turn to her until the two men were safely out in the hallway.

"What?" Mary asked her, irritated.

"He's cute," Lourdes asserted.

"I guess," Mary replied flatly as she busied herself with some papers on her desk.

"Could be an attraction there," Lourdes commented slyly.

"You're a married woman," Mary retorted.

Lourdes laughed. "You know very well what I'm talking about."

Mary thrust her arms toward the door. "I just met the guy!" she exclaimed.

Lourdes grinned and sauntered out of Mary's office. Without turning around, she called back, "I'm just saying—"

× × ×

Linus and Joe returned to Mary's office about twenty minutes later. Mary removed a bundle of papers held together with a large black clip from her desk drawer, and she placed it next to the one she had carried in from the storage room. She watched as the epidemiologists eyed the two stacks. If the volume of papers unsettled them, they did not show it.

"Okay," she began. "These are the documents I'd like you to review." She pointed to the thickest of the bundles and said, "This pile contains the norovirus outbreaks reported to us since the beginning of the year."

Linus looked at her as if he was deciding whether to say something. "What is it?" she asked him.

"You know," he began hesitantly, "nothing may come of reviewing these. The increase in outbreaks might just mean people are doing a better job of reporting them to us."

"I know," she replied.

"But something about this feels different to you?" Joe asked.

"Yes," she admitted. "I've got a nagging feeling I'm overlooking something, a key bit of information." She leaned onto her desk and added, "I just haven't had time to study the reports thoroughly."

Joe looked her squarely in the eye. "Okay, then. Tell us what you know."

Mary pointed to the second bundle. "These are the individual foodborne illness complaints that have been called into CD and Environmental Health since April. I used that month as the cut-off because that's when our cases rose above our baseline level. They don't seem to have any apparent connection to our norovirus outbreaks other than they occurred in the same time frame, so I don't know if they'll be of any help."

Linus picked up the clipped stack. "When did you have time to pull these together?" he asked.

"One night when it was nice and quiet here. And Steve in Environmental Health gave me access to their call log and complaint forms."

Linus flipped through the papers. "How many are there?" he asked.

"Between the two programs, fifty-four."

Joe's eyes widened. "Is that typical for a two-month period?"

Mary shrugged. "I don't know."

"Put that down as another reason we need a surveillance database," Linus commented. "We should be looking at trends in your calls."

Mary removed the rubber band from around the outbreak reports and said, "The first April outbreak, at the Valley Oak Alzheimer's Care

Center, was reported to us on the second of the month, but the actual illness onset was on March twenty-ninth."

"Another late reporter," Linus commented.

"Not even that," Mary stated. "A family member called it in. Forty staff and residents had become ill at the facility."

"How many total outbreaks have you had since that one?" Joe asked.

"Seven confirmed and one presumptive, and we're looking into a new report. Five were in nursing homes. Some of the other outbreaks were secondary to the nursing home outbreaks."

"Nine total since April?" Linus asked, looking worried. "You should have asked for my help sooner."

"Probably," Mary confessed. "At first I thought we were just having an extended season, like Phil suggested. Then I made the mistake of asking the wrong person for your time."

"Jonathan?" Linus said, and Mary nodded.

"Who's Jonathan?" Joe asked.

"I'll tell you later," Linus answered.

Joe looked back at Mary. "So you've probably had some hospitalizations and deaths with the nursing home outbreaks."

"Yes," Mary confirmed. "Eight hospitalizations and three deaths." She pointed to a sheet of paper that was clipped to the top of the outbreak stack. "I did manage to summarize the basic figures."

"Three deaths—how sad," Joe commented. "Dehydration?"

"Essentially," Mary replied. She knew what the epidemiologist was asking. The elderly were susceptible to complications from GI infections because of the loss of bodily fluids brought on by vomiting and diarrhea. Dehydration could bring about heart or kidney failure in frail individuals.

"Were any staff implicated in the nursing home outbreaks?" Linus asked.

"No," Mary answered. "They all reported symptom onset at the same time or later than the residents."

"That's odd," Joe commented, "and it seems unlikely across so many outbreaks."

Linus was studying Mary's summary sheet when he said, "Okay, what else do we need to ask you about? Can you think of anything, Joe?"

Joe took the summary sheet from Linus and looked it over. "Not at the moment," he said. Then he addressed Mary. "We may need to call around for more information. Is that okay with you?"

Mary smiled at him. "Of course," she said. She lowered her gaze when he smiled back at her.

As the two men stood to leave, Linus pointed to one page of outbreak notes and laughed. "What's with Cass' handwriting? Does she even know our alphabet?"

Mary grinned broadly. Cass had just entered her office and now stood directly behind Linus.

"I heard that, young man," she said.

Startled, Linus turned and mumbled an apology. He tried to leave, but the nurse grabbed him by his upper arm. "Where do you think you're going? You need to hear this. Sorry to interrupt, Mary, but I've got some news."

Now what? Mary thought. "I don't like the look on your face, Cass," she said.

"We have a meningitis case."

"Viral?" Mary, Linus, and Joe asked in unison. Viral meningitis gave people a very bad headache for a few days, and the investigation generally required only a couple of phone calls to ask how the person was feeling. Bacterial meningitis, on the other hand, could be fatal, and those investigations needed to be initiated quickly so that prophylactic antibiotics could be given to at-risk contacts. The news media usually took an interest too, if the case was a child or adolescent, and their stories would generate numerous calls to the CD Unit from anxious parents, school personnel, and the public.

"No, bacterial," Cass replied matter-of-factly. "Jane from Highland Hospital called it in. The patient is a fifty-two-year-old Mexican-American woman, and she's on life support."

"Damn," Mary muttered.

× × ×

"How can we have a meningitis case?" Mary asked to no one in particular. She, Joe, and Linus had moved to Cass' cubicle to hear the report with Stella and Erin. "We're nearly out of the season."

None of her staff answered the question because they knew she only asked it out of frustration. In the United States, most cases occurred during the winter and spring, but bacterial meningitis could strike at any time of the year.

"Are there any relatives we can interview?" she asked.

"Her husband," Cass answered, "but Jane said he's beside himself with grief. The hospital chaplain is sitting with him now. I'm not sure how much he is going to be able to tell us. Jane said Mrs. Hernandez, our patient, became septic very quickly, and her husband lost it when he saw the state his wife was in…with the purpuric rash and all."

"Does he speak English?" Mary asked.

"Un poquito," Cass replied. "Only a little."

"Is anyone else with him? Any children?"

"Just Mrs. Hernandez's brother and his wife, and they don't speak English well either," Cass added. "Jane said the chaplain called the family's priest to help. A son and daughter are on their way up from the city."

Mary sighed. "Then we'd better send Lourdes over there. Where is she?"

"She left for the clinic awhile ago to catch up on some TB charting," Stella answered. "She's not going to be happy about this."

"Well, it can't be helped," Mary said. Lourdes was the only CD nurse who spoke Spanish well enough to conduct the interview. "Nobody is going to die from late paperwork. We've got to find out who this woman's contacts were. I'll call Lourdes and give her the bad news. Cass, please call Suzanne and Jonathan and tell them about the situation in case the press takes an interest."

"Okay," she replied.

"Is there anything Joe and I can do, Mary?" Linus asked.

"No, just get started on those norovirus outbreaks. We'll let you know if we need help."

"What about Jackson's training?" Stella asked. "We're supposed to be there at one o'clock."

"Good Lord," Mary replied. "I forgot all about that. What time is it now?"

"12:05 p.m."

"Damn," she muttered. "Okay. After I call Lourdes, I'll find Jackson and tell him we can't make it."

As everyone began to disperse, Cass said to Mary, "Look on the bright side."

"What bright side?" Mary asked. Her response came out sharper than she had intended.

"Mrs. Hernandez is a middle-aged Latina. The press isn't going to take much interest in her."

Mary acknowledged the nurse's conclusion with a nod. She hated thinking about a human being's death in such crass terms, but she knew Cass was probably right.

⋊ ⋊ ⋊

"Mary? What am I doing here?"

The trim, muscled man spoke through clenched teeth. He was leaning against the table and gripped its edge hard with his weathered hands.

"What do you mean?" Mary asked, feigning innocence. She had found Jackson in the first-floor conference room. When she asked him to reschedule the training, the frustration and disappointment in his eyes was telling.

"Why am I in this job?" he asked her.

Mary squirmed inside. She knew what he was asking her. He wanted to know why he should show up every day to a place where he was given so little support, a place where he was often ignored and sometimes ridiculed.

"I'm wasting my time," he stated angrily, "and everyone else's."

Mary folded her arms defensively across her chest. She had not wanted a confrontation with this man, but now she realized it had been inevitable. "You and the people here," she began slowly, "you come from two very different cultures."

"I know that," Jackson replied irritably. He stood up and placed his hands on his hips, and Mary saw the former military police officer appear before her. He was well over six feet tall, in contrast to her five-foot-five-inch stature. Her impulse was to step backward, but she held her ground.

"Do you think I don't know that?" he added.

"Do you really, Jackson?" she countered, feeling her own anger rise. "Look, there are people here who can tell you how many public health programs could have been funded for a decade with the money that bought just one of those fancy fighter jets the military is so fond of crashing out in the valley."

"We all serve in our own way," the man grumbled.

Mary shook her head in frustration. "That's not it," she said. "You don't understand."

Jackson's eyes bore into hers. "Well, then explain it to me," he demanded.

Mary gripped the composition book in her hand so hard that it bent. "Public health..." she sputtered. "Public health is broken. We've been low man on the totem pole—at the bottom of everyone's priority list—for years." Anger took hold of her, and she spat out her words. "We lose out to the sheriff and the pretty boys in fire departments for county money, and any pittance of support we get from state funds is slashed in the next budget. If it weren't for the feds, public health would disappear overnight. And do you think anyone outside of this building would care?"

Jackson said nothing.

"And do we get any notice in the mudslinging between insurance companies and providers for healthcare dollars? Hell no! The medical community treats us like an irritating gnat they would love to squash."

Jackson's eyes softened, and Mary saw the tension along his jawline ease, but it did nothing to temper her words. She pointed toward the window as if the nation's capital was across the street. "Then along come the cowboys in this administration, and they find all sorts of money in their budget for bioterrorism. Bioterrorism, for Christ's sake! The military boys who get everything they've ever wanted, year after year, now get to tell us how to do our jobs? They want to militarize public health, and for what? What's the likelihood the stuff they want us to plan for is ever going to happen? Smallpox? That disease was eradicated from the planet a couple of decades ago—by public health, I might add. Where the hell is the logic in that, Jackson?"

Mary did not give him a chance to reply. "Twenty-five thousand people in this country die every year from the flu, and five times that many are hospitalized with foodborne illnesses. Upstairs, we're dealing with pertussis, bacterial meningitis, an intestinal virus that is killing the elderly, and a whole slew of other diseases, but that stuff isn't sexy or macho enough for the cowboys in DC, is it? No, only the fantastical will do for them. Public health is a mess, Jackson, and we may be run by half-wits, but we've still got real work to do. We don't have the luxury of sitting around in shiny buildings, playing with our hoses and polishing our missiles while we wait for something to happen."

Mary turned away, shaken by the strong emotions that had poured out of her. The last thing she had expected when she came looking for Jackson was to let loose her frustrations on him. She worked to regain control of herself. When she turned back, she stated in a calmer voice, "It might not be fair, Jackson, but that's what you represent to us. You're a nice man, but we don't need anyone telling us our business, and I resent the fact that we have to play these political games in order to get the funding we deserve on our own merits."

The two faced each other in silence for several moments. Jackson was the first to speak. "May I say something?"

Mary nodded, embarrassed that he felt he had to ask.

"Believe it or not, Mary, I get it. I get what you're talking about. Hell, I didn't even know what public health was or what you all did before I applied for this position. But this is a weird, sad kind of place, and from what I've seen, public health has to take a lot of the blame for the mess it's in."

"Thanks," she grumbled.

"Hold on," he protested. "You had your say. Let me have mine."

Mary steeled herself.

"I thought the army had some serious problems, but this place makes them look like masters of efficiency. Let's start with office supplies, shall we?"

"What?" Mary asked, incredulous.

"Never, in any other job, have I had to scrounge around to find a pencil like I do here. Every unit keeps their supplies under lock and key, terrified that a single paper clip might be stolen by someone. Can't trust our coworkers, can we?"

Mary kept quiet.

"And what's with needing permission to travel outside of the county, for Christ's sake? Do you know how many meetings I've missed with the state because the paperwork didn't go through in time? This place is hanging itself by its own anal-retentive bureaucracy, and no one seems to mind. In fact, the suicide is encouraged! If a person dares suggest an improvement, they're told to write a damn proposal, which has to be commented on by every single person in the department before it's pissed on by Administration."

Mary lowered her head and mumbled, "Well, that's not entirely true."

"And then there are the people!" he exclaimed. "Lordy! Altruists who put up with all of this crap because they have a save-the-world complex, nurses who are anxious control freaks and treat anyone who isn't a clinician with contempt, and a health officer who's obsessed with herself. And management? Champions of petty politics, obstructionism, and mediocrity."

The man paused to catch his breath. Mary looked sideways at him to see if he might be done, but his face told her that he had more to say about her bewildering profession.

He's obviously given this some thought, she grumbled to herself.

"And Jonathan?" he stated, eyes wide with disbelief. "The army is full of morons, but he tops them all." When Mary looked at him, surprised, Jackson declared, "Come on, woman. You can't think I'm that much of a dumb grunt to not see the man for what he is."

Mary lowered her gaze again. She recognized her own frustrations in his but wanted to argue back. Not about Jonathan, but to say that he was wrong about public health, to say that her profession performed good and noble works, but she could not muster the energy. Not now.

"So I ask you," Jackson persisted, "what am I doing here? Should I leave? Because I've got better things to do with my time."

Mary looked into the man's light-blue eyes and considered his question.

What am I doing here? she repeated silently. She had written the same sentiment, years ago, in a letter to her brother back home when she was a young, newly minted Peace Corps volunteer in Liberia, West Africa. She had been the first person ever assigned to her small, up-country village, and her job as a community development worker had come with an extraordinarily vague position description that left her and her village hosts at a loss as to what she would do for the next two years. For what seemed like a long time, the children ran away from her in fear and the adults watched her with great amusement and caution. Some accused her of being a CIA or FBI agent—or both. The isolation, cultural differences, language barrier, and unstructured, unproductive days had left her frustrated and depressed.

What am I doing here? she had cried to David from across the ocean.

But she persevered mainly because she had no other plans for her life. The villagers watched her and eventually came to know her, and she knew she had finally gained their confidence when the elders asked her to manage the money for a second water well in the village.

Mary looked at Jackson now and thought, *Have I really given him a chance?*

She had tolerated his presence in her unit because she had no other choice. But now she was forced to acknowledge that he cared as deeply about his work as she did about hers. In the short time he had been with the health department, her staff had developed a cautious fondness for the man. Lourdes had been the first to show signs of accepting his mission. After Jackson had once recommended they standardize the unit's protocols, Lourdes had taken her aside, and in her typically diplomatic manner, said, "We'll only look more professional, Mary, if we all follow the same procedures."

Mary took a deep breath and let it out. A sudden lightness came over her, and she laughed. "You picked up on all that in just a few months?" she asked Jackson.

"I'm an old man," he replied warily. "I've seen a lot."

Mary smirked. "Pencils, Jackson? Really?"

The man grinned. "Playing with our hoses and polishing our missiles? Where did that come from?"

Mary burst out laughing. "I'm not sure," she said.

"You can really get a head of steam up, young lady. I like that."

"Yeah?" she asked weakly.

"You better believe it. It lets me know where I stand, and it beats all the subterfuge that goes on in this place."

When she did not respond, Jackson said, "Look, Mary, I sit in my cubicle near your nurses all day long. I hear what's going on. I see what they're dealing with." He paused. "I think I can help. I'd like to help."

Mary met the man's gaze and was overcome with gratitude. Despite how he had been treated, he was still willing to stand by her team.

"How?" she asked.

He walked over to a chair, pulled it out from underneath the table, and beckoned her toward it.

She looked at him, perplexed, and thought, *When was the last time anyone did that for me? Was it Dad?*

"Come on, sit down," he encouraged her. "Just for a few minutes. You won't regret this."

Mary glanced around the room. She saw the notepads, folders, pens, and bowls of chocolates that Jackson had placed strategically on the conference room table. He had obviously put a lot of thought and effort into the training.

"I don't know, Jackson," she said. "I'm dealing with so much right now. One more thing might push me over the edge."

"Might?" He laughed heartily. "Young lady, you're already in free fall."

Mary's shoulders slumped with the truth of his words. She walked toward him, sat down, and let him help her scoot the chair underneath the table.

Friday, May 30

Raymond was drying his morning dishes when the telephone rang. He left the kitchen and entered the living room with the dish towel still in his hands. He looked at the old black phone as if it had suddenly started working after years of being broken. So few people called him.

He picked up the receiver. "Hello?" he said cautiously.

"Hello, Mr. Reynolds?" a man asked.

"Yes."

"My name is Joe Becker. I'm calling on behalf of the Revere County Health Department."

Raymond's heart began to pound. "Yes?" he replied.

"Do you have a few moments to talk with me about the norovirus illness you had earlier this year? We're seeing a sudden increase in cases, and I would like to ask you a few questions about your experience."

Raymond panicked. He did not know what to say. "Well, I, um—"

"I probably won't take more than five minutes of your time," Joe said.

Raymond did not know what to do. To cover his fear, he blurted out angrily, "Why is the government contacting me about such a private matter?"

Joe explained that, by law, the department was responsible for investigating cases of communicable diseases, and therefore, could talk with people about their illnesses.

Raymond rebuffed him, again. "I don't remember anything about it," he lied.

"Maybe my questions will—" Joe began, but Raymond cut him off.

"I said I don't remember anything."

The phone line was quiet for a moment. Then Joe said, "Well, please give the health department a call, sir, if something does come to mind. Your information may be of help to our investigation."

Rage surged through Raymond after he hung up the phone. He picked up a nearby crystal candy dish and threw it against the wall. Then he paced around the dining room table, cursing at the top of his voice.

"How dare anyone spoil my plan," he bellowed.

That past March, Raymond had gotten so weak from norovirus that his brother had insisted on driving him to the hospital. He was taken by wheelchair into an emergency department examination room for his intake interview. A nurse was the first to enter, and she introduced herself as Jane Holcomb, the hospital's infection control practitioner. She was tiny in stature and as dried up and tough as a piece of beef jerky.

"Sir," she said in a stern voice graveled with age, "you are the third person this evening to come here with severe diarrhea and vomiting. Is there any chance you were at the Heath Hotel in the past forty-eight hours?"

A painful cramp gripped Raymond's stomach and prevented him from answering her. He was doubled over when his brother asked, "Weren't you there for work, Ray? A conference or something?" Turning to the nurse, Paul said, "My brother works for the State Health Department."

"Yes," Raymond murmured when the pain eased, "I helped set up a training."

"Did you have anything to eat or drink, sir?" the nurse asked. He watched as she wrote on a form held firmly in place by her wooden clipboard's silver clasp.

"Yes. Lunch and a piece of cake." He remembered the dessert well: a cake in the image of a super hero. A piece had been cut for him from one of the black boots.

"I need to use the bathroom—now," he cried out in frustration, "or I'm going to mess myself right here." He hoped the declaration would cause the nurse to leave, but, instead, she helped him to the bathroom. As she waited outside, she said she suspected he had been infected with norovirus as had others who ate at the hotel. Before she left, she said she would recommend the doctor order stool specimen tests.

"I'm also going to report you to the Revere County Health Department as a probable case associated with this outbreak. They will call and interview you as part of their investigation."

"Why? Haven't you asked me enough questions?" Raymond grumbled.

The nurse did not answer him as she left the room. She simply said, "Take care, Mr. Reynolds."

It was on the way home from the hospital that Paul inadvertently planted an idea in Raymond's mind. Prompted by the nurse's mention of an outbreak, Paul recounted the time he and Maureen had lived with the Rajneeshees in central Oregon. Paul told him that in 1984, the year Skye was born, radical leaders in the group had plotted to influence the outcome of a local election by deliberately contaminating salad bars at area restaurants with salmonella bacteria. Paul said the Rajneeshees hoped the widespread illness would prevent a large number of locals from voting, thereby giving the winning edge to their candidate. He also told him that the health officials and law enforcement had not recognized the intentionality of the attacks.

"They didn't figure out that the salad bars were contaminated on purpose for a year," Paul said as he pulled up to Raymond's house. "Kind of scary, huh?" After he turned off the car's engine, he added, "And do you want to hear something really weird? The ring leader for the attacks, Ma Anand Sheela, ended up running two nursing homes in Switzerland. Can you believe that? She ended up in our line of business."

Raymond leaned onto the dining room table. "I need to sort this out," he said, aloud. And he knew the best place to do that was in his shed where he could prepare for his morning inspection. He went to the back porch and put on a pair of muck boots. Then he walked outside to the old weathered structure. Once there, he unlatched the door and stepped inside. He flicked on the lamp clamped to the workbench and glanced at the shed's small window to make sure the curtain was drawn. Then he began to perform his carefully honed procedures. He donned a lab coat and buttoned it up completely. Next he pulled large goggles over his silver-framed bifocals. He had first required reading glasses and good lighting to do close work when he turned forty. Now, in his fifty-eighth year, he wore eyeglasses all the time, especially for his work in this makeshift laboratory. Raymond double-gloved his hands, and from out of a small refrigerator, he pulled a small steel rack in which stood twelve glass test tubes that contained a murky fluid. He picked up one and strained to read its label.

You've got old-man eyes to go with your old-man body, he told himself.

The melancholy thought brought up one of his earliest childhood memories. He could not have been much older than four at the time. Pride burst from his chest as he ran through the apple orchard carrying a great silver sword to protect his castle and his fair lady from marauders. He chased after the imaginary foes, weaving in and out of the trees until he had slain every one. Then his damsel—his mother, Daisy—fell to her knees. She brought his head to her chest, and told him she knew he would always protect her.

But one marauder took years to banish. His stepfather, Alan, had taken hold of the little knight's arm and flung him away from his mother onto the dirt. Then he lifted Daisy to a standing position and grabbed her breasts roughly. "These are mine, kid," he jeered. "Go find your own slut." His mother had laughed nervously and looked at her son, as if to say, "What can I do?"

As a young man, Raymond's dreams had still revolved around the farm. He had planned to take it over from his family and open it up to the public for Octoberfest hayrides and apple picking and Christmas tree cutting. He even hoped to share that life with someone who loved him as much as he loved the farm. In those dreams he had never imagined nurturing a common, lowly virus, but it was the only way he could think to make things right—to return his life to what it should have been.

Raymond pulled a clean plastic spray bottle from a small box on the workbench. His thoughts turned to the call from the health department as he unscrewed the bottle's lid and filled it with the contents of a test tube. He smiled as an idea took shape in his mind. After replacing the lid, he dipped the bottle in a bleach solution and sealed it in a plastic bag. Then he returned the test tube rack to the refrigerator, removed one pair of gloves from his hands, and placed the plastic bag with the spray bottle into his briefcase. Raymond looked at his watch. He needed to leave for the inspection in forty-five minutes.

That should be enough time for the call, he thought as he disposed of the remaining pair of gloves.

Back on his porch, Raymond removed his boots and put on house slippers before he entered the kitchen. He opened the cabinet drawer that held a thick telephone directory and placed it on the counter. The local government offices were listed at the front, and he quickly found the appropriate number. Raymond wrote it on a small piece of paper and walked to the high-backed leather chair in the living room. He sat down, and began to dial the number. The rotary phone sang its familiar clicking and whirring sounds with each turn of the dial. His cat jumped onto his lap, and Raymond stroked it as he listened to the ringing on the other end of the line.

"Everything is going to be okay," he told the feline. Raymond felt the burn of arousal at his sudden confidence, and he dug his fingertips deep into the cream-colored fur along the animal's back. The cat responded by digging her claws into his thigh and leaping onto the floor. Raymond struck out at her with his foot and kicked her leg. She howled and limped away.

A pleasant voice greeted him. "Communicable Disease Control," the woman said. "Erin speaking."

Raymond's heart raced with excitement. "Um, yes, hello, Erin," he said. "I'm trying to locate a man named Joe Becker. Can you help me?"

× × ×

Mary finished typing the message for the Monday appointment. She marked it as *high priority* and clicked the send icon. During the meeting, she and Jackson would introduce the plan they'd put together to manage the unit's workload. She knew the proposal would be hard to sell to the group, but she was determined to try. The status quo was no longer effective, and the situation in her unit was deteriorating. That morning Stella had taken a call from Jane Holcomb. She reported that a sixteen-year-old girl had been admitted to the hospital with a presumptive diagnosis of bacterial meningitis.

"The child attends St. Joseph High School," Stella told Mary. The nurse waited for a response from her supervisor. When none came, she added, "Rosa Hernandez worked as a cook in the same school."

Mary suppressed the panic that shot through her mind with this news. The school connection between the two individuals was worrisome, but it did not yet meet the definition for a meningitis outbreak. Unlike outbreaks of other diseases, this definition depended on the number of sporadic, not epi-linked, cases that appeared in a given population.

Don't get ahead of yourself, she thought. *Wait for the case report and lab findings.*

She would worry if the former showed no social link between the two individuals and the latter indicated that they had been infected with the same serogroup of the bacteria. This new case was sure to generate media attention, though, so she asked Stella to tell Suzanne and Jonathan about it.

Lourdes entered her office a few minutes after Stella left it. Her appearance, usually impeccable, was unkempt. Her clothes were rumpled and her lively brown eyes were red and underscored with dark circles. The nurse angrily slapped a folder onto her desk.

"Sometimes, Mary…sometimes, I really hate my job."

Mary pulled Rosa Hernandez's case report form from the folder.

"I interviewed her husband, Marco," Lourdes snapped. "His wife was near death, but I had to ask him all of these questions that must have seemed so…stupid." The nurse slumped into the office guest chair. "But he said he understood. He told me I was a good person." Lourdes sighed and looked at Mary. "He sat between me and his priest and held our hands and sobbed quietly the entire time I was there. His wife was covered in that horrible purple rash, and her fingertips were blackened, and he kept asking me how someone could get so sick so quickly."

The fatigue and sorrow in Lourdes' words were palpable. Mary came around from behind her desk and closed the office door. She crouched down and placed a hand on Lourdes' forearm. Lourdes bowed her head and said, "Marco told me about the first time he met his wife, and how proud they were of their children—who are the same age as mine. He talked about how hard Rosa had worked to make a comfortable home for them and how excited they were about the birth of their first grandchild." Tears trickled down Lourdes' cheeks. "Mrs. Hernandez died while I was there, Mary. She was only a year older than me, and she worked hard all her life, and now she won't get to hold her first grandchild."

"I'm so sorry," Mary said. She took hold of Lourdes' hand and held it.

✕ ✕ ✕

Mary's desk phone rang shortly after Lourdes left her office, and she glanced at its little gray display screen. Jonathan's name appeared on it. She hesitated, but then picked up the receiver.

"Hello, Jonathan," she said softly. "What can I do for you?"

"I'd like you to come to my office for a chat," he answered.

Mary glanced at Rosa Hernandez's case report and ran the fingers of her hand roughly through her straight auburn-brown hair. "Can I come in about an hour?" she asked. "We're dealing with a new meningitis case."

"No, I want to meet now," he insisted. "It's urgent."

Mary knew from experience that Jonathan's definition of urgent did not match her own, but she was not in the mood to press the matter. It would be easier to hear what he had to say.

"Okay. I'll be there in a couple of minutes," she told him.

Jonathan's office was on the same floor as hers but at the opposite end of the building. As Mary approached it, she heard his baritone voice resounding over the cubicles. Its booming quality reminded her of mall Santas and politicians. He had been asked by others to keep his door closed when he had meetings or spoke on the phone, but he had refused, stating that to do so would go against his open-door management style.

Jonathan did not see Mary when she reached his doorway because he was facing the opposite wall, talking jovially on the telephone. She knocked, but he did not hear her.

"Yeah, Chuck, the board meeting went real well," Jonathan said with a laugh. He rested a supersized soda on the left arm of his chair. "I know they were real impressed with my bioterrorism plan." Jonathan paused a moment and then sniggered. "Of course Suzanne and Carl were there, but the board knows who's really in charge."

Instinctively, Mary turned around to see who else might be over-hearing this conversation. She had no idea who Chuck was, but she knew he was being duped. Carl was extremely controlling about what information was presented to the board, and by whom, especially when it dealt with significant sums of money like the bioterrorism funds.

Mary rapped on the doorframe, again.

"Maybe I'll be sitting up there some day," Jonathan continued. "Supervisor Cox. I like the sound of that."

Mary's eyes widened. Most of the arrogant people she had ever known were very insecure. They took offense when challenged and put people down in front of others to affirm their superior status, but their vanities usually had some basis in either a remarkable intelligence or talent. Jonathan had neither, but he did not seem to be aware of these limitations. Instead, his boundless ambition seemed to flow from a wondrous self-infatuation. As Mary watched him now, she struggled to identify a positive quality or two that might explain why he held his position. She could understand his initial appeal to others; she had ob-served that people often attributed strong leadership skills to men who had imposing statures and deep voices, despite their mediocre work histories. But, other than acknowledging that he was generally pleasant toward his colleagues, she could come up with no satisfying answer.

Mary was lost in these thoughts when Jonathan finally swiveled around and saw her standing in the doorway. He waved her into his office and did not seem the least bit concerned that she might have overheard his conversation.

"I've got to go now, Chuck," he said to the caller. "Let's do lunch soon when I get down to the city. Later."

"You wanted to see me?" Mary asked after he hung up the phone.

"Yeah," Jonathan replied. "Come on in and have a seat." He leaned forward and took a long slurp of his soda before placing the sweaty container on the large paper calendar that covered a good portion of his desk.

Mary took a step into the office but did not move any further toward the chair. She had learned from previous encounters that if she sat down, what should have been a brief discussion with Jonathan would extend to thirty minutes. "If you don't mind, I'll just stand."

"Suit yourself," he said.

Mary looked over his desk. The surface was free of clutter except for a stack of papers in his in-box. He took another slurp of his drink, and when he lifted his head, his face suddenly took on a grave expression.

"So, Mary," he began, "I saw the appointment you sent out this morning."

"Great!" she stated. "Can you make it?"

"Well, um, there's a problem with this that concerns me."

"What's that?" she asked.

Jonathan furrowed his brow and said importantly, "Mary, I want to remind you that I am your supervisor."

Mary steeled herself. On occasion, Jonathan would impart managerial advice to her during conversations that began with this same tone of voice. At first Mary found these lectures patronizing, but she learned to tolerate them, because afterward, he would leave her alone for a day or two, as if he had fulfilled a significant supervisory responsibility.

"Yes," she replied. "I'm aware of that."

"Good. And do you know about the management hierarchy in this department?"

"The what?" she asked, puzzled.

Jonathan chuckled. "The hierarchy, Mary. Your staff reports to you, you report to me, and I report to Carl and Suzanne."

"What's this about, Jonathan?" Mary asked with growing impatience.

Jonathan shook his head and tsked at her. "Why did *you* send Suzanne that appointment this morning?"

"What?" Mary asked.

"Why did *you* send Suzanne the appointment?" he repeated with exasperation.

"I checked with Rosalyn first, if that's what you're getting at," Mary answered. He smirked at her, and she added, "Look, Jonathan, I have a lot of work to do. Why don't you tell me what's on your mind?"

Jonathan took another sip of his soda. "I'm trying to, but we're being a little thick this morning, aren't we?"

Mary clenched her jaw.

Jonathan put his hands behind his head and smiled. "The point is, I'm your supervisor. You should have asked me first about the menstrual case—"

"Meningitis," she corrected him. "The word is *meningitis*, not *menstrual*." *For God's sake!*

He waved one of his hands dismissively. "Whatever. You should have talked to me first about this plan of yours and Jackson's, and then I would have called the meeting, if I felt it was necessary."

Mary's muscles stiffened. "Jonathan, as Suzanne has told you, I can contact her or call a meeting about CD without going through you. I'm not trying to undermine your authority, if that's what you are concerned about. I always include you on my communications with her."

"You should have talked to me first," he repeated. He plopped forward in his chair and leaned onto the desk. "I make the decisions about what Suzanne and Carl hear from this building, not you."

Neither person spoke, and during the pause, Mary became aware of a palpable silence in the cubicle area outside of the office. She closed the door. When she turned back to Jonathan, she said with controlled frustration, "I have never been required to seek permission from the operations manager, or whoever my boss might be, to contact the health officer on any urgent public health matter. CD moves too quickly to be stifled in that way."

"Well, things are different now," he declared. "You have me for a supervisor, and I'm responsible for protecting Suzanne's time."

"Protecting her from what, exactly?" Mary demanded. "Her duties as the health officer? And just how would you brief her on a situation when you haven't shown any interest in learning about my unit's work?"

Mary knew she came close to crossing a line with that question. She saw the surprise on Jonathan's face, but he said nothing about it. Instead, he returned to the topic of the appointment she had sent out.

"And why did you include Marni in the meeting?" he asked. "I'm her supervisor. I speak for her."

Marni Scheidt was the latest mental health manager to be transferred to the Public Health Department as a result of layoffs from budget cuts. A nurse herself, she had used her bumping rights and thirty years with the county to replace Kim Carter as the Public Health field nursing supervisor. Shocked about losing Kim, Mary learned from Stella that Marni could have bumped another mental health manager. The Human Resources Office had even set up a meeting with Jonathan and Isabelle Raposo, the director of the Mental Health Department, to talk with Marni about her two options. According to Stella, Isabelle had long desired Marni's removal from her department because she was a close friend of Supervisor Cahill. Isabelle urged Marni to move to Field Nursing, saying the position would be a better fit for her skills, and Jonathan did not argue the point.

"I did so because I need to ask for her staff's assistance. She knows their schedules and workload. You don't."

Jonathan picked up his soda and took a long sip. "I want you to retract the appointment," he said.

"Retract it?" Mary was not sure she even knew how to do that. "I will not," she declared.

Jonathan began to scribble on desk calendar. "Mary," he said, looking at her out of the corner of his eye, "you seem pretty emotional today. Are we having a little visitor?"

Mary's mouth dropped open in astonishment, and she charged his desk, leaning onto it fully. "Seriously, Jonathan?" she growled. "Do you really want to go there?" *You moron*, she thought.

Jonathan responded to her sudden move by rolling backward in his chair, completely off of the protective plastic floor mat that lay under his workstation. Their eyes locked, and Mary saw an emotion on his face that stunned her.

He's afraid of me, she realized. *He's actually afraid of me.*

Unnerved by this realization, she straightened herself up and took a deep breath. With a firm but calm voice, she said, "Jonathan, your comment was completely uncalled for." She looked around for the guest chair and sat down in it. "We need to talk."

Jonathan did not move. He looked at her with wide eyes. His soggy soda cup was cinched in the middle by his tight grip on it. Brown liquid threatened to burble onto his hand.

"Let me begin," she said. "Your management style is too controlling. I want you to treat me like the professional I am."

Jonathan slowly righted himself and scooted his chair back onto the mat with the drink still in his hand. He looked at her timidly. "But I'm a nice guy," he said.

Mary was both perplexed and touched by this admission. "This isn't about being nice or not," she stated. "Can we just put all this hierarchy stuff aside for a moment and talk?"

Jonathan avoided eye contact with her and scanned his desk, as if desperate to find something. "Okay," he said, opening a desk drawer and looking into it.

Mary relaxed. *Maybe something good will come of this*, she thought.

"It's unrealistic to think you can be an effective intermediary between my team and Suzanne on all matters," she said.

Jonathan mumbled a few incoherent words before grabbing the stack of papers from his in-box. Mary wanted to tell him to stop fidgeting but refrained from doing so. "Okay, maybe, I should have let you know about Jackson's and my plan," she admitted, "but I've always kept you informed about my unit's activities."

"Uh-huh," Jonathan murmured. Mary was not sure he had heard her because he appeared to be deeply focused on the papers in his hand.

"Have I given you any reason to think otherwise?" she asked, trying to engage him.

"Well," he said without look at her. Then his telephone rang. He immediately turned to the device and chuckled with palpable relief. "Oops! Excuse me, Mary. It's Carl. I'd better take this. It might be something important."

"But this conversation is important," she said. "You can call him back."

Jonathan looked at her as if she had blasphemed a god. He grabbed the soda and took a noisy slurp before he picked up the receiver. The sweaty container had left yet another soggy ring on his desk calendar.

"Hello, Carl!" He laughed into the phone, and positioned his body so that his wide back was to Mary. "What can I do for you?"

Mary studied him for a moment. She thought hard about the fact that he had the support of the highest ranking administrator in the department.

So this is how it's going to be, she thought.

× × ×

Mary did not return to her office after her encounter with Jonathan, and she had no intention of retracting the appointment. Instead, she decided to speak with Marni. The field nurses were busy enough with their own challenging work—making home visits to families with very young children, many of whom have special health needs—so she considered it only fair to give Marni some warning about the request she was going to make of her during the Monday meeting.

When she arrived in the section of the building that housed the Field Nursing Unit, Mary saw that all of the cubicles were empty. It was common for many of the nurses to leave the building after checking in and packing up their gear in the morning, but a handful usually remained to meet with clients or to catch up on their reports. The unit's small interview room was empty too. Then one of the field nurses emerged from Kim's old office. She was clearly upset.

"LaVonne?" Mary called out.

LaVonne hurried over to Mary. "I want Kim back," she stated angrily.

"What's wrong?" Mary asked.

"Marni," LaVonne sneered. "Kim never treated us like this."

Mary glanced down the hallway. "I haven't interacted with her much," she admitted. Mary was introduced to Marni when she first started her job, but later attempts to get to know her had failed. Marni would cancel meetings Mary scheduled with her, and Marni wasn't in her office when Mary stopped by.

"Well, I'm not surprised," LaVonne stated.

"What do you mean?"

LaVonne shook her head in frustration and stepped aside. With a wave of her arm, she presented Mary with a challenge. "Go on. Go talk to the woman that Administration thought was a suitable replacement for Kim."

Mary rapped on the closed door and waited for a response. When none came, she knocked harder. After a third knock, a faint voice answered, "Yes?"

Mary entered the room and saw Marni sitting behind her desk. A woman in her early sixties, she was flipping through the pages of a magazine.

"Hello, Marni," Mary said pleasantly. Marni looked up but then returned to reading the magazine. Mary stepped closer to her desk. "Do you have a moment to talk about an appointment I sent out a little while ago?"

When Marni closed the magazine and stood up, the image of a ghostly vapor arising from a vent in the floor popped into

Mary's mind. Everything about the woman was muted. She was tall and held herself regally, but she wore a garment whose colors were as bland as the institutional paint on her office walls. Her dress was two-toned, with an off-white bodice attached to a tan skirt. A thin faux-leather brown belt was cinched at her waist, and a tan jacket covered her shoulders. A simple strand of dull pearls hung around her neck; its curve matched that of the modestly scooped collar on her dress. Behind Marni's ashen-colored reading spectacles, pale-blue eyes barely pierced the backdrop created by her sallow facial complexion and her light turnip-colored hair. Marni lifted her chin further and extended her hand.

"It's nice of you to finally meet with me properly," Marni said coolly.

Mary's eyebrows rose at the condescending greeting, and also at the impressively strong nasal sound of the woman's voice. As they grasped hands, Mary fought an urge to recoil. Marni's handshake was limp and cold.

Mary forced a smile to her face and asked, pleasantly, "Were you named after Marni Nixon, by any chance?"

Marni looked down at Mary, over the top of her glasses. "I have absolutely no idea who that is," she stated.

"Really?" Mary said with genuine surprise. "Marni Nixon was the singing voice for Deborah Kerr in the musical *The King and I*, and for Audrey Hepburn in *My Fair Lady*. Her voice is stunning."

Marni shrugged and glanced back at her magazine, and Mary used the moment to look around the room. She was saddened to see no trace of Kim. "About that meeting," she began again, "I wanted to—"

"There's no need to talk about that now," Marni replied without looking up. "I have a different matter to discuss with you. An important personnel issue."

"Personnel?" Mary asked. "Certainly. What is it?"

"It's my understanding that Cass McGovern works part time for CD and part time for Field Nursing."

"Yes, that's correct."

"And her position has limited-duration status."

Mary laughed. "Yes, that's also correct, but typical of government, it hasn't really been limited. She's been here for six years."

Marni did not respond to Mary's attempt at humor. Instead, she said, "We're going to have to let her go, and you should do it since you've known her longer than I have."

Mary stepped backward. "Fire Cass?" she asked. "What for?"

A hint of a smirk appeared on Marni's face. "Her Field Nursing hours are paid out of county general funds," she stated calmly, "and I've been informed that those funds will be cut."

Mary sighed. "Budget cuts are always looming around here. Who told you about this one?"

"I can't tell you that," Marni huffed.

Mary was taken aback. She was used to speaking openly with Kim and other managers at her level about Administration's fiscal maneuverings. "Well, there are few secrets in this place," she said. "Can you at least tell me when the cuts are expected?"

"Sometime in the coming year," Marni conceded.

Mary relaxed further. "Oh, then we have time."

"Time for what?" Marni asked with some irritation.

"Time to consider our options," Mary replied. "Cass' position is safe for the moment. I have no intention of losing her."

Marni studied Mary, again, from over the top of her reading glasses and said the word *oh* in one long drawn-out breath.

Mary took another step back. The noise that had emerged from Marni's mouth sounded like the moo of a cow with adenoid problems.

Oh my, Mary thought, hiding her distress. *She is no Marni Nixon.*

Mary was so distracted by the strange vocalization that she forgot where they were in the conversation. It was Marni who spoke next.

"I see. You and Cass are close."

The implication that Mary and Cass were lovers was clear, and Mary responded swiftly, but without any rancor in her voice. "This isn't personal. Cass is a valued employee. I will do everything I can to find other funding for her position, if it comes to that."

Marni shrugged and began to flip through her magazine again.

After a few moments of being ignored, Mary wondered, *Is that it?* It appeared the conversation had ended, so she said, "Well, I'd better get back to my unit."

Marni did not look up as Mary left, and she did not even mumble a goodbye. A weight descended over Mary as she stepped into the hallway and closed the door behind her. She saw a bleak future with this new colleague.

What is wrong with this place? she thought.

Saturday, May 31

Mark ate a few spoonfuls of the vegetable soup that had been served for dinner, but he picked at the slice of rustic bread and did not touch his salad.

"Are you okay?" Paul asked him "You're not eating very much."

Mark sniffed and rubbed his eyes. "I just think everything's catching up with me. I'm really tired."

The small group was eating at the large, rough-hewn kitchen table. Paul sat at one end, and Willow sat to his right. She cradled her baby close to her chest. Her body was turned away from Raymond, who sat to her right. Mark sat across from Raymond, and Skye was to the left of his father.

"Why don't you go to bed after you finish?" Paul encouraged Mark. "It's early, but a good night's sleep should help."

"I will," Mark answered. "Thanks."

"Father knows best," Raymond said, taunting his brother.

"Ray," Paul warned him. "Leave it alone."

Mark sat back in his chair and studied Raymond. He remembered Skye saying there was only a couple of years age difference between his uncle and his dad, but Raymond looked at least a decade older, as if life had worn him down quickly. Raymond held some resemblance to his brother physically, but while Paul was outgoing and confident, Raymond was reserved yet jittery. He had an emotional edge that Mark found hard to define.

"Why did you ask me here?" Raymond said to Paul.

"Does there have to be a reason?" Paul replied. Mark could see that Paul was trying to remain calm. "We have company. I thought you might enjoy sharing a meal with us."

"So you're not buttering me up for another talk about the vineyard?"

Paul shook his head. "No, I'm not. Let's change the subject." He turned to Skye and said, "I have the weekend off. I thought we might show Mark around the area."

"That would be great," Skye exclaimed.

Mark caught Raymond's reaction as Paul touched his son affectionately on his forearm. Raymond's jaw muscles pulsed, and his eyes grew dark.

Thank God he doesn't live here, Mark thought.

Raymond stood up abruptly. He stacked his plate and bowl on top of each other, and carried them to the kitchen sink.

"I do have one favor to ask of you, Ray," Paul called out to him.

"Here it comes," Raymond muttered. He stood with his back to everyone.

Paul ignored the comment. "Could you come to a planning meeting tomorrow night about the fund-raiser?" he asked. "We could use your help figuring out how to arrange Maureen's art work in the school's gym."

Raymond's shoulders slumped noticeably.

"I'm sure your help would mean a great deal to Maureen if she was still alive," Paul added.

Raymond gripped the edge of the sink with both hands.

To Mark, Paul's manipulation of his brother was clear. He remembered Skye telling him that the conflict between the two men had something to do with his mom. Mark could see that Paul had used Maureen to get Raymond to help him. Mark's mother had used the same guilt-laced tactic on him. She would tell him how hard it was being a single mom working full-time when she wanted him to work around the house or run errands for her. But Mark wondered whether Paul, the kind man who had taken him in, was aware of what he was doing. The effect on Raymond was clear. Mark watched as Raymond grabbed a fistful of hair on the back of his head and yanked on it.

"I think so," Raymond replied softly.

Mark glanced at Paul to see if he had noticed this weird gesture, but Paul was looking at his bowl of soup, not his brother.

"Thanks. That will help a lot," Paul said.

Raymond walked to the door that led to the back porch and took his light brown jacket off of a coat hook. "I'm going home," he announced to no one in particular.

"Okay," Paul answered. "See you tomorrow."

Once Raymond was out of the house, Willow lifted the baby up to her face and nuzzled the child playfully. Paul and Skye began to talk animatedly. Mark glanced back at the door and wondered what had left the room along with Raymond.

× × ×

Raymond stepped off of Paul's back porch and gulped as much of the evening air into his lungs as his constricted chest would allow. But he did not feel much relief until he reached the gate of the chain-link fence that separated their two properties. He lifted the latch with a trembling hand and hurried through the grove of oak trees to the comfort of his home. His breathing grew shallow again as he traversed the large, unkempt garden behind his house.

Raymond had broken ground on the scrappy plot of land as a teenager. His stepfather had been found dead, and many praised the boy for creating such a beautiful memorial to him. But the garden had never served such a vulgar purpose. Rather, it had been a celebration of his freedom from that monster and his first step toward fulfilling his dream of owning the farm. He had attempted to structure the garden in the image of the precise, formal grounds of the great European castles he loved, but many of the plants could not survive in the shaded and dry environment. When he was a young adult, his mother had tried to maintain the garden while he was at work, but she had no talent for it, especially during her drunken stupors, and had placed new plants wherever she thought most convenient. As a result, the garden took on the appearance of a ragged, sprawling creature breaking free of its raised-bed cage. Raymond had cared little for the garden since his mother's death. The only pleasure he now found in it was the two-tiered stone fountain at its center, which he had once sat beside for an awkward conversation with Maureen after she and Paul had returned from Oregon. The memory of her hands waving over the heather spears that grew around the fountain's base aroused him still.

Raymond entered his house and headed to the second floor. He passed his mother's bedroom before reaching the staircase. As was his habit, he turned his head away from its closed door. Upstairs, he collapsed onto his bed and covered himself with a fading family quilt. He lay still for a long time, staring at the ceiling, and then masturbated without release until he fell asleep. When he awoke only an hour later, he rolled from his back to his side and looked out the window. The beauty of the rich light from the setting sun was softening the aging day, but he only saw the gray in the trunk of the massive oak tree that hovered over the house.

× × ×

Mark dragged himself up the steep stairs, following Skye to his bedroom. When his new friend turned on the overhead light, the first thing he noticed was that the room looked nothing like his own back home. The bunk beds were neatly made, and the floor was not cluttered with clothes, magazines, and crumpled snack packages. The only clue that the room belonged to a teenage male was the faint musky odor that hung in the air. Then Mark looked at the walls. They were covered with images of plants and animals of all kinds. Painted on the ceiling were stars and planets.

"Wow. What's all this?" he asked.

"I'll explain in a minute," Skye replied. "Let me grab some clean sheets for you."

"Hey," Mark called out after him. "You've got bunk beds. There's plenty of room for both of us. Why are you staying in another room?"

Skye stopped and faced Mark. "I think it's best," he said. He hesitated but then blurted out, "Mark, I'm gay. I thought you should know."

Mark's eyes widened. "Oh," he replied shyly, and then he looked at his feet.

"I just get the feeling you'd be more comfortable if I didn't stay in here with you."

"Does your dad know?" Mark asked, looking sideways at Skye. "About you being gay?"

Skye grinned. "Yeah. Actually, I think he knew before I did." After a moment, he added, "I'll be right back with those sheets."

Mark set his backpack against the wall and looked around the room at nothing in particular. His body suddenly felt like it was made of stone, so he laid down on the lower bunk. He shielded his eyes from the harsh lamplight and began to study the artwork on the walls. On the ceiling, he spotted an alien creature sitting on the Big Dipper. It was looking down at him with great amusement.

"What are you laughing at?" he said aloud.

When the ceiling light became painfully bright, he closed his eyes and was soon in a deep sleep.

Monday, June 2

"Why didn't you tell me that KZIV News wanted to interview me?" Suzanne demanded of Mary, who was standing outside of Cass' cubicle. The health officer was elegantly dressed in a navy-blue suit and matching high-heeled shoes that flattered her trim figure. She wore a laced-trimmed white shell under her jacket. A red-and-blue patterned scarf was tied around her neck, and under it, a diamond-encrusted cross dangled from a delicate gold chain. "I just got a call from them about our second meningitis case. As usual, the reporter knew more about it than I did."

Mary glanced over Suzanne's shoulder at the wall clock and was disappointed to see that it was only 9:45 a.m. The day had just begun. "Jonathan said he would tell you about it," Mary replied calmly.

Suzanne began searching for something within her soft leather briefcase. She pulled out a small black object and fiddled with it. "My pager's not working," she stated.

And that's my fault? Mary thought.

After a moment Suzanne said in a more subdued tone, "Okay, maybe there's been some sort of miscommunication, but I expect to be informed about these things."

"Did Jonathan say anything to you about this afternoon's meeting?"

"He told me to ignore it," Suzanne replied.

Mary looked away in frustration. *Damn it*, she fumed to herself. When she looked back, Suzanne was eyeing her suspiciously.

"Jonathan asked me to retract the appointment for it, but I didn't," she confessed.

"What's it about?"

"The situation here in CD," Mary answered. She was encouraged by the concern she heard in Suzanne's voice. "We're overwhelmed. Jackson and I have come up with a plan to manage the unit's workload more efficiently, and we wanted to present it to you this afternoon, but Jonathan keeps telling me that I shouldn't be contacting you directly."

Suzanne looked at her with a puzzled expression. "Why?" she asked.

"He keeps implying that I'm overstepping my authority. He says he needs to protect your time."

"Protect me?" Suzanne asked, amused.

"Yes," Mary nodded. She was sure Suzanne saw the absurdity in Jonathan's position, but then to her dismay, the health officer giggled. She had not heard that sound since she had once made an off-the-cuff remark to her young niece about the size of a Barbie doll's breasts in relation to its tiny feet.

"Oh, I see what's going on," Suzanne gushed.

"What?" Mary asked, disturbed by the blush on the woman's cheeks.

Suzanne leaned toward her. "I think he has a little crush on me," she whispered and then added too loudly for Mary's comfort, "He told me he's working hard so that I don't have to deal with petty interruptions from front-line staff."

Mary was stunned, not just at Suzanne's interpretation of Jonathan's actions but also at her lack of consideration for the people who were sitting in the nearby cubicles.

"Let's go to my office," Mary said in a tightly controlled voice. She resisted the urge to grab Suzanne by the elbow and lead her there.

Suzanne looked at her with surprise, but she walked ahead of Mary down the aisle that ran between the gray fabric-covered cubicles. The trip was slow because Suzanne's strides were shortened by the tight line of her skirt. Mary recalled the different attire that Suzanne had favored at the free clinic where they had first met. There, Suzanne wore flowing skirts, T-shirts, and flat shoes.

Suzanne entered Mary's office and placed her briefcase on the guest chair. While she smoothed the front of her jacket, Mary closed the door more forcefully than was needed and faced the health officer. "The CD staff has been working extraordinarily hard making sure the business of this department gets done," she said. "I won't let their work be dismissed as petty."

Suzanne sighed as if exasperated.

"Tell me," Mary continued, "how am I or my staff supposed to update you if my manager won't allow it, or if he won't do it himself? Just who is falling down on their responsibilities here?"

Suzanne laughed. "Mary, you're getting way too excited about this. Okay, *petty* was a poor choice of words. I'm sorry. Jonathan is still learning the job. Like he said, he's just trying to protect my time. I'm very busy, and he just wants to make a good impression."

Mary considered her situation. If Jonathan was the only person Suzanne was communicating with, the CD Unit would continue to suffer because of it. Never before had she gone over a supervisor's head to get help, but she could not keep quiet about Jonathan any longer.

"Suzanne," she began, "I have strong concerns about Jonathan's performance."

Suzanne appeared worried. "Have you talked to him about it?" she asked.

"I tried," Mary replied, "but the conversation didn't go well. I'd like to talk with you about my concerns."

Suzanne moved away from Mary and fiddled with the leaves of the schefflera plant that sat at one corner of her desk. "Well, I guess we could," she muttered.

"How about now?" Mary asked.

"Oh, no, I can't," Suzanne replied. "I have to get to a meeting in the city by one." She began to fumble again for something in her briefcase. "I don't have my Palm Pilot with me," she commented. "Why don't you make an appointment with Rosalyn?"

"I'll just take ten minutes of your time," Mary said eagerly.

Suzanne looked at her with anxious eyes. "No, I'd rather we'd not be rushed. Schedule a time with Rosalyn."

Mary stood with her disappointment for a moment. She realized she had probably pushed the limits of her working relationship with Suzanne for the day. "Okay, I'll do that," she said. "But may I have your permission to hold the meeting about the CD Unit's workload?"

"Yes," Suzanne replied.

"And will you be able to attend? It's at four o'clock. Your input is crucial."

"I don't see how. I'll be down in the city."

"You could call in," Mary suggested. "Carl let Jackson purchase a conference phone with the bioterrorism funds. We're going to try out it out today so that the regional lab can call in."

"You're involving them?"

Mary heard the dismay in Suzanne's voice, and it puzzled her. "Well, yes," she answered. "We've been working closely with the lab because of the specimen testing."

"I'll see what I can do," Suzanne answered grudgingly. She lifted her briefcase off of the guest chair, smoothed the back of her skirt, and sat down. "Now, may I have an update on the new meningitis case?" she asked.

× × ×

The telephone rang, and Mary looked nervously at its display screen. She was in no mood for a confrontation with Jonathan or anyone else. But she didn't recognize the number, so she assumed it was safe to pick up the receiver.

"Mary Campbell, Communicable Disease Control," she announced.

"Hello, Mary Campbell," replied a pleasant male voice she did not recognize.

"I'm sorry. Who is this?" she asked.

"Boy, you really know how to hurt a guy," the man replied. "It's Joe, your favorite state employee."

Mary laughed. "You're my only state employee," she corrected him. "Where are you?"

"I'm at Friar Bean's coffee shop. A little birdie told me you were having a rough morning."

"And just who is that little birdie?"

"Sorry. My epi vows require that I keep my sources confidential. But cheer up. News about your run-in last week with Jonathan may be all over the building, but the one you just had with Suzanne is only now starting to leak out."

"Great," Mary groaned.

"You're pretty feisty for a government slacker," Joe teased. "Would you like to get away for a while?"

Mary glanced at the papers strewn across her desk. "I can't. I'm swamped with work."

"Oh, this is work," he asserted. "Linus and I finished reviewing the information you gave us."

"Already?" Mary said, impressed. She realized they must have worked over the weekend to tackle her request.

"We think you're right," Joe continued.

Mary sat up straight. "Right about what?" she asked.

"We may have found a connection between the norovirus outbreaks."

"Really?" she exclaimed.

"Yep."

Mary stood up. "I'll be right over. Don't go anywhere."

"I wouldn't dream of it," he replied.

A bell over the door jangled as Mary entered the coffee shop. The interior decor, with its dark wood and dim lighting, reminded her more of an English pub than a cafe. She looked around for Joe and spotted him in a corner booth. He was studying some papers that lay on the heavily varnished table.

"Hi," she greeted him before looking around the room. "Where's Linus?"

"When Nettie heard I had arrived, she put him back on the grant work."

Mary scowled. "Damn it. I'm going to have to talk to her."

"Watch out for that one," Joe cautioned. "She's pretty scary."

"That she is," Mary agreed.

Joe moved to his right and patted the deep-red vinyl covering of the bench on which he sat. "Here, have a seat."

Mary glanced at his hand and slid onto the opposite bench.

Joe feigned hurt. "I don't bite, you know."

"This will be fine," Mary said. She waited for him to begin talking, but he just looked at her, amused. When the silence became too uncomfortable for her, she pointed to one of the papers on the table. It was a drawing of a small circle labeled *links* from which protruded several angled lines.

"What's that?" she asked. "It looks like a spider with way too many hairy legs."

"Very good," he said. "It's a mind map. Sometimes they're called spider maps. Have you ever done one?"

"I'm pretty sure I haven't," she answered as she picked up the paper.

"It's a technique for brainstorming an idea or problem in a nonlinear fashion. Since I wasn't familiar with the outbreaks, I drew this up to see if it could help me figure out how they might be connected."

"Interesting," Mary murmured.

"By the way, do you want coffee or something?" Joe asked.

"No thanks," Mary replied as she scrutinized the drawing. "I'm fine." She looked back up at Joe after several silent moments, and realized he had been watching her. "What?" she asked.

"Do you ever eat or drink?"

Mary knew why he was asking with the question. He had invited her out for coffee on the first day he arrived and for lunch on the second, but she had found excuses not to join him.

"Frequently," she replied, pointing again at the spider map. "So, did this help?"

Joe grinned and said, "Sort of. Let me back up a moment and tell you what Linus and I've been doing. We decided to look at all your norovirus outbreaks for the last three years—not just the ones since the beginning of the year—for comparison purposes."

Mary laughed lightly. "Only epidemiologists would go looking for more information to sift through," she said.

Joe smiled. "True," he replied. Then he grabbed a sheet of finely lined graph paper and handed it to her. "We reexamined the epi curves for each outbreak. Everything seemed to be in order for each individual investigation, so I looked at them in the aggregate. Meaning, I drew an epi curve that plots the number of outbreaks by the date they were reported to the health department. You can clearly see the seasonality of the illness. Most of your outbreaks over the past three years occurred between November and February."

Mary studied the figure. It consisted of a series of vertical bars rising up from the horizontal axis. Each vertical bar consisted of a stack of squares. The squares represented individual outbreaks and were color-coded for the year in which they occurred. The horizontal axis was labeled, *Epi Week*, with the first epi week being the first week in the calendar year. The vertical axis was labeled, *Number of Outbreaks*. Mary thought that, together, the shape of the series of vertical bars looked like a sea serpent about to slither off the page to her left. Its nose started in late September, when the number of outbreaks was lowest, and the curve of its back peaked in January, when the number of outbreaks was highest. The curve then dropped to a little bulge in the creature's tail, capturing their most recent outbreaks for the year.

"That looks right," she said, handing the epi curve back to Joe. "But how does your spider diagram fit into this?" She pointed to the words on the sections of the spider's legs closest to its body. "What are these?" she asked.

"They represent the various characteristics of the investigations. Some are pretty standard for describing outbreaks in space and time. I've got eight so far."

"So far?"

Joe shrugged. "I may be overlooking something."

Mary doubted that, but said nothing.

"And the words on the hairs of the spider's legs?" she inquired with a touch of repulsion. "I take it they're related to the characteristics?"

"That's right," he answered. "They're the values for each one."

Joe read off the characteristics in clockwise order, starting with the spider's upper right leg. "So there's *case status*, which is whether norovirus was confirmed, presumptive, or suspect. Then we have *time of symptom onset*, which I broke down by season and time of day. *Outcomes* refers to whether cases were hospitalized or died. And *source of infection* is whether food or something else was the vehicle for the virus. I was surprised you couldn't pin that down for more of this year's nursing home outbreaks."

Mary shook her head. "No, we couldn't," she said. "It was strange."

"I put the three characteristics dealing with location next to each other," Joe continued. "These are *geo-location*, which shows where in the county the outbreak occurred, like on the west or east side. *Setting* is the actual place where the outbreaks occurred, like a home or school or nursing home. *Exposure site* indicates where people were exposed within the setting—like, do we know if the outbreak started in one wing of a nursing home and spread to other wings? Your team had better luck getting that information."

"Yeah," Mary said. "And you'd think knowing where the outbreak started would've helped us figure out the vehicle of exposure, but it didn't."

"And the last characteristic I looked at was *people*," Joe said. "I treated that one a bit differently."

"How's that?" Mary asked.

"You know how we tend to lump everyone into one of two groups, like cases and controls, staff and residents, or employees and patrons?"

"Yes."

"Well, I added two other pairings." Joe pointed to one of the spider's legs from which two lines extended. "People can also be related to a case by whether they are paid to be around them. Nursing home staff or expo vendors would fall under the paid category. Relatives, customers, and others fall under the not-paid group. I also separated cases for this year's outbreaks into two groups based on whether your team was able to interview them. I didn't include the nursing home residents who couldn't be interviewed because they have dementia."

"Were there many we didn't reach?" Mary asked.

"Eight, which is a pretty small number considering all the outbreaks you've had this year. I tried to reach them again. Phone numbers were disconnected for four, my interviews with three didn't provide any new information, and one person refused to talk to me but then called back."

"Really?" Mary asked with surprise. "Did anything come of that?"

"Yes," Joe said with a grin.

Mary looked at him suspiciously. "What's with the impish twinkle in your eyes?"

"It must be the company."

"Or maybe you're just a big flirt," Mary said with a laugh.

Joe laughed too. "Okay, fair enough," he replied. "I'll tell you about that interview in a minute. But before I called around, I compared the names of the staff, residents, and cases across the outbreaks—the sick and healthy—to see if there was any crossover."

"Did you find something?"

"No," he replied, "not at first. I got excited when the same staff names popped up for two facilities, but then I found out they're owned by the same parent corporation, so they probably share staff regularly. But the guy who called me back, he said something that made me wonder if we had all of the information about temp staff at the nursing homes."

"Temp staff?" Mary asked. "They would've been listed on the staff rosters we were given."

"They should have been," Joe stated, "but as this fellow reminded me, many of those facilities don't have very sophisticated operations. Tracking information can be spotty."

"How does he know that?" Mary asked.

"He's in the business."

"Oh." Mary knew Joe's comment about the lack of sophistication to be true based on her efforts to find a care center for her father.

One facility she visited was a converted 1980s ranch home that had been expanded with modular extensions. It was clean, and run by a nice couple, but there was nothing modern about it. The aroma of cheap institutional cleanser permeated the home, and the decor was dull and shabby. The residents had sat glazed-eyed in the common room while she toured the facility. The monthly cost was within her family's budget, but she couldn't bear the thought of leaving her father in such a depressing environment.

"So I called the temp agency that employs ancillary staff like nurse's aides in this county and asked for their staff assignments for each of our nursing homes."

"And?" Mary asked eagerly.

The epidemiologist beat out a drum roll on the table.

"Joe!" she said, exasperated.

"Okay. It turns out one temp has worked at all of our nursing homes that have had outbreaks this spring, and he worked around the time of disease onset for each one."

"You're kidding!" Mary exclaimed.

"Nope." Joe grinned. "His name wasn't on all of the rosters."

Mary leaned back against the booth and enjoyed the sense of relief at having something tangible to move forward on. But the feeling was fleeting.

Joe noticed and said, "You're putting the pieces together, aren't you?"

"He couldn't have been sick all that time," she stated.

"True."

"Have you talked with him yet?"

"No, I wanted to run this by you first."

"Did he work before, during, or after symptoms began for each outbreak?"

"All of the above," Joe answered.

Mary leaned onto the table. "But if he was sick for one outbreak, he shouldn't have been infectious for too long. A person can shed the virus for several weeks, right? Could he have gotten reinfected? How long does the illness confer immunity?"

"It's hard to say. I've read that immunity is strain-specifc, and it's not life-long. And we're probably dealing with the pandemic strain in these outbreaks, so lots of people are going to be susceptible."

Mary leaned back against the booth and placed her hands in her lap. She thought for a few moments. "We need to talk to this temp worker and get more information. Would you like the honor, since you discovered him?"

"I'd be glad to," Joe replied.

"And can you make a copy of this spider map for me? I'd like to study it some more."

"Sure."

Mary slipped out of the booth as Joe gathered up his papers. When he stood up next to her, she said, "Thank you. This is great work."

The impishness returned to his eyes. "My pleasure," he replied.

× × ×

"Nearly half of our residents are sick, and a third of my staff are out," reported Ellen Randolph, the administrator for the Carriage House retirement community.

Erin put the woman on speakerphone so that Mary could join in the conversation. Ms. Randolph was giving them an update on the Carriage House's norovirus outbreak. Mary had called the facility the same day she had learned of the possible outbreak from the host of the soccer-team party. Ms. Randolph confessed that they had tried to contain the illness on their own, but she and her staff had since been cooperative.

"We're trying to stay on top of the disinfecting," Ellen stated, "but it's really hard. We've sent four residents to the hospital for dehydration, and one is in critical condition."

"How are you doing?" Mary asked.

The woman's voice quavered. "Just between us, I don't want to be the adult around here anymore."

Erin looked at Mary upon hearing the woman's distress.

"How much sleep have you gotten over the past couple of days?" Mary asked. Besides fatigue, she worried that Ellen would suffer the same fate of other administrators and nursing directors who led the response to outbreaks at their facilities. After several days of trying to keep their businesses going with limited staff and a runaway illness, they usually succumbed to the virus themselves and spent an additional exhausting day or two hanging around a toilet.

"Very little," Ellen replied. "I'm feeling a little more hopeful today, though."

"Why's that?" Erin asked.

"I never thought I'd be glad that a family member complained about us to corporate headquarters, but one woman did, and corporate finally contacted me. I gave them hell for ignoring my calls. I don't care if they fire me—they're finally sending in staff replacements, including someone for me."

"That's great," Erin said.

"Do you have any news for us?" Ellen asked.

"Just that the lab has received the stool specimens," Erin answered her. "We should get the results in a few days."

Ellen let out a long breath. "You know, we really do run a clean operation here."

Erin glanced again at Mary, who nodded her understanding about the defensive tone of Ellen's voice. Mary had warned Erin about the delicate political nature of conducting outbreak investigations. The greatest fear for businesses, whether they were a food stand at a county fair or a high-end restaurant downtown, was that the health department was going to shut them down. But in Mary's experience, only those businesses that willfully and belligerently refused to cooperate were served such notices.

"We know you do, Ms. Randolph," Mary replied, and Erin added, "Our environmental health specialist told us that your facility has a very good record. He said you take care of inspection findings right away."

"That's true," the administrator replied, sounding relieved. "And we just got good ratings on a state review."

"What review was that?" Mary asked.

"A licensing inspection. The nurse surveyor came here a little over a week ago."

"That must take a lot of prep work," Mary commented.

"Actually, the inspections are unannounced," Ellen said, "which makes them all the more stressful—and then the outbreak hit."

"I have one last question for you, Ellen," Mary said. "Did you happen to use any temp staff around the time your residents started to get sick?"

"Oh, sure," the woman declared. "We're frequently short staffed. We use this one temp agency all the time."

× × ×

"Okay, everyone," Mary began. "I've called this meeting—" She glanced at Jackson and realized she had not used the appropriate emergency management term for the gathering. "I mean briefing," she corrected herself, "to update you on what's happening in CD and to get your feedback on a plan that Jackson and I have developed to manage the work."

Mary scanned the room to take a measure of her colleagues' moods. Seated around the small conference table were Jackson, Joe, Nettie, Marni, Jonathan, Linus, Joe, Cliff Moore from Environmental Health, and the CD nurses. Suzanne and Asako Takata, the director of the regional public health laboratory, had called in on the conference line. Everyone appeared glum except for Jonathan, who was grinning broadly. Linus and the CD nurses projected stoic fatigue. Cliff, who was usually so relaxed and nonplussed during meetings that Mary was often tempted to tell him to sit up straight, sat today with his gangly legs tucked underneath his chair and his arms folded tightly across his chest. Marni wore a bored, distant expression, and Nettie emanated so much distress that Mary found herself actually worried about the woman.

Mary had arrived at the conference room just as another meeting was ending. Inside, she had found Jonathan and Nettie sitting at opposite ends of the table while Carl was preparing to leave. The tension between the three was palpable. Jonathan wore the somber pout he typically exhibited when he wanted to project that he was a serious professional, but flickers of delight pierced his facade. Nettie, in contrast, looked as if she struggled to contain a demon within; frustration and anger roiled across her face, and she appeared close to tears. Mary had never thought the woman capable of crying.

Mary had murmured a quick greeting to her colleagues at that earlier meeting and was startled when Suzanne declared her presence on the already-active conference line. "Oh, hi, Suzanne," Mary had said as she arranged her materials for the meeting. "Glad you could make it."

Something disagreeable had obviously transpired, but Mary was too anxious about the forthcoming conversation to give much thought to her colleagues' drama. She only hoped it would not spill over into her meeting. Her goal was simple: everyone would agree to at least try the new approach.

After Mary led introductions for Joe's benefit, she said, "To paraphrase the title of a recent movie, we are experiencing a near-perfect storm in CD. New cases and outbreaks are coming at us hard and fast, and I'm worried about our ability to stay on top of the work and prevent the staff from burning out."

"As if we haven't already," Cass said, and others in the room laughed nervously.

Mary let the moment pass. "Besides the ten norovirus outbreaks reported since early April," she continued, "we're also dealing with the ongoing pertussis outbreak and investigating a potential bacterial meningitis outbreak, in addition to the usual hodgepodge of individual case reports we receive on a daily basis. The CD staff have worked to the best of their ability to manage all of this, for which I am grateful, but we've reached our threshold. Actually, we probably passed it a while ago, and I'll take responsibility for not acting on that sooner. Sometimes it's hard for us—for me—to let go and ask for help, but that's what I'm doing now."

Mary stopped speaking because she was afraid she had started to ramble. She was encouraged to see that her colleagues were still listening attentively. "The CD Unit needs a smarter way to work," she said. "We need additional support, and we need a way to set priorities and improve communications between ourselves. Our routine approach is not efficient under the present circumstances. We're falling behind, which may ultimately lead to new cases and more work for us."

Mary paused and then said, "Jackson has been watching the CD Unit, and he understands what we're dealing with. He has suggested a new approach that I'd like us to try."

Mary felt a shift in the energy of the room. The CD nurses glanced from her to Jackson, and she knew their thoughts. They had watched her interactions with him since his arrival, and they had followed her lead in maintaining a polite but obvious distance from the man and his work. She braced herself. "What we are proposing," she told the group, "is that we work under a temporary emergency management structure."

Mary studied her fellow managers for any signs of unease. Jonathan squirmed in his chair, and someone on the conference line cleared her throat, but no one said anything. "The approach is called the Incident Command System," Mary continued, "or ICS for short. ICS is a tool used in the emergency management world to structure and organize responses. And, like I said, it's temporary. We'll only use it until our workload returns to a normal level."

"Emergency?" Jonathan snorted.

Mary ignored him and looked at her staff. She was most worried about resistance from them. She valued the nurses tremendously, but she was very aware that their strengths were also their weaknesses. They were strong-minded, smart, and independent, and they needed little hand-holding to carry out their duties. They could, however, also be controlling and stubborn and slow to change. These traits had presented more than a few management challenges for her over the past four years.

Mary also worried about Nettie's and Suzanne's reactions. Neither of them liked being told what to do. She did not concern herself with Jonathan or Marni. Mary knew that Jonathan would go along with any decision of Suzanne's. Marni was still too much of an enigma for her to guess what position she might take.

Cass was the first to raise her hand.

Here it comes, Mary thought, bracing herself.

"Command?" the nurse said. Defiance laced the simple one-word question. "Really, Mary?" Cass had been leaning on the conference room table, but she now reclined in her seat and draped one arm casually over the back of her chair.

"Yes," Mary replied simply. "I know it sounds strange to our public health ears, but let's not get hung up on terminology."

"Come on," Cass said. "What are we playing at? I'll agree that having some extra warm bodies to help out would be great, but why do we have to complicate our work with this military shi—" The nurse stopped speaking when she suddenly remembered who, other than her CD colleagues, was listening to her. She finished her sentence by saying, "Jargon?"

"Actually, Cass," Jackson offered, "ICS was developed by the fire service, not the military."

Cass turned her head slowly toward him. "Okay, then, paramilitary jargon."

Undeterred, the man asked, "Remember the recent fires in southern California? The fire service used ICS—which they call SEMS, the Standardized Emergency Management System—to organize their resources and operations. What they accomplished was very impressive given the geographic scope of the fires."

Cass said nothing and shifted her torso away from Jackson.

"So, how does it work?" Linus asked.

Mary smiled at him, grateful for the way he refocused the conversation. "Good question," she said. "It's much easier to describe using a diagram." She lifted a large sheet of poster board onto the table and said, "This is the structure that Jackson was going to explain to us during his training that was cancelled. You start with a basic organizational chart that assigns people to specific roles and responsibilities. This structure also lays out the lines of formal communication between everyone."

Drawn on the poster board was an organizational chart that contained one rectangle at the top and four others lined up in a row underneath it. A single line dropped from the top box and broke off in two directions to connect to the lower row of four boxes. Mary began to describe it for the benefit of the people on the conference line. "The top rectangle represents the incident commander, who is in charge of the overall response. There are four chiefs who report directly to that person. One chief oversees the staff assigned to the Operations Branch. These are the people who are out in the field; the boots on the ground, or the doers, so to speak. Another chief leads the planning efforts, such as—"

"Mary?" Suzanne interrupted.

"Yes?"

"I need to leave soon. I appreciate your efforts, but I hardly think we need to take on an elaborate new scheme just to help you get back on your feet. Let's just reassign some staff to your unit for a couple of days."

Mary fought back a familiar feeling of defeat. Suzanne always began her rebuffs with an expression of appreciation.

Jonathan slapped his hand against the edge of the table. "I agree," he declared. "There's no need to make a big deal of this."

"Make a big deal of what, Jonathan?" Nettie asked pointedly.

Jonathan looked at Nettie, startled. "About…you know…what Mary's been talking about," he replied with a laugh. "This coincidence stuff."

Nettie's eyes shown with victory as Jonathan tripped over his words.

"Suzanne," Mary interjected, "this isn't just about the number of staff. It's also how we organize our work and how we communicate with each other. After talking with Jackson, I'm confident ICS can help us in those areas."

"It might also be helpful for—" Linus began, but Suzanne cut him off.

"It's nice to see you enthusiastic about something for a change, Mary," she said, "but I'm afraid a new approach will only further diminish your ability to manage the CD Unit's work."

Jonathan nodded his head vigorously. "I agree," he declared.

Mary prickled at the public insult, but she was heartened to hear Cass whisper to Stella, "What the hell?"

Linus tried to speak again. "Suzanne, the CD Unit is working under some extraordinary circumstances. It's not any one person's—"

Suzanne interrupted him. "I'm not finished," she declared. "I have two more points to make. First, we shouldn't be investigating every norovirus outbreak that is reported to us."

"That's so true!" Jonathan chortled.

"What?" Lourdes blurted out uncharacteristically.

"DePaul County doesn't," Suzanne continued, "and by the time we receive a report of an outbreak, there's not much we can do but let the illness run its course. Second—"

Mary ran her fingers through her hair. One of her fears was starting to come true. Suzanne was derailing the meeting. Mary needed to get it back on track while she could. "Excuse me, Suzanne," Mary stated firmly.

"I'm not done talking," Suzanne countered.

"I realize that, but we need to return to the topic at hand. Your point about DePaul County is interesting but requires a separate discussion. And I'd like to note that DePaul County does investigate norovirus outbreaks in high-risk populations, such as the elderly. At this point, our outbreaks are primarily in nursing homes."

No one said anything. Mary had just shut down the health officer, and they were waiting to see what happened next. In the ensuing silence, Mary glanced at Joe and was embarrassed to see him grinning at her.

"Second," Suzanne continued stonily, "I attended a presentation on ICS at a statewide meeting of the Conference of Local Health Officials. Nettie was there too, as I recall."

Nettie did not react to the mention of her name.

"The majority of attendees agreed that working under ICS would be too much of a distraction during true public health events."

Jonathan leaned toward the conference phone. "I couldn't agree more," he stated gravely.

Cliff groaned audibly.

"Suzanne?" Jackson asked. "At this meeting, did they mention that ICS is scalable?"

After a moment, she replied, "I don't remember."

"Well, I see some confused expressions here in the room. Would you mind if I took a moment to explain that term? I'll be brief." Suzanne said nothing, so Jackson continued. "Scalable means that an ICS structure can be expanded or contracted to fit the size of an incident. For example, the first patrol officer on the scene of a freeway chemical spill may start off as the incident commander but then pass that responsibility off to someone else as others become involved in the response, such as fire crews, hazmat teams, transportation workers, and medical personnel."

"What's your point?" Suzanne asked.

"You're concerned about the time ICS will take away from your work. Is that correct?"

"Yes, among other things."

"Would you allow the CD staff to try it out on a smaller scale?" Jackson looked to Mary as if he were making the request to her as well. "Doing so would help us meet a state preparedness exercise requirement, and it would give the unit the opportunity to see if ICS is a good fit for them under these circumstances. In a scaled-down version, Mary could be the incident commander, and in that role, she would communicate with you as the senior health policy advisor. She would keep you up-to-date on the situation and seek your input on decisions."

The meeting participants were quiet as they waited for Suzanne to respond, but then a new voice entered the conversation. It was Asako.

"Mary?" she asked calmly. "May I say something?"

"Certainly, Asako."

Asako had only held her job with the regional Public Health Laboratory for two years. But in that time, she had come to be highly regarded by staff and management in the six local health departments that her lab supported. The lab's testing services were one of the few revenue-generating activities within public health, and as Mary had learned from Suzanne, after only eighteen months under Asako's guidance, the lab had increased its revenue by fifteen percent.

"Before I discovered microbiology," Asako began, "I was a natural resources major in college. One summer I got a job with the state's Department of Forestry, and I helped with their seasonal fire-fighting efforts. We worked under ICS, and I can tell you the system really does improve communications and ensure that resources like people and equipment are used efficiently. Suzanne, it's easier to learn ICS during small rather than large-scale emergencies. My lab staff and I have been working with your CD Unit on their outbreaks, and even we've noticed the pressure they're under. If you have a requirement to exercise ICS, I recommend you let them try it out. I'd also like my staff to participate."

Mary and Jackson looked at each other, astonished. Neither had any knowledge of Asako's background. Suzanne relied heavily on the lab. She was unlikely to threaten her good working relationship with Asako by brushing her recommendation aside. Mary suddenly felt more confident.

After a long pause, Suzanne said, "I'm still not sure I see the need for even a scaled-down version, but if it helps meet an exercise requirement, then I can agree to a trial run. But I want Jonathan to be the incident commander. That will better reflect our current management hierarchy."

Numerous shoulders slumped around the table, while Jonathan beamed at the compliment. Dismayed, Mary looked at Jackson, but he only shook his head and whispered to her, "Don't worry about it."

Nettie then startled the meeting's participants with a brisk and authoritative pronouncement. "I agree. Given Jonathan's impending promotion to the Manager E level, it would only be right that he assume all responsibility for this challenging situation."

As if on command, all eyes except for Joe's filled with silent shock. Jonathan, in turn, straightened his posture importantly.

So that's what happened during the last meeting, Mary realized. Now she understood why Nettie was so upset. Such a promotion was an astounding accomplishment for a new hire who was still on probation. Currently, both Nettie and Jonathan were at the Manager D level. Nettie had been at that ranking for a decade, despite the numerous accomplishments and accolades she had brought to the agency.

As a Manager E, Jonathan would have authority over Nettie and her programs and would be the second-highest ranked manager in the Public Health Department. Nettie could tolerate Jonathan while he supervised others, but she would never allow him to supervisor her.

Of course she's outraged, Mary thought.

Suzanne's response was swift and angry. "Nettie, that information is not for public discussion. The decision is not yet final."

Nettie leaned toward the phone. "But Carl usually gets his way in these matters, doesn't he?" she replied. "There's no reason to keep Jonathan's promotion a secret. Wouldn't you agree?"

Mary was unsettled by the steely determination in Nettie's eyes. She looked at Jonathan. Unbeknownst to him, a battle had just commenced. Mary now likened the grinning man to a farm animal on its way to the slaughter house. Nettie would seek out the means to see him fail dramatically, and the incident commander position would provide an enticing opportunity for her to do so. From now on, all of Nettie's energy would go toward preventing his promotion, and Mary knew that Nettie did not care whose lives she made hell in order to ensure his ruin.

× × ×

"Mom?" Mary called out. She peered into her mother's house through the open window in the door that lead from the carport to the kitchen. "I'm going to see Dad. I was wondering if you wanted to come along." Mary could see her mother sitting in the tiny living room, reading a book. Her back was to the door. Carol made no move to greet her daughter.

"Mom, why are you doing this?" Mary pleaded. "Can't we at least talk?" She stared at her mother, willing her to turn around. When she did not, Mary sat down on the stoop. She was exhausted from the day's events. "Okay, I'm just going to wait out here until you change your mind," she said stubbornly.

Mary laid a bouquet of flowers across her lap. Her mother always said flowers reminded her of the dances from *The Nutcracker*

Suite. Mary took a whiff of their fragrance and then lowered her head to her knees. Tears welled in her eyes as they often did when she allowed herself to rest. She sat for several minutes and felt the weight of her grief. She was overcome with a sadness that seemed to dissolve her bones and muscles.

The faint music of an ice cream truck grew louder as it drove through the neighborhood. Mary lifted her head when it stopped in front of the house next door. A little boy ran to meet it, and he pulled his father along by the hand. Mary was instantly reminded of David and her own father.

Mary watched as the man lifted his son so that he could look at the pictures of the frosty delights on the side of the truck, and she remembered that orange creamsicles were David's favorite treat. The little boy waved to the ice cream man after their purchases were made.

I never got the chance to say goodbye to David, she realized, *and now I don't know how to say goodbye to Dad.*

She glanced over her shoulder and thought about her parents. Her father, not her mother, had been the one who dispensed most of the sage advice to her over the years and had guided her through the vagaries of life. An unfailing optimist, her mother had never been the parent who handled change or conflict well. What others considered as living in denial, her mother had regarded as focusing on the beauty in life. Mary sat with this realization for a while. If her mother was as broken as she was with grief, then Mary's anger would not help. It would take more time for her mother to sort through the swirl of emotions she must be feeling.

Mary looked around at the yard and house. Everything she saw brought up memories of happier times with her family: the birthday parties with friends under the carport, running through the sprinkler on the front lawn, and helping her parents tend the vegetable garden out back. She raised her head and spotted a metallic mount attached to one of the carport's overhead beams. A punching bag had once been suspended from its eye ring. Her father had used it to teach his children how to fight. He'd had a practicality born, he often told her, of being a professional male dancer in a sports-obsessed culture. And he had justified the training to his disapproving wife by saying he did not want his children to learn how to defend themselves like he had, in street fights. Mary smiled at the memory of her father reminding her to keep her thumb on the outside of her closed fist as she hit the bag, even though the heavy object barely budged when she struck it.

Mary decided to leave. She peered one more time through the door's window and could no longer see her mother. "I'm going now, Mom," she called out. "Let me know if you need anything. I've left you a little something out here." She kissed one of the blossoms in the bouquet, laid the flowers on the stoop, and walked down the driveway to her car.

× × ×

Mary spotted her father sitting on a couch in the common room with a few of the other nursing home residents. The television was on, but he was not watching it. Instead, his eyes darted around as if he was trying to understand who everyone was and why he was there. A nurse had warned her that her father had been struggling with his anxiety that day, so Mary approached him cautiously.

"Hello, Dad," she greeted him.

When he looked up, she saw the lack of recognition in his eyes, but he responded pleasantly. "Hello, young lady," he said. "How are you today?"

"I'm fine, and you?"

"Would you like something to eat?" he asked in a halting voice. "I don't know what we have, but we can probably find something."

"No, thank you. I've already eaten," she reassured him. "May I sit down next to you?"

"Of course," her father answered. He patted the sofa cushion, just like he had when she was a child and he wanted to talk with her. "It's not every day that a pretty girl wants to sit with me."

Mary smiled at the pleasantries. He had been so good at these that it had taken her and her mother quite a while, during the early stages of his dementia, to realize he was using them to cover up the confusion of his failing mind.

"How are you?" he asked her again.

"I'm okay, but we're very busy at work. It's been hard."

Her father nodded. "Hmm," he said.

"How about you?" she asked. She fumbled around in her mind for something to say, a topic that would not cause him distress, but it was her father who spoke next.

"Where's David?" he asked fretfully. "Why isn't he home from school yet?" He began to wring his hands. Fear filled his eyes. "I'm worried. He's been gone too long."

Mary bit her lip. She took one of her father's hands in her own. She and her mother had stopped reminding him about David's death because it felt cruel to do so. He mourned anew each time he was told. Thinking quickly, Mary said, "He's spending the night with a friend, Dad."

"Who?"

"Billy Thompson, from school. David will be home in the morning."

"Oh!" her father exclaimed with relief. "That's why. Thank you, young lady. You're very kind. I've been so worried."

Mary lowered her head and began to cry softly. To her surprise, her father placed one of his hands on top of her head. "What's wrong?" he asked lovingly as he stroked her hair.

Mary heard something familiar in his voice. She looked up and saw the father of her childhood reappear in the limpid brown eyes that gazed back at her. She felt him in the warmth of his touch.

"I'm tired of being a good girl, of always trying to do the right thing, of being alone," she confessed.

Her father laughed. "Well, whoever said you had to, Cricket?"

Mary drew in her breath, elated he had spoken his long-used endearment for her. She hugged him and buried her face in his chest. He grasped her forearm and exclaimed, "Oh, my!" She held him until a nurse's aide spoke.

"I'm sorry to interrupt, Donny, but it's time for your bath."

With difficulty, Mary loosened her hold on her father. He looked up at the nurse's aide, and Mary watched him disappear again.

The aide placed a walker in front of him. As he stood with her help, he asked Mary, "How are you today?"

Mary kissed her father on the cheek. "I'm much better now thanks to you," she said. "Goodnight, Dad. I love you."

Tuesday, June 3

Mary and Jonathan were the only managers from yesterday's meeting who reconvened to work out the details of the ICS structure. Mary was propping up the draft diagram when Jackson, who was standing next to her, cleared his throat. She looked at him, and he nodded in the direction of the door. Mary turned and saw that Jonathan had gathered up his belongings and was making his way to the exit.

"Whoa, Jonathan!" she called out. "Where are you going?"

With his back to her, he said, "I have a pressing matter to attend to."

"But Jonathan," she implored him, "you're in charge of this response. We need you to help us develop the ICS structure. Otherwise, we'll just be guessing at what you want."

Jonathan took another step, but he turned his head toward the sound of her voice. "It's very important," he said meekly.

"Well, can you take care of whatever it is and come back?" she asked.

Jonathan turned his body just enough so that she could see the side of his face. "No," he replied before mumbling a string of incoherent words.

Mary overheard Cliff whisper to Stella, "He's probably got to go find his brain."

Mary studied her supervisor. He seemed so anxious she actually felt sorry for him. She had come into the meeting with low expectations that he would work any differently with her under ICS. Jackson had even warned her that ICS did not resolve personality conflicts, but she had not thought Jonathan would disengage from the process entirely. As he continued to inch his way toward the door, Mary came up with an idea that would ease his discomfort, honor Suzanne's request that he remain in charge, and selfishly, minimize her interactions with him.

"Okay, then," she said. "Why don't we just plan on giving you a daily update from now on? That way you can let us know how we're doing."

Mary glanced at Jackson and saw his disapproval, but she ignored it. She knew what she had to do.

Jonathan turned around fully. "That's a great idea," he exclaimed.

"What time is best for you?" she asked.

"Well, that depends," he said. "I have lots to do."

"Just a rough estimate," she encouraged him. "We can be flexible."

"How about at nine am, when I get in," he suggested. Then he scowled. "No, wait. That's before I meet with Carl. Um, how about ten, after I've had a chance to check in with him?"

"Ten is fine," Mary replied.

Jonathan looked up at the ceiling. "No. Let's make it nine, before I check in with Carl. That way I can let him know what's going on."

"Okay," Mary agreed. She had averted her gaze because it was so painful to watch him make this simple decision.

"Great! See you all later," he bellowed as he stepped from the room.

"Well, that's an auspicious start to our new management structure," Stella said. "We have no incident commander."

Cass ignored Stella's comment and asked Jackson, "So, what's your role in all of this? You're not a nurse or an epidemiologist—or even someone like Cliff."

"Geez, thanks," Cliff said.

"I'm going to be your coach since you haven't had any formal ICS training," Jackson answered with enthusiasm. "I'll help everyone understand their roles and responsibilities and how to stay in their own lanes, so to speak. I'll also act as the safety officer. This is really an exciting opportunity."

"An opportunity for what, Jackson?" Cass snarled at him.

Mary watched as Jackson opened his mouth, as if to speak, but then said nothing. The anger behind Cass' question was clear. Mary had no idea whether ICS would help her unit, but she knew she had to confront Cass' attitude if the management tool was to have any chance of success. Cass' professional arrogance was blinding her to the realities of their situation.

"Cass," Mary began, "do you think we're working effectively now? And you had better say no, because you're in my office often enough complaining about one problem or another."

Startled, Cass paused before answering. "No," she said bluntly.

"And do you have any different ideas about how to manage our workload?" Mary persisted.

"Just get us some warm bodies," the nurse replied forcefully. "That's all we need."

"That's all we need?" Mary asked, taking on the woman's defiance. "Then I want you to step into my shoes for a moment. Say we get those warm bodies. We get two nurses, two health educators, and an administrative assistant reassigned to us. Given that they're new to CD, what work will you assign them? Who will train them? And who will they report to? You? Are you going to manage five new staff in addition to your other responsibilities? And how will you know when we're caught up enough on one outbreak so that we can reassign them to another? And do you really think Nettie is going to lend you her people indefinitely? And who knows what Marni will have to say about her field nurses working CD? There's a good chance at least one of those two managers will be breathing down your neck to get her staff back as soon as possible."

Cass glanced away. She said nothing.

"And how do you expect to give Suzanne and Jonathan regular updates on top of your other duties?" Mary continued. "And I'm not talking about individual case reports. I'm talking summary statistics. We don't have a surveillance database, so someone is going to have to compile that information by hand on a daily basis and put it into some sort of format that is simple enough for Jonathan to understand yet answers all of the questions that Suzanne and the press might ask of us."

Cass' expression was now subdued, and she gazed at an indefinable point across the room. Mary saw her discomfort and took her attention off of her. She addressed the entire group. "ICS is not just about our case investigations, although its primary function is to support that work. We'll use it to conduct daily planning sessions, work on talking points and press releases, and track staff hours and supplies. And then there are safety concerns. It's not like we have an unlimited supply of personnel. Take Cliff, for example. We need to make sure he stays healthy while he's out doing his inspections."

"Amen to that," Cliff declared, and a few people laughed.

Mary glanced around the room. "Does anyone have another approach, a realistic one, they'd like us to consider instead of ICS?"

Mary glanced at each person while she waited for a response and was reminded of how far the group had come over the years, despite their differences. She had started as a CD staff nurse, but after only six months with the unit, Mary almost left her job because she had become so frustrated with the chaotic behavior of her predecessor and former supervisor. She had applied for another position with Monroe County, which lay just north of Revere County, but then her supervisor unexpectedly announced she was moving to Alaska. The operations manager at the time, Nora York, encouraged Mary to apply for the CD Nurse Supervisor position. Nora had treated her to coffee one morning at Friar Bean's and said she saw in her someone who could help the management team advance the department. Nora laid out a vision for moving Public Health into the Information Age that took hold of Mary's imagination. The ideas Nora had presented to her that morning gave her hope she might finally become part of a team that strove to do great work. She had some reservations about her ability to supervise others, but she put those aside to compete for, and win, the position.

It had taken her three years to rebuild the CD Unit. Her first task had been to develop a strategic plan for the unit with her team. Her second had been to put one nurse on a work plan. This nurse had been nicknamed Eeyore by her coworkers because of the cloud of complaints that enveloped her every word and inaction. After a year, the nurse finally gave notice, and Lourdes was hired in her place.

Mary had been devastated when Nora announced she was leaving the department. Her official reason was an early retirement, but Stella told her Nora had challenged Carl one too many times. As a result, Carl had shut her out of the decision-making process. Soon after Nora's departure, senior management disappeared into its own realm. Mary eventually regrouped, and she saw no reason not to continue to move her team forward. Now, as she looked around the table, she felt a surge of gratitude. Everyone in the room, including herself, had their quirks, but they were here with her now, willing to work.

"Look," Mary began again. "I don't know if ICS is going to work, but we're drowning. If it can get us back into the boat and steering the damn thing up the river, then we should give it a try."

"Interesting metaphor," Erin said with a grin. "Are we talking about a rowboat or a navy cruiser?"

Mary laughed.

"It's going to work," Jackson stated emphatically.

Cass shook her head. "Good God," she moaned. "Could this man be any more persistent?"

"I wouldn't put that to the test, if I were you," Stella answered. She looked at Mary and said, "I'm in, boss."

"Me too," Lourdes called out.

Others around the table nodded their approval, and Mary looked expectantly at Cass. The nurse threw up her arms and said, "Oh, well, why the hell not?"

The team spent the next half hour making adjustments to the ICS structure. Cass, Lourdes, Stella, Erin, and Cliff were assigned, respectively, to direct the pertussis, meningitis, norovirus, duty nurse, and environmental health branches under the operations unit. Asako would oversee the lab branch. Each branch director would report to Mary in her role as the operations chief. Linus became the planning chief, and

INCIDENT COMMAND SYSTEM STRUCTURE

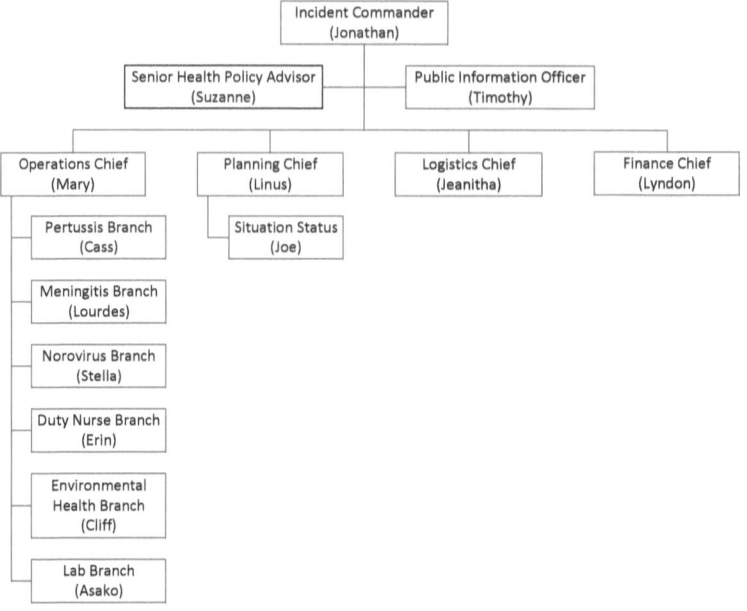

he would supervise Joe in the situation status, or sitstat, unit. Planning would collect, compile, analyze, and report on information for each operational period, which was one work day. Jeanitha would serve as the logistics chief, since she was most familiar with ordering and managing supplies. The department's fiscal manager, Lyndon Perry, was assigned as the finance chief. Jackson learned that Lyndon had previously been employed by the county's Emergency Management Office and had worked under ICS for flood responses. Lyndon gladly agreed to participate. The group also decided they would ask Nettie and Marni for two health educators, a nurse, and an outreach specialist to assist with the response.

"So that just leaves three command staff positions to fill," Jackson noted. He pointed to an area of the diagram between the incident commander position and the row of chiefs. "I'll serve as the safety officer, and Suzanne will be the senior public health policy advisor, but we don't have a public information officer. Got any ideas who could fill that role?"

Mary thought a moment. Suzanne had always served as the department's media spokesperson, but as Jackson had explained, they needed someone who had enough time to liaise with reporters, monitor news reports, and write press releases.

"Perhaps Timothy O'Conner could help us out?" Mary said, remembering the county's public information officer who had spoken at her news media training.

"He's pretty high up in the hierarchy, Mary," Stella warned her.

"I know," she replied, "but he might have some ideas or could suggest someone else."

"Can you talk to him?" Jackson asked her.

"Lord, no." Mary laughed. "That wouldn't go over well with Carl. I'll ask Jonathan to run it up the chain of command."

"Can you trust him with that?" Linus asked.

"He needs something to do as incident commander," she replied. She turned to Jackson. "Is there anything else we need to do, or are we done here for now?"

"I think we're done."

"Great!" Everyone began to stand up from the table. "Remember, our end-of-day briefing is at four p.m.," Mary told the group.

"That's sixteen hundred hours," Jackson called out.

Linus walked over to him, put a hand on his shoulder, and said, "Don't push your luck, buddy."

× × ×

"Focus," Raymond muttered to himself. "Focus."

A telephone rang in the cubicle to his right, and he jumped at the sound. After taking a few deep breaths, he reached with shaky hands for his cup of tea, hoping the hot liquid would comfort him. Then a coworker let out an explosive sneeze, startling him again. The cup's contents spilled toward his lap. He leaped from his chair so forcefully that it rolled out of his cubicle into the aisle and bumped into a woman who was talking to another coworker.

"Ow!" she exclaimed, grabbing her ankle. "Get a grip, Reynolds."

The previous evening, Raymond had helped Paul transport Maureen's paintings to the elementary school that bore his mother's name. Back and forth they had gone, from the farmhouse to the school. He had felt like he was in a tortuous infinity loop, holding Maureen close and letting her go, over and over again. Nighttime had been worse. Memories had flooded his mind and tormented him, depriving him of sleep. The next morning he was exhausted but anxious to go to work. There he could find relief.

After cleaning up the spilled tea, Raymond opened up a spreadsheet on his computer that contained a listing of nursing home facilities. He scanned the names and was content to see there were still several in Revere County where he could make unannounced inspections. He chose one, Valley Village, and copied the name of its administrator and the address on a small piece of paper. As he slipped this into his wallet, his body trembled with relief.

× × ×

Mary, Joe, and Linus were listening to Jackson when Jeanitha poked her head into the room. The BT coordinator was instructing them on how to put together a daily Incident Action Plan, or IAP. The document would contain the latest summary of their investigations, as well as their objectives for the response.

"Mary?" Jeanitha said. "Can I speak with you?"

Mary looked up and saw an expression on the woman's face that worried her. "What's up?" she asked.

Jeanitha approached with a pink message slip in her hand. "You need to return this call," she said. "It's about a suspect measles case."

"Measles?" Mary asked skeptically. Because of high child immunization rates, the only cases of measles seen in the United States were brought in by unvaccinated people travelling from countries where the disease was active. And these imported cases were few in number. "It's not Monte again, is it?" Monte was a gentleman who called the

CD line about once every three or four weeks to express his concerns about a rash on his body.

Jeanitha shook her head. "No," she replied. "It's Dr. Hansen."

"Dr. Hansen?" Mary asked. She took the pink paper from the administrative assistant and studied it, hoping to find an error. "Erica Hansen out in Mill Creek?"

"Yes," Jeanitha replied sympathetically.

"Damn," was all that Mary could think to say.

× × ×

Mary navigated her white 1994 Honda Civic through the stands of giant pine trees along the two-lane road that followed the curve of the river. Joe was sitting in the front passenger seat.

"It's a good thing I don't get car sick," he said. "We've been winding along these roads for forty minutes. Do you know where you're going?"

"Ha ha," Mary replied. "It hasn't been that long. We're only a few minutes away." She glanced quickly at him. "Haven't you been out here before?" she asked. "It's a popular weekend getaway for city dwellers."

Joe shifted in his seat and placed his right ankle on top of his left knee. "No, I haven't," he replied. "I'm new to this area. I'm from the East Coast."

"Ah, that explains a lot," Mary teased.

Before Joe had a chance to protest, a red-tailed hawk swooped across the car's path, carrying a mouse in its talons.

"Wow," Joe exclaimed softly. He craned his neck in an attempt to follow the bird's flight. When he turned back, he said, "So, tell me about this Dr. Hansen. You seem to have a lot of confidence in her."

"I do," Mary said. "She's seen measles before."

"Really?" Joe asked. "When? Most docs haven't."

Mary steered the car around a large branch that lay partially across on the road. "About two years ago, a resident of our county traveled to Mecca in Saudi Arabia on hajj and was exposed to the virus during his travels."

"Interesting. What happened?"

"Erica made the diagnosis. The patient was admitted to Highland Hospital with fever and a rash of unknown origin, and the resident physician who was managing his care presented the case during morning rounds the next day. Erica, who is a community faculty member with the residency, was there and asked the resident if he had ruled out measles. I heard from my friend Katie that the resident laughed at her suggestion."

"Why be so rude to a faculty member?" Joe asked.

Mary motioned with one hand to a dilapidated house that was typical of the others nestled along the river. "Erica is a family physician who practices in a small town," she said, "and she's probably seen as old in the residents' eyes. They can be pretty cocky."

Mary slowed her car to a stop on the side of the road at the entrance to an old one-lane bridge that crossed a tributary of the river. She waited for a truck to cross and then proceeded over the bridge into Mill Creek.

"This area is incredible," Joe marveled. "It's so green."

"You're in a temperate rainforest," Mary informed him. "They get a lot of moisture out here. Every few winters, the river floods the town. If you look close enough, you can see some of the high-water marks on the front of the buildings."

Mary stopped her car at the single stoplight that hung from a thick cable over Main Street. When the light turned green, she drove straight through the intersection and entered the parking lot of a one-story, whitewashed building. Covering one entire wall of the clinic was a colorful, detailed mural of whales breaching and slapping their tails in the ocean.

Mary put the car's gearshift into park and announced, "Here we are."

"Wait," Joe said as Mary began to open her door. "What made Dr. Hansen think the patient had measles?"

Mary grinned. "Erica had worked at a Lutheran mission hospital in West Africa for a couple of years—"

"Ah! And she probably saw lots of infectious diseases," Joe said, finishing Mary's thought. "She sounds like an interesting woman."

"She's the best," Mary declared. "And very gracious too. Katie said that after the resident laughed, Erica calmly began to list out the risk factors and presenting symptoms for measles. The resident blanched visibly. She could have rubbed the young man's nose in his error, but she didn't."

"I take it your unit was involved in the investigation?"

"Yep, and what a nightmare that was. If only the patient had been a social recluse," she recalled, "but he wasn't. By the time the diagnosis was made, he had gone to work, religious services, and a school play. He was also seen in his doctor's office and the hospital emergency department—all during his infectious period."

"Any secondary cases?" Joe asked.

"No, thankfully. Fortunately, the man didn't live in west county, where, as you know, our immunization rates are low."

Joe smirked. "And where we're at right now, huh?"

Mary laughed and said, "Correct." She returned Joe's smile but suddenly felt shy after holding his gaze. Looking away, she said, "We should go inside."

× × ×

It was 6:30 p.m. when a young woman in a pink flowered medical smock let Mary and Joe into the clinic. She introduced herself as Celia and led the pair through the empty reception area to the examination rooms. As they entered the hallway, a woman of medium height with white hair and a trim build stepped out of the farthest room. She was wore a white lab coat over a blue paisley dress. A stethoscope, the perennial sign of a clinician, was draped around her neck.

"Mary Campbell!" Erica exclaimed with delight. "Measles brings us together yet again."

"What are you trying to do?" Mary laughed as she hugged the woman. "Become our resident expert?"

The physician shook her head. "I don't know. Maybe I'm working through some bad karma."

A wide smile broke across Mary's face. "Or maybe the universe just trusts you with these things." Turning to Joe, she said, "Erica, I'd like you to meet Joe Becker, an epidemiologist with the State Health Department. He's helping us with our outbreaks and asked if he could come along. I hope you don't mind."

"Not at all," Erica replied, extending her hand to Joe. "It's nice to meet you."

"You too," Joe said.

Erica opened the door of the examination room to her left. "Let's step in here so I can catch you up before you talk with the patient."

Mary was the first to enter the cramped space. She sat down on a brown-cushioned stool, while Joe found a place to stand between the white sink and the silver floor lamp. Erica leaned against the side of the exam table. As she did so, the stiff white paper that ran its length crinkled noisily.

"So, what we have," the physician began, "is a fifteen-year-old Caucasian male named Mark Sullivan. He says he traveled across the country from the East Coast to join his father here in Mill Creek, but I suspect he's a runaway."

Mary was relieved to hear that the boy was fifteen because that meant he could seek medical care in her state without the consent of a legal guardian.

"Other than his present illness," Erica continued, "he is generally in good health, but he is underweight, probably due to his time on the road."

"How did you end up seeing him?" Mary asked.

The doctor looked up from her notes. "He was befriended by long-time patients of mine," she answered, "Paul Merrill and his son, Skye."

"Paul Merrill?" Joe repeated.

Mary glanced at him. He looked surprised. "Something wrong?" she asked him.

"Uh, no," he answered, shaking his head. "Sorry to interrupt."

Erica glanced from Joe to Mary and then continued her report. "The boy states that he started experiencing fatigue and cold-like symptoms about two or three days ago. He woke up late this morning with a rash at his hairline that descended down his body."

"Really?" Mary asked excitedly. "That's classic." She stopped talking after realizing she too had interrupted Erica's report. "Sorry."

Erica laughed. "No problem. He may be experiencing a mild course of the disease. His rash is light, and his temperature is 101.8 degrees. There appear to be faint Koplik's spots on the inside of his mouth. I asked him about his immunization history, and he reported that he was up-to-date on his shots. When I asked him how he knew that, he told me he turned in his immunization record himself to his school's front office this past fall."

Mary swiveled on the stool and asked, "Any idea how he might have contracted the virus?"

"That I don't know," the doctor replied. She shifted her weight, and the table's paper crinkled again. "I almost ruled out measles when he denied any international travel. Then he told me he hitched a ride with a couple of German students on his way out here."

Mary sat up straight. Europe was experiencing a measles resurgence because people were rejecting immunizations. "Now that's a possibility," she said before turning to Joe. "Has the State CD Program received any measles alerts from the CDC?"

"For this region?" he asked. "Not that I know of, but I can ask."

"Please do," Mary replied. She next asked Erica, "How about the boy's current contacts? Are they up-to-date on their immunizations?"

"Yes, Paul and Skye are fully immunized," Erica stated. "But what worries me is that Paul runs a new age enterprise called Dovestone. He hosts a lot of visitors, and our patient was around a six-month-old infant, a girl. I told Paul you will want to contact the mother."

Mary furrowed her brow. Children under twelve months of age were not routinely immunized for measles because their immune systems might not mount a robust response to the vaccine. "Are you the child's physician, by any chance?" she asked.

"No. The mother and baby flew back to their home in Arizona late Saturday night."

"So, by the time we contact the mom," Mary said, "it may be too late to give the baby a postexposure vaccination, but we can give her immunoglobulin."

"What about your patients and staff?" Joe asked. "Was anyone exposed in your waiting room?"

Erica shook her head. "No. Fortunately, Paul called me before bringing the boy in. He suspected measles."

"Really?" Mary responded with surprise. "The owner of a new age enterprise in the west county can identify measles?"

Erica laughed. "Paul was a medic in Vietnam and saw the illness over there. I thought measles was a long shot, but just to be safe, I asked him to bring the boy in after-hours and through the back door."

"Smart move," Joe said.

"Experience is a great teacher," Erica replied. "And the room he's resting in now is not connected to our ventilation system, so there isn't much chance the virus will spread through it. Is there anything else you need?"

Mary stood up from the stool. "Nasal, urine, and blood specimens."

"And we should take a picture of his rash," Joe added.

"Is he well enough to talk with us tonight?" Mary asked Erica.

"Yes, I think so."

Mary heard the reservation in the woman's voice. "What's wrong?" she asked.

"He's very skittish. I wouldn't be surprised if he's running away from an abusive home. He refused to give me his home address or his mother's name. He also appears to have had a rough time getting out here. His ribs show old bruising, and he has a poorly healed gash on his forehead that should have been stitched up."

"Poor kid," Joe murmured. "He went through all that, and now he has measles."

Mary studied Joe for a moment before saying to Dr. Hansen, "Well, at least he found you and has a place to stay. You mentioned something about a father?"

"Yes, he's the reason the boy traveled out here."

"Has he been in contact with him?" Mary asked.

"No, but he's adamant about finding him."

"Maybe I should hang back," Joe wondered aloud.

Mary looked to the physician for her opinion.

"I think it will be okay," Erica said. "He's very intelligent. Just go slow and don't spook him or Skye, who's keeping him company. Skye is very protective of his new friend."

"Okay," Mary replied. "We definitely don't want an active case of measles running around the west county."

× × ×

As Erica knocked on the door to the exam room, Joe whispered into Mary's ear, "Paul Merrill is the name of the nurse's aide I'm going to interview about the norovirus outbreaks."

Mary turned to him. "You're kidding," she said, and Joe shook his head.

A young voice called out from the exam room, "Come in."

Erica entered first. "The visitors I told you about are here."

The room was dimly lit because the bulb of the standing floor lamp had been turned toward a wall. Mary guessed the patient's eyes were sensitive to light. Photophobia was a sign of measles. As she and Joe stepped farther into the room, a lanky adolescent with dark-brown hair pushed himself upright from a fetal position on the exam table. An older teen, dressed all in white, sat on the chair next to the room's sink cabinet. Mary moved to face the patient, and they exchanged a look of surprised recognition. Mark was the boy she had seen last week on the grassy plaza downtown. He was even wearing the same outfit, although both he and his clothes were now clean.

"Hi," she greeted him casually as she extended her hand. "I'm Mary Campbell, a public health nurse with the Revere County Health Department, and this is my colleague, Joe Becker. He's an epidemiologist."

"A skin doctor?" Mark asked Joe.

Joe smiled. "No, I study communicable disease in communities."

Mark looked at Mary's extended hand. "Is it okay if I touch her?" he asked Dr. Hansen.

"Oh, sure," Erica teased. "Mary's an old pro at this."

"Who are you calling old?" Mary asked, feigning insult.

Mark accepted her hand tentatively. She could feel the heat of his fever through his skin, and she saw the trepidation in his eyes.

"Mark Sullivan," he said.

"And that young man is Skye Merrill," Erica announced. "Mark has been staying with his family."

"Nice to meet you, Skye," Mary said. "Dr. Hanson told me about your family's generosity toward Mark."

After Joe and Skye exchanged greetings, Joe searched for a place to stand that was not already occupied by a human body or object. Erica noticed his dilemma and said, "It's cramped in here. Why don't I step outside for a while and let you talk?"

"Can Skye stay?" Mark asked the physician anxiously. Erica looked at Mary, who said, "It's fine with me." Mark's shoulders relaxed visibly.

"Skye," Erica said as she opened the door, "Celia or I will let you know when your dad gets back."

"Okay, Doc," the teen replied. "Thanks."

After the door was closed, Mary grabbed the room's brown stool and sat down in front of Mark at a respectable distance.

Immediately, he asked her, "Am I in trouble?"

"For being sick?" Mary replied. The expression in the teen's eyes touched her deeply. *He looks just like David at that age*, she thought.

Mark nodded, and Mary let the memory of her brother fade. "No, not at all," she reassured him. "Do you know what public health nurses do?"

Mark shook his head.

"Well, I work with the county health department's Communicable Disease Control Unit, and our job is to make sure that infectious diseases, like measles, don't spread to other people."

"So you're disease cops?" Skye asked from his side of the exam table.

"Not quite," Mary replied calmly.

Skye seemed unconvinced by her answer. "You're not like Dustin Hoffman in the movie *Outbreak*?"

Mary forced herself not to laugh. "Didn't he play some sort of military specialist?" she asked. When Skye nodded, she said, "I saw that movie with a couple of coworkers. Believe me, we don't come close to being that glamorous or dramatic. We just figure out how someone got sick and make sure the person receives the appropriate treatment. We also work with the person to identify who might be at risk for catching the disease, such as friends or family members—" Mary saw Mark flinch at the mention of family, so she added quickly, "Or coworkers and close acquaintances."

Skye straighten himself up in his chair. "So you're more like detectives," he asserted.

"Something like that. Except that we don't carry guns or throw people in jail because they're ill."

Skye studied her. After a moment he said, "Okay, that's cool."

"But isn't that what Dr. Hansen is doing?" Mark challenged her. "She's asked me all sorts of questions."

Mary thought for a moment. Then she remembered a story one of her professors had used in an introductory public health class. "Think about it this way," she began. "Imagine it's summer, and about once a week, someone is rescued from drowning along the same stretch of the river. Each rescue involves plenty of action: lots of first responders, sirens, flashing lights, and trips to the hospital. While all that flash is going on, public health workers are the ones who go up the river to figure out why people are falling into it in the first place."

"That spot would be the Addicts Grotto out here," Skye laughed. "It's about a quarter mile from my house. People get high and fall into the water all the time."

Mary grinned. "I think I've heard of that place."

"So you're trying to prevent illnesses, not treat them like a doctor would," Mark said.

Mary nodded. "That's right."

Mark turned to Skye, and Mary watched the unspoken interplay between the two teens. Mark was clearly monitoring his friend's impression of her. Then he blurted out, "I just don't understand how I got measles. I've been vaccinated."

"Well, there are a couple of possibilities," Mary began. "Your immune system may not have responded fully to the vaccinations you received. That's unusual, but it can happen. Or the vaccine might not have been stored properly, making it ineffective."

"None of this is your fault, though," Joe added.

"Then why didn't I get the measles when I was a little kid?"

"Probably because you weren't exposed to the virus until now," Mary answered.

Joe took a small step forward. "Mark, most of the measles cases we see in the United States are imported. People bring the disease here from other countries, where it's common."

"And because our vaccination rates are so high in this country," Mary continued, "other people formed a protective barrier around you. If any of them had been exposed to the measles virus, they wouldn't have gotten sick and passed the virus on to you, because they had been vaccinated. It's called herd immunity."

"Oh!" Skye said. "So that's how it works."

Mark lowered his gaze. "But Willow's baby," he worried aloud. "She's going to get sick, isn't she?"

Mary felt a surge of sympathy for the boy. He really did appear to be emotionally and physically exhausted. He had prominent dark circles under his eyes, and she estimated that he was ten to fifteen pounds underweight. The gash above his left eyebrow was thick and scabby. *And now he's beating himself up about the baby*, she thought.

"Mark, look at me," Mary said firmly. "Yes, the baby might get sick, but we'll have diagnosed your illness in plenty of time to give her a treatment to boost her immune system. It will help her fight the disease and may even prevent it."

Mark raised his head a little and peered at her. "But I've heard that babies can die from this."

"Yes, they can," she replied, "but that's usually children who are malnourished or have an underlying medical condition or poor access to health care."

"You mean like kids in developing countries," Skye commented.

"That's right," Mary answered, impressed. "But we also take the disease seriously in this country because of the serious complications it can cause. Mark, the baby will have lots of good, smart people watching over her, so try not to worry. You've got plenty to deal with on your own. Okay?"

Mark held her gaze and nodded. Then Mary asked Skye, "How long have you two been here?"

"What time is it now?" Skye asked.

Joe looked at his wristwatch. "Seven fifteen," he said.

"Almost an hour and a half," Skye answered.

"You know what, Mark?" Mary said. "Dr. Hansen and her staff have done a great job of pulling together most of the information we need. I was going to ask you a few more questions tonight, but I think you need to go home, have a little something to eat, and get to bed." She asked Skye, "Would it be all right if I stopped by your home tomorrow to check in on Mark?"

The teens exchanged another silent communication, and Skye said, "Sure, I don't think my dad would have a problem with that."

"Good. And Mark, would you mind if we took a picture of your rash now? It will help us make the diagnosis. We'll only photograph your forehead and hairline, and we'll only show the pictures to other health officials involved in the investigation."

Mark nodded. "Sure."

"Thank you."

Mary stood up and pushed the stool back against the wall as Joe pulled a small camera from his satchel. "After we take the pictures, I'll let Dr. Hansen know we're done for the night. Just one last thing, though." Mary stepped a little closer to Mark. "Dr. Hansen told me that you're looking for your father," she said softly. "Is there anything I can do to help with that?"

Mark looked directly into her eyes. For a brief moment, she saw the same plea she had seen when he stood on the plaza, but he lowered his gaze and shook his head.

"All right," she said gently. "Let me know if you change your mind."

Wednesday, June 4

Mary glanced at the break room's wall clock again. The end-of-day briefing had been rescheduled for 3:00 p.m. so she could go out to Dovestone and check on Mark. It was now 3:10 p.m, and Jonathan had not shown up. That morning, he'd told her Suzanne wanted him to lead the briefing. Mary decided to start without him. She did not want the now thirteen members of the response team, who sat or stood before her, to wait any longer. Mary gave her measles report and asked for an update from the lab. Then she addressed Lourdes, who sat with Irini, a health educator reassigned from Nettie's teen pregnancy prevention project. "How's the Meningitis Branch doing?" she asked.

Lourdes smiled. "We've got some good news for a change."

"Really?" Mary asked, excited. "What's that?"

"Irini figured out the link between our three teen cases."

Cheers and applause erupted in the room.

Mary was stunned. Two additional cases of bacterial meningitis cases, both boys, had been reported to the unit shortly after they learned about the first. The second teen was a fifteen-year-old from Jefferson High, and the third attended Fairview Middle School. The three students had been infected with the same serogroup of the meningitis bacteria, but the CD staff had not been able to determine if the teens had a common exposure. As a result, the health department was planning a mass vaccination clinic with the school district to prevent further cases. Determining the link would eliminate the need for the clinic.

"It's not a big deal," Irini said shyly.

"Yes, it is," Lourdes scolded her. "She's too modest, Mary, so I'll tell you what happened. Irini got permission to talk with the best friend of our first case. That child told her they had attended what you might call an underground party in the reception hall at the Hidden Valley Baptist Church. Do you remember the news story about a teen being stabbed there?" she asked.

"Yes," Mary replied. The *County Courier* had identified the perpetrator as the child of a church deacon. Fortunately, the victim's stab wound had not been serious.

"Well, that happened as the party was breaking up," Lourdes said. "Irini heard students talking about it before a health class at the high school." Lourdes nudged Irini. "You tell the rest."

Irini blushed but said, "The party was a hot topic, and the kids were talking about the usual stuff. You know, who made out with whom, who got high, who puked…that sort of thing. I thought there might be a chance our three cases had been there."

Lourdes took over the story. "So Irini reinterviewed our second case and asked him about the party." Lourdes nudged Irini again. "Tell her what you found out."

"He admitted to sharing a marijuana joint with the others," Irini stated.

"Ah, so the smoking gun was a reefer," Linus quipped.

Joe laughed. "Coffee and donuts must have had an interesting perfume after service that weekend."

"What a relief," Mary said. "Well done, Irini. You may just have saved us and the school district a lot of work."

Irini's blush grew. "Thanks," she said.

"So, will you two spread the word about the party?" Mary asked.

"Definitely," Lourdes answered. She was looking with pride at Irini. "We just wanted to let you know first."

Mary thanked her and then addressed Cass. "Anything new for pertussis?" she asked.

"Not too much other than the work with the Legal Office," the nurse answered. "Linus and Joe are handling that information request."

She glanced at Holly, a second health educator from Nettie's team, who was sitting next to her. "I've oriented Holly to the disease, and she's been tackling the follow-up work with cases and contacts."

"Wonderful. Do you need any help?" Mary asked.

"No, I think we're good," Cass answered.

Mary turned to Stella. "What about norovirus?"

"We're still working on the Carriage House investigation," she answered. "And Monroe County gave us a call. They have an outbreak they think is secondary to one of ours. A staff person was the likely vector."

Mary crossed her arms over her chest and stared straight ahead.

"Something wrong?" Stella asked after a few moments.

Mary looked at her. "Doesn't it feel like these nursing home outbreaks are coming at us in a slow but steady trickle?"

"Are you wondering if there's a pattern to them?" Joe asked.

Mary shrugged. "Maybe."

"Well, we plotted them by reporting date and didn't see anything unusual," Linus said.

"But that was for all the outbreaks," Mary noted, "and the reporting dates were by epi week, right? We've also had some late reporters. What about looking at them by the date of disease onset—just for our nursing home outbreaks?"

Linus looked at Joe, who nodded. "That would be easy enough to do," Linus answered her.

"Good," Mary replied. "It may be nothing, but I'll feel better if we cover all our bases."

"Mary," Stella said, "I'm worried about the Carriage House. The nursing director said they've isolated the wing where the outbreak started, but for all its fancy airs, the facility is very poorly designed. It's laid out in a spoke-and-wheel design. The nursing station, utility room, and rec center are at the hub, and the four residential wings form the spokes. The staff are probably dragging contaminated bedding down the hallway to what is essentially the building's highest traffic area. The virus is going to keep spreading."

Mary glanced at Cliff, who was lounging in a chair with his long legs stretched out in front of him. His hands were clasped behind his head. "Any ideas, Cliff?"

"I've given them recommendations about managing soiled items, but I can check in on them this afternoon, to see how they're doing."

"That would be good," Stella said. "Could you also update the line-listing of sick staff and residents while you're out there? We don't have a good handle on their case count."

"Sure," Cliff answered.

Jackson, who was standing to Mary's right, cleared his throat. "Mary, may I ask something?"

Mary looked in his direction. His feet were planted shoulder-width apart, and his arms secured a yellow legal pad against his chest. "Of course," she said.

"Cliff," he began, "how do you protect yourself during these inspections?"

Mary grinned at the man's perseverance. In the short time they had implemented ICS, he had taken his role as safety officer very seriously. He made sure hygiene and equipment protocols were being followed and had programmed the health department's new twenty-four-seven emergency phone number into the managers' cell phones. Some on the team had even started calling him Mom after he placed bottles of hand sanitizer in their cubicles.

Cliff smirked. "My kind are pretty good at opening doors and the like with our pinky fingers, shoulders, and butts—so we don't pick up any cooties."

Jackson laughed lightly along with the others in the room. Then he asked, "Has anyone ever gotten angry at you?"

"Oh sure," Cliff replied. "But not at the nursing homes. No one's come after me with a cane yet. It's the restaurants you have to watch out for. I've been threatened with meat cleavers after telling cooks to throw out bowls of underheated food."

Jackson studied him for another moment. "Do you carry a cell phone in case you get into a tight spot?" he asked.

The question captured Cliff's attention in a way that Mary had never before witnessed. The young man sat straight up in his chair and eyed Jackson cautiously. "No," he answered. "Field staff in my program aren't allowed to carry cell phones, only managers."

"Well, that's stupid," Erin said. "They sit in meetings all day. No one's coming after them with meat cleavers."

"You haven't attended many management meetings here, have you?" Linus remarked.

"I'll see if I can get you one," Jackson told Cliff, and he wrote a reminder for himself on his notepad.

Cliff's lower jaw dropped open. "That would be great," he replied, stunned.

Mary smiled. Jackson had just won over another person. Wanting to keep the briefing moving, she asked Stella, "Do you need more help?"

Stella looked at LaVonne, who had been assigned to her branch. LaVonne nodded. "Yes," Stella replied. "Maybe Holly could give us a few hours of her time?"

Mary looked at Cass expectantly.

"We can make that work," Cass said.

"Great," Mary said. She glanced around the room. Everyone was more relaxed and confident than she had seen them for a long time. "We're actually making some progress here, aren't we?" Then she turned to Erin. "How's everything with the duty nurse branch?" she asked.

"We're busy but okay," she replied. "Artie has been fielding a lot of calls from the public."

Mary looked at the handsome, middle-aged HIV/AIDS outreach specialist who had been assigned to work with Erin. "It's been a trial by fire," Artie said, "but I'm learning a lot. Erin has been taking baby steps with me. I can't believe how many diseases you people need to know about."

"Excellent. And planning?" Mary asked Linus.

"Today's incident action plan will be ready for distribution shortly after this briefing," he said. "And Joe has an interesting update."

"What's that?" Mary asked.

Joe began to flip through the pages of his spiral notepad. "I interviewed Paul Merrill, the fellow who worked at each of the nursing homes," he began. "He's fifty-four years old and lives in an unincorporated section of the west county. He works as a part-time nurse's aide through a temp agency, but he also owns a business called Dovestone."

"Did you get his work history? What's it look like?" Stella asked eagerly.

"It's a mix. His shifts began within twenty-four hours before, during, and after people started to get sick."

Jackson turned to Mary. "Wait," he said. "Isn't Paul Merrill the name of the guy who's hosting our measles case?"

"Yes," she replied.

"And you're saying he's also a possible connection between our nursing home outbreaks?"

"That's correct."

Jackson gave Mary a disapproving look.

"Did I forget to tell you that?" she asked, meekly.

"Yes," he grumbled.

"Well, then, it's a good thing we have these briefings, isn't it?" she said.

Stella came to Mary's rescue. "What about his health history?" she asked Joe.

"He hasn't been sick. No abnormal stools, no vomiting, not even any nausea."

"You mean he claims he hasn't been sick," Jackson stated.

Mary glanced warily at the BT coordinator. The room was quiet until Erin asked, "Can someone be a carrier of the virus without experiencing symptoms?"

"I'm not sure," Mary said. "I'll look it up." She scrawled a reminder in her composition book and then asked Joe, "Is Mr. Merrill willing to provide a stool specimen?"

"He is," the epidemiologist answered, "although he doesn't see the need for it. Do you want me to follow up with him about that?"

"No," she answered. "You have your own work to do. Let's have Stella's branch handle that." She turned to Stella and said, "I'm going out to Dovestone this afternoon to check on Mark. I can take the specimen containers for Mr. Merrill with me."

Jackson pivoted and faced Mary fully on two firmly planted feet. More than one nerve had obviously been activated in the mind of the former military police officer.

"Hold on, young lady," he warned her.

Mary was about to caution Jackson not to get excited when Jonathan lumbered through the doorway.

"Have you started yet?" he chuckled. "Did I miss anything?"

× × ×

Mary excused everyone from the briefing but Jackson. Joe and Linus remained without being asked, and Jonathan departed happily after she told him the incident action plan would be emailed to senior management within the hour.

"Mary," Jackson began. His expression was one of stern control. "Doesn't any of this strike you as odd?"

"Well, sure," she said lightly, willing the man to relax. "But right now the fact that our measles case is staying with a man associated with our norovirus outbreaks only strikes me as a crazy coincidence."

"Okay, I'll give you that," he conceded, "but what about Mr. Merrill himself?"

Mary knew where his questions were leading, but she said stubbornly, "What about him?"

"I want you to consider that Paul Merrill might be lying." Jackson spoke with more than a hint of exasperation in his voice. "We shouldn't rule out that possibility."

"When you hear hoofbeats, think zebras, not horses?" Joe asserted.

"Exactly," Jackson replied. He crossed his arms over his chest and nodded at the epidemiologist. "Thank you."

Mary scowled at Joe. The phrase he recited about zebras was used to remind people in her profession to consider intentionality, like bioterrorism, when confronted with unusual circumstances. To emphasize the point, Jackson had gifted Linus and the CD Unit with stern-looking little wooden zebra toys shortly after he began his job.

"You're not helping matters," she told Joe, but he only grinned at her. "Look," she said to Jackson. "I agree that we're dealing with an odd situation, but none of our present information indicates any wrongdoing by Mr. Merrill."

"How do you explain the man's work history?" he asked her.

"I can take that one," Linus offered. "The outbreaks began on or near weekends. Regular employees take these days off. Mr. Merrill told Joe that he's often called in to cover staff shortages."

Jackson countered with a question: "Then why are we even considering him as a possible link—or vector for the virus? From what I know about this bug, if he had been sick, he couldn't have contaminated facilities for more than a couple of weeks."

Mary looked at Jackson, impressed. A few months ago, she could not have imagined discussing exposure and infectious periods with a former security expert, and she realized how much progress everyone had made in understanding each other's perspectives.

"That's an excellent point, Jackson, and we can't explain it right now," Mary said. "We need more information."

Her response seemed to mollify him, until he said, "But you're planning to go out to Dovestone."

"Yes. I want to check in on the boy and drop off the specimen containers. I hope to meet Mr. Merrill and talk with him."

Mary immediately saw that this plan did not sit well with Jackson. "Take someone with you," he commanded her.

Mary prickled at the tone in his voice, and she lowered her face to hide her annoyance. *I'm not your daughter,* she thought. But when she looked up, she saw the concern in his eyes, and she checked her emotions. "We can't spare anyone," she replied.

"Let me go. You can spare me."

Mary shook her head. "No, I can't. I want you to stay here and cover for me as operations chief—or would that make you deputy ops chief?"

Jackson's eyes widened, and he looked to Linus and Joe for help. They just grinned at him. "You're putting me in charge of the nurses?" he asked Mary nervously.

"Yes," Mary affirmed. "I've met Mark. He knows me and is expecting me. Everyone here needs to focus on our investigations and epi work. I would appreciate it if you made sure the team is supported and troubleshoot any problems that come up." She smiled at him and added, "Thank you for your concern, Jackson, but I've been doing field work for years. I'll be fine."

⚹ ⚹ ⚹

Mary turned left off of River Road onto the gravel driveway that led to the Merrill residence. She nearly ran into a battered blue pickup truck that was stopped at the driveway's entrance because she was momentarily blinded by the contrast in light between the bright sky over the open road and the deep shade created by the oak trees at the property's entrance. She waved her apologies to the driver as she passed by, but he did not seem to notice her. He was staring at something straight ahead. When Mary glanced in her rearview mirror for what that might be, the only thing she saw was the name on the front of the elementary school across the street.

The driveway was longer than she expected. It traversed a narrow woodland that created a buffer between the road and farmland. When she cleared the trees, she spotted a large white farmhouse situated on the edge of a field that rolled toward the west. She pulled up next to a white twelve-passenger van that sat in an informally designated parking area, and climbed out of her county-issued car. A path to her right led to the home's front door, and the one directly in front of her led to the back of the house. She chose the former and approached the broad porch. The wide veranda had an inviting tropical ambiance despite its run-down appearance. Lush potted ferns sat on two small round tables whose colorful mosaic tops were made from broken tiles. The wooden strips of the porch's creaky floor had once been a mossy green color, and two weathered wicker chairs were positioned on either side of the front door. Ancient flowering bougainvillea vines encircled the porch's pillars and traveled along its eaves. Mary thought the setting only lacked a lounging cat. Then she spotted one lying under a chair. The black-and-white feline lifted its head and gave her a bored look. It stretched its body luxuriously.

"Don't get up on my account," she murmured to the animal.

Only a screen door, its frame outlined with a delicately hand-painted but faded trail of ivy, stood between her and the home's small inner foyer. A hallway ran directly from it to what Mary assumed was the kitchen. She peered through the dark mesh wire but did not see anyone.

"Hello?" she called out. When no one answered, she opened the door and leaned inside. "Hello?" This time a tall male figure leaned backward into the frame of the kitchen's doorway and peered at her from down the hall. "Be right there," he said.

Mary recognized Skye's youthful voice. He disappeared for a moment and then reappeared with a glass of juice and a plate of food. "Come on in," he said walking toward her. "I was just fixing Mark a sandwich."

Mary moved through the doorway. "How's he doing?" she asked.

"Pretty good," he answered enthusiastically. "I think you and Dr. Hansen might be right about him having a mild case. He's not feeling great, but it's not like he's been knocked flat on his back either."

Skye began to climb the staircase to the left of the foyer and Mary followed him. "Good," she said. "I'm glad to hear that. It's really very fortunate that you and your father took him in."

"Well, we're used to guests, and it's nice having him around."

"I'm sure it is. Is your father here, by the way? I'd like to talk with him too."

"No, he had a meeting in town, but he should be home pretty soon."

As they climbed the stairs, Mary took note of the floral artwork flowing above the baseboard on the wall to her right. "These artistic touches are charming," she said.

Skye stopped and turned around. "My mother painted them a long time ago," he said. "She's dead. That's why they've faded. I've started to touch them up."

"I'm sorry about your mother," Mary said, surprised by Skye's matter-of-fact statements.

"It's okay. I was young when she died," he replied. He began to climb the stairs again and added, "If you like these, wait until you see what she did with my room."

Skye turned to his right at the top of the staircase and led Mary to a door halfway down the hall. It was slightly ajar. "Hey, man, are you decent?" Skye yelled into the opening. "The nurse from yesterday wants to check you out."

Mark laughed. "Come on in," he said.

Skye pushed the door open with his shoulder, and Mary followed him into the room. "Hello," she greeted Mark. She was about to ask him how he was feeling when her senses were overwhelmed by the images on the walls and ceiling. "Wow," she declared in a hushed tone. A hand-painted mural covered every inch of space except for the hardwood floor. The style of art was familiar to her, but she could not recall where she had seen it before. Mary moved closer to one wall. "Look at this detail," she exclaimed.

"What did I tell you?" Skye said, pleased by her reaction.

Mary stepped back into the middle of the room and slowly turned around in place. Each of the earth's major ecosystems were drawn on the walls in maddening detail, and all manner of creatures were depicted under and on the ground, and in the flora and the sky. A chilly polar landscape merged with a sweltering desert vista, and it flowed into a rolling prairie that fused with a tropical rainforest. On the wall with the window, a red-tailed hawk soared above the clouds with the sun to its right. The hawk directed her eye to the thin layers of the earth's atmosphere, which gave way to the dark void of space. The solar system's planets floated overhead on the ceiling, as did the only piece of whimsy she spotted in the creation: an extraterrestrial being sat cross-legged on the handle of the Big Dipper and grinned down at her. She tilted her head back farther and glimpsed a small spiral galaxy swirling above the light fixture at the ceiling's pinnacle. Mary stood silently in the midst of this masterpiece, unnerved by the contradictory sensation of being both insignificant and at the center of the universe.

"What was your mother's name?" she asked.

"Maureen Durand."

"What an amazing artist she was," Mary commented.

"We're actually holding a remembrance of her in a few days," Skye mentioned. "It's a fund-raiser for Dovestone, and I'm going to show some of my work."

Mary looked from the mural to Skye. Something in his voice made her realize it was not easy for him to talk about his mother, despite his casual comments, so she changed the subject.

"So, how are you doing this morning, young man?" she asked Mark as she pulled a chair up to his bed.

"Okay," he replied. "I slept hard last night, and Skye keeps nagging me to eat and drink." As if to emphasize the point, Mark lifted the glass and sandwich that his friend had just handed him.

Mary laughed.

"Isn't that what you're supposed to do?" Skye asked in his own defense.

"Yes," Mary reassured him. "Fluids are especially important when someone has a fever. You need to stay hydrated, Mark."

Just then, the sound of a car's horn caught everyone's attention. "Maybe that's my dad," Skye said. "I'll go get him."

As he left the room, Mary began to rummage in her satchel for a copy of Mark's case investigation form. "I'd like to ask you those last few questions," she said, as she pulled it out, but when she looked back at him, he was picking at the crust of his sandwich.

"Is something wrong?" she asked gently.

Mark looked at her tentatively. "Can I ask you a question?" he said.

"Of course."

"Yesterday," he began, "you said something about helping me find my dad. Can you still do that?"

"I can certainly try."

"Ms. Campbell, Skye and Paul have been great. It's just that—" He set down the plate and glass and then leaned over to lift his backpack from the floor to his lap. He pulled a folded piece of paper from a small front pouch. "This is from my father," he said, and pointed to the address on the letterhead. He told her, "Skye went out to the resort, and they said they wouldn't give him any information about their guests. And the other day, Skye told me he's gay, and he asked if my dad was gay because he stayed in Mill Creek—at this place." Mark hung his head and began to cry. "I don't want to bother anyone anymore. I just want to find my dad, but I don't know what to do next."

A stillness fell over the room, and Mary gently grasped of one of Mark's hands. "It's okay, Mark," she reassured him. "We'll figure this out."

He looked at her with red-rimmed eyes. "I can't go home," he pleaded.

"I know," she said.

He looked away. "And what if my dad is gay? I don't know anything about that. What if he is, and that's why he left me and my mom? Maybe he doesn't want anything to do with me. Then what do I do?"

Mary held onto his hand. "Did he ever give you that impression?"

Mark shrugged. "I don't know."

Mary let go of his hand and said, "Do you mind if I read this?" Mark shook his head and gave her the letter. After a few moments, she said, "Mark, look at me. These are not the words of a man who wants nothing to do with his son. Quite the contrary, in fact."

Mark wiped his eyes with the bed's top sheet. "You think so?" he asked.

"I do."

"When he left, he said I would always be welcome wherever he was."

"Well, then, there you have it. There could be any number of reasons why you haven't been able to connect with him. I'll do my best to help you find him. Just remember that you're not alone in this, okay?"

Mark nodded, and they both turned toward the door when they heard footsteps rapidly approaching. Mark wiped his eyes again, and then Skye entered the room. He addressed Mary.

"Something weird's going on outside," he said anxiously. "A bunch of women are here with their kids. They say they're friends of Willow's, but I don't recognize any of them."

"What do they want?" Mary asked.

Skye looked at Mark. "They want to meet you and have a party."

"Me?" Mark asked, astonished.

"Yeah. They even brought cupcakes."

"Oh, no," Mary murmured.

Both boys looked at her. "What?" they asked.

"Some people believe it's better for a child to build up their immunity by getting sick with the actual disease than to be vaccinated against it. They believe it's a more natural process," Mary explained.

"What does that have to do with these women?" Skye asked.

Mary placed Mark's case investigation form back in her satchel. "My guess is that they want to expose their children to measles by having them sit in the same room with Mark. They call it a party because it's usually a group of friends and acquaintances that gets together. They bring treats for the children to share with the sick child. At the chickenpox parties I've heard about, the sick child will suck on lollipops, which are then given to the other children to eat."

"They get their kids sick on purpose?" Skye asked.

"Yes, but with measles," Mary continued, "the virus is so hot, or infectious, that just being in the same room with the ill person is enough to transmit the disease. You don't need lollipops or cupcakes."

"There's no way I'm going to do that," Mark declared. "I probably already got one kid sick. I'm not doing that to anyone else."

"It's okay," Mary reassured him. "I'll go down and talk with them." Then she asked Skye, "Is there any way we can reach your dad? As the owner of this property, he could tell them to leave."

Skye shook his head. "No, he doesn't carry a cell phone."

Mary stood up from the chair and thought a moment. "Are there any other adults around?"

"Uncle Raymond is home from work. He stopped by before you got here. He lives next door. Want me to call him?"

"Yes," Mary replied. "Tell him what's going on."

Skye moved quickly out of the room. When Mary looked back at Mark, he said firmly, "I don't want to see them."

"I know. I'll be back shortly to finish up that form with you."

Skye caught up with Mary as she reached the front door. "Uncle Raymond didn't answer his phone," he said, "but I left a message."

"Okay," Mary replied as she reached for the screen door. She motioned for Skye to stop when she saw that he intended to follow her. "I'd like you to stay inside for now," she said, "in case your uncle calls back." He nodded, and when Mary stepped through the doorway onto the porch, she saw a much larger crowd than she had expected. Seven women, three of whom held babies, mingled with each other under the large oak tree to her left, and as many as twenty toddlers and school-age children chased each other around their mothers' legs. Two of the women looked like twins; they wore matching powder-blue jogging suits and sported pink visors. Each held a plastic cake carrier that Mary assumed contained cupcakes. An eighth woman, dressed in a summery baby-doll dress, stood off in the distance at the back of a black Mercedes SUV. She was changing her child's diaper. When she finished, she lifted the toddler onto her right hip and walked toward the others.

Mary took a step forward. "Hello!" she called out. "May I help you?"

Mothers and children alike turned and took a step toward her. One of the women holding the cupcakes looked Mary up and down from under the brim of her visor. "Who are you?" she asked.

"My name is Mary Campbell. I work for the county."

The woman in the baby-doll dress now moved hurriedly to the front of the crowd. She was beautiful and statuesque and walked along the gravel path in kitten-heeled shoes. The child on her hip played with her cascading blond locks as she pushed her way past the others. "What are you doing here?" she called out to Mary.

"I'm here on a work-related matter," Mary replied calmly.

Another woman in the crowd yelled out, "We want to meet Mark. We brought him some treats and a present."

"I'm afraid you can't come into the house," Mary stated.

"Why not?"

"The owner isn't home," Mary replied.

A voice in the back of the crowd yelled, "Well, if someone is sick in there, we don't mind." The other women laughed, and the children mimicked their mothers with a chorus of giggles.

The woman with the toddler moved closer to the porch. Mary stepped forward and said, "May I ask what your name is?"

"That's none of your business," she stated, pointing a red manicured index finger at Mary. "Let's not skirt around the issue, all right? Mark has measles, and we intend to meet with him."

Mary was taken aback by the woman's sense of entitlement. She studied her and considered her options, which were few. She only had the power of persuasion and the little authority that working for the health department bestowed upon her to convince these women to leave. She could tell them she would not allow them to expose their children to a serious illness, but they would say she had no right to do so. She could warn them about the risks associated with the illness, but she knew that approach would be futile. People who were concerned about vaccinations but were open to learning about them would not be standing in front of an ill person's home, ready to storm it. She could also tell Skye to call the police.

Mary made her decision as the woman took another step forward. The rest of the crowd moved with her. "Please consider your actions here," she said, holding up both of her hands in appeasement. "Measles is not a benign disease. Children can develop serious, permanent complications from it."

A mother with curly red hair in the back of the crowd yelled, "That's nonsense. You're just some government worker spewing the party line. Tammy, push the bitch out of the way."

The vitriol in the mother's voice stunned Mary, but she forced herself to stand firm. "The owner isn't home," she said. "You can't come into someone's house without their permission. The people inside say they don't know you."

It was then that the presence of another woman caught Mary's attention. She looked familiar, but Mary did not know why. She was leaning against the large oak tree and writing in a notepad.

"Well, we intend to get to know Mark," Tammy said as she lifted a foot onto the lowest step of the porch. She was now less than ten feet away from Mary. The toddler in her arms was yanking on one of the dress' spaghetti straps, threatening to remove the last bit of coverage over the woman's ample cleavage. "Move aside," Tammy insisted.

Mary heard the screen door open behind her but did not turn around. "She's telling the truth," Skye called out behind her. "You can't come into the house."

"Skye!" a woman called out.

Mary looked to her right and saw a mother with a sweet face move through the crowd. She waved her hand in the air to catch the teen's attention. "It's me, Lou Ann. I'm a friend of Willow's. Let us in."

"I don't know you," he yelled back to her.

The crowd surged forward as if someone had sent out a silent command, and it formed a half-moon shape on the lawn along the length of the porch. Two mothers encouraged their preschool-aged daughters to climb through the porch railings.

"Lock the doors and call the police," Mary whispered to Skye. Then a movement to her right caught her attention. A bespectacled man jogged to the back of the house. She hoped he was Skye's father.

Skye closed the door just as Tammy stood face-to-face with Mary. The woman's son smiled shyly at Mary and then buried his face into his mother's shoulder. He began to cry when two quick blasts of a siren sounded from the driveway. Mary heard the peel of wheels on the gravel driveway, and she looked behind Tammy. A sheriff's patrol car had arrived. The mothers and children turned to the car, and almost immediately, the group shrank in upon itself like a sea urchin when poked. Tammy pivoted elegantly and retreated to her friends. She left a delicate trail of floral scent in her wake. Her son waved at Mary as he was carried away.

Mary watched as the patrol car veered to the right and parked perpendicular to the driveway, effectively blocking anyone from entering or exiting the area. The vehicle's doors opened simultaneously. A female deputy stepped from the driver's side, and a male officer climbed out of the front passenger seat. The bulletproof vests under their uniforms gave both the telltale barreled chests of law enforcement. Even at her distance on the porch, Mary could see the rifle positioned to the right of the steering wheel, and she heard the squawk of the officers' radio.

Mary was impressed, but also jealously annoyed, by the effect of the deputies' presence on the crowd, which now looked like a dysfunctional football huddle on the sparse lawn under the oak tree. The male deputy took a position between the women and their cars. He was a young man, perhaps in his late twenties, with dark, closely cropped hair. The female officer was very tall and impressively built. Her sandy-colored hair was pulled back in a tight, short ponytail at the base of her neck. She approached the porch. After glancing over the crowd, she addressed Mary.

"I'm Sergeant Stacie Fielding," she said, standing on the porch's steps. "We got a call from a Raymond Reynolds about an unruly crowd."

Skye emerged from the house. "That's my uncle," he told the deputy. "He must have gotten my message," he said to Mary.

"And your name is?" Sgt. Fielding asked the teen.

"Skye Merrill."

The officer took a rapid visual assessment of the farmhouse and asked him, "Do you live here?"

"Yes, ma'am," he replied.

The officer glanced at the county ID badge that Mary wore on a black lanyard around her neck. "And who are you?" she asked.

"Mary Campbell, Officer. I'm a public health nurse with the Revere County Health Department."

"Can you tell me what's going on here?"

Mary thought a moment. Given Mark's status as a likely runaway and knowing how skittish he was, she chose her words carefully. "Yes, I can," she began. "A young man, who is a guest in this home, is sick with the measles. These women would like to visit with him so their children can be exposed to the disease."

Sgt. Fielding turned and studied the group. Many of the women had regained their composure and now wore defiant expressions, but all remained quiet. Mary suspected their attempt to meet Mark had been a new tactic for them. Chickenpox parties were usually arranged quietly within a network of like-minded acquaintances. But given the rarity of measles in the United States, Mary guessed this group had not wanted to pass up the opportunity and had decided to act more boldly.

But how did they find out about Mark? she wondered.

Sgt. Fielding turned back to Mary. "I take it you don't think that is a good idea."

Mary shook her head. "No, I don't, and I'm sure our health officer wouldn't either."

"Is the patient under quarantine?" the sergeant asked.

Mary shook her head again. "No, we're just recommending that he stay away from—"

"Let me guess," the officer interrupted, "susceptible people, like kids who haven't been vaccinated."

Mary's eyes filled with surprise. "That's right," she replied.

Sgt. Fielding saw the expression on Mary's face and said, "I've lived in this part of the county for eleven years, and I'm very familiar with the attitudes out here." Then she faced the crowd. "Okay, ladies, you're not infecting your children today…not on my watch. Get back to your cars and leave the premises immediately."

Sgt. Fielding silently signaled her colleague, who climbed into the patrol car. He maneuvered the vehicle expertly so that it faced the property's exit but was parked on a grassy area just to the side of the driveway.

As Sgt. Fielding began to corral the group toward the parking area, the woman with the notepad approached the porch, and Mary realized why she looked so familiar.

"Whoa," the officer stated, returning to the porch. "Where do you think you're going?"

The woman flashed an identification badge. "I'm Trish Matthews with KZIV News. I'd like to interview Ms. Campbell."

Sgt. Fielding looked to Mary for an answer.

"How did you find out about this?" Mary asked, incredulous.

"We got a tip," Ms. Matthews stated casually as she flipped open her notepad.

When? Mary wondered. Then she said, "You'll have to speak with our health officer. She can be reached through the health department, but wait a half hour so I can brief her on what just happened."

Ms. Matthews scribbled in her notepad as Mary spoke. "Why go to all that trouble?" she challenged her. "Can't I talk with you? I've got a deadline to meet."

There's always a deadline, Mary thought. "Dr. Henderson is our official spokesperson," Mary replied firmly. "She'll give you the interview."

"But—"

"You heard the lady," the sergeant stated as she pointed to the now departing cars. "No interview. Move along."

As Sgt. Fielding and Ms. Matthews walked toward the cars, Mary noticed the second officer examining her county vehicle. He said something to Sgt. Fielding, who motioned for Mary to join them. She saw nothing unusual until she was about fifteen feet away and spotted the flat tires on the passenger side of the vehicle. Closer up, she noticed the jagged gash that ran from just above the front tire fender through the rising sun of the county's logo on the door to the bumper of the rear wheel. Her mouth fell open when the second officer, who introduced himself as Deputy Martin, pointed out the smashed headlamps, tail lights, and outside mirrors. The driver's side of the vehicle was equally damaged.

"I take it the vehicle was not in this condition when you drove it here," Sgt. Fielding said.

"When did this happen?" Mary asked, astonished. "Just now?"

"Unlikely," Sgt. Fielding replied. "We would have seen or heard something. Were you out here when the crowd arrived?"

"No," she replied, flabbergasted. She paced around the vehicle. "I was talking with the sick boy."

She and Sgt. Fielding were suddenly distracted by Deputy Martin's stern voice. Ms. Matthews had gotten out of her car and had begun taking pictures of the damaged county vehicle. After Deputy Martin saw to it that the reporter left the property, Sgt. Fielding said, "Chuck, please call county fleet for a tow."

Mary was fingering one of the car's gashes when the sergeant addressed her again. "Ms. Campbell?"

Mary raised her head and looked at the officer.

"If you have any future business out here, I suggest you not come alone or in a county car."

Mary nodded her agreement. "Damn," she murmured. "Jackson's going to kill me."

× × ×

Raymond stopped running when he reached the river's edge, and he bent over to catch his breath. He had fled to this narrow strand of coarse sand because he was afraid the sheriff's deputies would go to his house after he called them. He trembled despite knowing it was his brother who would soon hold their attention, along with that of the county health department and the news media.

Raymond tried to calm himself by taking in the beauty of his surroundings. The river was still running high from the spring runoff, and the clouds raced across the sun, blocking its light for fleeting moments. But the opposing currents of the water and clouds, the play of shadows in the sky, and the silver sparkles on the water only further stimulated his racing mind. He heard a sound from behind and jerked his body around, falling onto the sand. He peered into the shadowy natural shelter that was called the Addicts Grotto by the locals. It was composed of pine trees and shrubs that grew at the base of a hill. Raymond angrily willed the source of the sound to make itself known. When he was satisfied no one was there, he stood and turned back to the river. He laid his eyes upon a familiar large rock. Its smooth black surface was flecked with yellow and red, and it lay partially submerged in the water. As a boy he had imagined it to be the back of a great sea turtle that would someday awaken from its slumber, lift itself out of the sand, and swim down the river to the ocean. As an adult, he once dreamed the turtle had saved Maureen. Now the recollection released a cascade of memories about her that flowed through his mind like the river before him. He kneeled on the sand and began to strike his temple with the butt of his hand. With each blow, he moaned, "Stop it."

Raymond had not brought Maureen to his home until that night, and he had never spoken about her to his mother. Their relationship had started with coffee after an art class she taught at the community college. She had leaned in close to him during one class to explain the importance of perspective, and he found the courage to ask her on a date. He was stunned when she accepted his offer.

Raymond's ego was buoyed by Paul's response to his choice almost as much as Maureen's attention to him. On another occasion, Paul ran into them at the same coffee shop, and he had flirted with Maureen a little when he introduced himself. The next day Paul had slapped Raymond playfully on the back and praised him for making such a hot catch.

On the night Raymond brought Maureen home, she had taken him to a party where she seemed to know everyone and he knew no one. He found a corner in the run-down house where he drank a beer and waited dutifully for her to return from her frequent excursions to a back room. After one of these trips, she stumbled over to him and fell into his arms. She laughed, and he nuzzled her long, red locks. When she whispered that she wanted him, the longing that had festered in his soul for so long threatened to overwhelm him.

But Maureen was not able to tell him where she lived, so he drove her to his house. He left her dozing in his car while he went inside to make sure his mother was in bed. He found her sleeping in the high-backed leather chair. The glow of the light from the television screen illuminated the room and the shabby, immodest nightgown that barely covered her body. A bottle of peppermint schnapps sat on the side table next to the chair. Paul was asleep on the couch.

Raymond quietly turned off the television and then heard, "Where have you been?"

He glanced, worried, at the front door and then responded to his mother. "Out," was all he said.

"That's not like you," she commented.

"I'm a grown man," he said, and his mother began to cry. "Did I say anything? Why do you talk to me like that?"

Raymond reached for the open bottle. "You're drunk again. Why don't you go to bed?"

His mother grabbed the bottle and wagged her finger at him. "No, no, no, handsome. This one's mine," she teased.

Their conversation roused Paul, who sat up and rubbed his eyes. When he became aware of his surroundings, he declared, "I'm outta here."

Raymond panicked at the thought that Paul might leave through the front door and spot Maureen in the car. Thinking quickly, he said, "You left some smokes on the kitchen table. Why don't you pick them up on your way out the back?"

Paul acknowledged the suggestion with a salute, and when Raymond was confident that Paul had left through the back door, he turned his attention back to his mother. He slipped his arm under her shoulder and lifted her to a standing position. "Come on, Mom," he said. "Let's get you to bed." He moved her along so quickly that her feet dragged behind her.

"Slow down," she giggled. Raymond stopped, but only because he thought he heard a car door slam shut.

"What are you doing?" his mother asked.

"Hush," he scolded her.

She began to play with the buttons on the front of his shirt. "Want to know something? You'll never find anyone who loves you as much as I do," she cooed.

"Yeah, yeah," Raymond muttered as he dragged her to the bedroom. He laid her down on the bed and covered her with a quilt. Then he stopped to listen again. Something felt wrong, and he grew even more anxious. He tried to leave, but his mother drew him close by pulling on the front of his shirt. "Why don't you join me, my little white knight?" she said, slithering further under the cover. "Just like old times."

"Get your hands off of me," Raymond growled at her. "God, you're disgusting."

A deep pout appeared on his mother's face, and she began to sob. "What did I do?"

Raymond shook her violently by the shoulders. "Stop crying, for God's sake!" he yelled. When he released her, she pulled the quilt up to her chin. "You know I can't sleep alone," she sobbed. She looked at him with panic in her eyes. "The nightmares—"

Fury filled Raymond's being. "You want to sleep?" he shouted. He reached for the medicine bottle on her night stand and poured some tablets into his hand. "I'll get you to sleep." Pulling down the quilt, he grabbed her jaw and began to shove one pill after another into her mouth. She shook her head and tried to spit them out, but Raymond pinched her mouth shut with his hand. He only removed it to pour schnapps down her throat. She fought him again when he squeezed her jaw shut.

"Swallow, damn it!" he yelled at her. She tried to twist her head away, and he jerked it back. "I said, swallow!"

Raymond left his mother sobbing on her bed when he ran out of the house to his car. As he had feared, Maureen was gone. He searched the front yard and the back garden, but did not see her or Paul. Then he picked up a faint aroma of tobacco smoke and realized where they had gone.

Raymond ran to the river, and when he neared the grotto, he stepped off the path and crawled through the undergrowth toward the clearing. He peered through the shrubs and saw Maureen sitting near a small campfire with Paul and another couple. Maureen's face was lit up strangely by the flickering flames, and Raymond watched as Paul teased her with a bottle of an amber-colored liquid. The second couple sat on a log with their backs to him, and he watched as the woman plunged a needle into the crook of her left arm. She soon fell into a stupor.

Raymond seethed when Paul put his mouth to Maureen's chin to stop a dribble of the alcohol from trickling down her neck. He nearly leaped from the undergrowth at that point but backed away when the second man dragged his companion closer to where Raymond was crouched in the shrubs. The man stripped the unconscious woman and lowered his pants. Raymond turned away and covered his ears to block out the sounds of the man's groans and the slapping of flesh against flesh.

After several minutes, Raymond listened again and only heard sounds of the forest night. The second man was gone and had left his prey where she lay. Raymond looked for Maureen and Paul. They were no longer near the fire. He crawled forward to get a better vantage point and finally spotted them. They had moved further into the grotto's shadows. Paul was on his back, and Maureen straddled his pelvis. Her long skirt was hiked up above her knees, and her hips moved in a rhythm that Raymond had hoped would be only for him.

The focused rage of a single kick to Paul's temple easily rendered him unconscious, and Raymond stood briefly above the dazed Maureen before yanking her up violently by her red mane. With her back against his chest, he clamped his hand over her mouth and hauled her toward the water. When her dulled senses finally awoke to the assault, she fought her tormentor by going limp and slipping down his body, but the weight of her petite frame was of little counterforce to Raymond's farm-hewn strength. He lifted her again, easily. Then he clasped his hand over her mouth and twisted her neck threateningly to keep her still.

At the river's edge, Raymond released his hand from Maureen's mouth. She screamed and thrashed wildly. He punched her in the side of her head and commanded her to be silent. Both stumbled with the force of the blow and fell into shallow water. Raymond landed hard on his left shoulder, which loosened his grip around Maureen's waist. She twisted away from him viciously and stood to face him, but she swayed, as if buffeted by forceful winds.

"You bastard!" she screamed with a bloodied, garbled tongue.

Raymond took a step toward her and she retreated. "You came with me," he growled, thumping his chest. "You were with me!"

Maureen took another step backward and stumbled again. She looked upon Raymond with unfocused eyes, and he watched her with sudden worry. The river's current plastered her thin skirt against her slim thighs. He waited for a chance to grab her. For a moment, she seemed to grow steady, but then she suddenly bent over, as if struck in the stomach. Seeing his chance, he moved toward her, but she vomited, and the force of her retching caused her to stumble backward again.

"Don't move," he called out, now frightened, but his voice scared her, and she took another step back. Then her eyes closed, and it appeared as if she simply decided to sit down onto the cushion of water. She disappeared momentarily except for the crown of her head and floating tendrils of hair. When the river returned her to the air, it unfolded her body gracefully, and she looked as if she were enjoying a moonlight swim.

Before Raymond had a chance to react, he felt something hard strike the back of his head. The resulting pain caused him to drop to his knees. Another blow forced his torso and face onto the sand. He sensed a movement at his side and managed to raise his chest for a brief moment. The last thing he saw before passing out was Paul splashing into the water after Maureen.

Raymond had awoken in the dawn light near his turtle rock. Two blood-caked lumps protruded painfully from the back of his head. He left the grotto and returned home where he feared the police were waiting for him. But the house and its surroundings were quiet. He quickly showered and thought about running away. He was so distracted that he did not realize, until after the cuckoo clock sounded noon, that his mother had not yet made her appearance for the day. He went to her bedroom to check on her. He opened the door slowly.

"Mom?" he said, softly.

His mother was laying on the bed, and he knew from the childlike bliss on her face that she was dead.

× × ×

The next time Raymond saw his brother was in a law firm's waiting room just before the reading of his mother's will. It was there that Paul told him he and Maureen were leaving for Oregon. Raymond had simply nodded at this news.

The lawyer began the reading with a statement about how Daisy had died from an accidental overdose of alcohol and sleeping pills. Then he announced she had left her house and a third of her property to Raymond, which included the apple orchard. Paul was bequeathed her grandparents' house and a second third of the land. The lawyer said the remaining third had been donated to the local school district. When the brothers asked him for an explanation about the school donation, he looked at them pointedly and said, "Daisy had wanted to be remembered for doing one good thing with her life."

Raymond drove home after the reading and sat for many hours in the high-backed leather chair. When the sky grew black, he retrieved a bottle of schnapps from the kitchen and sleeping pills from his mother's medicine cabinet. Then he went to her bedroom and sat on the edge of her bed. He swallowed the pills and drank the bottle dry before slipping underneath the quilt. He awoke nearly two days later and realized the full extent of his failed life.

Thursday, June 5

"Ms. Campbell?"

Mary raised her head and was surprised to see Timothy O'Connor, the county's public information officer, standing in her doorway. She raised an index finger to signal she would be with him in a moment. She was speaking on the phone with an epidemiologist from the State CD Program who was serving as the intermediary between the county and the CDC on the measles case.

"Okay," Mary said, "so we can transport the specimens to the regional lab, and they'll send them on to the CDC for us, right?" She paused for the response and then said, "I think that's it for now. Thanks for your help. I really appreciate it." Mary lowered the phone's receiver and looked up again at the stylishly dressed man, who was now waiting anxiously at the edge of her desk.

"I'm Timothy O'Connor, the county public information officer," he said, extending his hand.

"Yes, I know." Mary smiled at him. "You spoke at the news media training I attended shortly after I became a manager."

The man glanced at his watch. "Oh good, you've had the training. Excuse me for being abrupt, but I'm in a tight spot."

Mary stood up. "What's the problem?"

"Reporters from two television stations and the *County Courier* are here in the building, and I need someone to talk to them."

"What about?"

"Your nursing home outbreaks."

"Really?" Mary asked. The news media had shown little interest in the outbreaks, despite a press release about norovirus that the health department had issued just before Memorial Day weekend, urging the public to practice good hygiene. The statement had only resulted in a one-paragraph article in the *County Courier*'s Metro section.

"I'm confused," Mary said. "Why is a press conference being held?"

The man glanced at his watch again. "The daughter of an elderly resident called various news outlets to complain about her mother's care. Her mother got sick with norovirus at an assisted living facility, fell, and broke her hip. Then she was sent to a skilled nursing facility to recuperate, and it also had an outbreak."

"I know who you're talking about," Mary said. The woman's daughter had contacted her CD Unit. She had demanded detailed information about each outbreak, including individual case information. Stella's explanation about the need to maintain patient confidentiality had not appeased her.

"The daughter is claiming that the health department didn't do anything to prevent these outbreaks," Timothy continued. "She also told the press that the county is suppressing information."

Mary's stomach knotted. She could see where the accusations were leading. Her unit did not yet know why the county was experiencing an unusual number of outbreaks, but the public never cared much for nuance or uncertainty. The department would be forced to defend its actions.

Timothy leaned onto her desk. His moist forehead glistened under the fluorescent lights. "The reporters are in the conference room downstairs, expecting to hear from a health official," he said pointedly. "Suzanne was supposed to attend, but she's stuck in traffic coming out of the city. I asked Nettie if she could do it, but she said she's not familiar enough with the situation. She sent me up here to talk to you." Timothy paused and then said firmly, "I need you to speak at the press conference."

"Me?" Mary gasped. "What about Carl?"

"He's having dental surgery."

"What about you?" Mary asked. "Isn't that your job?"

"Not for something like this. I need a subject matter expert. Someone who knows what's going on."

"Can't you reschedule it?"

Timothy shook his head. "No. They want to meet today's deadline."

Mary threw up her hands. "There's always a deadline," she complained.

"We need to address this woman's accusations as soon as possible," Timothy insisted. "If we don't, the press will think the county is stalling, or worse, that we're covering something up. They'll write their stories based on the daughter's account."

Mary looked at him anxiously. "I understand that, but the rule here is that no one gives interviews unless they get permission from Carl. He and Suzanne will have my head if I do a press conference."

Timothy glanced at his watch for a third time. "Given the circumstances, I think they'll understand. And I'll take the blame." He moved around to her side of the desk. "We really need to get going," he said. "We only have seven minutes."

"But I've never done a press conference before," Mary protested.

The man stepped behind her and placed his hands on her shoulders. "You'll be fine. Just remember your training."

Mary looked at the man, aghast. "My training? That was nearly four years ago."

"It will be okay," he reassured her as he gently pushed her toward the door. "Just give them the facts as you know them." Once they were out in the hallway, he added, "You've got a very attractive, intelligent face—the girl-next-door type. I think I even see some freckles on that nose of yours. You look very trustworthy."

Timothy let go of her shoulders once she began to move forward of her own accord, but he kept glancing at her as if he was afraid she might bolt away from him. As they descended the stairs, Mary became queasy trying to recall the statistics around the outbreaks: the number of affected nursing homes, confirmed cases, deaths, and hospitalizations. She forced herself to breathe deeply when the figures threatened to become a jumble in her mind. "What if I can't answer a question?" she asked.

"Just say you'll look into it and will get back to them. It's that easy," he replied with a smile. "And for future reference, please give me a heads up when you have something this big going on. No one likes to be blindsided."

Mary cursed to herself. She had asked Jonathan to complete just one task as incident commander, which was to talk with Carl about contacting the County Administrator's Office for public information assistance. He had not done so despite numerous reminders from her and Jackson.

As they approached the first-floor conference room, Mary saw two white news vans parked on the street through the double-glass doors at the entrance to the building. She had seen those vans in the same location many times before but had always slipped by them as a nameless employee. She longed to do so now.

Timothy opened the conference room door, and Mary wiped her sweaty palms on her pants. She swallowed hard when she saw a cameraman standing just inside the door, and she peered over his shoulder to look at the reporters. She was surprised to see Nettie standing at the far end of the room, staring out at the street as if she were looking for someone. Just as the cameraman stepped to his right to let them pass, Mary heard a loud, familiar voice call out for Timothy. She turned and saw Jonathan pushing his way through the building's front entrance. He hurried over to them.

"I came as soon as I could," he said to Timothy. Then he glowered at Mary. "What're you doing here?"

"Timothy asked me to take Suzanne's place at the press conference," she whispered. "It's about the nursing home outbreaks."

"You?" Jonathan bellowed. He pushed past her and stumbled into Timothy, which caused Timothy to fall forward against the conference room table. The startled reporters turned at the commotion, and Mary saw that Trish Matthews was among them.

"Why you?" Jonathan bellowed.

"Shush!" Timothy whispered sternly after regaining his balance. He pushed Jonathan and Mary back into the hallway and closed the door behind them. "What's the problem?" he whispered sternly.

"If anyone's going on TV, it's me," Jonathan declared. "I'm your supervisor."

Mary looked at him with dismay. As much as she welcomed the idea of not being interviewed, she dreaded how Jonathan might characterize the outbreaks to the press. She tried to catch Timothy's eye, but he was focused on Jonathan. "Do you know enough about the situation to give an update?" Timothy whispered.

"Of course I do," Jonathan replied loudly. He lifted himself to his full height and stated, "I'm the incidence manager."

Mary tried to reason with him. "But Jonathan, I don't think—"

"What?" he snapped at her. "You don't think what? I'm the boss around here. Nettie told me Carl and Suzanne couldn't do the interview, so I'm going to do it."

Nettie? Mary wondered with alarm. She swiveled her head in time to see Nettie enter the hallway. She approached the trio with an uncharacteristically pleasant expression on her face.

Timothy glanced from Jonathan to Mary. He was red-faced with anger. "Someone needs to get in there now," he growled.

Nettie touched Timothy's upper arm gently. "Jonathan is in charge when Carl and Suzanne are out," she said. "He's the responsible party."

"Fine," Timothy whispered testily. "Just go do it," he told Jonathan.

"But, Jonathan—" Mary implored him, but her supervisor turned away from her.

Nettie touched Mary on the shoulder. "Let him go," she said.

Mary shrugged off the woman's hand and walked over to a wall. She slumped against it. Nettie returned to the open conference room door. Only after a reporter asked the first question did she close it. Then she walked over to Mary and stopped directly in front of her. Despite her high-heeled shoes, the top of Nettie's jet-black bouffant hair only reached the bridge of Mary's nose. Nettie tilted her head back and locked onto her colleague's eyes.

"And that, Mary, is how the game is played," she said proudly.

Friday, June 6

Mary glanced at the time display on her computer. It read 3:11 p.m.

I'd better get going, she thought.

She rolled her chair to the right and unlocked the gray, two-drawer filing cabinet that was positioned under her desk. From its top drawer, she pulled out a file labeled *JF.* It held the one-page summary of her concerns about Jonathan she had given to Suzanne three days earlier. Then she retrieved her satchel from another drawer and walked to the small, erasable whiteboard that hung on the outside of her office door. On it, she wrote a brief message stating she had a 3:30 p.m. meeting with Suzanne.

Stella walked up to her. "Mary, can I talk to you when you get back?" she asked quietly.

Mary looked at her, worried. "Anything wrong?"

Stella leaned toward her and whispered, "No, I just have an idea about how to handle Marni's threat against Cass' job."

Mary raised an eyebrow. She had told Stella about her disturbing encounter with Marni the previous week. "Sure," Mary said. "I should be back before you leave for the day."

As Mary walked through the Seventh Street building to its front exit, the events of the previous twenty-four hours consumed her thoughts and senses. If she could have foreseen the future, she would not have chosen this day for her meeting with Suzanne, but no one could have anticipated the consequences of Jonathan's interview. The silence in the building was palpable. Everyone was digesting the sting of public condemnation in private. The interview's aftermath even seemed to have pierced Jonathan's delusion of himself as a rising executive. Mary had seen him only once that day, from a distance, as he returned to his office from the bathroom. The joviality was gone, and he walked with his head down. Once inside his office, he closed the door and lowered the window's shade.

The press had shown little mercy in response to his performance. Jonathan had imparted so few facts and had spoken so incoherently that the reporters interpreted his words as a smokescreen. And, as Timothy had feared, they based their stories on information given to them by the daughter who had brought the outbreaks to their attention. During a live interview with Trish Matthews, the daughter cried while describing in detail how she found her mother on the floor of the nursing home.

"My mom was so sick she fell and broke her hip on the way to the bathroom. I found her sitting on the floor, leaning against a wall in her room. She must've slid down it because it was smeared with blood, and the skin on her arm was torn. Her legs were spread apart, and the right one was turned in funny. And she was moaning, even though her eyes were closed. There was a stream of poop running from her favorite chair near the window to where she'd fallen, and vomit was all over the front of her robe. And I thought her roommate was dead. She had this blank stare in her eyes, and her head was twisted to the right. It was pressed up against the bed's metal bars. She'd puked through them. Vomit was on her lips and in a puddle on the floor. The smell in the room was horrible."

Jonathan had not limited his statements to the norovirus outbreaks, either. Instead, he had titillated the reporters with misinformation about the department's other investigations. He substituted the word *menstrual* for *meningitis* and confused their pertussis case count with measles, effectively declaring that the county had sixty-seven cases of the rash illness, which Mary knew was more than the measles case count for the entire United States.

The *County Courier*'s morning headline, *Local Health Official Dismisses Death of Elderly*, was no more bearable than KZIV's running scroll for the previous evening's newscast. It had read, *County health department incompetent in face of multiple outbreaks*. During that station's editorial spot, Trish Matthews raised "grave concerns about the department's bewildering internal workings and unwillingness to engage the public." To Mary's dismay, the reporter used her as evidence of the latter.

"KZIV News has also uncovered a connection between a teenager with measles, and the series of devastating nursing home outbreaks dismissed by Mr. Cox," the news anchor had stated. "The ill teen is staying at Dovestone, a new age enterprise in the town of Mill Creek. I was at Dovestone when a group of mothers attempted to meet with the boy. Measles can be prevented by vaccinations, but these women have concerns about the safety of vaccines. They wanted their children to get measles from the teenager in an attempt to build their immunity to the disease naturally. A county public health nurse, Mary Campbell, was present, and with the aid of sheriff deputies, prevented these mothers from entering the home and exposing their children to the measles virus. I spoke with one of the mothers, Tammy Walters, about her concerns at her east-side home shortly after the confrontation. Ms. Walters is the wife of Peter Walters, the prominent local lawyer and environmentalist."

Mary watched as Ms. Matthews next appeared on-screen in front of a sprawling, elegant home with the woman who had confronted her at Dovestone. Ms. Walters wore a fitted black suit with no blouse under the buttoned-up jacket. Her long blond locks were tied up in a neat chignon, and fashionable black-rimmed glasses rested on her nose. She looked directly into the camera with a pouty expression and stated, "Ms. Campbell's behavior is typical of the petty bureaucrats who are paid by vaccine manufacturers and professional medical organizations to cover up the dangers of vaccines. We mothers ask nothing more than to not have our children's delicate immune systems overwhelmed by dangerous chemicals."

Trish Matthews then turned to the camera and added, "For the record, this reporter asked Mary Campbell for an interview, but she declined." She ended her editorial with the challenge, "What is happening inside our health department? The public deserves an immediate and detailed accounting of the department's actions surrounding these events."

The news anchor's words had their intended effect. Mary had never seen Administration respond so quickly. Fifteen minutes after the end of the broadcast, Carl called her at home and said that he and Suzanne expected an update on all of the unit's activities, including the most current statistics, at 7:30 a.m. the following morning. Surprisingly, Mary found herself counting her blessings after he hung up. If this public relations crisis had happened prior to implementing ICS, Carl's request would have been impossible to fill. But under ICS, the outbreak information was updated daily for the incident action plan. Tomorrow, she would simply hand Carl the document Linus had emailed him earlier that day.

At 7:00 a.m. the next morning, the damage-control activities began in earnest. Carl sent out a department-wide email reiterating that under no circumstances were health department employees to speak with the press, and he stated that he, Suzanne, and Timothy were working with news agencies to schedule a second press conference for early that afternoon to clear up the misunderstandings.

Mary's meeting with Carl and Suzanne had been brief. Carl was satisfied with the contents of the IAP, and to her surprise, he insisted she attend an emergency session with the County Board of Supervisors at 9:30 a.m. Before that meeting, he directed her and Suzanne to sit on either side of him, and he made it clear they were not to speak unless he instructed them to do so. During the meeting, Mary observed with grudging admiration the control he maintained over the proceedings despite being the focus of the board's ardent displeasure. Suzanne, however, wore a sour expression as she listened in silence to the board's inquiries.

News media reports about Jonathan's initial press conference had garnered such high interest from outside the county that the second press conference was moved to a large auditorium at the community college. Mary slipped unnoticed into the venue, and she sat in the shadows of the back right-hand corner of the auditorium, away from the brightly lit stage. From that vantage point, she watched Carl and Suzanne offstage, in the wing, as they waited for Timothy to complete his introduction of them. Carl wore a classic dark-gray suit, a pale shirt, a bold red tie, and highly polished shoes. Suzanne checked her makeup in a mirror and smoothed her jacket and skirt before following Carl onto the stage.

The pair handled the event expertly and gave concise and clear answers to every question that was thrown at them. Carl began with a statement of sympathy for the daughter of the elderly resident who had broken her hip and for those with family members who had become ill or had died in the nursing home outbreaks. He also apologized for the confusion and misunderstandings that resulted from the previous day's press conference. As for Jonathan's role, he merely stated that he was not qualified to give the interview. When Trish Matthews asked how the department could assure the public that it had the expertise and capabilities to contain the outbreaks, Suzanne boasted that they had activated their bioterrorism response plan when the outbreaks first started and were now working under the Incident Command System.

"We've been practicing for just such an emergency for many months," she declared proudly. "ICS, long used by the fire service and emergency management, is proving to be an effective tool in directing our resources and actions." When another reporter asked who was in charge of the response, the health officer stated firmly that she was the incident commander.

Early that morning, Mary had called Rosalyn to cancel her meeting with Suzanne about Jonathan because it felt inappropriate to hold it after his very public failure. But after the Board of Supervisors meeting, Rosalyn called her back and said that Suzanne still wanted to talk to her.

Suzanne was sitting at her desk, signing papers, when Mary knocked on the open office door. She wore the same pink suit she had worn for the press conference, but she had removed the matching silk scarf from around her neck, which fully revealed the diamond-encrusted cross necklace. When Suzanne glanced up, Mary saw a mix of emotions on her face and heard a gritty tension in her voice. "Come in, Mary," she said. "Please close the door behind you."

Mary did so but said, "Shouldn't we reschedule this meeting? I'm sure you've had a long day."

"Take a seat," Suzanne said firmly.

Mary sat down at the small round table near a wall filled with books. She kept the folder labeled *JF* in her satchel, which she placed on her lap. Suzanne walked over from her desk and sat across the table from Mary. She brought with her a copy of Mary's one-page summary.

Suzanne looked Mary directly in the eyes. Her anger was evident. "You've had it in for him every since he arrived, haven't you?" she growled. Suzanne crumpled Mary's summary and threw it at the door.

"What?" Mary asked, stunned.

"You set him up yesterday, didn't you? I know you were at the press conference."

"I did no such thing," Mary declared.

Enraged, Suzanne said, "You let him get up there and make a fool of himself and this department."

Mary pushed away from the table, her own anger rising. It would have been so easy to tell Suzanne about Timothy's request and Nettie. It would have been so easy to plead her case, to say it was not her fault, but she no longer cared what this woman thought of her.

"You set him up, I know you did," Suzanne yelled at her.

Mary stood and walked to the door, intending to leave. Then she saw her crumpled summary on the floor. She picked it up and returned to the table. When she spoke, the steadiness in her voice came not from steely nerves but from a deep sense of loss.

"Jonathan insisted on doing the interview," she said calmly. "He ordered me to leave the press conference."

"I don't believe you," Suzanne replied.

Mary looked at Suzanne with disappointment. She smoothed out the crumpled sheet of paper on the table and said, "Suzanne, you only have yourself to blame for Jonathan's performance. You supported Carl's decision to hire him and to place him in a position of authority. You chose to overlook his lack of training and his incompetence." Then Mary walked away, but at the door, she turned back around. "Jonathan ordered me to leave in a very loud voice. I know I can find witnesses, even members of the press, who will back up my story," she warned the health officer. "So don't even think about pursuing this accusation further."

× × ×

Mary was overcome with hurt and frustration as soon as she left Suzanne's office. Tears welled in her eyes. She moved quickly to the narrow stairwell that led to the north exit of the courthouse and headed back to the Seventh Street building. Once there, she realized she was in no condition to return to her office, so she walked into the quiet neighborhood of 1950s bungalow houses just west of the health department. But the tidy little homes reminded her of her family and all they had lost, and her tears began to flow in earnest. She tried to stifle the sobs, but the effort only made her throat constrict painfully.

Mary walked along the tree-lined streets, and after some time, began to find solace in the neighborhood's end-of-day activities. A blue minivan released a load of small children into one driveway. Their wet hair and tiny swimsuit-clad bodies were wrapped in enormous, colorful beach towels. A few houses away, an elderly couple weeded the garden beds that bordered the walkway of their home, and two young teens lounged on a lawn with their bicycles lying close by. A man in a business suit loosened his tie as he retrieved the newspaper from his driveway and read the day's headlines.

But then a ringing jarred Mary's growing calm. By reflex, she grabbed the phone at her waist. Only as she said "Hello?" did she wonder why she felt the need to answer the call.

"Hi, Mary. It's Lourdes. Are you coming to the afternoon briefing?"

Mary panicked at the oversight. "Oh, God," she replied. "I forgot all about it."

"That's okay," Lourdes reassured her. She paused and added, "Are you all right, chica? You sound congested."

The worry in Lourde's voice was clear, and Mary's eyes welled with tears again. *Damn nurses*, she thought. *Why're they so perceptive?*

Mary tried not to sniffle into the phone. "I'm fine," she said, "but I'm not in the building. Could you ask Jackson to lead it?"

"Sure," Lourdes answered softly. "Is there anything else I can do for you?"

Mary swallowed hard. "No, thank you." Her voice broke as she spoke.

"Okay," Lourdes replied, "but why don't I change the message on your door to read something vague like 'in a late meeting,' just in case someone comes looking for you?"

Mary smiled. Lourdes was very savvy about appearances, political and otherwise. "That's a good idea," she answered warmly. "Thank you."

"Promise me you'll get some rest over the weekend?" the nurse asked.

"I promise."

Distracted by the conversation, Mary had turned back toward the city's center and now found herself at the northern edge of the downtown area. She spotted the sign for Friar Bean's coffee shop and decided it was a good place to pass the time until the Seventh Street building emptied for the day. She crossed the four-way intersection and was unnerved to see Carl sitting with Supervisor Cahill in the eating area outside of the Golden Leaf restaurant. They were deep in conversation and neither glanced her way.

At Friar Bean's, Mary forced a smile to her face when she ordered a cup of coffee but then wondered why she had done so, given that her eyes and nose were likely puffy and red. The contrast must have looked odd to the young man who waited on her.

She sat down in the dimly lit booth she had shared with Joe when he presented his spider diagram to her. Wanting to look purposeful, she opened her satchel and pulled out a folder, but quickly returned it when she saw that it held her notes about Jonathan. She looked around for other reading material and spotted stacks of free local circulars in black wire bins near the front door. She chose one with a colorful front cover and returned to her booth. Then she picked up the large white ceramic mug of steaming coffee with both hands and took a cautious sip. The earthy flavor and warmth of the liquid grounded her. Still holding the cup, she studied the picture on the magazine's cover and was drawn into the artist's lovely, otherworldly vision. At first she saw only the image of a mountain, but as she looked closer, she began to see that the peak was formed by the bodies of a man and woman. The woman stood with her back to the viewer. Her arms were held out low to her sides, and her face was lifted to the sun. The man kneeled behind her and rested his right cheek against her low back. Life teemed on and around them.

"I know this artist," Mary murmured to herself. She searched for confirmation on the circular's cover. At the bottom, a caption read, *Remembering the art of Maureen Durand, p. 26.*

Skye's mother, she thought with delight.

"Would you like a refill?" a man asked, interrupting her concentration.

"No, thanks," she replied politely, continuing to study the image.

"How about something stronger? Like a shot of single malt whiskey?"

She looked up and saw Joe standing before her. He grinned and slipped into the booth across from her. "You're deep in thought," he said.

Shaken by his presence, Mary could only mutter, "Yeah, well..." She felt her face redden, so she turned her gaze back to the circular.

"Care to talk?" he asked.

"About what?" Mary replied. Her attempt at indifference sounded insincere even to her. She felt Joe watching her. After a few uncomfortable moments, he said, "About your run-in with Suzanne."

Mary looked at him with alarm.

Joe laughed. "Do you really think there're any secrets in that department?" he asked. "As soon as Lourdes suspected something was wrong, inquiries were made."

Mary sighed. "Did someone tell you to come find me?"

"Nope," Joe answered, leaning forward onto the table. "I offered. The team gave me a couple of suggestions about where you might be, and here I am."

Mary smiled weakly, and the two sat in silence for a while. Finally, she gave up her pretense and wiped her eyes with her now damp, crumpled paper napkin.

"How did I become the bad guy in all of this?" she asked him.

"Are you really?"

"Suzanne thinks I am."

Joe reached out with his right hand but did not touch hers. "She's just one person, and not much of a leader, if you ask me." He gazed at her with such intensity that she had to look away. "What kind of person jumps all over someone who has the guts to stick out her neck and speak the truth, even if it's just the truth as she sees it?"

"No one wants to hear the truth," Mary mumbled.

"Maybe not, but it comes out eventually, right?" Then he laughed. "Jonathan's media debut is proof of that."

Mary could not help but laugh too, and she dabbed her eyes again with the soggy napkin.

Joe reached into a pocket and handed her a piece of cloth. "Here, use this," he said.

Mary studied the white material. Its decorative border was heavily threaded, and a subtle pattern was ingrained in the fabric.

"What's this?" she asked.

"I think they call it a handkerchief," he teased.

Mary smirked. "Yes, I know that, but who uses these anymore?"

"I do," he replied, feigning insult.

Mary touched the soft, well-worn cloth to the skin under her eyes. "Thank you," she said. After a moment, she sighed and asked, "How can I work with Suzanne after this?"

"Have you done anything wrong?"

"No," she said confidently.

"Well, it might help if you see her for who she is," he suggested.

"Which is?"

"You tell me."

Joe sat back in the booth and was quiet as Mary thought about Suzanne. She had always felt a sense of shared purpose with her, even years ago when they worked together at the free clinic. But now she realized that connection may have just been wishful thinking on her part.

Mary had heard grumblings over the years that Suzanne only paid attention to others when she wanted something from them, but she had brushed those accusations aside, attributing them to bitterness about the ousting of Dr. Castillo, the previous health officer. Now she wondered if she had dismissed their resentments too quickly.

"At least he didn't chase after every opportunity that put him in the spotlight," LaVonne had once said about Dr. Castillo. "And he was in the office most days." On another occasion, she overheard Cass imitating Suzanne giving a television interview. She had mocked her. "Don't I look *mahvelous* as I save the world?"

Mary had thought the accusation of false modesty out of line, but then Jonathan arrived, and she watched him use Suzanne's desire for adoration to his advantage. And now, despite Jonathan's very public and self-imposed failure, Suzanne was willing to lay the blame for it on someone else.

"I've been stupid," she told Joe as she rested her head in her hands.

"Nah, you're just human," he assured her. "We all have our blind spots."

"Well, mine's a pretty big one."

He shrugged. "So you're a nice person," he said. "You give people the benefit of the doubt. That can be a double-edged sword."

"It still doesn't answer the question of how I can work with Suzanne after today."

Joe grinned but said nothing.

"You're not going to help me with that one, are you?"

"Nope."

Mary opened her clenched fist and revealed his wadded handkerchief.

Joe pointed at it and said, "I don't want that back anytime soon. At least not until you've washed it."

Mary laughed. "Spoken like a true public health professional." She held his gaze and realized just how often she found herself laughing in his presence.

"Can I buy you a cup of coffee?" she asked him.

One of Joe's eyebrows rose ever so slightly. "I'd like that," he answered.

Monday, June 9

At 8:25 a.m. Mary left her office to attend the morning briefing. The weekend had been restful, and she felt confident about accomplishing her one goal for the day, which was to have an uneventful first encounter with Suzanne. After the second press conference, Suzanne had sent out a department-wide email reaffirming that she was the new incident commander for the response, but Mary did not see her when she entered the briefing room. But she was impressed to find Timothy O'Connor chatting with the team. He had called her after Jonathan's ordeal, and once Mary described ICS to him, he offered to fill the public information officer position. She was talking with him when Jackson walked over and asked her about Suzanne.

"Is she coming?" he said. "We should get started."

Mary glanced at the wall clock. "That was my assumption. I'll give her a call. If I'm not back in a couple of minutes, start without me."

Mary left the room and walked to an empty cluster of cubicles. She unclipped the cell phone from the waistband of her pants and dialed Suzanne's number. *Just get this over with*, she told herself. After the fourth ring, Suzanne answered the phone by saying, "Good morning. Dr. Henderson speaking."

"Hi, Suzanne. It's Mary."

"Oh, hello. What can I do for you?"

Mary relaxed a little when she heard no acrimony in the woman's voice. "The team was wondering if you'll be leading this morning's briefing," she said. "We can delay the start time if you've been held up."

Suzanne did not respond, and after a long pause, Mary wondered if they had been disconnected. "Suzanne? Are you still there?" she asked.

"Yes, I'm here," Suzanne answered. Her voice had sharpened considerably. "Why in the world would I run a briefing?"

"Well," Mary began, "since you're the incident commander—"

Suzanne laughed. "God, you are so incredibly naive."

To Mary's surprise, the insult did not sting. But she wanted to know what Suzanne was thinking, so she asked, "How's that?"

"Don't you get it? This so-called president of ours is going to be gone in another year, and then the BT funds will dry up. Don't go wrapping yourself up in the ICS flag. This nonsense is not going to last."

"Actually, we're finding it pretty helpful," Mary countered. She did not add, *Just as you had mentioned at the press conference.*

"Why am I not surprised?" Suzanne scoffed.

Mary thought for a moment. Suzanne's attitude saddened her, but she was happy she had accomplished her goal for the day. "How about this?" she suggested. "We'll continue to send you the incident action plans. They contain situation updates and our daily objectives."

"You do that," Suzanne replied, "and I expect to be consulted before you make any important decisions."

Mary suppressed a chuckle at the petulant command. "Of course," she stated. "Have a good day."

Mary returned to the meeting room and took a seat along a wall. She listened intently to the concise plans that each branch outlined for the day. When it was her turn, Jackson asked, "How about measles? Anything new to report?"

Mary gave a brief accounting of Mark's health and the status of his lab tests. Then she added, "I need to go out to the west county today. Would you mind serving as deputy operations chief, Jackson?"

Jackson lowered the clipboard he had been holding against his chest. "Wait a minute, young lady. Why are you going out there again so soon?"

"I want to follow up on a lead that might help us find Mark's father."

"Well, you're not going alone," Jackson insisted. He turned to Joe. "Becker, you have business in the west county, correct?"

Startled, Joe looked up from his notebook. "Um, I guess I do," he replied, not daring to counter the man. The rest of the team laughed.

"Really, Jackson, I don't need a babysitter," Mary admonished him. "I'll be all right. That car incident was an aberration."

"Don't start with me, Mary," Jackson warned her. "I spoke with Sgt. Fielding."

"You did?"

"Yes, and the family that owns Dovestone and the surrounding property has a sketchy history. Mainly domestic disputes and drug use. No one's going out there alone."

Mary started to protest again when, to her surprise, Cass said, "Jackson's right, Mary. Why take chances?"

Mary glanced around the room. As their safety officer, Jackson had every right to impose this restriction on her. She had asked the others to abide by the ICS rules, and they had done so, even if reluctantly. She needed to follow their example. Feigning anger, she said to Jackson, "I just have one question."

"What's that?" he asked. He returned the clipboard to his chest as if bracing himself for a fight.

Mary grinned impishly. "My car's in the shop. Who wants to loan me theirs?"

× × ×

"There it is," Mary exclaimed, pointing to a small wooden sign on the right side of the two-lane highway. It was tacked to a tree, partially obscured by a low-hanging branch. The words *Pine Ridge Resort* was carved into it, but the letters were nearly weathered away.

"How is anyone supposed to see that?" Joe asked, dismayed. "Just how exclusive is this place?" He slowed the car and maneuvered it onto the highway's shoulder. Then he turned onto a wide, flat area at the base of a forested hill. It was covered with pea gravel. Two unpaved roads extended up and around the rise in opposite directions. "Which way now?" he asked.

Mary scanned their surroundings for a clue. Metal road gates stood open in both directions, and she spotted a second wooden sign. It was nailed to the tree directly in front of the car, but its faded, red-painted arrow pointed unhelpfully downward. She considered their options and pointed to the right. "Let's go that way."

Joe looked at her skeptically. "You're just guessing, aren't you?"

Mary nodded sheepishly, and Joe reluctantly put his foot to the gas pedal. The engine revved as the rear tires spun in protest against the deep gravel. He backed off the gas a little, and on the second attempt, the tires found traction and the vehicle moved forward. But Joe stopped the car again when they arrived at the point where the gravel met the dirt of the ascending road. He pointed straight ahead and exclaimed, "We need a four-wheel drive to get up that."

Mary peered into the shaded region ahead of her. A deep but now dry, rain-formed groove ran down the center of the unpaved road. Thinner channels extended off of it at various angles and dropped into a brush-filled ravine.

"We had a lot of rain this spring," she stated as if defending the road. "But it only looks bad for about twenty feet."

Joe looked at her in disbelief. "Twenty feet? That's because we can't see the road after that point."

"Well, do you want to try the other side?" she suggested. "Or we could park and walk."

"How far away are we?"

Mary shrugged her shoulders. "I don't know," she confessed. "I've never been here before. Some of these resorts are close to the main road, and others are set back a few miles."

Joe let out a long stream of breath.

"Where's your spirit of adventure?" Mary teased him.

Joe furrowed his brow but took on her challenge and drove the car forward a few feet. The vehicle slipped with a jerk to the left as a groove in the road gave way. In response, he turned the wheel in the opposite direction and found solid ground for a short distance before the car dropped hard to the right.

Mary gripped the handle above the passenger door and laughed.

"Having fun, are we?" Joe asked, focusing intensely on the road.

Mary tried to suppress another laugh as she pointed to the left. "It looks solid over there."

"Says the woman who didn't offer up her own car," Joe retorted.

"Hey! That's not fair," Mary protested. "My car's in the shop, and you offered because you said you wanted to learn the roads out here."

Joe gingerly applied the gas and headed in the suggested direction until the vehicle's left side dropped and its undercarriage scrapped hard against the dirt. The man winced. "Paved roads," he insisted. "I meant paved roads."

Mary's attempt to stifle another laugh resulted in a snort escaping from her nose.

Joe took a quick glance at her. "How do you feel about pushing cars uphill, Nurse Mary?" he asked.

"We've only got a few more feet to go."

"A few more feet? You have a strange sense of distance, woman."

The car jerked hard to the right, and Mary laughed again. To her surprise, so did Joe. "Damn!" he exclaimed. "This is as bad as a money bus in the rainy season."

Mary turned to him, surprised. "A money bus?" she asked. She had not heard anyone use that term since her Peace Corps days. In Liberia, money buses were utility trucks that ferried passengers between the capital city and upcountry towns and villages. Typically, the driver would sit in the cab blaring African music so loudly that he could ignore the pleas of his passengers, who were crammed onto two benches in the bed of the truck. The passenger area was open to the air except for a roof mounted a few feet above their heads, onto which most of their possessions were secured. She had used this mode of transportation often to visit her fellow Peace Corps volunteers in other parts of the country. During the dry season, the trips on the hard roads were pleasant despite the overcrowding in the suppressive heat, the occasional inebriated driver, the military checkpoints, the passengers who used her shoulder as a pillow, and the urine that trickled onto her outstretched arms from the goats strapped to the roof above. During the rainy season, if the vehicles ran at all, they skated perilously over the slick, gooey red-clay of the roads or got trapped in the substance like a mammoth in the La Brea Tar Pits. Those road trips had made such an impression on her that now, whenever she heard the upbeat rhythm of African music, she was immediately transported to a seat on a money bus. She could clearly recall the passing vista of dense greenery made vivid by the contrasting red clay dirt, the pungent aroma exuded by herself and her fellow passengers in the cramped space, and the lovely, graceful sway of the women and children who walked along the sides of the roads balancing impossibly heavy loads on their heads.

"What do you know about money buses?" she asked Joe.

"Peace Corps, Ivory Coast, 1987 to 1989."

"No kidding?" she exclaimed. "I'm an RPCV too."

"I know."

Mary was puzzled. Returned Peace Corps volunteers had a knack for identifying themselves to each other early in an encounter, and this usually led to an instant connection, even if they had served on different continents. "Why didn't you say something?" she asked.

Without taking his eyes off the road, Joe said, "I got the feeling you thought I was coming on too strong, so I decided to back off a bit."

Mary blushed at this frank admission that his interest in her was more than collegial. She said nothing and turned her face to the passenger window.

The car jolted again, and Mary winced at the sound of rock scraping against metal.

"Crap!" Joe laughed. "Mary, if I break an axle, you're gonna owe me big time."

Mary called out, "Look!" They had rounded the bend and now had a partial view of the lodge. It sat in a clearing on a wide grassy lawn at the top of the hill.

"Hallelujah," Joe said with a sigh.

Mary and Joe were greeted with a stunning view when they entered the lobby of the rustic yet elegantly decorated lodge. The wall directly opposite where they stood was made entirely of glass. Through it, they could see an expansive vista that began with a swimming pool on the lawn and extended over the tree line to the meandering curves of the distant river. Mary walked farther into the room. Everything from the walls to the door handles seemed to be made from massive pieces of polished timber. The decor included fine tapestries and furnishings with accents in red and gold hues. To the left of the windowed wall, an immense stone fireplace soared to the second story.

"Nice place," Joe commented, and Mary nodded in agreement.

They approached the heavily polished reception counter, and the clerk greeted them with a confused expression. He was exceptionally small, and Mary wondered about his age. He looked to be in his early teens, but she thought he must be older, given that he was employed.

"Good morning," the clerk said, glancing from her to Joe. "Are you here for a room?"

Joe let out a nervous burst of laughter, and Mary fumbled for the county ID badge that hung around her neck. "No," she hurriedly corrected him. "We're with the Revere County Health Department. May I speak with the manager?"

"Sure," the clerk replied. He walked with an uneven gait to a door behind the counter, which Mary assumed lead to a back office. A moment later, a middle-aged man with white hair and caramel-colored skin stepped through the door. He appeared surprised to see them, but when he spoke, he did so cordially.

"Forgive me. When Brady told me the health department was here, I was expecting someone else."

"Cliff, by chance?" Mary asked.

"Yes," the man replied. "Do you know him?"

"Yes, he's a colleague of ours."

"Are you here to see our kitchen, then?"

Mary smiled. "No. That's Cliff's expertise. We've come about another matter." She handed him her business card, and he looked at her with concern. "I'm Mary Campbell, a public health nurse. And this is Joe Becker. He's an epidemiologist with the State Health Department."

"Nice to meet you," Joe said as he extended his hand.

The man hesitated but eventually took Joe's hand in his own. "Steve Carlisle. I own this place with my partner. Are we in some sort of trouble?"

"Not at all," Mary reassured him. "We're hoping you can help us."

The man glanced back over his shoulder and then offered, with some trepidation, "Well, I'll try."

"We're trying to locate the father of one of our clients, a teenager who is ill," Mary began.

"Ill?" the man asked with alarm. "Did he get sick here at the resort?"

"No," Mary said. "I'm sorry. Let me back up and explain."

At that moment, another man stepped into the reception area from the office. He walked to Steve's side and said to him, "Brady told me we had company."

"This is my partner, Evan," Steve announced warily. "Evan, this is Ms. Campbell and Mr. Becker. They're from the health department."

Joe extended his hand, but Evan did not respond in kind.

"I was just explaining to Steve why we are here," Mary said in an attempt to break the tension. "A client of ours, a teenager, traveled from the East Coast to Mill Creek to find his father. The only contact information the boy has for him is the address of this resort. His father wrote him a letter on your stationery. We're hoping you can help us locate him. The boy has no other family in the area."

Evan turned to Steve. "Is this the boy Brady mentioned the other day?"

"I believe so," Steve affirmed, and he turned to Mary. "A young friend of your client's was out here asking for the same information. We're an exclusive gay resort, Ms. Campbell. I could not give him the information because of client confidentiality. I'm sure you understand that."

"I do," Mary began, "but I was hoping you might share it with me or contact his father on our behalf because—"

"I'm sorry," Evan interrupted. "Maybe you didn't hear my partner correctly."

Mary saw the anger in the man's eyes and braced herself.

Evan gripped the counter's edge with both hands. "Even if we could give you the information," he said, "I'm not inclined to help the health department in this or any other matter."

Mary saw Evan clench his jaw. He brushed aside something unseen on the counter, and Mary was glad for the physical barrier between the two of them. She let a moment pass before saying, "May I ask why?"

"Because of how your so-called health board feels about gays," he replied through gritted teeth.

"You're talking about Supervisor Cahill," Mary said.

Evan glared at her, and she glanced at Steve, who was watching his partner with concern. Steve's eyes told her that he was not comfortable with this confrontation.

"Supervisor who?" Joe asked, and Mary began to explain.

"Virginia Cahill is a longtime local politician who had been in the minority on the County Board of Supervisors until recently. A conservative majority was elected last fall, and Supervisor Cahill was appointed as the head of the Health Board. For years, she's talked about reducing government services to communities that have offended her not-so-thinly-veiled religious sensibilities. And recently she pressured the Mental Health Department to use conversion therapy for their gay clients. The department's director, Isabelle Raposo, publically refused to do so. Supervisor Cahill hasn't been able to impose her changes yet, but—" Mary paused and looked Evan straight in the eyes. "Her verbal assaults have hurt a lot of people, haven't they?"

Evan lurched forward onto the counter toward Mary so suddenly that the others leaned back reflexively. Joe thrust an arm in between Mary and Evan. "Hey, watch it," he warned the man.

"Evan, please calm down," Steve pleaded with him.

Evan ignored his partner and focused his anger on Mary. "We're not going back to the days when the government chose to let us die," he stated, nearly spitting out the words. "Do you have any idea how many friends I lost to AIDS? How many funerals I've attended? I'm not going to let some shriveled up right-wing hag who sits on some hick town board of supervisors take us back to that nightmare." Shaking, he pushed himself away from the counter. "I thought this place was different."

Mary was momentarily distracted by Brady, who peered out of the office door. The boy quickly retracted his head when Evan turned to follow Mary's gaze.

"It is different," she stated softly. "We're not all like that."

"Then how could such a hateful person get elected and get away with what she plans to do?" he growled.

Mary had wondered about that many times herself and had not come up with a satisfactory answer. "People aren't paying attention," she offered feebly.

The man scoffed at her.

"Please know," she beseeched him, "that my colleagues are just as appalled as you are with her statements."

Evan laughed derisively. "I don't buy that for a minute. You're just a bunch of automatons who'll do anyone's bidding to keep your paychecks and benefits."

Steve grabbed his partner's forearm. "Evan, that's uncalled for. They're just trying to help a kid."

Evan shook off his partner's hand. "You need to leave now," he demanded of them.

Joe leaned toward Mary. "Come on. Let's go."

But Mary summoned her courage and asked Evan, "Do you have any children?"

Evan was startled by the question. "That's none of your business," he replied, but the expression in his eyes gave Mary her answer.

"Yes, he does," Steve confirmed, defiantly. "A daughter from a previous relationship."

"The boy we're trying to help is only fifteen years old. He's sick, and he's staying with strangers."

"That's none of my concern," Evan stated. "If he came here with just an address, he must not be very bright."

"Or he's desperate," Mary added.

Her words had little effect, and Steve spoke next. "As you can see, Ms. Campbell, we're at an impasse. I have your card. If we can help, we know how to find you."

Mary acknowledged Steve's assessment of the situation with a nod. She turned to Joe and said, "Let's go."

In the parking lot, Mary heard the crunch of irregular footsteps behind her in the gravel as she and Joe walked toward his car.

"Hey," a voice called out. Mary turned to see Brady running up to them. His physical frailty was even more transparent against the majestic backdrop of the surroundings.

"I'm really sorry about that back there," he said, winded. "Steve and Evan are actually really good guys."

"That's okay," Mary reassured him. "I'm sure they are."

"They treat me well, like Skye did. Will you tell him I said hi?"

"Sure," she answered.

The young man kicked at the gravel with one of his sneakers. "I wish I could help him," he added shyly. "He got me out of some tight spots in high school."

Mary said, "Skye strikes me as a very caring young man."

Brady smiled at her and pointed to the lodge. "Well, I'd better get back," he said.

"Okay," Mary replied as he began to walk away. "Thank you."

"Oh, wait!" Brady called out. He swiveled around, off-balance. "I almost forgot to tell you. You came up the wrong side of the hill. That road is barely good enough for our horses." He pointed to the side opposite of the hill and said, "Go that way. You'll have an easier time of it."

× × ×

After leaving the resort, Mary and Joe spent the next few hours re-viewing medical charts at the West Hills Pediatric Clinic. They were gathering vaccination dates for the cases and contacts associated with the pertussis outbreak. Afterward they travelled to Dovestone. Their plan was for Mary to check on Mark and pick up Paul's stool specimens while Joe taught the new secretary at the Daisy Merrill Elementary School how to determine if incoming kindergarteners were up-to-date on their school-required immunizations.

Mary swung a small specimen cooler in her hand as she enjoyed the walk along the long driveway to the farmhouse. The air was crisp and fresh under the oak trees, and a gentle breeze lifted her shoulder-length hair lightly. As she approached the residence, she heard voices coming from the backyard, so she walked to that part of the house. But when she drew closer, she realize that two men were arguing. She stopped before making her presence known.

"I don't care how much money a vineyard will bring in," one man shouted. "You can't have my land. It's all I've got."

"Don't you see?" said the second man. Mary recognized his voice as belonging to Paul Merrill. "This is our chance to make something of our lives."

"Not we, you. My life is fine the way it is."

"Really?" Paul asked him. "You sit over there, all by yourself, day after day, never seeing anyone except at work. What kind of life is that?"

"And whose fault is that?" the first man growled. "Who made sure I was alone?"

"Oh, for Christ's sake, when will you let that go? Maureen never loved you," Paul said. "You could've moved on—we never reported you—but you turned into a bitter old man instead."

"Says the favored child," the first man jeered.

I forgot, Mary thought, *Paul has a brother.* She remembered the day when she was confronted by the antivaccination mothers at Dovestone. Skye's uncle had called the Sheriff's Office about the crowd.

"You don't know what I've been through," Paul growled. "You're not the only one who's struggled."

Paul's brother laughed, and the cruelty in his voice gave Mary a chill. "This is all about you. It's always been about you. Well, brother, I've got a plan for my future, and it doesn't involve desecrating our family's land."

"No one's desecrating anything," Paul countered, exasperated. "I'm just trying to pull us out of this lame existence of ours. I can grow grapes on just my land, but we'll do better if we work together on this."

"Never," his brother fumed.

Silently, Mary backed up several feet before moving forward again. She kicked purposefully at the gravel in the path to signal her presence. "Hello?" she called out well in advance of reaching the two men.

Paul's brother turned on her when he saw her. "Who are you?" he asked threateningly.

Paul held up a hand. "Relax, Ray. This is Mary Campbell, the nurse I told you about. She's from the health department. Hello, Mary. How are you?"

"Fine, thank you," Mary said. Paul looked drawn. He had dark circles under his eyes.

"Mary, this is my brother, Raymond Reynolds," he said.

A half brother, Mary realized upon hearing his last name. She extended her hand to Raymond, who shook it. His grip was neither strong nor weak. He looked at her through silver-framed glasses, and she held his gaze, curious to see if his eyes revealed anything. She saw suspicion in them, which was not unusual when she was introduced in her professional role. Turning away, she said to Paul, "I came to pick up your stool specimens and to see how Mark was doing."

"Oh, sure," Paul said, lightly. "The specimens are in the refrigerator. Follow me. Mark's feeling a lot better. He and Skye went on a short walk down to the river." Paul led Mary through the screened-in back porch. "Did you know that Raymond is in the nursing home business too?"

"No, I didn't," Mary replied, cordially. She was going to ask Raymond what his job was when something shattered behind her. Both she and Paul jumped at the sound. Mary turned around and saw

Raymond looking at a broken clay pot on the floor. A purple African violet plant, with its roots bound in a clump of dirt, lay next to it.

"Sorry about that," Raymond said. "I knocked it off the ledge." He stooped to pick up the broken pieces.

"Just leave it," Paul replied, and Mary heard the tension in his voice. She understood its source when she spotted the childlike drawing of a bird and Skye's name on large shards of the flowerpot. "I'll take care of it later."

At the refrigerator, Paul opened the door, took out a small brown paper bag, and handed it to Mary. The top edges were neatly folded over, and the bag was clearly labeled with his name and the date. "I also labeled the containers like you told me," he said.

"Thank you," Mary replied, appreciatively.

"You suspect my brother of wrongdoing?" Raymond asked.

Startled, Mary turned. Her body stiffened when she realized just how close Raymond was standing to her. This time when she looked into his eyes, she saw that he had enjoyed surprising her. She stepped away from both men and set the cooler onto the kitchen table. "Not at all," she replied. "This is part of our standard outbreak procedures." Mary placed the specimen bag in the cooler and asked Paul, "Did you hear the news about Willow's baby?"

"Yes," he answered. "It's too bad she got sick, but it sounds like she'll be okay."

Mary nodded. "I wanted to make sure Mark knew," she said. "I know he was worried about her." She looked from one man to the other and said, "Well, I'd better get going. I have a colleague waiting for me at the elementary school. We need to get back to the office. Please tell Mark I'm glad to hear he's feeling better and that I'll stop by again soon."

"Let me see you out," Paul offered, and Mary followed him to the living room. "I hope you're still planning on coming to our fund-raiser—the art exhibit."

"I am," Mary replied enthusiastically. "I'm looking forward to it.

As Paul opened the front door for her, Raymond called out, "Paul told me your father is in a nursing home. The Covenant Hill, I believe?" Mary turned and saw Raymond standing in the shadow of the small hallway that ran between the kitchen and living room. "You'd better figure out what's causing these outbreaks before something happens to him."

Mary glared at the man. She had heard a veiled threat in his words.

"I'm sure he's safe," Paul said reassuringly. He smiled and added lightly, "No doubt your dad's facility is taking extra precautions, considering they're caring for the relative of a health department employee. I know I would."

Paul opened the screen door for Mary. She stepped onto the creaky porch but looked back at Raymond. He had moved further back into the shadow.

"I'll be around," she said.

Mary walked to the elementary school and met Joe at his car. She placed the cooler in the trunk, but before she climbed into the passenger's seat, she took in the school's surroundings. The structure had been built to preserve a grove of elderly oak trees along the back of the property. They stood like protective sentries over the lovingly tended grounds. Shrubs filled the curved border gardens that hugged the school's main building, and four young plum trees dotted the lawn between the school and the front sidewalk. A vine of pink-and-white flowers, which Mary did not recognize, grew along and softened the harsh chain-link fence that enclosed the playground and the field next to it. A tower of bark chips stood next to the slide, waiting for someone to spread it around to create a cushion for the little bodies that would fling themselves from the swings onto the ground. Behind the playground, a half-sized basketball court was outlined in yellow on the blacktop, and a safe distance away from it, six raised garden beds lay in perfect alignment at the edge of the open field.

Mary's thoughts flashed to her childhood. She could almost see her friends scampering onto the playground after walking from their classroom in single file. When her eyes alighted on the monkey bars, a memory of her brother filled her senses. As a second grader, a classmate had once tried to pull her off of the apparatus by yanking on her skirt. David had pushed him away, but Mary's grip had already slipped. She collapsed on top of her brother and landed with her skirt covering his face. Mary had stood up quickly, worried that he would be angry and embarrassed. But he had laughed instead.

Mary smiled and looked past the oak trees to the clouds floating across the blue sky. *You were a wonderful brother, David. Thank you.*

"Penny for your thoughts?" a voice asked.

Mary woke from her reverie to find Joe looking at her across the roof of the car. She smiled at him warmly. "Just indulging in a memory," she said.

"A good one, I hope," he said, and Mary nodded. Then he added, "Mind if we stop and get something to eat on the way back? I could use some food."

"Can it wait?" she asked. "We've been away from the office for a long time."

"It's almost four, and that's a forty-minute drive," he said irritably.

"Sheez. Do you always get cranky when you're hungry?"

"Yes."

The expression on Joe's face told Mary that he was serious. "Well, okay, then," she said. "I don't want to mess with anyone's blood-sugar level."

"Thank you."

After a short drive into town, Mary pointed to a line of shops. "Look. There's a deli," she said, "and it even has a parking space out front."

"Do they sell meat?" Joe asked. "The people in this town don't look like they eat a lot of meat."

"It's a deli, for heaven's sake."

"But it's a west county deli," he corrected her. "Home of the alternatives. Their pastrami is probably made of pressed tofu."

Mary laughed. "Alternatives? You're really not from around here, are you?"

"Nope, and I like my meat pink and from an animal."

Mary raised an eyebrow at him. "You might just want to keep that bit of information to yourself while we're here."

Joe held the door open for Mary as they entered the deli. She glanced around the tiny establishment and saw that it had only four tables. An elderly couple shared a sandwich at the table to her left, and two women were holding an intimate conversation at the table behind them. Three farm laborers chatted in Spanish at the table to her right. They looked up as Mary and Joe walked by.

"Buenos dias," Mary said to them.

A narrow black floor mat ran from the door down the center of the room to a wood-trimmed deli case that displayed an array of salads, pickles, cheese, and desserts. Two dark chalkboards—on which menu items were written in white—hung from the ceiling by chains. A slender young man with wild dark curls and a woman with long, thin white hair staffed the counter.

Joe nodded at the chalkboards. "What did I tell you?" he whispered. "Tofu."

Mary followed his gaze. The daily special was minestrone soup and a BLT sandwich made with bacon-flavored tofu. She hurriedly scanned the rest of the menu items. "Look," she said. "They have tuna salad. Do you like tuna?"

"I guess," he grumbled.

As Joe placed his order and devoured a banana, Mary heard a familiar voice from across the room. She turned and saw Trish Matthews on the screen of a small television mounted high on the deli's front wall. Words scrolled by quickly under the reporter's image. They read, *KZIV 4 O'Clock News Update: Deadly diseases threaten Revere County.*

Uh, oh, Mary thought.

"Five days ago," the news anchor began, "KZIV News presented information to our viewers about the Revere County Health Department's investigations into the deadly diseases that have stricken our community."

Mary tapped Joe on the arm and pointed to the television. "You might want to watch this," she suggested.

"This station now brings you the findings of its own investigation into two outbreaks that are sickening our teenagers and the elderly."

Mary walked forward. Transfixed, she stopped at the edge of the table occupied by the three farm laborers. They looked at her with curiosity, and one of the men glanced at the health department badge that hung from the lanyard around her neck.

"We begin with the bacterial meningitis outbreak," Ms. Matthews stated. "A fourth case of the disease has been uncovered by this station."

A picture of a middle-aged woman materialized on the screen to the right of the anchor, and the name Rosa Hernandez appeared under it.

"Rosa Hernandez, fifty-four years of age at the time of her death from bacterial meningitis, was a Mexican national who entered this country illegally and received U.S. citizenship through amnesty in the 1990s."

Joe joined Mary. "This can't be good," he said as he took a bite of his sandwich.

"This reporter has learned," Ms. Matthews continued, "that the Latina worked in the kitchen at Franklin Middle School, one of the schools that a teen victim attended."

"Damn," Mary grumbled. She watched as the reporter's face disappeared and Mrs. Hernandez's picture was shifted to the top center of a yellow screen. The photographs and names of the three teen meningitis cases appeared. Their pale Caucasian features were in distinct contrast to Mrs. Hernandez's heritage. Thick red arrows connected Mrs. Hernandez's image to the other photos.

"Who gave them permission to use the kids' information?" Joe whispered. "They're minors."

Mary shrugged. "I don't know," she answered. "Their parents?" She cursed to herself when the reporter asked her viewers, "Is Mrs. Hernandez the source of the deadly disease that nearly killed these children? Although she was ill one month before the students, she handled the food of one of the teen victims. Are we dealing with a Latina Typhoid Mary? Parents are asking if she transmitted this disease to their children."

"Good God," Joe stated incredulously. "Everything she just said was wrong."

Mary became uncomfortably aware of the three men sitting at the table next to her. They now ate in silence.

"Lo siento," she said to them. "I'm sorry."

"Revere County's health officer, Dr. Henderson, says no," Ms. Matthews continued. "She claims that a link has been identified between the three teens that explains their illness, but she could not share the nature of that link with this reporter. She also claims that the Latina had no contact with the teens during her infectious period and that her illness was caused by a different serotype of the bacteria."

"Well, at least she talked to Suzanne," Mary muttered to Joe.

"But this reporter also spoke with George Murray, a former laboratory manager, who had this to say about the link between the Latina and the children."

"What link? There is no link," Mary whispered angrily.

"Who is George Murray?" Joe asked.

"I have no idea," Mary replied.

A middle-aged man in a frumpy suit appeared on the screen. He stood outside an unidentified building, and each time the wind gusted, his thin, black, combed-over hair lifted ever so slightly to reveal a bald scalp. Someone off-camera held a microphone to his face. "There's a possibility of error in every lab test," he said. "No test is ever 100 percent valid or reliable."

The camera shot widened to reveal Ms. Matthews standing next to him. "Could the health department's lab have made a mistake?" she postulated to the audience. "Could this Latina actually have had the same deadly bacteria as our children?"

"Stop calling her 'this Latina,'" Mary grumbled. "How does she get away with this stuff?" she asked Joe. "She's supposed to be a journalist."

Mr. Murray disappeared from the screen, and the camera came in for a close up of Ms. Matthews' now grave expression. "We may never know the truth, but this reporter will continue to ask the hard questions in search of it."

"Bigot," Mary said. Adrenaline surged through her. She felt for the cell phone at her waist. *I should be at the unit. Why didn't anyone call me?*

"Let's get out of here," she told Joe.

Joe pointed to the screen. "She's not done yet," he said.

"In a related story, KZIV News has also uncovered stunning information about the norovirus outbreaks that have devastated our local nursing homes. I've learned that the Revere County Health Department has been investigating a person of interest. He is a nurse's aide who tended to the residents on the very day the outbreaks began at each facility."

Mary gasped, and Joe leaned closer to her. "Where's she getting this information?" he asked.

Mary shrugged. "I don't know."

"I also spoke with Dr. Henderson about the situation," Ms. Matthews said. She was shown standing outside of the Seventh Street building with Suzanne at her side, and she held the microphone close to Suzanne's mouth.

"We're working very closely with nursing homes to prevent these outbreaks," she said. "No one is under suspicion. Some residents and staff at the facilities are undergoing testing, as is typical for these types of investigations."

Nicely stated, Mary thought, but her relief lasted only a moment. Ms. Matthews next appeared at her anchor desk. Her intense gaze penetrated the camera. "My source states otherwise. Given the health department's questionable performance in recent weeks and the vulnerability of nursing home residents, who are our most beloved and fragile elders—"

"Man, she can really lay it on thick," Joe whispered.

"This station is calling for local law enforcement to conduct an independent review of the health department's investigations."

"Good Lord," Mary exclaimed. She nudged Joe forward. "Come on. We've got to go."

As they reach the door, one of the farm laborers called out, "*Buena suerte, señora.*"

× × ×

Erin had tried to reach Mary, but Mary did not receive the message until she and Joe were within range of a wireless signal, about ten miles outside of Mill Creek. "Damn phones," she muttered, striking the instrument against her left hand. Erin's message said that a briefing had been scheduled for five o'clock and that Carl would be in attendance.

Back at her office, Mary checked her desk-phone messages while her computer slowly loaded its programs. The first voice spoke with controlled anger.

"Mary? This is Paul Merrill. Do I need to get a lawyer? Call me."

Mary returned Paul's call, and she reassured him that, as far as the health department was concerned, he was not under suspicion for any wrongdoing.

"But do I need to get a lawyer?" he demanded of her.

Mary's thoughts flashed to the many calls she had taken over the years from people who worried about catching the most obscure of communicable diseases—and then to the warning Nora York had given her when she first joined the CD Unit. "Never underestimate the level of anxiety in the general population," she had said, "or the actions some people will take in response to that anxiety."

Mary also remembered the antivaccination mothers' response to the sheriff's deputies at Dovestone and some legal advice her brother had once given her. "A legal shot across the bow, like a cease and desist letter," he had said, "can be very effective against bullies."

She told Paul, "Yes, get a lawyer, just to play it safe."

At 4:55 p.m., Mary entered the conference room and took a seat at the table. Everyone on the team was present except for Suzanne, who was calling in on the conference line. Jonathan sat against a wall away from the others. When Cass arrived, she took a seat next to Marni, who then stood up and joined Jonathan.

Cass noticed and Mary heard her whisper to Lourdes, "Do I smell or something?"

Once Carl entered, he immediately took charge. The man had no interest in any topic other than that of Paul Merrill and the nursing home outbreaks. He peppered Mary with questions. When anyone else attempted to offer an answer, he told them to keep quiet. The onslaught finally ended with the question, "In your opinion, is there is any reason to suspect that Mr. Merrill intentionally infected the residents of these nursing homes?"

"No," she replied firmly. "We have no evidence of that. It's all circumstantial."

He stood up and leaned on the table. "Well, the Board of Supervisors doesn't want to take any chance that you're wrong," he growled at her. "They've instructed the sheriff to send deputies over here tomorrow to talk with you."

"Holy crap," Cass muttered.

Carl ignored Cass. Before he left, he glared at Mary and said, "You and your staff will cooperate fully with the sheriff. Is that understood?"

Mary bristled at the directive. *When have I ever not done so?* she thought.

Tuesday, June 10

Mary woke up with the dawn light, and her mind immediately began ruminating over her 9:00 a.m. meeting with the Sheriff's Office. She lay in bed wondering what they might ask her and how she might respond.

This isn't helping, she told herself, so she decided to go to work. By 6:38 a.m., she had logged onto her computer. By 7:50 a.m., she had answered emails, listened to the messages left on the CD line, and filled out intake forms for the disease reports that had come in over the fax the night before. At 8:10 a.m., she walked over to Lourdes' cubicle to join her team for the morning report. Then she returned to her office. She pulled a yellow legal pad out of the shallow center drawer of her desk and placed it before her. She had been told to expect two deputies and wanted to have her thoughts together before they stepped into her office. Mary picked up a black pen, and for a moment, listened to her surroundings. She heard the sounds of people quietly settling into their day's work.

The calm before the storm? she wondered.

Mary stared at the paper for a few moments before she began to write down the reasons why Paul Merrill should not be implicated in the outbreaks. She stopped after listing four: he had not been sick, the results of his stool specimens were not yet in, he had not always worked on the day of exposure, and he had been good to Mark. The explanations looked small and lost on the multilined sheet.

What do I really know about this guy? she wondered as she tapped the point of her pen on the pad. He had opened his home to Mark, he saw to it that the boy received medical care, and he had cooperated with her unit on the nursing home investigations. To her, those actions did not fit the profile of someone who would purposefully sicken others.

Mary had read accounts of people who had killed patients under their care; Angels of Death was what these doctors and nurses were called, because of their proximity to their victims when they died. *Serial killers don't need a motive,* she thought, *but is Paul Merrill one of those?* Her instincts told her no.

Joe stepped into her office at 8:40 a.m. and handed her a single sheet of paper.

"What's this?" she asked.

"It's the analysis you asked for. The list of our nursing homes, but by the likely date of exposure to the virus for each," he told her.

"Why not the date of disease onset?"

"Just look," he replied. "You'll see why."

Mary studied the table on the page. Its title indicated that Joe had included the norovirus outbreaks from the beginning of the year to the present day. The first column listed the nursing homes by name. A second column showed the likely dates of exposure for each nursing home. Written in parentheses next to each date were the corresponding names of the days of the week. *Thursday/Friday* was noted for every nursing home outbreak that had been reported since early April.

Mary's eyes widened, and she looked up at Joe. "Am I reading this right? Starting in April, the likely day of exposure for these outbreaks was a Thursday or Friday?"

"Yep," he said. "That's one pattern. Now look at the actual dates. What do you see?"

Mary studied them a minute. "They occurred every other week?" she asked, puzzled. She looked up at Joe. "Coincidence?"

"Not likely," he replied.

After Joe left her office, Mary returned to writing on her yellow legal pad, but a man's voice soon interrupted her musings.

"Excuse me. Ms. Campbell?"

Mary looked up and smiled as she pulled from her mind the name that belonged to the face of the young, uniformed man standing in her doorway. "Hello. Deputy Martin, isn't it?"

"Yes," he said as he walked to the front of her desk.

Mary stood up and shook his hand. "We met at Dovestone," she said nervously. "And here you are again. I usually don't come to the attention of law enforcement this much."

The deputy made no reply, and Mary glanced at the clock on her wall. "Nine o'clock exactly. You're very punctual."

"The sheriff made it very clear that this was an urgent matter," Deputy Martin stated. He hooked the thumb of his right hand behind his thick black belt. Then he placed the rest of his fingers lightly over the grip of his holstered gun. The movement was so casual that Mary was certain it was an unconscious act.

"Us?" she asked.

"Sgt. Fielding came with me," the deputy explained. He nodded to the right. "She's using the ladies room."

Mary began to offer him a seat when Cass stepped into her office. She looked at the deputy and blurted out, "Did you really need to bring a gun into this building?"

"Cass!" Mary scolded her, and she moved quickly to the nurse. "Excuse me a moment," she said to the officer as she maneuvered Cass into the hallway. Once there, she whispered to her, "Don't you have any sense of self-preservation?"

Just as Cass was about to respond, someone behind Mary caught her attention. Mary turned and saw Sgt. Fielding standing in the doorway to her office. Her impressive stature nearly filled the frame. "Good morning, Sergeant," Mary called out. "I'll be right with you." Then she turned to Cass. "What do you need?"

Cass did not hear her question. "Who is that?" she whispered. "She's magnificent."

Mary looked back at Sgt. Fielding and then at Cass, again. *Well, she must be feeling better*, she thought. And she whispered, "You don't even know if she's a lesbian."

"I can look, can't I?" Cass replied dreamily.

Mary placed her face directly in the nurse's line of vision. "Cass, focus. Why did you come to my office? Do you need something?"

The spell was broken, and Cass looked at Mary. "I just wanted to say good morning."

Mary shook her head in amusement. "That's it? Well, from now on could you please refrain from speaking the first words that pop into your head to our guests?" She glanced behind her and said, "I'd like to start off on the right foot with these people."

Back in her office, Mary and Sgt. Fielding exchanged greetings while Deputy Martin retrieved a third chair from an empty cubicle.

"So," Mary began, "we've been directed to talk to you about the nursing home investigations."

"Correct," the sergeant answered briskly.

"Would you like me to brief you on our activities to date?" Mary asked, and then she laughed to herself. *I sound just like Jackson.*

"Please," the sergeant responded. Her expression revealed nothing.

But before Mary could say anything, Cass entered the office, again. She walked past Deputy Martin to Mary's desk and said, "I thought your guests might want to see a copy of our latest incident action plan."

Mary looked at her with surprise. "Um, thanks, Cass," she replied, holding out her hand for the report. Cass held onto it, though, and glanced at Sgt. Fielding.

"You're working under ICS?" the sergeant asked Mary.

"Yes," Cass answered quickly. "It's been very helpful."

Mary pinched her lips together hard to prevent herself from laughing aloud.

"May I see it?" Sgt. Fielding asked.

"Sure," Cass replied. Her smile broadened, and she gave the IAP to the officer. "I'm Cass McGovern, by the way. One of the CD nurses."

Cass' gaze lingered on the sergeant until Mary said, pointedly, "Thank you, Cass."

The nurse correctly interpreted her supervisor's instruction and turned to leave. At the door, she said, "Let me know if you need anything else."

Mary spent the next twenty minutes giving the two officers an overview of the nursing home investigations, and she also told them about the table Joe had shown her that morning. Their demeanor grew more relaxed as she answered each of their questions.

"What we'd like to do, Ms. Campbell," Sgt. Fielding began, "is to conduct a preliminary investigation of our own. We'll start by interviewing your contacts at each nursing home."

"Okay," Mary replied. "What do you need from us?"

"A point of contact. Someone we can reach out to for information. Would that be you?"

"Yes," Mary answered, "but I'll also introduce you to Linus, the department's epidemiologist. He's our planning chief and is in charge of keeping our information current."

"Good." Sgt. Fielding glanced at the IAP again and said, "Based on what you've told me, it's likely we're dealing with odd coincidences and an overly ambitious news reporter. But I'm curious about one thing."

"What's that?" Mary asked.

"Personal medical information is confidential, right, even during outbreak investigations?"

"That's correct."

"So where is Trish Matthews getting her information?"

Mary remembered Joe's question at the deli. "Someone else asked me that recently," she said.

"And?"

Mary looked the sergeant directly in the eye. "I don't know."

× × ×

Raymond woke to a beautiful morning that held no pleasure for him. His senses were dulled to the rich palette of colors in the dawning sky, and they were muted to the glorious birdsong that pierced the fresh, clear air. The night before, he had drunk an entire bottle of whiskey to numb his mind. Now, as he lay in bed, he may as well have been entombed in the darkest of winter days. His mood paralyzed him, and when a long-neglected child buried deep within his psyche realized he was immobile, and vulnerable, it reacted with terror. Panic flooded his being, and a memory burst into his consciousness that he had fought hard to suppress.

"Get up, you lazy little shit," his stepfather, Alan, had yelled at him before smacking him on the back of his head.

"Dad," a young Paul called out fearfully from across the room. "It's okay. I'll get him up in a couple of minutes."

But Alan hit Raymond again. "I said get up. Look at your brother. He's already dressed."

Raymond's young teen body, still heavy with sleep, lay prone on the bed. Only his mind stirred, and with it, a bold voice slipped from its prison into the unguarded space between his dreams and reality.

"Old man," he grumbled, "if you hit me one more time, I'll break your face."

The beating his fifteen-year-old body and spirit endured that morning lasted no longer than a few minutes, but during that tiny interval of his life, the sum of all the loathing from previous attacks did not compare to the hatred and humiliation his stepfather pummeled into him. Raymond remembered Paul crying out weakly when Alan pulled him off of the bed, but he had no memory of how he got to their family doctor's office, fully dressed. Through tears, his mother told the physician he had been ambushed on his way to school. Later, when the police asked Raymond if he recognized his attackers, he saw the panic in his mother's eyes through the slits of his swollen ones. "No," he told them. "But I think they were field hands."

He missed two weeks of school because of the concussion and the labored breathing caused by his busted nose and ribs. When he did return, he struggled to hold a pencil with his splinted fingers. At home, his model cathedrals and castles lay untouched for weeks. No one in the house spoke, and his stepfather slipped in and out of the rooms like an animal hearing, but not seeing, a predator.

Seven months later, shortly after Raymond's sixteenth birthday, Alan Merrill was dead. The man's drunken outings were so predictable, Raymond had marveled at how easy it had been to kill him. As was his habit, Alan had left the farm on a Monday evening and headed to a bar several miles outside of Mill Creek. Raymond arrived at the establishment at 10:00 p.m. and waited in his car for the drunk to stumble to his vehicle. He followed him first along the lower, foggy portion of River Road that traversed a wetland. Then he stalked him up its dark, winding climb. On the descent, Raymond only had to pull up next to his stepfather's car on a sharp curve and show his face to attain his revenge. The man was so startled by the vision that he took the curve too short and drove into a deep, forested ravine. Not until that fall, when the foliage had dropped, was his stepfather's vehicle discovered by hikers. The only regret Raymond felt was seeing his mother's reaction upon learning from the police that a woman had died in the car along with her husband.

The weight now pressing on Raymond's chest was so intense that he feared he was dying. His heart pounded against his breastbone, and he gasped for air. When the trembling began, he curled up into a fetal position and covered his entire body with the quilt, clutching it with both hands beneath his chin. Then, through the blurred vision of his fear, he spotted his favorite painting of Maureen's and focused on the image as if it were his salvation. The magnificence of the mountain image, in all its colorful detail, soothed him, and his breathing began to ease. He lay back down on the bed, exhausted, and stared at the ceiling.

Saturday, June 14

Mary sat in the nook that served as the dining area in her apartment and stared at the spider diagram she had fashioned after Joe's to figure out who might be feeding confidential information to Trish Matthews. She tapped the eraser end of her pencil against the paper with ever greater frequency as her frustration grew. The question had wormed its way into her psyche after her meeting with the deputies. She had written on the diagram the name of every person she knew who had been sent the incident action plans. All were county employees, which meant she was at a loss for a motive. The department had investigated numerous outbreaks over the years, so she did not know why anyone would want to excite the press now. She studied the diagram a few more minutes and then pushed it aside.

"I'm wasting my time," she said aloud.

Mary carried her breakfast dishes to the sink, rinsed them off, and put them in the dishwasher. She wiped down the counter, and after squeezing out the hand sponge, looked back at the table. She recalled the statement on the first page of every IAP. It warned the recipient against distributing or forwarding the document to anyone else. *Why would someone give Trish Matthews the information?* she wondered. *What for? Money?*

"Oh, hell," Mary grumbled as she returned to the nook and began to study the diagram again.

× × ×

Raymond stepped out of the stairwell behind Judy, the administrator for the Lakeview Village skilled nursing facility. She pointed to her left and said, "Constance's room is that way. She's easily confused, so be patient with her. I'll join you there shortly. I just need to check in quickly with our nurse about some ill residents."

Raymond thanked her, and she reentered the stairwell. Energy flooded his body as he watched her descend and disappear through the first floor door. He had altered his plan because he could not wait another week to see his mother. Instead of proceeding left, as Judy had instructed him, he turned to his right and walked down the hall to room 231. The nameplate on the door read *Agnes Sanders*. Raymond entered the room and found a woman sitting up in bed, covered by a light blanket. She was modestly dressed in a nightgown and a day robe.

"Hello," he called out.

"Tommy?" Agnes asked in a raspy voice filled with delight. "Is that you?"

Raymond closed the door. "No, Mom," he said. "It's me, Raymond. Who's Tommy?"

"Raymond?" Agnes laughed. "Who's Raymond? Stop teasing me, Tommy, and come closer."

Raymond walked over to the bed and sat down. He placed his briefcase near her feet. "How are you?" he asked.

Agnes did not respond right away. She looked as if she were trying to sort something out in her mind. "Who are you?" she asked, and she reached out her hands to feel her visitor.

"You've been drinking again, Mom, haven't you?" Raymond said as he took her hand. "You don't even know who I am."

Agnes recoiled at his touch and reached for the call button near the head of her bed.

Raymond grabbed her wrist and pulled her arm down forcefully. "Ah, ah, ah!" he scolded her. "You don't need that."

Agnes cried out in pain. "I want Judy. Let me call Judy."

Raymond clamped a hand over her mouth. "Hush! Who's Judy? I don't know any Judy. Be quiet, Mom. Are you going to be quiet?"

Agnes nodded. When Raymond released her, she whimpered and rubbed her wrist. Raymond snapped open his briefcase.

"You know, Mom, I want to be a good son, but you make it so hard sometimes. You really messed everything up for me."

Inside the briefcase lay a bottle of peppermint schnapps, a box of latex surgical gloves, a bottle of sleeping pills, a stack of pill cups, a one-ounce spray bottle, and a clipboard. Each rested neatly in a nest of hard foam. Raymond gloved his hands, opened the schnapps, and set it on the bed stand.

"I mean, first there was Alan—" Raymond twisted the cap off of the medicine bottle and poured some tablets into a pill cup. "And then you let Paul get to Maureen."

He scooted closer to Agnes, and she held up her frail arms to shield herself. "But the worst of it was when you gave away my land," he said. "That really tore me apart, Mom."

Agnes pushed against him and screamed. Raymond lowered her arms and pulled her head back by her hair. "I told you to keep quiet," he growled. "God, you're disgusting. Stop crying, for God's sake. How many times do I have to tell you?"

Raymond slowly released his grip on her hair and began to stroke it. "But I know you've suffered too," he said.

Agnes swatted at his arm.

"I was too hard on you the night I brought Maureen home, wasn't I? I'm really sorry about that, but like I said, you can be so difficult. I still want to be your little white knight. I really do. Let me give you something to help you sleep and keep the nightmares away."

"No," Agnes whispered at her unseen assailant.

"It will make everything better," Raymond said. "I promise. We'll curl up together, just like we used to."

"No!" Agnes yelled. Raymond did not see the terror on her face.

"You need to sleep, Mom," he repeated.

Agnes' eyes filled with tears. "No, I don't want to," she yelled out.

"Keep quiet," Raymond admonished her. He lifted the pill cup to her lips. "Open your mouth."

Agnes shook her head vigorously from side to side.

"Stop moving!" Raymond growled at her. He set the pill cup on the bedside stand, grabbed the woman's jaw, and pried open her mouth. "I don't want to bruise you." With one hand holding her jaw open, he picked up the pill cup with the other and poured the tablets onto the back of her tongue. Agnes choked on them, and Raymond poured the schnapps into her mouth and closed it shut. He held it shut.

"Swallow!" he demanded of her.

Agnes struggled against him, pushing at his forearms with her frail hands. He responded by pressing her against the bed. "I said swallow!"

She struggled to breath through her nose, and he stroked her throat as he would a pet's. Only when he felt her tongue give way did he release his grip on her.

Agnes wailed. Raymond grabbed her lower jaw and turned her face to his. He gave her a full, long kiss on the mouth. When he released her, the woman looked at him in horror, laid on her side, away from him, and sobbed.

Raymond returned the items to his briefcase and set it on the floor. When Agnes' cries began to subside, he slipped under the blanket and curled up against her. He caressed her body in long strokes.

"That's right, Mom," he said. "Go to sleep. Everything will be good again. We'll start all over again, tomorrow. You'll see."

Thursday, June 19

Mary hung up the phone after letting it ring eight times. No one had answered her calls at Dovestone since the *County Courier* published its latest article about Paul Merrill yesterday. The Sheriff's Office had arrived at the same conclusion as she: the evidence against Paul was circumstantial at this point, particularly given that his stool specimen had come back negative for the virus. He remained a person of interest only. The reporter had quoted Paul's lawyer as saying his client was cooperating fully with the authorities and that no charges had been filed against him.

Mary was eager to connect with Mark, though. The State CD Program had called her that morning about his test results. The CDC had identified the measles virus as a German strain associated with a small outbreak in the Midwest. They could not give her many details about that investigation, so she tracked down her local counterpart, Sheri Lawson, in Indiana.

"We only had three cases, thank God, but even that was a lot of work," Sheri said. "The source case was a German high school student who attended a two-week exchange program at the university. He infected his host father, who travels around the Midwest for his employer."

Mary was skeptical. "Really? An American adult got sick with the measles?"

"Yes. The man was born in 1957, which, as you know, is right at the

CDC's cut-off year for assuming natural immunity. He had no record of being immunized, and he didn't recall having the disease as a child."

"What a lousy break," Mary said.

Sheri did not respond to that comment. Instead, she asked, "So, how do you think your young man is tied to our outbreak?"

Mary heard the hesitant curiosity in Sheri's voice. "He hitchhiked out here from the East Coast," Mary explained. "He must have crossed paths with one of your cases."

"Hmm. How old is he?"

"Fifteen."

"Crap," Sheri whispered.

"What's wrong?" Mary asked.

"I hope it wasn't our adult case he ran into."

"Why?"

"Because the guy is a real creep, a sexual predator," Sheri hissed. "Our third case was a fourteen-year-old homeless boy. He came to our attention when the police took him to a hospital emergency department. His initial diagnosis was pneumonia with a rash of unknown origin, but the docs also found a couple of cracked ribs and days-old contusions. The boy said nothing about who beat him up, or why, until the virus tied him to his perpetrator."

Mary shivered as Sheri relayed her story, and she recalled her first encounter with Mark at Dr. Hansen's clinic. She remembered the healing gash on his forehead, his tender ribs, and his wariness. *And now he's dealing with Paul's situation.*

Mary thanked Sheri for the information. She hung up but quickly picked up the phone again to call the Merrill residence. Then she thought better of it. The news she had for Mark should be given in person. The Dovestone fund-raiser was scheduled for tomorrow evening. She would attend the art exhibition and find a quiet moment at the end to speak with Mark.

× × ×

"Media reports about Mr. Merrill slowed today," Irini told Mary. "I've only counted seven compared to eighteen for yesterday. And today's content is mostly repeats of old information or speculation."

"Okay. Thanks, Irini," Mary replied. The number of people at the end-of-day briefing was no higher than at previous meetings, but new assignments had been made within the ICS structure. Irini was now monitoring news media reports for Timothy, since the meningitis investigation was nearly complete. Sgt. Fielding was leading the new law enforcement branch under operations, and LaVonne had been reassigned to the sitstat unit. She was reviewing medical charts to support the effort to determine why the nursing home outbreaks were occurring with such regularity.

"Linus? Do you have anything to report?" Mary asked.

"Yes," he answered. "We're almost done analyzing the location and timing of the medical outcomes associated with the nursing home outbreaks. And LaVonne found something really interesting in her chart review." Linus leaned closer to the conference phone and said, "Sgt. Fielding, are you still on the line? I'd like you to hear this."

"I'm here," the officer responded.

"Go ahead," Linus encouraged LaVonne.

"Overall," the nurse began, "eleven deaths, due to any cause, occurred around the time of the six nursing home outbreaks. Of these, five have documentation in their charts of norovirus-related gastrointestinal symptoms contributing to their deaths. But these GI symptoms were not noted in the medical records of the remaining six deceased individuals. They were reported as having died of natural causes. We decided to look at those further."

"Why?" Cliff asked. "That doesn't sound like a lot, and we're talking about old people."

"But when you think about it," Joe explained, "nursing homes don't experience deaths every day or even every few days. We wanted to make sure the deaths really weren't associated with norovirus."

"Where did these natural deaths occur?" Sgt. Fielding asked.

"There was one at each nursing home," LaVonne answered.

"Each one?" Lourdes stated. The tone in her voice reflected the surprise on everyone else's face.

"Did you look at any other characteristics of the deaths?" Mary asked.

"Yes," LaVonne replied. "They were all females in their eighties. They had various physical ailments, but all had vision and mobility limitations."

Mary glanced at Joe. His face was solemn. "What's wrong?" she asked him.

"Each of the natural-cause deaths occurred on the second day after disease onset for each outbreak," he said. "That seemed really odd to me and could have been due to chance alone. Just coincidence. But—"

He paused.

"Go on," Mary encouraged him.

"I decided to test that. I started by designating five-day periods around each of the six natural-cause deaths, with the third day in the period being the actual date of death—two days before and two days after the death. Then, using the county's death-record data," Joe continued, "I took a count of how many deaths occurred within those five-day periods over the past five years for each nursing home."

"Why five days?" Erin asked.

"It makes for a more conservative test," Joe answered.

"We'll take your word on that," Stella said with a slight smile.

"And what did you find?" Mary asked eagerly.

"The difference is statistically significant. It's unlikely the natural-cause deaths for the present year occurred due to chance alone."

The room was silent until Cass spoke the words others were thinking. "What does this mean?" she asked anxiously. "Are you saying someone did this on purpose? Who would want to hurt old women?"

"Did Paul Merrill really do something?" Lourdes asked.

"Hold on," Mary cautioned them. "Let's not jump to conclusions. LaVonne, was there any other information on the death certificates—like secondary causes of death—or autopsy results that might clear this up?"

LaVonne shook her head. "No, and autopsies weren't conducted."

"Why not?" Jackson asked.

"Why perform an autopsy on an elderly, infirm woman who died in her sleep?" LaVonne told him. "There would be no reason to do so."

Mary addressed Stella. "Did the administrator of our latest outbreak give any indication that anything unusual was going on before their outbreak started?"

"You mean Lakeview? No," Stella answered her. "And I really challenged him about it."

"Nothing at all?" Mary asked.

Stella scanned through the notes she held on her lap. "There were no staffing changes, no outside contractors working on the building, no new food suppliers—nothing was different. He did mention the state licensing agency conducted an inspection, but I didn't think anything of that."

"Really?" Mary replied, her curiosity piqued. She was about to ask Stella a follow-up question when Sgt. Fielding interrupted her. "Ms. Campbell?" she said.

"Yes?" Mary answered.

"I'm going to get off the line now so I can call the county medical examiner about these deaths."

"Understood," Mary replied.

⚹ ⚹ ⚹

Back in the unit, Mary walked over to Stella's cubicle and waited while she finished a call. After she hung up, Stella turned around and found Mary staring into space, deep in thought. "You okay, boss?" she asked.

Stella's question broke Mary's reverie. She looked her squarely in the eyes and asked, "Did any other nursing homes, besides Lakeview, report an inspection around the time of their outbreak?"

Stella shook her head. "Not that I'm aware of."

"Are you sure?" she persisted, and Stella nodded.

Mary began to fiddle with the wooden toy zebra that sat on top of the filing cabinet in the cubicle. "I just have this nagging feeling there was another one."

"Well, maybe you should sleep on it," Stella suggested. "It's the end of the day, and you're exhausted."

"Yeah, maybe," Mary muttered. She turned to go but bumped into Erin.

"Excuse me, Mary," Erin said as she handed Stella a pink message slip.

Mary looked at Erin intensely.

"Something wrong?" Erin asked.

"Do you remember hearing anything about state nursing home inspections when you were working the outbreaks?" Mary asked.

"Oh, sure," Erin replied. "About two weeks ago—you and I talked to Ellen Randolph from the Carriage House—she mentioned they had just had one. I remember because she mentioned the title *nurse surveyor*, which I had never heard before."

"That's right!" Mary exclaimed. "Thank you!" She left the cubicle saying, "I knew I wasn't crazy."

"You're welcome," Erin called out after her. Then she and Stella exchanged worried glances.

✕ ✕ ✕

Mary sat down at her office desk and looked at the time on her computer. It was 4:20 p.m. *What next?* she asked herself. She closed her eyes and thought about what she knew. Two of the six nursing homes that had norovirus outbreaks over the past eleven weeks also had licensing inspections around the same time. A logical next step would be to call the other nursing home administrators and ask if they had inspections, too. *But what would it mean if they had?* she wondered. *Would that explain anything?* Mary realized she did not even know what took place during one of those inspections. She needed to talk to someone who did.

Mary remembered how helpful Ellen Randolph had been when

they last spoke. She dialed her office number, and Ellen picked up the phone on the second ring. After exchanging greetings, Mary said, "You certainly sound more rested than the last time we spoke."

"I am," Ellen replied. "I took a few days off once the corporate office sent in a replacement for me. Now I'm working with our nursing director on revising our outbreak response procedures. We learned a lot from that last one. Would you be willing to take a look at them once we're done?"

"I'd be happy to," Mary replied, impressed with Ellen's diligence. Then she told Ellen she had called to learn more about what takes place during a state nursing home inspection. Ellen spent several minutes describing the process for her.

"Okay, let me see if I can summarize what you've told me," Mary said. "Skilled nursing facilities need to be certified for compliance every fifteen to eighteen months to receive Medicaid funds. The inspections are unannounced and are conducted by the state. A full inspection consists of a life-safety survey and what's called a standard survey. The life safety survey is like a fire-safety inspection of the building, and the standard survey looks at things like pharmacy and kitchen services and quality of life for the residents. Residents and staff are also interviewed. Is that right?"

"Yes," Ellen answered. "I would also add that abbreviated surveys can be conducted when a complaint is filed against the facility."

"Are those unannounced too?"

"Yes."

"Would you mind giving me the name of the nurse surveyor who conducted your last inspection?"

"Not at all, I've got his card right here," Ellen said. "His name is Richard Schroeder. I'll give you his cell phone number. He told me to call him on it if I had any questions. He's away from his office a lot. Do you know, he even came back a few days after his inspection because he heard about the outbreak and wanted to know what happened. He's an odd one," she mused. "I remember he kept tugging at his hair. He must have a stressful job."

"Has he always done your inspections?" Mary asked.

"I don't know," Ellen replied. "I've only been here for about a year." She laughed and said, "We'll see if I make it through another."

After Mary wrote down the inspector's cell phone number, Mary thanked Ellen and glanced at the time after she hung up. It was 4:50 p.m. She stared at the nurse surveyor's number and wondered if she should give him a call. If he was assigned to Revere County, he could tell her about all recent inspections. *Why not go straight to the source?* she thought. She picked up the phone and dialed the number.

"Hello? Who's calling?" a man asked.

Mary was taken aback by the emotion in his voice. It's gruffness sounded familiar.

"Mr. Schroeder?" she asked. "This is Mary Campbell with the Revere County Health Department. I'm the nurse supervisor for the Communicable Disease Control Unit."

Mary heard a click and the line went dead. She looked at her phone, puzzled. It had been a long time since someone had hung up on her. She redialed the number in case it had not been intentional.

The man answered the phone after four rings, and his voice was now pleasant and polished. "Hello. Richard Schroeder speaking."

"This is Mary Campbell again."

"Ms. Campbell, I'm so glad you called back," he said with relief. "I think I hit the 'off' button with my chin. How may I help you?"

"Thank you for taking my call," Mary replied, mimicking his excessive politeness. "The health department is investigating several gastrointestinal illness outbreaks at nursing homes. I recently learned that you conducted a licensing inspection at the Carriage House facility around the time of their norovirus outbreak. We've not been able to identify the source of the infection. I was wondering if you noticed anything unusual during your inspection that might help us."

Mr. Schroeder cleared his throat. "Let me think a moment."

While Mary waited, she listened to the sound of his breathing. It was as if he was holding the phone up to his nostrils. His breaths were surprisingly short and rapid.

"Now I remember," he stated. "Ms. Randolph is the administrator there. They received high marks on my assessment. Everything was in perfect order."

Mary raised an eyebrow. *Perfect* was not a word used by any of the regulators or inspectors she had ever known in her career. "Do you inspect all of the facilities in Revere County?" she asked.

"Revere is one of counties I cover," he stated.

"I'd like to ask you about other facilities that have had norovirus outbreaks," Mary said.

"What exactly do you need to know?"

Mary heard the stiffness in his voice and realized she had to tread carefully. She did not want to imply that he was not doing his job adequately. She needed his help.

"It's just the same question as for the Carriage House facility," she said. "I'd like to know if you saw anything unusual during other inspections that might help us understand why the outbreaks are occurring."

"Certainly," he replied. "Let's schedule a time to talk."

"By any chance, do you have time now?" Mary persisted. "We're feeling a strong sense of urgency about these outbreaks because of the illnesses and deaths associated with them."

"Of course I would help you if I could," he said, "but it's just about five o'clock, and I'm anxious to leave for a personal engagement."

Mary found herself growing irritated by Mr. Schroeder's oily manner of speaking.

"Let's talk first thing in the morning," he suggested, "when I can give you my full attention."

Mary sensed she was being manipulated, but she decided not to press him any further. "All right," she replied. "What's a good time for me to call you?"

"It's best if I contact you," he said. "Say around 10:00 a.m.? I have two early morning meetings."

"That's fine. Let me give you my office number."

"There's no need for that, Ms. Campbell. I have access to county information. I know how to find you." And he hung up the phone.

× × ×

Raymond sat in his battered blue pickup truck in front of the Covenant Hill nursing facility. He snapped his cell phone shut and slipped it into his shirt pocket. *She's getting too close,* he thought. Panic flooded his mind. He grabbed a fistful of hair on the back of his head and yanked on it. His brain felt like it was cramping, and the truck's cab felt like it was closing in around him. He climbed out of the vehicle and gasped for air. While he paced, he stroked his tie between the thumb and forefinger of his right hand. *Figure something* out, he told himself. After several minutes, he rested his head against the frame of the passenger-side window. He glanced inside and saw the flyer for the Dovestone fund-raiser—Maureen's art exhibit—laying on the floor. He smiled as a solution presented itself to him.

Friday, June 20

Richard Schroeder did not called Mary that morning, and after several attempts to reach him, she decided to contact the other nursing home administrators. By 2:00 p.m. she had spoken with all of them. Each told her they had had an unannounced inspection that began just before their outbreaks and all were conducted by Mr. Schroeder. He had told them the inspections were the result of complaints filed with the state against their facilities. Mary called Sgt. Fielding and gave her this information.

"Whatever you do, don't talk with him again," she warned Mary. "Chuck and I will look into this. We'll give you an update during the briefing this afternoon."

But at 2:45 p.m., Sgt. Fielding called her back. "Like you, we tried to reach Mr. Schroeder on his cell phone," she reported, "but no one answered. Chuck had that number traced, and it's listed with a licensing program within the State Health Department. I spoke with Ms. Chen, the manager for the program. She told me Richard Schroeder retired to Costa Rica eleven months ago."

"What?" Mary replied, stunned.

"The program hasn't replaced him yet because of the state's hiring freeze. We called the real Mr. Schroeder in Costa Rica. He confirmed his identity by giving us the numbers for his U.S. driver's license and passport. He said he hasn't traveled to the United States in over a year. Chuck is confirming that."

Mary shivered. "So who was I talking to when I spoke with Richard Schroeder?" she asked.

"We were wondering the same thing," Sgt. Fielding replied. "Do you have any idea?"

"No. There was something familiar about his voice—something about the tone or inflection—but nothing I can place."

"Well, keep thinking about it and let me know if anything comes to you."

"I will," Mary told her.

After the briefing, Mary returned to her office and was pleased to find a message on her answering machine from Paul Merrill. In it, he apologized for not returning her calls and said they had unplugged their phone because of all the media attention. He also said that Skye and Mark were doing well and that they hoped she would come to the art exhibit that night. Mary was relieved to hear this and began to tidy up her office for the weekend. She filed away some of the papers on her desk and made a to-do list for Monday. Linus and Erin stopped by to say goodnight just as she was returning from emptying her trash and recycling bins. They found her humming a tune. Linus looked at her, amused.

"What?" Mary asked him.

"You're in a good mood," he stated. "It's nice to see."

"I feel great," she said, emphatically. "I heard from Paul Merrill, and Sgt. Fielding told me not to do anything about Richard Schroeder."

Erin grinned. "So you can relax for a change."

"Yep!"

Mary's telephone rang as Linus said to her, "Want to walk out with us?"

"Sure. Let me just get this." She picked up the phone, and Joe greeted her with a scolding. "Why are you still at work?"

"Who is this?" she teased him.

"Ha ha. Very funny. You're not standing me up, again, are you?"

Mary laughed. "When have I ever done that?"

"I count all the times you said no to coffee."

"Wow. You are one tough customer."

"Look who's talking," he countered. "So, are you coming? I'm hungry."

Mary laughed again. "What else is new? I'll be right over."

Mary met Joe at the Gold Leaf restaurant. She ordered salmon with rice pilaf and seasonal vegetables, and he ordered chicken schnitzel with garlic mashed potatoes and French-style green beans. They talked about everything but work. At one point, Mary intertwined her fingers with his and felt the same electric warmth as when they had first shaken hands. When their waiter approached the table with their meals, Mary reluctantly let go to make room for the plates.

× × ×

Mary drove to the Daisy Merrill Elementary School after dinner. The parking lot was full by the time she arrived, so she left her car on a nearby side street. She walked to the school's front entrance and followed others into the gymnasium. A square area in the center had been converted into a cozy art gallery for the weekend. Easels holding paintings of various sizes defined the boundaries of the exhibit, and tall potted plants had been placed strategically on each corner of the square to soften the shape. Twinkling lights strung overhead created a festive ambiance.

Mary found Mark at the ticket table inside the gymnasium doors. "Hi there," she greeted him. "How are you doing?"

"Good!" he exclaimed. He gestured at the metal cash box on the table and said, "It's nice to feel useful for a change." He handed her a ticket and said, "No charge. It's on the house."

Mary smiled at him. "Thank you. Mind if we talk when you're done here?" she asked. "I've got some information to share with you."

"No problem. I'll come find you," he replied.

"Okay. Where's Skye?" she asked, curious.

Mark pointed to a small galley near the refreshment table and told her he was on kitchen duty. "Paul's here too," he said. "He's out in the crowd mingling somewhere."

Mary passed the refreshment table on her way to the paintings. She waved to Skye through the small kitchen's opening as she picked up a homemade chocolate chip cookie. She was immersed in the details and vivacity of one image when she felt a tap on her shoulder. She turned and saw Paul standing behind her. He greeted her warmly.

"How are you holding up?" she asked.

"Okay," he said quietly. "If anything good can come from being a *person of interest*, it's that this crowd is about three times what I expected. People have been giving me odd looks all night."

"Well, I can't really tell you anything, but you probably won't hold that status much longer."

"Really?" Paul said. "I'll keep my fingers crossed." He laughed and added, "You've probably investigated enough outbreaks over the past few months to last a lifetime."

"It certainly feels that way," she admitted.

"Did you ever find out what caused the Heath Hotel outbreak?" Paul asked.

Mary paused. "The Heath Hotel?" she asked, surprised.

"Yes. The one back in March."

Mary looked at him, intrigued. Then she closed her eyes and tried to recall the details of that particular investigation. March seemed so long ago. "One of the kitchen staff had been ill," she told him. "We think he contaminated the cake he cut and served. How do you know about that outbreak?"

"My brother was part of it," Paul answered her. "He got so sick I took him to the hospital. A nurse mentioned the health department was investigating it."

"That would be your brother Raymond?" she asked.

Paul nodded and said, "Yes."

Mary recalled the day she met Raymond at Dovestone. She remembered a shattered clay pot and a line of conversation that had not been finished. She remembered a veiled threat as she left the farmhouse.

"He never did say what he did for a living," she commented, casually. "Didn't you mention he was in the nursing home business too?"

242

"That's right. He works for the state agency that licenses them. "

Mary's heartbeat quickened, but she tried to keep her voice calm for her next question. "Does he inspect them, by any chance?" she asked.

Paul shook his head. "No, he's an administrative assistant. Why do you ask?"

"Oh, just curious." She hoped her face did not reveal her growing concern. "We've be trying to contact the nurse surveyor for our county," she said, "hoping he could help us figure out why we've had so many outbreaks."

"Well, I don't know if Raymond can help you, but if you want to talk to him about it, he's here somewhere." Paul glanced around the gymnasium. After a moment, he pointed to his brother, who stood about twenty feet away. "There he is," he said. "He's standing in front of Maureen's *Whales Breaching* painting."

Mary looked to her right. The crowd parted momentarily, creating a narrow tunnel through which she saw Raymond. He stood with the right side of his body toward her and was studying a large painting similar to the mural on the outer wall of Erica Hansen's clinic. Mary inhaled sharply when he lifted his right hand to the back of his head, threaded his fingers through his hair, and yanked downward.

He's an odd man, she recalled Ellen Randolph saying about the nurse surveyor who had conducted her facility's inspection. *And he kept tugging on his hair.*

Raymond turned, as if he sensed someone watching him. His eyes met hers just before the tunnel filled with people. A chill ran through Mary's body.

× × ×

Mary gave her excuses to Paul for leaving early and asked him to tell Mark she would contact him tomorrow. Then she hurried to her car. On the way she pulled out her cell phone to call Sgt. Fielding, but she could not get any reception. "Damn," she grumbled as she snapped the phone closed. She looked around and thought about her options for reaching the officer. The school office was closed, and she did not want to ask Paul, Mark, or Skye to let her use the phone at Dovestone. She did not want to chance an encounter with Raymond.

I'll call once I'm outside of Mill Creek, she decided, remembering the location where her phone usually picked up a signal.

After opening the car door, Mary glanced briefly into the dark sky. It was the last night of spring. The air was clear, and the stars were plentiful. She spotted the Big Dipper and nearly expected to see the whimsical creature from Skye's bedroom ceiling laughing down at her. She tossed her satchel onto the passenger seat and was startled by a crunching sound on the gravel behind her. She twirled around and saw two exhibit visitors making their way to their own car.

Get a grip, she told herself as she climbed into the vehicle. She started the engine and drove the short distance from where she'd parked to River Road. She passed the entrance to Dovestone, but did not notice the white van sitting in the driveway with its engine idling and its headlamps off.

× × ×

When Mary woke to a chilly, pitch-black world, she fought back panic. The cool wind rushing across the back of her neck told her she was outside, but she could not make sense of why her face was pressed hard against a stiff material that stank of chemicals. She tried to lift her torso but could not. Something rough and heavy lay across her upper back and had her left arm pinned painfully in place. She searched gingerly with her free right hand for something familiar and found a circular object underneath the material. She grabbed it, and a horrible blast of sound crashed through her skull. Her head throbbed, not just from the sound, but from the pressure of being inverted. She realized she was dangling from her waist and searched her torso until she recognized the shape of the restraint that held her.

It's a seat belt, her brain told her.

Mary was overcome with fatigue, and let her face sink into the foul-smelling material. She closed her eyes, wanting nothing more than to sleep deeply. But the discomfort caused by a small, hard object kept her awake. It jabbed her in the side of her right rib cage. And her brain kept pestering her.

Seat belts are in cars, it told her.

Mary reached back to rid herself of the object.

Your car is pointing downward.

She felt the gadget and recognized it as her cell phone.

This is not good, her brain insisted.

Mary unclasped the phone and brought it close to her face. She flipped it open and pressed the first digit on the keypad.

Saturday, June 21

"Fred Astaire was okay," Mary heard a man say in hushed tones.

"Okay? Just okay?" a woman argued in a loud whisper. "The man was a genius."

Mary told the pair to shush, but they did not seem to hear her.

"If I have to pick, though, I would go with Gene Kelly. He could have survived a rugby scrum."

"Fred Astaire could run circles around any rugby player," the woman countered angrily.

Please be quiet, Mary persisted. *I'm trying to sleep.*

"Yeah, that's about all he could've done," the man chuckled. "And at least rugby is based in reality. Who breaks into song and dance while they're doing the laundry?"

And turn off that infernal beeping, Mary demanded.

"Lots of people," the woman declared. She was no longer whispering. "And musicals are an art form. They don't have to be realistic."

Mary reached out her hand. *Mom, he's teasing you*, she tried to say. *Joe, stop teasing my mom.* The bickering ceased, and Mary was pleased. She could go back to sleep.

"Did you see that?" Carol asked anxiously. "She moved her fingers."

Not again, Mary thought.

"And she muttered something," Joe added.

"Mary?" Carol asked.

Mary groaned but rolled her head toward the familiar voice. She felt a tender squeeze on her right hand.

"Wake up, dear."

With effort, Mary began to open her eyes.

"That's right," Carol encouraged her. "It's time to wake up."

Mary's eyes opened, and she focused on her mother. "Mom? What are you doing here?" she asked, looking around at her surroundings. "Where are we?"

"You were in a car accident, and now you're in a hospital." Her mother glanced to the other side of the bed. "This young man brought me here."

Mary turned her head slowly. It felt like it was made of lead.

Joe grinned at her. "Hi there," he said.

"Hi," she replied softly. "I'm in a hospital?"

"Yes. Highland Hospital."

Mary searched for the source of the beeping and saw a cardiac monitoring machine to Joe's right. She started to scoot herself up on the bed but realized she had the use of only one arm. Her left arm was in a splint, strapped to her chest.

"What happened?" she asked.

"Like your mom said, you were in a car accident," Joe answered. "Amazingly, you only have a mild concussion, that broken arm, and a few cuts and bruises." Mary heard both irritation and concern in his voice. "Do you remember anything about it?" he asked her.

Mary closed her eyes and saw a man's bespectacled face in her mind. Not knowing what that meant, she tried again. "I remember something about the Big Dipper and Skye's bedroom ceiling." She opened her eyes and saw her mother and Joe exchanging worried glances. She thought harder. "I remember leaving the elementary school," she said, after a moment. "Where did I crash?"

"Off of River Road, outside of Mill Creek," her mother told her. "You drove into a ravine."

Mary was stunned. She had driven that road hundreds of times. "How is that possible, and how did anyone find me?"

Joe leaned onto her bed. "You managed to call the health department's twenty-four-seven line, and Jonathan answered. He didn't know what to do, so he called Jackson, who called the sheriff and me and lots of other people."

"Jonathan? Really?" she asked. "I'll have to thank him for that."

"Me too," Joe murmured.

"But I don't remember talking to him," Mary said puzzled. "Did I know where I was?"

"No, but Joe figured it out," Carol answered. "He told the police you were probably on your way back from Dovestone and that your phone only gets reception outside of Mill Creek. That narrowed their search."

Mary smiled weakly at Joe. "You're a smart man."

"Well, they also heard your car horn blast a few times." He grinned. "That helped."

Mary cringed and raised her right hand to her head protectively. "I remember that. It was loud."

Joe laughed lightly, but Carol began to cry. "The paramedics said you must have a very nimble guardian angel." She choked out the words through her tears. "Your car missed half a dozen trees and was stopped by some stumps. A few more feet, and you would have fallen to the bottom of the ravine."

Carol lowered her head to her daughter's forearm and began to sob. Joe kissed Mary on the forehead and said, "I'll leave you two alone for a while. I'll let the nurse know you're awake."

After Joe left the room, Carol whispered, "I'm so sorry, Mary. I've been so horrible to you, and then I almost lost you too."

Mary lifted her hand to her mother's head and stroked her hair. "It's okay, Mom. You've been through a lot."

"But so have you."

Mary let her mother cry in silence. She was thrilled to have her close by again. Eventually, her mother's tears ceased, and she blew her nose and wiped her eyes. Then Carol moved unexpectedly from her chair to the edge of the hospital bed.

"So, why didn't you tell me about Joe?" she asked her daughter.

Mary looked at her, a little bewildered. "You weren't talking to me, remember?"

Carol gently brushed aside some strands of her daughter's hair that had gotten caught in the bandage on her forehead. "Well, that's no excuse," she replied, and they both laughed.

A short time later, a nurse entered the room with Joe following close behind.

"Mary Campbell," she called out. "You're finally awake! Aren't you quite the drama queen, stirring up such a ruckus? Do you know how many calls we've had from people who are worried about you? Two sheriff's deputies even stopped by."

Mary looked over at her nursing school friend. "Katie McLaren," she said softly because her head was throbbing. "Did you ever learn how to do an NP swab?"

The tall, red-headed nurse stopped and laughed. "Boy, you just won't let that go, will you?" She walked to the side of the bed and wrapped a blood pressure cuff around Mary's upper arm. "Seriously, sweetie, how are you feeling?" she asked gently.

"I've been better."

"I don't doubt that. We need to get you up and moving around soon. Then we can start your discharge papers."

"Discharge?" Carol asked horrified. "She just woke up! I stayed in this hospital for a week after I gave birth to her."

Katie laughed. "Times have changed, Mrs. Campbell. She's lucky they didn't send her straight home from the emergency department."

Emergency? Mary thought. Katie helped Mary scoot herself into a seating position using her one good arm and adjusted the pillows behind her. Mary wondered why that word seemed so important.

"That's just wrong," Carol complained.

"Mom, it's okay."

"No, it's not," she scolded her daughter.

Mary caught her mother's eye and smiled. "It's nice having you on my side again." Then a memory flashed through her mind. She was standing in a crowd, watching a man.

"If it makes you feel any better, Mrs. Campbell," Katie said, "the process takes a couple of hours." The nurse pulled the bandage on Mary's forehead away from her skin a little to check underneath. "Girl, you are so lucky that tree branch didn't slice your face a few inches lower." She began to write a note in Mary's chart but said, "Shoot, I forgot my glasses."

Mary focused on the nurse's face. *Glasses?* She saw in her mind's eye the profile of a bespectacled man, shrouded in darkness. His face and eyeglasses were illuminated by a faint green glow. He held something in his hands.

Katie touched Mary's forearm. "I'll be right back to help you to the bathroom."

Mary did not answer her. She was deep in thought. *He's in a car,* she realized.

When Katie reached the door, she turned and said to Joe and Carol, "Don't let her go anywhere."

"Like we have any say in that," Joe called back to her.

Memories flooded into Mary's mind. *The Heath Hotel, the State Health Department, the school gymnasium. Paul's brother!*

"Katie! Wait!" Mary yelled after her friend.

× × ×

Raymond watched the sheriff's deputies question his brother from the safety of the oak trees that separated his property from Dovestone. But he did not watch long because he had an appointment to keep. Raymond returned home and entered the kitchen. He washed his hands and double-checked the contents of his briefcase. Then he picked up his wallet and keys and headed to his pickup truck. He felt a keen sense of hope.

I will succeed this time.

× × ×

"Sgt. Fielding, it's his brother!" Mary exclaimed. She was sitting in the passenger's seat of Joe's car. A wave of nausea washed over her when Joe turned a corner.

"Slow down, Ms. Campbell," Sgt. Fielding said. "It's whose brother?"

Mary held the cell phone away from her ear as the officer spoke. Every sound that entered her brain was magnified tenfold. "Paul Merrill's brother, Raymond Reynolds. He works for the State Health Department."

"Why does that matter?" the sergeant asked. "And why aren't you in the hospital?"

"They released me," Mary told her. Then she described her conversation with Paul and how Raymond was part of the Heath Hotel outbreak. "That's probably how he got the virus to infect people. He used his own poop." She also told the sergeant that Katie had obtained Raymond's original discharge papers from the hospital's medical records office. They confirmed he had been seen for a gastrointestinal illness and was reported to the county health department.

"But you don't know what we've discovered here at Dovestone," Sgt. Fielding said. "While I was talking with Mr. Merrill, Chuck found a small biological refrigerator and laboratory glassware under a tarp in the barn."

"It's a diversion...or set-up...whatever you call it," Mary said excitely. "Joe tracked down Ms. Chen from the state licensing office, the same woman you talked to. He asked her if she knew a Raymond Reynolds, and she said he's an administrative assistant with their program. Sergeant, I think Paul's brother has been impersonating a nurse surveyor. That's how he's been able to access the nursing homes."

"And why he'd have one of their cell phones too," Sgt. Fielding added. Neither woman spoke for a moment, and Mary could tell the officer was pulling together the facts in her own mind.

"One last thing," Mary said. "Ellen Randolph, the administrator for the Carriage House facility, told me the person who performed their inspection had a nervous habit of tugging the hair on the back of his head. I saw Raymond Reynolds do that last night at the Dovestone fundraiser."

Sgt. Fielding let out a long breath. "Where are you now, Mary?" she asked.

"Joe is driving me and my mom to see my dad," she answered. She squinted to keep the bright sunlight out of her eyes. "I need to see him."

"As I recall, Raymond Reynolds lives on the property that adjoins Dovestone," Sgt. Fielding said. "Is that right?"

"Yes."

"All right, then, Chuck and I will have a conversation with him as soon as we're finished here."

"Thank you, Sergeant," Mary said, relieved.

Mary closed Joe's cell phone. "Please drop me off at the front entrance," she asked as he pulled into the Covenant Hill parking lot.

"Mary, let me park the car," he said. "We can all walk in together."

"You just got out of the hospital," Carol reminded her. "There's no hurry. When I called, they said your father was fine."

"I know, but I need to see him myself. Raymond Reynolds knows he lives there. Please drop me off at the front," she insisted.

Joe let Mary out at the entrance after she agreed that her mother would accompany her. They walked through the lobby together, but when Carol stopped to check in at the reception center, Mary hurried to the elevator.

"Mary!" her mother called out after her, exasperated.

The elevator did not arrive immediately, so Mary entered the stairwell to its right. Her body felt three times its normal weight as she climbed the steps. With effort, she opened the heavy door to the third floor with her one good arm. Then she leaned against a wall to catch her breath and allow her nausea to subside. Her eyelids drooped, but she pushed forward to her father's room. She found him lying flat on his back on his bed. He was motionless, and his eyes were closed.

"Dad?" she yelled out in fear.

Donny did not move.

Mary hurried to his bed. Using a thumb and forefinger, she pried open one of his eyelids. The pupil underneath contracted normally to the sudden light.

"Ah!" her father cried out in fright, and Mary pulled back her hand. Then he rolled to his side and fell back asleep.

Mary sat on the edge of his bed and began to sob. Soon, she felt someone sit down next to her and gently take hold of her shoulders. She turned to her mother and cried against her chest. "I can't let him go. It hurts too much."

"You're going to be all right, Mary," Carol consoled her. She rocked her daughter and said, "We're both going to be all right."

Mary stayed in her mother's arms until a strong wave of nausea surged upward from her stomach. "I feel sick," she said. "I'd better go to the restroom."

"Do you need my help?" Carol asked.

"No, I'll be okay."

Carol placed a steadying hand on her daughter's back as she stood up from the bed, and Mary made her way to the tiny bathroom. At its entrance, she looked back and saw her mother pull the bedsheet and blanket farther up around her father's shoulders. She kissed him tenderly on his cheek. Then Mary heard a faint, anguished cry. It came from outside of her father's room. She stepped into the hallway and listened.

"Swallow," she heard a muffled voice demand.

Adrenaline surged through her body, and her nausea disappeared. She walked in the direction of the sound and entered the first room to her right. No one was inside. She stepped back into the hallway and heard another plaintive cry. Mary moved toward a room two doors down from her father's on the opposite side of the hallway. The door was barely ajar. She pushed it open cautiously and peered inside. She heard spitting and gurgling noises. Mary stepped into the room. Against the far wall, Raymond Reynolds sat on the edge of a bed. He was leaning onto a frail woman who lay on her back. He held her jaw open with one hand and was trying to pour something down her throat with the other. The tiny woman fought him.

"Stop!" Mary shouted.

Raymond did not even flinch at the sound of her voice, and Mary stepped closer to the bed.

"I said, stop," she demanded, but Raymond seemed to be in a trance. He neither saw nor heard anything but the elderly woman who struggled against him.

Mary raced to the bed. She set her sights on his temple and made a fist with her right hand. But when she drew her arm back, she heard her father say, *Thumb out, Cricket, or you'll break it*. Mary slipped the digit from its hiding place just before her knuckles connected with Raymond's head. The force of the blow flipped him against the wall. She heard a satisfying crack when his head struck the windowsill.

Sunday, June 22

Mary sat in the passenger seat of Joe's car as he drove along River Road toward Dovestone. After Raymond was taken into custody the day before, she had asked Joe to take her to see Mark. But Joe said he would only do so if she promised to rest for twenty-four hours. Now, as they approached milepost forty two, Joe pointed to the opposite side of the road and said, "It was around here that they found you."

Mary quickly scanned the area. She shivered when she saw a pair of black tire marks that lead into the dark forest, and she performed a mental check of her body, as if to reassure herself that she had survived. Her broken arm throbbed more than her head, which she took as a good sign that she was recovering from the concussion. The bandage covering the gash on her forehead was pressing down onto her eyebrow. When she raised her right hand to adjust it, the stiffness in her fingers reminded her of the blow she had stuck against Raymond. She had knocked him out just long enough to get help from the facility's staff in restraining him.

Mary and Joe found Paul sitting alone in the farmhouse when they arrived at Dovestone. To Mary, he looked like he had aged considerably since the art exhibit. His face was drawn, and he seemed to have trouble holding himself upright. He said they had come at a good time because the press had finally left for the day. When Mary asked if she could speak with Mark, Paul said that he and Skye were at the elementary school taking down the art work. Paul asked Mary if she would stay and talk with him for awhile. Mary agreed, and Joe left to help the boys.

Paul thanked her for her support through everything, but he trembled and cried as he tried to understand what his brother had become. He described how cruel his father had been and how his mother had never protected herself or her sons from him. He told her he had welcomed being drafted into the war because he was so desperate to get away from his family. He'd had no money for college and no place else to go. He also told her how he started doing hard drugs in Vietnam and how his drug problem worsened when he returned home. He sobbed when he described running away with Maureen to live in Oregon. He told her Maureen had managed to stay drug-free during her pregnancy, but not afterward. She had lived with him and Skye for a short while when they returned to Dovestone but then had run back to Oregon and died on the streets of Portland from an overdose. Paul said that he and Raymond had driven her to it.

"She was like a savior for Ray and me," he said. "But I was a selfish bastard. I took Maureen for myself, and I got her into the hard drugs. It was Skye who saved me. I fell in love with him when he was born. I turned my life around only because of him. He brought me the light, Mary. I'm sure that's all Ray ever wanted, but I stole it from him."

× × ×

Mary walked to the elementary school with a heavy heart. She found the two teens and Joe in the gymnasium and asked to speak with Mark alone. They went outside to the playground and sat on the swings. Mary explained that the contents of the envelope she held contained the epidemiological evidence linking his illness with the measles outbreak in Indiana. Mark opened it. He pulled out a copy of his case report form, Dr. Hansen's clinical notes, and the photographs of the rash along his forehead, which captured the healing gash over his eye.

Mary also told him about her conversation with Sheri. "You don't need to tell me anything about why you left home and what happened while you were on the road, but you might want to share your experience with someone else someday—maybe even the Indiana prosecutor. Talking about these things can be very healing."

Mark sat quietly for a few moments with the envelope on his lap. Mary was deeply moved when he looked at her and said, "Maybe I will, if it keeps someone else from getting hurt."

Mark was kicking at the ground with the toe of his shoe when Mary spotted a vehicle pull into the driveway to Dovestone. Very little time passed before it returned to the street. Mary watched the car warily as it parked in front of the school. By then, Mark had noticed the vehicle too. He stood up suddenly. Anxiety filled his eyes. Mary also stood to get a better look at the vehicle's occupants. The driver and front-seat passenger were the first to step out of the car. It was Brady and Evan from the Pine Ridge Resort. The vehicle's back right passenger door opened next. The man who emerged stepped onto the grass and took three steps forward to the sidewalk without taking his eyes off of Mark. Worry and fear emanated from him.

"Dad?" Mark whispered.

Mary looked at the teen, surprised.

A second man from the backseat walked around from the other side of the car and placed a supportive hand on Mark's father's shoulder.

Mark turned to Mary. She saw the hesitation and apprehension in his eyes. Then she smiled and said, "What are you waiting for?"

Mark grinned, and in a flash, leaped forward. "Dad!" he cried out as he bounded through the playground to the street.

Mark's father nearly fell over in the act of catching his airborne son, but the man standing behind him laughed and lent him a pair of steadying hands. The father spun his son around and buried his head in the boy's shoulder, overcome with emotion. As Mary walked toward them, she saw he was fighting to compose himself. When he finally held Mark at arm's length, he began to remark about how tall he had grown and expressed concern that he was not eating enough.

He introduced Mark to the man who stood at his side. His partner, Howard, extended a cautious hand to the teen. Mark began to shake it in a very professional manner, but then, to the man's surprise, hugged him too.

Mary walked over to Evan and Brady. "Thank you," she said to each with sincere gratitude.

Evan shook her hand and gripped Brady's shoulder playfully. The young man lowered his head out of shyness, but Mary could tell he was very pleased.

Wednesday, July 2

Mary sat in the guest chair next to Sgt. Fielding's desk. She was helping her summarize the epidemiological evidence for the case against Raymond. As a result of his attacks, 48 staff and 222 residents had become ill across the 8 affected nursing homes. The authorities were preparing to indict him on seven counts of first-degree murder for the women he overdosed with sleeping pills, five counts of second-degree murder for the elders who died from norovirus-related complications, and one count of attempted murder for his last attack on the Covenant Hill resident. When Mary asked Sgt. Fielding if they had figured out his motive, she referred to a conversation between Deputy Martin and Raymond a day after his booking.

Sgt. Fielding stood up from her desk and walked over to a tall filing cabinet. She opened the top drawer and said, "Mr. Reynolds asked Chuck about his last victim. When Chuck told him she was alive, Mr. Reynolds slumped to the ground and cried out, 'Thank God, I was so worried. Everything's going to be okay.' And then he asked to see her."

"See who?" Mary asked. "The woman he attacked?" The thought made her skin crawl.

Sgt. Fielding shook her head as she pulled a file from the drawer. "Not quite. He asked to see his mother. And he continues to ask about her." She returned to her desk and placed the file in front of Mary. "Nineteen years ago, Daisy Merrill, Raymond Reynolds' mother, died of an overdose of alcohol and sleeping pills. Her death was ruled accidental, even though Mr. Reynolds admitted to playing a role in it. He said he gave her a couple of pills when she told him she was afraid to go to sleep. He also said he hadn't realized she had drunk so much alcohol."

"Are you saying it was his guilt over her death that drove him to commit these murders?" Mary asked.

"We asked Paul Merrill that question."

"And?"

Sgt. Fielding leaned onto her desk. She glanced at the cast on Mary's arm as if she was trying to decide how much to tell her. "Let's just say there are a number of tragic reasons why Raymond Reynolds might have become who he is today. His brother believes the opening of the Daisy Merrill Elementary School last fall, along with preparations for Maureen Durand's art exhibit—Mr. Reynolds had been in love with her, apparently—may have triggered some long-buried conflicts in his brother that resurfaced and overwhelmed him."

"Did Paul try to do anything about that?"

"Apparently not. Mr. Merrill said his relationship with his brother had been superficial and tenuous since he returned from Oregon with Ms. Durand and their son."

Mary thought of Skye. "And that son would have been a constant reminder for Raymond of what he had lost," she said. "But what about his motive?"

"Paul Merrill was not in the best emotional state to speculate about that. But the psychologist who performed Mr. Reynolds' mental health evaluation thinks he was reenacting his role in his mother's death with the hope that she—that is, his victims—might survive."

"Really?" Mary said. "How sad."

"Well, don't feel too sorry for him. Mr. Reynolds was sane enough to know that what he was doing was wrong. He attempted to frame his brother by timing his attacks according to his brother's work schedule. Paul Merrill usually worked weekends, and Mr. Reynolds had Fridays off."

"Ah," Mary mused. "That's why the likely days of exposure for the outbreaks were on Fridays."

"Mr. Reynolds also planted incriminating evidence on his brother's property," Sgt. Fielding said, "and he tried to kill you with a method he may have used successfully in the past."

Mary looked at Sgt. Fielding with curiosity. The officer opened the folder she had placed before her and showed her two photographs. One was of a wrecked car at the bottom of a ravine. The other was of two decomposed bodies leaning against the dashboard of the same vehicle.

"Mr. Reynolds' stepfather, Alan Merrill, and a woman who was not his wife, died in a car crash when Mr. Reynolds was sixteen years old. At the time, the police ruled the crash as an accident. Mr. Merrill was known to be a heavy drinker, and he was last seen in a bar. The accident happened a few months after Mr. Reynolds had been brutally beaten, by field hands, according to his statement. No evidence was ever found to support his story. Alan Merrill's car was discovered on the same stretch of River Road where you were found, only on the opposite side."

Mary swallowed hard at the images of what could have been her fate. "So you think Raymond drove his stepfather off the road in retaliation for the beating?" Mary asked.

"Let's just say we're reopening that investigation," Sgt. Fielding answered her.

After their meeting ended, Mary received two back-to-back calls. She answered them while sitting on a wooden bench in the lobby of the Sheriff's Office. The first was from Kerry Roberts, a reporter with the *County Courier*. Mary recognized his name from the newspaper's coverage of the conflicts between Supervisor Cahill, Isabelle Raposo, and the gay community about conversion therapy. Mr. Roberts was one of the few reporters she felt had written balanced articles about the issue. He asked her for an interview about the nursing home outbreaks.

"Please ask Timothy O'Connor if it's okay," she told him. "All of the health department's media requests are being routed through him now. But I'm pretty sure he'll let me do the interview."

The second call was from Suzanne and Phil. They wanted to talk to her about writing up the nursing home outbreaks for publication in a professional journal.

"We're confident we can get the article published in the CDC's *Morbidity and Mortality Weekly Report*," Suzanne said, "but we'd like to try for something more prestigious, like *The New England Journal of Medicine*. Bioterrorism is a shoo-in for publication."

Mary laughed to herself at the health officer's newfound enthusiasm for the topic.

"So here's what I want you to do," Suzanne instructed her. "I want you and Linus to summarize all of the outbreak information for Phil and me while it's still fresh in your mind. And I want a draft article in a month. We'll take it from there. Of course, we'll recognize the two of you in the acknowledgements section."

A soft snort escaped Mary's nose at this minimal offer of recognition.

"Is something funny?" Suzanne asked. When Mary did not reply, Suzanne said, "I'd like some assurance that you'll get started on this immediately."

A sheriff's deputy walked past Mary and glanced at her. He may have seen the determination on her face when she said, "Suzanne, let's do this instead. If we move forward on an article, Linus and Joe get full authorship. In fact, given the critical role they played in solving these outbreaks, they should be the lead authors. And we'll acknowl-edge the entire response team."

Mary waited for Suzanne's reaction. She began to imagine an ex-change of indignant glances between Suzanne and Phil but stopped herself. It did not matter what they thought of her. The response team had successfully conducted the investigations. They should get the credit.

Phil might understand, she thought. She had learned from Joe that Phil had used his influence to clear away a number of roadblocks that might have otherwise slowed their response.

"Mary," Suzanne began, "I appreciate your suggestion, but—"

Mary shook her head at the woman's predictable dismissal. "Excuse me, Suzanne," she said, "but I'm sitting in the lobby of the Sheriff's Office. I really need to get back to the health department. I'll send out an appointment to talk more about the article in a couple of weeks. This is not a high priority. The team needs some time to regroup and recharge."

Suzanne began to argue, but Phil jumped into the conversation. "Mary," he said, "I like your plan. Get some rest, and we'll talk in a couple of weeks.

× × ×

Mary made it back to her office just in time for a meeting with Jackson to work on an outline for the response's after-action report. The incident command system structure had been dismantled, and everyone had returned to their normal duties. The end of the school year had broken the transmission of pertussis, and the bacterial meningitis investigations were complete. Only one norovirus outbreak had been reported to the CD Unit since Raymond's arrest, and it was secondary to the Covenant Hill outbreak.

"We'll also need to include a timeline of major events and decisions," Jackson said to her. He was leaning against a wall in her office with one cowboy-booted foot crossed casually over the other. "And once we have a solid draft," he continued, "let's ask the lab and Sheriff's Office to review it."

"Sounds good," Mary said. "Thanks for taking this on. It's going to be a lot of work to write this up."

"Glad to do it," Jackson replied. He secured his pen to the clipboard that held his notepad and lowered it to his side. "So, are you coming this afternoon?"

Mary laughed in disbelief. "After all we've been through, you're worried I won't show up for our final briefing?"

Jackson grinned broadly. "Well, yeah," he teased. He pointed at her with fake sternness as he left. "Be there. Fifteen hundred hours. I'm bringing chocolate."

Seconds later, Stella poked her head into Mary's office. "Did you read Carl's email?" she asked.

Mary looked up and saw the fatigued resignation in Stella's eyes.

"No, I haven't," she said with concern. "Have a seat." She pointed to the guest chair and then swiveled in her own to face her computer.

Mary scanned the lengthy list of unread emails in her in-box. She was surprised to see one from Phil. It had been sent shortly after their conversation with Suzanne. Mary opened it. Phil's brief message read, *In case you know of anyone who might be interested.* A job announcement for a public health nurse with the State CD Program was attached to the email.

I'll read this later, she thought.

Then she spotted the email from Carl. It was entitled, *Announcements.* She opened the message and saw that it had been sent to nearly everyone in the Revere County government. The text was terse and to the point, as was Carl's style.

Effective immediately, it read, *the Revere County Health Department will merge with the Department of Mental Health to form the county's new Department of Health and Human Services. I have been appointed the interim director.*

Mary drew in her breath sharply. "You were right, Stella," she said. "Carl was after something big."

"Keep reading," Stella told her.

This reorganization is occurring under the direction of the County Board of Supervisors. The board has taken this action to streamline our operations, reduce costs, and improve services to the community. Health Department staff will be given the opportunity to discuss their questions and concerns with Dr. Henderson at the next all-staff meeting. In the meantime, Mental Health personnel will begin relocating this week from their Salmon Street location to the Seventh Street building.

Mary leaned back in her chair and clasped her hands behind her head. "I should have seen this coming," she said. She now realized how the events of the past two years fit together. Public Health had moved into a larger building, presumably because the department's previous site had not met county codes. But half of the cubicles remained vacant despite Carl's insistence that the extra space was needed for the future expansion of Public Health programs. Then Public Health management positions were filled with Mental Health personnel, and before that, the county had transferred Public Health general funds into the Mental Health budget, supposedly as an emergency stopgap measure. And she remembered Jonathan talking about reducing Public Health to only the minimum functions required by law. At the time, she thought his comment reflected his ignorance, but now she realized he was probably repeating what he had heard from Carl.

"Public Health and Mental Health aren't being combined as equals into one new agency," Mary told Stella. "Mental Health is absorbing Public Health."

Stella nodded, and Mary leaned forward to reread the sentence about Suzanne being available to address concerns at the next all-staff meeting. "I wonder if Suzanne even put up a fight for Public Health," she said.

"I wouldn't bet on it," Stella replied.

Mary continued to read Carl's email. *Jonathan Cox has decided to return to his former position. I'm sure all of us wish him the best of luck and thank him for his outstanding performance during recent events.*

"Outstanding performance?" Mary groaned.

"They have to say things like that," Stella commented.

"Well, we do have one thing to thank Jonathan for," Mary said. She feigned a frown and thrust a personnel action request form at Stella.

"It came back from Human Resources already?" Stella asked nervously.

Mary nodded.

"And?"

"Look for yourself."

Stella scanned the bottom of the form. "Yes!" she exclaimed, throwing back her head.

Mary laughed. "Who says the union and management can't work together effectively?"

The form contained all of the necessary authorizing signatures—hers, Jonathan's, and the head of Human Resources—to make Cass' position permanent. Stella had come up with the idea after Mary told her that Marni wanted to let Cass go presumably because her job had limited-duration status. Stella suggested that if she retired, Cass could be transferred quietly, via paperwork, to her position. Doing so would weaken Marni's ability to remove Cass. While Mary hated the thought of losing Stella, she knew her retirement was inevitable. Mary easily sold the idea to Jonathan by pointing out that the transfer did not incur any cost to the agency.

Mary read the last paragraph in Carl's memo.

Also, please join me in welcoming Marni Scheidt as the Operations Manager for the new Department of Health and Human Services. Marni has had a long and distinguished career with the county, and she brings a wealth of expertise to the position, including her most recent experience as the Public Health Field Nursing Supervisor. She will assume Jonathan's responsibilities.

The memo was signed simply, *Carl.*

Mary slumped backward in her chair.

"What is it?" Stella asked.

"Marni is my new boss." She sighed and confessed, "I don't think I have the energy to deal with her."

"Maybe you shouldn't," Stella said. Her eyes were full of sympathy. "Look, have you thought about taking some time off—to recover and think about your future given all that's happening here?"

"No," Mary said, shaking her head.

"Well, you should."

"How about I take a lunch break instead?" Mary suggested.

Stella smiled. "Well, it's a start."

Mary called Lourdes, who was covering the CD phone, and told her she was going out to get something to eat. But before she did so, she read Phil's job announcement. Her eyebrows rose when she saw that one of the position's duties would be to serve as an intermediary between a software developer and local health department personnel in developing a statewide communicable disease surveillance database.

× × ×

Two men offered Mary their table on the sidewalk as she exited the crowded cantina with her order. She thanked them and eased herself into a chair. Then she raised her face to the sunny sky and took several deep breaths. She felt some of the tension in her body slip away. When her stomach growled, she expertly folded one end of her soft-shelled taco so that its spicy red sauce would not dribble out when she picked it up. She took the first bite just as she spotted Linus and Erin walking toward her. They were holding hands, obviously no longer trying to hide their relationship.

"Sorry to get you midbite," the epidemiologist apologized. "Mind if we join you?"

Mary shook her head because her hands and mouth were full.

"Nice spot you have here," Erin commented, as she sat down.

Linus knocked over the table's flower vase as he lowered himself into a chair. After he righted it, he jostled the table with his knee. Mary had never seen him so nervous.

"It is nice," he said, looking around the plaza.

Mary regarded the couple suspiciously. Both were avoiding eye contact with her. She put down the taco and wiped her mouth with the thin white paper napkin that had come with her meal. "Okay, you two," she said playfully to cover her anxiety. "What's up?"

Linus glanced at Erin, who smiled at him encouragingly. He swallowed visibly and said, "May I use you as a reference? I'm in the running for a job, and the hiring manager wants to talk with my references."

Mary's heart sank, but she forced herself to speak evenly. "Of course," she replied. "What's the job?"

"I'll be an epidemiologist on an HIV/AIDS intervention project in East Africa," he said. The painful expression in his eyes mimicked her own.

"East Africa?" Mary asked. "Is it with the CDC?"

"Not directly. The project is CDC-funded, but I'll be working with a university team."

Mary glanced at Erin, who was watching her with sympathy. "Please don't look at me like that," she said. "Do you want me to start crying?" She turned back to Linus. "I guess I'm not surprised that you're leaving, when I think about it. I know you've been unhappy for a long time."

Linus nodded. "It's just that working with Joe these past few weeks made me realize how much I want to work with others who understand and value what I do. Not that you didn't—just everyone else."

"I know," Mary said. She felt deeply the sting of losing Linus. He was more than a coworker. He had been a confidante and a friend who shared similar dreams for their profession. *And now he's another person I have to let go.* She pushed that thought aside and asked, "But why an international job?"

"I have you to thank for that," Linus teased.

"Me?"

Linus laughed. "You've been telling me stories about your Peace Corps service ever since I've known you."

Mary looked surprised. She was aware that she thought about Liberia often, but now she worried she had given Linus an overly optimistic impression of her time overseas.

"It's going to be tough," she warned him, "and I don't just mean physically. It took forever to get anything done. I was always scrounging around for materials and equipment, and there were always setbacks." She waved a hand in the air and added, "And then there was the politics. Well, that was just way beyond me."

Erin and Linus looked at each other and burst out laughing.

"What?" Mary asked innocently.

"Listen to yourself!" Erin exclaimed. "Setbacks, limited resources, politics—"

"Doesn't that sound familiar?" Linus suggested.

Mary thought a moment and then she laughed too. "I guess you have a point." But the moment of levity passed, and a dark curtain fell over her mind. She looked into Linus' eyes. "You do understand why you haven't been appreciated here, don't you?"

Linus shook his head.

"You're a threat to the status quo, my friend."

"Me?" he asked nervously.

"Not you personally," Mary said, "but what you represent." She glanced at Erin. "I've been thinking about a lot of things lately. People like Suzanne and Nettie—and maybe even me—we're old school. We're from the old paradigm of Public Health as a social service, one that's all about providing health care for people who fall through the cracks."

"What's wrong with that?" Erin asked.

"Nothing, except that it will go away. Someday this country will figure out how to provide health care for everyone."

"When's that ever going to happen?" Erin asked.

"When the system implodes—or comes close to doing so," Mary answered firmly. "And then other agencies, like nonprofits and hospital systems, will take over Public Health's outreach and clinical work because they're better at it than us. Strip that away and what's left?"

Linus looked at her with genuine curiosity. "What?" he asked.

"A new paradigm," she said. "One that's based on information and securing the public's health. It's the work you and Joe did in the sitstat unit. Public Health could be the information hub for the health care system. Surveillance, monitoring, analysis—all of that could be used for strategic planning, response operations, and evaluation. It's your work, Linus, expanded twentyfold. Public Health at the center of our health care system."

"Wow," Linus replied. "You really have given this a lot of thought."

Mary leaned toward him. "With your analytic skills, Linus, you represent that future," she said, "and it scares the heck out of people like Suzanne and Nettie. That's why they've worked so hard to control you."

Linus' face reddened as if she had put him in the spotlight for too long.

"Then why can't they get out in front and lead the way?" Erin asked.

"That takes vision and courage," Mary pointed out. "I've only seen that in one person since I've been here—my mentor, Nora York—and she was pushed out of the department."

Mary gazed down at her food. The two small soft-shell tacos had unfolded, and the contents of each lay in soggy, unappealing lumps on her plate.

"And what about you?" she asked Erin. "I had so hoped to offer you a position with our unit at the end of your internship."

Erin replied with the frankness Mary had come to appreciate in her. "To be honest," she said, "I had my doubts about the job early on. I kept asking myself, 'Is this as good as it gets?' I believe in working within a system to change it, but I'm not sure that's possible in some cases."

Mary pushed her plate away.

"Why do you stay?" Erin asked her. "A nurse with your experience could have her choice of jobs."

Mary regarded the couple. They were two very smart, decent, hard-working people whom she was going to miss very much. "Believe me," she replied, "I've asked myself that question more than once over the past few weeks. I guess I feel like I can still do some good here."

× × ×

Mary saw Mark and Skye approach the health department as she returned from lunch. Mark's father, Dale, and his partner, Howard, were with them. She called out to the teens, and they waited for her. Mark appeared to have grown another inch since she last saw him. Skye had cut off his ponytail and was now wearing blue jeans and a U2 T-shirt instead of his Dovestone tunic and pants. He also carried a package wrapped in brown paper under his arm.

"What are you doing here?" Mary asked. She was genuinely pleased to see them.

Mark spoke first. "We wanted to come by and see you before we left."

"You're leaving?" she asked, looking at the two friends. "Both of you?"

"I won't be gone long," Skye said. "I'm going to check out some colleges. My dad never went, but he wants me to go."

"Of course he does," Mary said. "You're a remarkable young man."

"He is, indeed," Dale commented, and Mary saw the deep appreciation in the man's eyes for his son's protector.

Mary turned to Mark. "And what about you?" she asked.

The teen glanced from his father to Howard. "We're going to spend the rest of the summer packing," he said excitedly, "because we're moving back here. Dad and Howard really like this area, and they think it's better for me to go to school up here than in the city."

The boy beamed when his father put an arm around his shoulder and gave him a quick hug.

"That's great, Mark," Mary replied. "I'm so happy for you."

"Yeah and, um…" Mark's voice trailed off. Mary saw the familiar anxiety return to his face, but he did not lower his head this time or turn away from her. She waited patiently while he found his words. "Thank you for the records you gave me," he said. Then he glanced shyly at his father's partner. "Did you know Howard is a lawyer?" When Mary shook her head, Mark said, "He talked with the prosecutor in Indiana, and they're going to use my information against the guy who assaulted me." Mark's face brightened when he declared, "It's really handy having a lawyer in the family."

Mary felt the familiar but now softer ache as she thought of her brother, David. She smiled at Mark and said, "Yes, I know." Then she looked at the two older men. Dale was watching his son with the painful expression of a parent who could not bear to think of his child having been harmed in such a manner, and Howard returned her gaze with a knowing expression.

Mark added somberly, "And Dad wants to go after my mother's boyfriend."

"How do you feel about that?" she asked him gently.

"A little scared, but I'll be okay."

Mary had a strong urge to hug the boy, but she held herself back.

Skye spoke next. "Would you mind if I stopped by sometime to talk?"

"Sure," Mary replied, surprised by the request. "Is there something in particular you're interested in?"

"Mark and I think your job is pretty cool."

"Cool?" Mary grinned. "No one has ever told me that before."

"Are you kidding?" Skye said. "Tracking diseases, working with the CDC and law enforcement, helping people—"

"Well, when you put it that way," she mused.

"Except for, you know, people getting sick and dying," Mark noted. "That's not so great."

Mary smiled. "No, it's not."

"I need to start thinking about a career," Skye continued, "and I'm wondering what it takes to work in public health. What do I major in, what kind of jobs are there, that sort of thing. That's what I want to talk to you about."

Mary recalled her conversation with Linus and Erin, and she wondered if it would be hypocritical of her to encourage Skye to consider public health as a career. She thought a moment. *Well, it's his choice,* she decided. *Who knows what the future holds.*

"I'd be glad to talk with you, Skye," she answered. "Give me a call anytime."

He grinned. "Great!"

Dale broke into the conversation. "Boys, we should probably let Ms. Campbell get back to work."

"Just one last thing," Mark said to his father. He nodded at Skye who handed Mary the package he had been holding. "We want you to have this," he said.

"Open it," Mark encouraged her.

Mary tore off the paper eagerly. She was stunned to see the original Maureen Durand painting of the image she had first seen on the cover of the circular at Friar Bean's coffee shop after her clash with Suzanne.

"Do you like it?" Skye asked.

"It's magnificent," Mary said. She kissed Skye on the cheek. "I will treasure it. Thank you very much."

Mary turned to Mark. He appeared stuck, as if he did not know what to say or do. But before she could help him find the words, he threw his arms around her.

"Thank you," he whispered, and she held him close.

× × ×

At 4:00 p.m., Mary reluctantly left the small conference room to head back to the unit. The final briefing had turned into a bittersweet celebration of endings and beginnings: Stella's pending retirement, and Linus and Erin's engagement. To Mary's dismay, the team honored her with a massive chocolate cake on which was written, *To Mary, Our Fearless Hero.* The confection's only other decoration was a mound of chocolate-covered raisins contained within a specimen cup in the center of the cake. Mary glanced at Linus suspiciously.

"Don't look at me," Linus said. "It was Lourdes' idea."

Lourdes slapped him playfully on the arm. "You're a bad boy," she teased.

As Mary neared her office, she heard her desk phone ring, and she quickened her step to answer it. "Mary Campbell," she greeted the caller.

"There you are," Marni said.

Mary's grip on the phone's receiver tightened at the high-handed tone in Marni's voice, but she asked politely, "Have you been looking for me?"

"Obviously," Marni answered her. "Did you read Carl's email this morning?"

"Yes, I did."

"Well, I would like to talk to you about these developments."

"Certainly," Mary replied. "Shall I ask Rosalyn to schedule an appointment for us?"

"No, I want to speak with you now."

Mary pinched the bridge of her nose. The party had lifted her spirits considerably, and she wanted nothing more than to conclude this challenging day on a positive note. "Could we meet on Friday, after tomorrow's holiday?" she asked. "I have some work to finish before the end of the day."

"No, we can't," Marni said. "And perhaps you should hold fewer parties with your staff if you're having trouble managing your time."

Mary thought about the fashion magazines Marni always carried with her. She sighed quietly and resigned herself to a meeting. "Well then, I guess I'll come right over," she said.

"Please do. And by the way, my office is in the Administration suite now."

Mary's eyes widened at this news. She had assumed Marni would move into Jonathan's old office. "Thank you for letting me know," she said neutrally. "I'll be over in ten minutes."

Marni was waiting for Mary just inside the entrance to the county courthouse, and she lead her to the Administration Office after greeting her with, "Follow me." As expected, Rosalyn was sitting at the reception desk, but Mary was disturbed to see the alteration in her usually impeccable appearance. Everything about her was askew. The lines of her makeup melted messily into each other, her hair had collapsed noticeably on one side, and her peach-colored sweater set was wrinkled and puckered. Rosalyn shrank away when Marni passed by, but she managed a timid smile for Mary.

Mary followed Marni into the center of the suite. The serene silence that had once filled the elegant space now felt thick with resentment and fear. Suzanne's office was dark and empty. Carl's door was closed, but Mary could see him through the window next to it. He was hunched over his desk, and did not see her walk by. Mary peered to her right and was surprised to see Lyndon, her team's ICS finance chief, sitting in a cubicle. He turned his head in her direction but did not make eye contact. It was then that Mary realized where Marni was leading her.

"Please close the door and take a seat," Marni insisted with rigid politeness, as they entered Lyndon's former office. Mary left the door open a crack, and Marni walked to the other side of her desk.

"I'd rather not sit, if you don't mind," Mary said.

Marni, who had begun to lower herself into her chair, returned to a standing position and fingered the pearls that hung from her neck.

"You have something to tell me?" Mary asked.

"Carl left out a few details in his email that I wanted to make sure you understood."

"What's that?" Mary asked with genuine curiosity.

"I want to make it clear that in my new role, I will be your supervisor," Marni said imperiously.

Yes, I know, Mary thought, and she again felt the weariness that had settled deep into her being. "I understand. Is that all?"

A fashion magazine lay on Marni's desk, and she began to trace the outline of the cover model's image with her forefinger. "No. I'm glad you understand," Marni said, "because—" Her voice trailed off.

"I'm sorry," Mary prompted her. "I didn't catch that."

Marni raised her head and spoke as if she was giving a well-rehearsed speech. "The state budget is continuing to experience significant problems. As a result, the county needs to eliminate personnel. Cass will be let go despite your manuevering to get her into a permanent status job. She has the least official seniority in your unit. Also, authority for your vacant PHN position has been transferred to Mental Health to cover their staff shortage."

"What?" Mary gasped. "You're cutting my nursing staff by half? Who made this decision?"

One corner of Marni's mouth curled into a slight smile. "That's not something you need to know."

Mary took a step toward Marni's desk. "What I need are those positions," she declared. "This county is growing rapidly. How is my unit supposed to meet its responsibilities without them?"

Marni straightened up to her full height. "Your staff did just fine with help from others under ICS."

"That was a temporary, emergency situation," Mary said angrily, "and you know it. I'm talking about our routine work."

Marni glanced down and began stroking the magazine cover, again. "You'll just have to make due."

"Stop fiddling with that thing," Mary insisted, "and look at me when I'm speaking to you."

Marni looked up, shocked. "Who do you think you are?" Her words were venomous. "Don't you get it? Public Health is no longer in charge."

Mary stepped to the desk's edge.

"In charge?" She laughed. "When has Public Health ever been in charge of anything? I get it that this latest reorganization is about two sad little disciplines competing with each other for scraps on the bottom of the funding barrel. It's pathetic, but understandable given the priorities in this county."

Mary leaned onto the desk, and Marni's already sallow skin paled.

"Tell me the truth, Marni. How real are these budget problems? Or is this just an excuse to get rid of people you don't want around? What are your friends up to?"

Marni stomped her foot. "I don't answer to you."

"No, you don't," Mary said. "You answer to a bunch of self-righteous bigots." She slapped her hand on the desk. "What's their agenda?" she insisted.

Marni pick up her magazine and held it tightly against her chest.

"What is it?" Mary demanded. She pounded her fist on the desk.

Marni shook her head furiously from side to side but then screeched, "You want to know? Okay, here it is." Her words sliced the air. "We're cleaning out the filth that has infested this once beautiful county." She twisted the magazine. "As a first step—effective immediately—we're implementing a new policy. The department will cease all HIV/AIDS activities."

A chill spread through Mary's body at the high-pitched proclamation.

Marni lifted her chin high and shrieked, "Everything is to stop immediately. Do you understand me?"

"You can't do that," Mary growled.

Marni ignored her. "As I told Nettie earlier today, you will no longer send any staff out into the community to do intervention work."

"Why are you doing this?" Mary demanded. "You're a nurse, for God's sake! We're talking about human beings who are sick."

Marni now held the magazine with shaky hands. She laughed nervously but said nothing.

"Why?" Mary persisted. "How can you live with yourself pushing through Cahill's hateful agenda?"

Marni's body grew rigid. Her wrinkled, pinched lips turned white and her eyes narrowed.

"Well, let me tell you what I think," Mary said. "People who hate gays and lesbians, like Cahill and her supporters, fear a sexuality they don't understand. They're so horrified by their own sexual urges they're willing to destroy the powerless to prove their piety."

"How dare you?" Marni growled.

"I do so gladly," Mary replied. "You, on the other hand, are the worst of them all. You may not even care about their political agenda. You only do their bidding because of the power they give you to exact your revenge."

Marni gasped at the accusation.

"Oh, don't act so offended," Mary said. "In this new position of yours, you can now inflict on others whatever real or imagined insults you've endured as a result of sucking up to your superiors and supporting their petty politics over your long and undistinguished career."

The features on Marni's face contorted with indignation. "I am your supervisor," she squealed. "I will write you up for insubordination."

"Go ahead," Mary said, and she dug deeper into her disgust. "Tell me this, Marni. Did you ever give any thought to the people our two disciplines have tried to help all these years? Like the traumatized vets and runaway kids who live on our streets and shoot drugs to cope with their distress? They're at risk for HIV. Do they deserve to be judged so harshly?"

Mary waited for a response, but all of Marni's emotions seemed lodged in her throat, blocking her voice.

"Don't you get it?" Mary asked. "You can't base policies on what group gets a disease first because that disease will spread to others—even to people who look a lot like you and Cahill. That's how nature works."

Mary again waited for Marni to say something, but Marni just looked at her with frantic, angry eyes. Mary straightened herself up. "Why am I wasting my breath?" she asked. "You know this. You just choose to ignore it."

Mary turned to leave, and Marni let loose with a piercing sound Mary had never heard before from a human being.

"Where are you going?" Marni screeched. "I haven't dismissed you."

Mary opened the door without saying a word.

"Your job is to listen and obey, Marni!" her supervisor screamed after her.

Mary halted her step and waited, but Marni did not appear to notice her verbal slip.

"Do I make myself clear?" she added.

Mary did not reply. As she closed the door behind her, a tiny spider scurried over the doorframe and out of the room. The insect's movements drew Mary's eyes to Carl's office. Then, to her surprise, she heard a welcome voice.

"Mary?"

She turned and saw Joe watching her from Lyndon's cubicle. The expression on both men's faces was of pale shock. Joe stepped toward her, but Mary held up a hand, warning him to stay back. She walked over to Carl's office, knocked on the door, and stepped inside without waiting for an invitation to enter.

"Carl?" she said.

The man looked up from his work. "Not now," he replied. He gave no indication that he had overheard any of Mary's exchange with Marni.

"This will only take a moment," she said, closing the door behind her.

Carl let out an exasperated sigh. "For God's sake, what is it?" he asked without looking up from his papers.

"How long do you think you're going to last in your new job with Marni in the next office and her best friend sitting on the Board of Supervisors?"

Carl raised his head slowly. His eyes bore into hers with their usual steeliness.

Is that the best you can muster? Mary thought. She walked to the man's desk and leaned onto it. "I'd say you have about six months, perhaps eight, if you're lucky. Then Marni will be the one sending out an email announcing you're taking early retirement—for health reasons, or perhaps to spend more time with your family."

Ever so subtly, Carl smirked, and Mary saw the condescension and victory in his eyes. Their faces were so close she could smell the mingled odors of mints, stale cigarettes, and alcohol on his breath. The stench triggered a memory of seeing him smoking outside the Golden Leaf restaurant with Supervisor Cahill.

Mary blinked at the sudden recognition of her error. She stood up and struck her hand against her forehead. "I'm as much of a dolt as Jonathan," she said.

She now realized the key to her spider map, and the question of who had been stirring up controversy about the department's investigations by feeding information to Trish Matthews. Carl had not hired Jonathan because he found him to be an exceptional candidate. He had used the man's oversized ego and limited intellect to do his bidding. Carl not only knew Jonathan would fail, he planned on it. During Jonathan's short tenure, Carl created a pathway for Marni to rise to her current position. Kim got bumped as the field nurse supervisor, the operations manager job was reclassified to a Manager E level, Jonathan was ousted, and Marni became second in line to run the new department. Carl did all of this for Supervisor Cahill so that she would have an ally, Marni, in a high-level position over a discipline that had thwarted her efforts for so many years. In return, Cahill appointed Carl as the director of the new department over Isabelle Raposo, who had publically rebuked the supervisor's call to adopt conversion therapy.

Mary thought of Jonathan and almost felt sorry for him. Almost.

"I've been so stupid," she told Carl. "You don't think Marni and Cahill will last, do you? You know there will be political fallout for their extreme positions. In fact, you're counting on it."

Carl's lips formed a deep frown.

"They'll be ousted, but you won't," Mary continued, "and the board will keep you as the head of the newest and largest department in the county. You'll be back near the top," she added giddily, "just like in Florida. You'll have redeemed your career."

"You know nothing about this—nothing," Carl growled at her. "I'm in the political fight of my life."

Mary winced but realized Carl's words were probably the most honest he had ever spoken to her. "Your life?" she puzzled. "Your life? What about Public Health, Carl? What about the people in this department who are trying to make a difference? What about the communities we serve? Did you think about any of that during all of your scheming?"

Anger poured from the man's eyes. "You have a future here, Ms. Campbell. Don't test my goodwill any further," he warned her.

"Does any of what I said matter to you?" she persisted. "Will you do anything to claw your way back to the top?"

"Your time is up," he declared, turning his attention back to the papers on his desk.

Without taking her eyes off of him, Mary said, "Don't worry. I'm leaving. But tell me this, Carl? Who stops these games?"

Carl said nothing. He only shook his head.

Mary walked to the door and grabbed its handle. She turned to him once more and said, "Selling out, Carl—selling out Public Health—that will be your legacy."

Carl looked up at her and laughed. "Get over yourself," he said. "It's just Public Health. Who cares?"

Mary held his gaze. "I do," she said, as she closed the door behind herself. "I do."

Outside of his office, Mary pressed her forehead against the closed door and stared at a swirl of wood. Someone in the suite cleared their throat, and Mary looked in the direction of the sound. Marni was watching her from her office. Mary turned back to the swirl on Carl's door. Finally, she walked over to Joe, who was still at Lyndon's cubicle. With her back to Marni, she grabbed his hand and asked quietly, "May I treat you to dinner tonight?"

"Sure," he answered. Deep concern etched his face. He began to speak, but Mary stopped him.

"Give me an hour," she whispered. "There's something I need to do."

Mary smiled discreetly at Lyndon, aware that Marni might make life difficult for him if she thought they were on friendly terms. But she was touched when he called out as she walked away, "See you around, chief!"

Rosalyn swiveled 180 degrees in her chair and watched Mary approach her desk. Mary saw the receptionist straightened her posture and lifted her chin when she shifted her line of sight from Marni to Mary.

"Rosalyn, you always look so lovely," Mary said as she drew near. "You quite put the rest of us public health women to shame."

Rosalyn beamed and smoothed out her sweater. "Why, thank you, Mary! Have a wonderful Fourth of July."

Mary grinned broadly. "You too!"

Wednesday, July 9

The CD team gathered in Mary's office and sat in a semi-circle in front of the portable television that Stella had brought from home. Mary found the station for KZIV News and turned down the volume while the commercials played.

"You made popcorn?" Lourdes asked Cass, who had appeared with an exceptionally large mixing bowl filled with the white puffy kernels. "It's only 9:00 a.m."

"Of course!" Cass exclaimed. "It's not like it's alcohol." She began to pass around napkins and the bowl to the others. "This is going to be fun. I can't wait to see how our fearless administrators gets out of this mess."

"Sometimes we're our own worst enemies," Mary said softly.

Stella peered at her from over the morning newspaper.

Jeanitha entered the room carrying paper cups and two bottles of sparkling lemon-flavored water left over from the previous week's celebration. "Anyone want some?" she asked, and several hands shot up.

Stella lowered the newspaper and told the group, "It says here they've moved the press conference to the community college auditorium again because of the nationwide interest. Who would have thought sleepy ol' Revere County could get so much attention for something other than its wine."

Erin pointed to the image of Trish Matthews on the screen. "Mary, it's starting," she said. "Can you turn up the volume?"

Timothy O'Connor began the press conference by introducing Suzanne as the person who successfully uncovered the identity of the perpetrator of the nursing home outbreaks.

"Really?" Cass asked, dumbfounded. "That stinks. Was she even around for a tenth of the response?"

"Where's Carl?" Lourdes asked. "He's not going to talk? That's a first."

"It's called distancing yourself from the situation," Stella replied, and she winked at Mary.

Suzanne was dressed in a dark-blue suit. A red scarf was knotted at the side of her neck. Her outfit declared that she was trustworthy, intelligent, and decisive, but Mary thought she looked unsettled, even shaken. Suzanne began with a statement assuring the reporters and audience that Revere County was dedicated to promoting the health and well-being of all its residents, regardless of a person's sexual orientation. As proof, she said the Board of Supervisors welcomed a review by gay and civil rights leaders of the department's policies on equity. She also said that the source for the *County Courier* story was likely a disgruntled employee who was upset by the effect of the reorganization for the new department on her position.

"I'm dying to know who that is," Lourdes said. "Any ideas, Mary? When did you find out about the new policy?"

Stella glanced again at Mary from over the newspaper.

"Marni told Nettie and me last Wednesday," Mary answered, and she offered no more information.

"The first *County Courier* article came out on Sunday, so you could be the one," Lourdes teased.

Mary smiled and shrugged.

"Does it really matter?" Stella asked, and Mary silently thanked her for the diversion. "Cahill and her cronies want to discriminate against a whole class of people. Did she really think this wouldn't get out to the press and the public?"

"Well, I for one hope that employee isn't revealed," Erin said. She looked at Mary out of the corner of her eye. "Things never work out well for whistleblowers."

"Look," Lourdes said, pointing at the television screen. "It's Cahill's turn to speak."

The television camera followed Supervisor Cahill's tiny figure as she walked confidently across the stage. She stepped onto a box behind the podium so that she could be seen.

"I have grave concerns about how taxpayer dollars are being used to promote immoral behavior in our communities," she asserted.

"Whoa!" Cass exclaimed. "She just evaporated Suzanne's smokescreen."

Erin laughed. "You've got to give her credit for sticking with her beliefs, as distasteful as they may be."

"As head of the Health Board," Supervisor Cahill continued, "I directed the new department to cease specific activities. I'm confident the voters who elected me will support this action."

"We'll see about that," Stella said. "The newspaper says the gay and lesbian community has already started a recall effort against her."

"And I heard on the radio," Lourdes added, "that the county's Legal Office wants to look into who gave protected health information to KZIV News."

The press conference ended with Timothy thanking everyone for their time and asking that further questions be directed to him.

Mary turned off the television and said, "Okay, everyone, let's get back to work. It's time for our morning report."

"I'll go cover the phones," Jeanitha said, leaving the office.

Mary thanked her, and began to scoot her chair back behind her desk. But one of the wheel casters attached to the base of her chair ran into her satchel, which lay on the floor. A large manila envelope jutted out of the bag. It contained her application for the public health nurse position with the State CD Program. She intended to mail it during her lunch hour.

It had taken little time for Administration to figure out who had leaked the story about the new department's internal power struggle to the *County Courier*, and on Monday, the day after the front page article appeared in the newspaper, Mary's superiors began a concerted effort to push her out of the department. She had expected this, but was surprised at its swiftness. First, she received numerous meeting cancellations. Then Marni began checking on her whereabouts. Every two hours, she would telephone Mary and ask her what she was doing. Marni also directed Mary to include her on every email she sent to others. Suzanne would not return any of her calls, and in an email to the CD team, said that all questions from the CD Unit should now be directed to her only through the CD duty nurse.

Mary looked from the envelope to the nurses sitting in front of her and felt a profound sadness at the thought of leaving them. Their respect and trust—and even love—for each other had deepened greatly during the response. They had put their differences aside and come together as a team under challenging circumstances to protect their community. She would miss their wonderful quirkiness and exemplary dedication, and she worried she might never again find such camaraderie. But Mary knew she could not stay in her job and serve these women well. It was time to move on. Until that day, though, she intended to enjoy every remaining minute she had with them.

Mary picked up a pen and opened her composition book. She smiled and said, "Okay, Cass, what do you have for us?"

About Norovirus

According to the Centers for Disease Control and Prevention (CDC), norovirus is the most common cause of acute gastrointestinal illness and food-borne outbreaks in the United States. The CDC estimates that, each year, the virus causes 19–21 million illnesses and contributes to 56,000 hospitalizations and 570–800 deaths. Worldwide, norovirus is thought to cause approximately 200,000 deaths annually with at least 70,000 of those deaths occurring in children in developing nations. More than half of all norovirus outbreaks in the United States occur in nursing homes, and norovirus costs the United States $2 billion annually in healthcare and lost productivity from foodborne illness. Norovirus, as a member of the Caliciviridae family of viruses, is a Biodefense Category B pathogen on the National Institute of Allergy and Infectious Diseases (NIAID) pathogen priority list. Work on a vaccine to protect individuals from norovirus is underway. To learn more, visit the CDC and NIAID webpages at www.cdc.gov/norovirus/about/ and www.niaid.nih.gov/topics/bio defenserelated/biodefense/pages/cata.aspx.